# FitzRam Family Trilogy

## CARRIED AWAY

## SWEET TASTE OF LOVE

## WILD VIKING PRINCESS

ANNA MARKLAND

Copyright © 2013 Anna Markland
Cover Art by Steven Novak
All rights reserved.
ISBN: 978-1-927619-03-2

| | |
|---|---|
| CARRIED AWAY | 1 |
| PROLOGUE | 1 |
| CHAPTER ONE | 4 |
| CHAPTER TWO | 9 |
| CHAPTER THREE | 19 |
| CHAPTER FOUR | 28 |
| CHAPTER FIVE | 34 |
| CHAPTER SIX | 37 |
| CHAPTER SEVEN | 40 |
| CHAPTER EIGHT | 44 |
| CHAPTER NINE | 51 |
| CHAPTER TEN | 56 |
| SWEET TASTE OF LOVE | 71 |
| PROLOGUE | 71 |
| CHAPTER ONE | 74 |
| CHAPTER TWO | 77 |
| CHAPTER THREE | 81 |
| CHAPTER FOUR | 83 |
| CHAPTER FIVE | 88 |
| CHAPTER SIX | 93 |
| CHAPTER SEVEN | 96 |
| CHAPTER EIGHT | 100 |
| CHAPTER NINE | 104 |
| CHAPTER TEN | 108 |

CHAPTER ELEVEN ................................................................. 114
CHAPTER TWELVE ............................................................... 119
CHAPTER THIRTEEN ........................................................... 122
CHAPTER FOURTEEN .......................................................... 126
CHAPTER FIFTEEN ............................................................... 130
CHAPTER SIXTEEN .............................................................. 133
CHAPTER SEVENTEEN ........................................................ 136
CHAPTER EIGHTEEN ........................................................... 141
CHAPTER NINETEEN ........................................................... 149
CHAPTER TWENTY .............................................................. 154
CHAPTER TWENTY-ONE ..................................................... 158
CHAPTER TWENTY-TWO .................................................... 163
CHAPTER TWENTY-THREE ................................................ 166
EPILOGUE .............................................................................. 172
MEDIEVAL MEAD RECIPE .................................................. 173
WILD VIKING PRINCESS ..................................................... 175
PROLOGUE ............................................................................ 175
CHAPTER ONE ...................................................................... 179
CHAPTER TWO ..................................................................... 182
CHAPTER THREE .................................................................. 188
CHAPTER FOUR .................................................................... 192
CHAPTER FIVE ...................................................................... 195
CHAPTER SIX ........................................................................ 198
CHAPTER SEVEN .................................................................. 201
CHAPTER EIGHT ................................................................... 205
CHAPTER NINE ..................................................................... 207

# FITZRAM FAMILY TRILOGY

*CHAPTER TEN* ............................................................. *211*
*CHAPTER ELEVEN* ...................................................... *214*
*CHAPTER TWELVE* ..................................................... *219*
*CHAPTER THIRTEEN* .................................................. *222*
*CHAPTER FOURTEEN* ................................................. *225*
*CHAPTER FIFTEEN* .................................................... *229*
*CHAPTER SIXTEEN* .................................................... *231*
*CHAPTER SEVENTEEN* ................................................ *234*
*CHAPTER EIGHTEEN* .................................................. *240*
*CHAPTER NINETEEN* .................................................. *244*
*CHAPTER TWENTY* .................................................... *249*
*CHAPTER TWENTY-ONE* .............................................. *252*
*CHAPTER TWENTY-TWO* ............................................. *257*
*CHAPTER TWENTY-THREE* .......................................... *261*
*CHAPTER TWENTY-FOUR* ............................................ *264*
*CHAPTER TWENTY-FIVE* ............................................. *267*
*CHAPTER TWENTY-SIX* ............................................... *271*
*CHAPTER TWENTY-SEVEN* .......................................... *274*
*CHAPTER TWENTY-EIGHT* ........................................... *278*
*CHAPTER TWENTY-NINE* ............................................ *280*
*EPILOGUE* ................................................................ *286*
*HISTORICAL POSTSCRIPT* ........................................... *288*
*GLOSSARY* ............................................................... *289*
*LEXICON* .................................................................. *297*
*ABOUT THE AUTHOR* ................................................. *299*
*FAMILY TREE* ........................................................... *300*

**A NOTE TO MY READERS,**
This book is a compilation of three novellas in the series entitled **The FitzRam Family**. These stories grew out of **The Montbryce Legacy Series**. If you have read the Legacy books you will already be familiar with many of the characters and events in this book. If not, you will meet them for the first time.

A glossary of characters and a lexicon of foreign words and phrases used in my books can be found at the end. There's a helpful Family Tree too, but don't peek yet!

I hope you come to love my heroes and heroines as much as I do!

**The Montbryce Legacy**
Conquering Passion
A Man of Value
If Love Dares Enough
Passion in the Blood
**Sons of Rhodri**
Defiant Passion
Dark and Bright
The Winds of the Heavens
**FitzRam Family**
Carried Away
Sweet Taste of Love
Wild Viking Princess
**Montbryce~The Next Generation**
Dark Irish Knight
Silent Knights (Sept. 2013)
Dance of Love
**Medieval Sampler Boxed Set**

If only my heroes and heroines had revealed their stories to me in chronological order, it would have made life so much easier for my readers! If you prefer to read sagas in chronological order, here's a handy list.

1066—Conquering Passion
1066—If Love Dares Enough
1066—Defiant Passion
1087—A Man of Value
1097—Dark Irish Knight

1100—Passion in the Blood
1106—Dark and Bright
1107—The Winds of the Heavens
1107—Dance of Love
1113—Carried Away
1120—Sweet Taste of Love
1124—Wild Viking Princess

If you like stories with medieval breeds of dogs, you'll enjoy **If Love Dares Enough, Carried Away,** and **Wild Viking Princess.** If you have a soft spot for cats, read **Passion in the Blood.**

Looking for historical fiction centred on a certain region?
English History—all books
Norman French History—all books
Crusades—A Man of Value
Welsh History—Conquering Passion, Defiant Passion, Dark and Bright, The Winds of the Heavens
Scottish History—Conquering Passion, A Man of Value, Sweet Taste of Love
European History (Holy Roman Empire)—Carried Away
Danish History—Wild Viking Princess
Spanish History—Dance of Love
Ireland—Dark Irish Knight

If you like to read about historical characters:
William the Conqueror—Conquering Passion, If Love Dares Enough, Defiant Passion
William Rufus—A Man of Value
Robert Curthose, Duke of Normandy—Passion in the Blood
Henry I of England—Passion in the Blood, Sweet Taste of Love
Heinrich V, Holy Roman Emperor—Carried Away
Vikings—Wild Viking Princess
Kings of Aragon (Spain)—Dance of Love

# CARRIED AWAY
*Nothing matters but being with you,*
*Like a feather flying high up in the sky on a windy day,*
*I get carried away.*
*~George Strait*

*For my daughter-in-law, Samantha,*
*one of the most creative people I know*

## PROLOGUE
*Bolton, Northumbria, 1113 A.D.*

Caedmon FitzRam was more than distraught. Four years ago it had been a source of pride for his family when their fifteen year old daughter, Blythe, had been chosen to go to King Henry's court as a lady-in-waiting to Princess Adelaide. Now Blythe had been commanded by the Princess to accompany her to Germany where she was to wed the Holy Roman Emperor.

Caedmon had made the long journey south to Court and tried every diplomatic move he could think of to extricate his reluctant daughter from the obligation, but the spoiled Adelaide was having none of it.

"I'm afraid, FitzRam, my little girl has dug in her heels," Henry had drawled. "She insists Lady Blythe attend her in Mainz."

Blythe had not blamed her father, but her unsuccessful determination not to cry at their farewell had made his gut clench. He might never see her again as a result of this dreaded journey. He had failed her.

Caedmon imparted this bitter news to his wife as she welcomed him home. He enfolded her in his cloak in the bailey of their manor to protect her from the biting east wind sweeping across the moorland on its journey from the North Sea.

Agneta sagged against him, her last hope gone. "Blythe has been forbidden to marry as a lady-in-waiting to the Princess. She's nineteen. What are her chances of marrying if they carry her off to the Holy Roman Empire? Adelaide is no doubt taking many ladies-in-waiting, surely she wouldn't miss Blythe?"

Once inside the shelter of the front hallway, Caedmon put his hands on his wife's shoulders. "There is no other recourse. I'm sorry. I did what I could. Adelaide is going to marry Heinrich and she intends to take Blythe with her. Henry is adamant about building alliances, as evidenced by his betrothing his ten year old son to the daughter of *Comte* Fulk of Anjou. Think of it. A Norman prince, grandson of the Conqueror, betrothed to an Angevin! William of Normandie must be turning in his tomb."

Agneta wiped her eyes and blew her nose as Caedmon escorted her into their solar. "You of all people should remember that old enmities can be put aside. Your hatred of Normans almost got you killed."

Caedmon chuckled as he handed his cloak over to his steward, Alain Bonhomme. "Ironic, isn't it? When I discovered I was the illegitimate son of a Norman Earl, I despised myself and Ram de Montbryce. Now, here we are bearing a Norman patronymic and proud of my Montbryce heritage."

Agneta motioned to a maidservant hovering in the doorway with a jug of ale. She filled a tankard and gave it to her husband. "Your father was indeed a man to be proud of, Caedmon. I loved him. We wouldn't have this beautiful manor house were it not for his influence. I was nothing to him, yet he saw to it my family home was rebuilt."

Caedmon slumped into a chair near the hearth and eased off his boots. "My father loved you, Agneta."

She stood behind him and put her arms around his shoulders, watching him drain his tankard. "I'm glad you're back. I miss you when you're away."

He smiled, swiped his hand across his mouth and belched. Stretching his legs out to the fire, he leaned his head back against her and pressed his hands atop hers. "It's good to be home. You have the other children here to keep you company. By the way, where are they?"

Agneta took the tankard and refilled it. "They don't warm my bed, husband! Aidan is particularly upset about his sister's move. He's never lived in a different country to his twin. He fears he'll never see her again. He's gone to assist with repairs of a cottage in the village. He'll be home soon. Edwin is with him."

"What about Ragna?"

Agneta scoffed. "She's the only person in the household green with envy. She desperately wants to go in her sister's stead."

"She's only thirteen! What makes her think—oh, wait, this is Ragna, our wild Viking princess!"

Agneta laughed. "Exactly!"

As they talked, Ragna burst into the chamber, her flaxen hair streaming like a banner. "Papa! You're home. No one told me. I would have greeted you."

Caedmon came to his feet. She threw herself into her father's arms and he kissed her. "I've missed you, my wild Viking princess."

Ragna pouted and pushed away from him. "Would you have me be anything other than myself? *Maman* is proud I remind her of my Danish grandmother. Papa, why can't I go in Blythe's stead? She doesn't want to go."

Caedmon put his arm around his youngest child's shoulders. "You are too young. It would break your mother's heart if you went to Germany."

Agneta burst into tears. "We won't even have Blythe home for Yuletide." She fled the Hall.

# CHAPTER ONE

On the Seventh day of January in the year of our Lord One Thousand One Hundred and Fourteen, Adelaide, the daughter of King Henry of England, married the Holy Roman Emperor, Heinrich the Fifth. The marriage took place in Mainz. Adelaide changed her name that day to Matilda, and was crowned Empress. She was twelve years old. Heinrich was twenty-eight.

As the lengthy wedding and coronation ceremony of her mistress proceeded, Lady Blythe Lacey FitzRam stood in awe in the basilica, recalling the detailed history she had been regaled with upon first arriving in Mainz. The voice of the young priest had choked with pride as he conducted Adelaide's ladies-in-waiting through the *Mainzer Dom*.

Only recently arrived after a long and cold journey and full of resentment because she had missed Yuletide with her family, Blythe had not appreciated the compulsory history lesson. Now, however, she looked with admiration upon the massive gold cross commissioned by Archbishop Willigis, the heavy bronze doors made by Master Berenger, and the stunning stained glass windows illuminated by the bright winter sunshine. She recalled the guide's explanation that the cathedral was not simply one church, but a complex which included those dedicated to Sancta Maria ad Gradus, and Saint Johannis, the latter built five hundred years before. It was a most appropriate place for a coronation.

A pang of jealousy and annoyance surged through her as the twelve year old Adelaide was bound to Heinrich. Some of her fellow ladies-in-waiting shared her resentment.

"She's twelve and getting married, but I'm not allowed to marry because I'm in her service. She thinks of no one but herself," Blythe whispered to the widowed Lady Dorothea Le Roux. "I'll die a spinster. My younger sister will probably be wed before I'm released from this obligation."

She had felt isolated since arriving in this foreign land. Sharing confidences with other ladies-in-waiting was all very well, but could be dangerous. Whom to trust? While Adelaide's entourage were French speaking, Heinrich's courtiers spoke German, a harsh sounding language she had never learned.

Her parents had raised her to be tolerant. Her father, Sir Caedmon FitzRam, had fought in the First Crusade and experienced firsthand how intolerance led to needless bloodshed. Her mother often told the story of almost losing Caedmon because of her resentment of exiled Saxons who had helped the Scots slaughter her family. The FitzRams had come to terms with their prejudices and hatreds and had passed their belief in the power of love on to their children. Blythe was torn between wanting to be accepting of the foreigners in whose midst she found herself, and disdain for their alien tongue and temperament.

As she watched the Emperor repeat his vows, she leaned close to Lady Dorothea's ear. "Poor Heinrich, he looks so bored—a twenty-eight year old man marrying a child. He's quite handsome, despite his long nose. He'll no doubt find solace with a mistress—as our own King Henry does—often!"

Lady Dorothea gave her a conspiratorial grin, but put her finger to her lips.

Blythe shifted her weight on the hard pew and recommenced her perusal of the historic surroundings, but her mind was on her discontent. Blythe's parents were intensely loyal and faithful to each other. She longed for such a relationship for herself, but had discovered during her years at Court that most men were only interested in one thing from ladies-in-waiting. They knew the women were not allowed to marry and looked upon them as potential liaisons without entanglements. Blythe suspected the Germans would be no different. She would have to keep braiding her hair so tightly in crown braids it made her wince.

*I look like a harridan.*

She tightened her mouth into an unattractive pout and creased her brow, transforming her face into an ugly scowl. "This is the *fraulein* face I'll present to the ogling Germans. They're used to seeing the same expression on the faces of their own women!"

The strident sound of a trumpet fanfare rattled her from her reverie. "The end must be in sight!" Her long legs were stiff from standing and kneeling—up and down, up and down. She stifled a yawn, concealing it with her kerchief. "What a long ordeal! Adelaide will need a nap," she whispered to Dorothea. "I suppose we must call her Queen Matilda now." A cold shiver crept down her spine. She had striven unsuccessfully over the years to find love in her heart for her mistress. Adelaide had been arrogant enough as a mere Princess.

The rehearsals for this grand rite had been lengthy and tedious. Blythe fell into her assigned place in the long procession out of the cathedral, squaring her shoulders to face whatever lay ahead.

As predicted, Queen Matilda fell asleep upon regaining the imperial chambers and before the banquet. Blythe was kept busy helping with the disrobing, preparing the bath and redressing her mistress. A worry nagged at her and she wondered if anyone had explained to the infant queen what would be expected on her wedding night. Had Adelaide's mother prepared her? Would Heinrich expect his conjugal rights from a twelve year old? If so, she hoped he was a gentle and considerate man. Blythe's mother had hinted to her daughters of the exhilarating passion of the marriage bed when a man and woman loved each other.

"Not that I'll ever need the knowledge," she lamented bitterly.

~~~

Emperor Heinrich was preoccupied with events within the borders of his empire that involved revolt rather than union. He faced a rebellion initiated by the citizens of the ancient city of Köln, along with allies from the Saxon nobility.

While he waited for the summons that all was in readiness for the banquet, he met with his advisors. "I have naught but disdain for the rebellious upstarts in Köln. Is the army assembled to march against them?"

The commander of his forces bowed. "Yes, sire, mostly Alemannians and Bavarians. It's a grand army."

Heinrich rubbed his finger along his moustache. "*Gut!* I vow to reduce Köln to shame and insignificance. They arrogantly think they are one of the great cities of the Empire. Be ready to march on the morrow."

"But sire, your bride?"

Heinrich snorted. "She's twelve! What am I supposed to do with her? I'll come back when she's grown up a little."

The assembled noblemen snickered with sympathetic laughter.

~~~

Spring turned to summer, bringing sweltering heat. Queen Matilda whined constantly about the weather and Heinrich's absence, though she did not seem concerned for his safety. The clothing Blythe had brought from England was completely unsuitable for the climate in Mainz, and she had never felt so uncomfortable. Lady Dorothea had thrice mentioned nervously to their mistress the discomfort of all the English ladies-in-waiting, but nothing had come of it so far. The elderly woman was reluctant to bring up the subject yet again.

Blythe's tightly braided auburn hair was a crown of thorns that grew more painful when she was obliged to listen to Matilda's regurgitation of the accounts of Heinrich's campaign as they were brought to her.

She sat, dwarfed by her massive throne, boasting of her husband's prowess. Though her Imperial robes touched the mosaic floor, the occasional bulge in the heavy fabric indicated the tiny Empress was swinging her feet. She paused, making sure everyone was paying attention. "It took His Highness two days to march with his army from Mainz to Tuitium, a fortified town on the opposite side of the Rhine to Köln established by the Roman Emperor Constantine eight hundred years ago."

Blythe resisted the temptation to roll her eyes. Matilda was a scholar repeating her lessons as she prattled on. "A bridge connects Tuitium to Köln and His Highness planned to capture the town and from there lay siege to Köln. Tuitium is an important centre of learning and its Abbey home to several noted theologians."

*Saints preserve me and rescue me from this child.*

Blythe had already learned Heinrich had captured Tuitium. It was common knowledge. Apparently Matilda was the last to be told anything.

Oblivious to the uncomfortable shuffling around her, Matilda carried on. "Once he captured the town, he stationed a garrison there and was able to cut Köln off from all river trade and transportation."

She smiled and looked smugly down her nose at the assembled courtiers. "That should teach them a lesson they won't soon forget."

Pleased with her husband's military success, she was apparently unaware of subsequent events. Blythe was not going to be the one to tell her, and the nervous glances of her fellow ladies-in-waiting told her they too would keep silent. Lady Dorothea swayed and clutched Blythe's arm.

Everyone listening to the Empress was aware that Köln had mustered a sizeable army of young men who had crossed the Rhine with a strong force of bowmen. They had anticipated the Emperor's attack. It was rumoured, and later substantiated, that Heinrich had met with his advisors and decided to draw out the battle until evening, thinking the exhausted enemy would withdraw.

There were a few indecisive skirmishes, then suddenly a great cloud of arrows came showering in from the Köln side and a large number of Heinrich's men fell dead or wounded. Because of the sweltering heat they had removed their armour of horn.

*Let someone else tell the child Queen that!*

Heinrich had decided to yield the field and retreat behind the improvised military camp he had set up. The next day he had directed his army against Bonn and Julich, two fortified places belonging to Köln, and plundered and burned everything within reach.

On his return, heavy fighting ensued and Heinrich was apparently gaining the upper hand, having captured several noteworthy prisoners. Then Count Frederick of Westphalia came up with heavy reinforcements. Heinrich was forced to give way and barely escaped the pursuing enemy. Reports were that he was exhausted. Taking Köln was proving to be more difficult than he had anticipated.

Blythe hoped someone informed the Queen of events before her humiliated husband returned to Mainz.

# CHAPTER TWO

The tension in the small chamber exhilarated Dieter von Wolfenberg. A cadre of young noblemen within the city of Köln, supported by journeymen and apprentices, were gathered to confirm details of their plot to take advantage of Heinrich's absence from Mainz. They wanted to be free of the Empire and resented the Anglo-Norman child who had been made Empress. They intended to kidnap Queen Matilda and ransom her for their city's freedom.

They planned to make their way to Mainz, overpower Matilda's guards and spirit her away. Dieter, a Saxon count, vassal of Duke Lothar von Süpplingenburg, was their leader.

As the men prepared to leave on their mission Magnus Braunschweig approached him. "Can we trust Süpplingenburg?"

Dieter owed allegiance to his Duke, a powerful new force in Saxon politics, but he had to be evasive. There was much he could not reveal about his overlord. "He's been fortunate in expanding his own lands through inheritance."

Magnus eyed him suspiciously. "I know you are his man, Dieter. It was he who made you *Graf* when he extended his authority into the north and west. But isn't he in the Emperor's pocket?"

Lothar had effectively transformed himself into the head of a Saxon nation, but Dieter knew he schemed to be perceived as a supporter of Heinrich. Lothar was in fact incensed by taxes imposed by the Emperor, and plotted secretly to free Saxony from Imperial rule. Dieter was ambitious and saw great benefit in being of service to his Duke. It was the reason he had left his home in

Saxony and come to Köln. The clandestine nature of his activities on the Duke's behalf appealed to his darker side. It had been relatively easy to scheme his way into a position of trust among the disaffected noblemen.

He had been torn by the decision to leave Wolfenberg, a place filled with bitter memories of a loveless marriage. But his son, Johann, was there, in the care of Dieter's father and sister. Johann was the one good thing to come from the years of erratic behaviour on the part of his wife. Madness had eventually driven her to take her own life. Now his son was motherless, but better that than the future he would have had at Frederika's hands. Johann was a bright, happy boy who exhibited no outward signs of his demented mother's lunacy. But when Dieter and Frederika had been betrothed as children, she had seemed normal too.

By now, several of the conspirators had drawn close, anxious to hear his reply. He must get his mind back on the business at hand and consider his words carefully. "We owe the Duke our fealty and must trust in his judgement. In any case, this is our plot, not the Duke's. It is for us to free Köln from the blockade."

A few nodded, others mumbled; Magnus remained silent. However, most of them seemed satisfied and prepared to embark on the mission. He breathed a sigh of relief. The sooner the Emperor was removed from power, the sooner he would return to Wolfenberg.

~~~

Dieter and a score of handpicked men left Köln under cover of darkness. Clad in the black tunic, hauberk, leggings and boots he typically favoured, he had left off the long white cloak he often fastened to his shoulders. The scabbard and hilt of his sword were black. His jet black hair and swarthy complexion would ensure his invisibility in the dark.

They completed the two day journey to Mainz and arrived in the city without challenge, much to their surprise. "Heinrich is so preoccupied with Köln he leaves his own nest unprotected," Dieter observed to Magnus.

They stole into the cathedral under cover of darkness and took up their positions. The plan was to seize Queen Matilda when she came to the Emperor's private chapel in the cathedral for morning mass, which she was known to do daily. To take her in the palace would be nigh on impossible.

Dieter rehearsed over and over in his mind the details of how the abduction would proceed. Nervous dread and anticipation warred within him. He dozed intermittently, waiting impatiently for dawn, leaving his station only occasionally to prod a snoring comrade.

~~~

The daily excursion to accompany the Queen to morning mass was at least a relief from the boredom of Blythe's routine. She was learning a few German words, but finding it difficult. The Queen was bored too and spent most of her day changing outfits, for which Blythe was responsible. She supposed she should be flattered to be the Queen's 'favourite'! In all the years she had been in service to Matilda, she had never taken a liking to the child, who had grown more arrogant as time went on. Her Majesty had done nothing to provide her ladies with a more suitable wardrobe. She refused to learn German and complained constantly about the German courtiers who surrounded her.

Blythe wondered how Matilda and Heinrich were ever going to communicate.

*Perhaps he doesn't care about communicating, only getting her with child.*

Her attention wandered quite a bit these days. Homesick for England, she missed her family. She knelt for the Invocation of the Holy Spirit, the droning voice of the priest lulling her to sleep. She stifled a yawn, but was abruptly jarred awake by a gloved hand pressed firmly over her mouth. She struggled and tried to scream, but tasted leather. Heart racing, she was dragged unceremoniously over the back of the bench by a strong arm clamped around her ribcage. Her attacker kept his other hand over her mouth. Screams rent the air. Blythe squeezed her eyes tight shut, hoping when she reopened them, this nightmare would be a dream.

It was only too real. Lady Dorothea lay in a crumpled heap a few feet from the altar. Five Imperial guards had formed a shield in front of their Empress and were fighting off a group of masked men. Booted feet echoed off the stone floor, running, coming closer. Male voices shouted in anger and alarm. Matilda cowered behind her guards with the priest, pressing herself up against the altar, a terrified little girl. "I should have been with her," Blythe thought wildly. "I could have protected her."

Breathing became difficult. Her eyes watered. Her feet touched the floor for an instant, then she was hoisted over a broad male shoulder, forcing the air out of her lungs with an *oomph*. The man carried her out of the cathedral, moving quickly. His shoulder jarred her belly as he loped along. She pounded his back with her fists. It was like hitting a wall. She braced her hands against him, trying to get air into her lungs. Even through the leather of his hauberk he was rigid, hard-bodied, all muscle. A thrill of fear coupled with indignation swept over her. Now free to scream, she did so—loudly. Without warning, she was jerked back to her feet. The cold blue eyes of a swarthy man bore into her. He pulled down his mask, smiled at her laconically and said in French, "You will deafen me if you scream in my ear, *milady*."

She gulped air as he coolly appraised the décolletage of her dress, his deep voice penetrating to her belly. Her mind whirled. Before she could utter a word he had gagged her and she was back over his shoulder, his right arm wrapped around her thighs, his left fending off another Imperial guard with his sword.

A deadly lunge dispatched the guard and the man loped on, sword in hand, towards the ancient church of St. Johannis. He paused for a moment behind a pillar, listening. Blythe forced down the bile rising in her throat.

She tried to catch her breath, but then he was moving again, with greater stealth. Blood rushed to her throbbing head and fleeting images swirled. The man reached a small door, opened it carefully, and bent to clear the jamb. Her skirts rustled against the wood as he eased her through. She made the mistake of raising her head, and banged it hard on the wooden frame.

Still clinging desperately to his hauberk with one hand, she touched the other to her head, half expecting to feel blood oozing. The gag prevented anything more than a grunt.

"My fault."

*A gentleman bandit!*

He stepped outside and reached to untie the reins of a tethered black stallion. He set her on her feet and mounted the horse. For one blessed moment she hoped he would ride away without her, but he leaned down and held out his hand. He must have seen the flicker of hesitation in her eyes. "I will kill you if you run," he said softly in English.

Who was this brigand who spoke both her languages? A shiver went through her. She averted her eyes and held out her hand, squealing involuntarily when he pulled her up effortlessly and sat her in his lap. On a clipped command in German, the horse cantered away, carrying them, no doubt, to a rendezvous point outside the city arranged with his confederates. She had no choice but to cling to him as he held her fast, his arm tight around her waist. She heard the steady beating of his heart. Hers was probably deafening him. She closed her eyes in an effort to overcome her dizziness. Her frenzied mind filled with memories of family stories of the attack by Scots that had taken the lives of her grandparents. Now she understood the terror her mother must have experienced that day long ago.

Her breath caught when she thought of her parents. She wanted to cry out, to weep with fear, but determined to be brave. This bandit must not know she was afraid. She was a descendant of Vikings. She closed her eyes to conjure an image of the ceremonial dagger that hung on the wall of her home in Kirkthwaite Hall and of the Danish ancestor who had carved its hilt. She called on his aid, just as her mother had done when her father left to join the Crusade.

The man shifted his weight in the saddle, jolting her out of her trance. He moved her arms to around his neck—no choice but to rest her head against his chest. She had never been this close to a man's body. His legs were like iron and a strange hardness pressed against her thigh. She had often seen her brothers' male parts when they were all children, but did not recall anything so—big. She still tasted the leather of his gloves on her tongue. He smelled of leather, and something else—sweat, fear? Was he afraid too? She dared a glance at his face. His jaw was clenched, his stern expression unreadable in the early morning light.

After what seemed like an eternity, they arrived at a small church. It looked deserted, but as they approached a young man emerged to grasp the horse's reins. Her captor said something in German, then released her and she slid into the arms of the youth. Her knees buckled as her numbed feet hit the ground.

The boy seemed flustered as he helped her regain her balance. "*Kaiserin* Matilda?" he asked her captor.

The Black Knight dismounted, shook his head, took his prize from the boy and carried her into the ancient church in his arms. Setting her back on her feet, he looked at her. Some of the stress had left his features. Her heart fluttered—he had the face of an angelic devil. His high cheekbones and aristocratic nose bespoke a man of noble birth. She had a momentary notion to touch the dark stubble of his morning beard. He smiled the same naughty grin as before. Had he read her thoughts?

"Do you promise not to scream if I remove the gag, my lady?" His deep voice, speaking a language not his own, somehow soothed her. There was no threat in it.

She nodded mutely, her eyes wide, feeling completely dishevelled, alone and defeated.

He untied the gag. "If you scream, no one will hear you—only the ghosts."

She could not speak.

"*Vous parlez la langue normande?*" he asked.

Tears welled in her eyes and she blinked rapidly. "*Oui*, I speak Norman French and English—but not German."

He nodded his understanding. "What is your name?"

His ability to speak several languages bespoke an educated man. His French was flawless. This reassured her that at least she was not in the hands of a brigand. But what was she doing here? Why had he taken her? Summoning up her courage, hoping her voice would not betray her terror, she allowed him her name. "I am Lady Blythe Lacey FitzRam."

He nodded, a strange half smile on his lips. "So you are indeed a Norman?"

Blythe clenched her fists nervously, nails digging into the flesh of her palms. "My father is half Norman, half Saxon. My mother is of Saxon and Danish descent."

"Quite a mixture," he quipped. "So you're from the northern part of England?"

It seemed incongruous to be standing in this ancient church having a conversation as if they were recently introduced acquaintances at some courtly function. She took another deep breath. "No, but my mother was born there. I was born in the Welsh Marches. I have a twin brother, Aidan. We do live for part of the year in the north, at my mother's ancestral home of Kirkthwaite Hall."

Why was she telling him these personal details? Who was he? Why had he kidnapped her? She remained silent, fearful of the answers. Her heart was still beating too fast, but was it because of her fear or his overwhelming maleness?

The smile left his face. "And you came to our land with Heinrich's child bride." It was not a question and she could not fail to hear the sarcasm in his voice.

She averted her eyes from his steadfast gaze. She wanted to explain that she had been brought against her will, but that would be disloyal to her mistress. "Yes, I'm one of her ladies-in-waiting."

"What is it you're waiting for, Lady Blythe Lacey FitzRam?"

The question took her by surprise and she wondered if he perhaps didn't understand the term *lady-in-waiting*. He was too refined for that, too much a man of the world. What did he see when those blue eyes pierced her? The truth? She almost blurted out the secret longings of her heart.

*I'm waiting for a handsome knight to sweep me off my feet, carry me away and make me his wife in every way possible.*

What was she thinking? She felt her face redden, and he smiled again. Suddenly she swayed, overwhelmed by the heat and fear. He caught her and carried her over to a bench.

"My lady, I'm a terrible host. I should offer you a beverage. You've had an ordeal. Ale, perhaps? I can summon the boy."

She had regained some of her equilibrium now she was seated. She used her hand as a fan. "No, thank you. I'm just so hot."

He raked his gaze over her from head to toe. "Forgive me, Lady Blythe Lacey FitzRam, but your attire isn't suited to our summer climate."

She smiled ruefully. "You're absolutely right. It would be good to be wearing less."

His blue eyes lit up with suggestive delight—had she no control over her words?

*Think before you speak. Be on your guard.*

"Your hair is too tightly braided. My apologies if it appears rude to say so, but it is fashioned in a style that doesn't suit your beautiful face."

He raised his hand to touch her hair. "I regret bumping your head as we left the cathedral. How does it feel now?"

*Instantly better with his touch.*

"Perhaps if you took down your hair you would feel more comfortable?"

A shiver raced up and down her spine. "I cannot, sir," she whispered, wishing fervently she could. "It wouldn't be seemly to take down my hair in your presence."

He laughed. "Lady Blythe, it's not *seemly* of me to have carried you off!"

His laughter reverberated down to her toes and she took courage from his teasing. "Who are you, Black Knight?"

He looked away. "My name is of no importance, but you can call me your *Black Knight* if you wish."

*My Black Knight.*

"*Schwarze ritter,*" she attempted and he laughed again. "Very good. You have a good ear for my language."

The silence stretched between them before she had the courage to ask, "Why have you brought me here?"

His eyes pierced her. "We need you to take care of your child Queen. She knows you. She'll feel safer."

Her mouth fell open. "You've kidnapped the Queen? Why?"

He leapt to his feet. "Do you English know nothing of German politics, of our realities?"

She looked away from him, stunned by his vehement reply.

He took her hand and bowed to kiss it. "Forgive me, Lady Blythe, I didn't mean to be rude. We've come from Köln. Heinrich has laid siege to the city and blockaded it, cutting us off from the Rhine. We don't wish to be his subjects, so we've rebelled. We'll hold Matilda until he withdraws. We wish harm to neither her, nor you."

She looked up nervously, wanting for some incomprehensible reason to lift her hand to her lips and lick the still-wet warmth of his kiss. "You're from Köln? I know of the struggle there."

He shook his head emphatically. "*Nein*, I'm from Saxony. Like you I have Saxon blood. We're allies of our friends in Köln. I'm a vassal of Duke Lothar von Süpplingenburg of Saxony."

All of this was beyond her. Who was this Duke Lothar with the unpronounceable name? She laced her fingers together and looked anxiously toward the door. "But where *is* Matilda? Is someone bringing her? She must be terrified."

His brow furrowed as he rose to his feet. "*Ja*, you're right to be concerned. They should be here by now."

He strode to the door, leaving her alone in the silent church. She was grateful the stone pillars made it cooler here, but now she was trembling, despite her heavy gown. The sweat of her fear became clammy. Several anxious minutes later she heard horses approaching fast. Men shouted at each other in German. The Black

Knight's deep voice was raised in anger. Strangely, hearing it again calmed her. Abruptly he came back into the church, grasped her elbow and urged her towards the door.

She lifted the hem of her dress, afraid to stumble. "What's happening? Where are we going now?"

He did not look at her. "Köln."

Panic seized her. She would never be rescued if he took her to Köln. She tried in vain to pull her arm from his tight grasp. "But where is Matilda?"

He stopped suddenly and turned her to face him, his hands gripping her shoulders. His blue eyes glinted with anger. She held her breath. "Lady Blythe, I'm not accustomed to explaining myself to women, especially foreign women. Neither am I accustomed to failure, but it seems my men have failed me. Matilda escaped with her guards. Six of my comrades were killed, and several wounded."

A wave of relief swept over her. Now she would be freed. "But if you don't have Matilda, why do you need me?"

She regretted the words instantly. They would kill her now.

He stared at her for long moments. "We don't, but you'll come with us anyway."

She lowered her eyes and her heart plummeted. "I'm to be a hostage? They'll give you nothing for me. I'm of no importance to them."

He touched her hair again. "You're right," he replied gently. "But you're of importance to me."

He mounted his stallion and held out his hand. "Ride behind me."

She glanced around. Wounded men slumped against the backs of several riders. Perhaps she could aid them. With no hope of escape or rescue, she obeyed. She hitched up her copious skirts, straddled the horse behind him, grateful for many hours spent riding with her brother, and flung her arms around his waist. They rode off into the late afternoon sun.

~~~

The fear and hopelessness in his captive's eyes saddened Dieter. He was not a man who kidnapped innocent young women, and he had no doubt Lady Blythe Lacey FitzRam was indeed an innocent. But she was brave, had not whined or wept once, despite her obvious terror, and had maintained a dignified bearing.

"Why should I care what this Norman wench thinks?" he

wondered, trying to decide if her eyes were green or brown. He had untied the gag to allay her fear and admitted ruefully he had flirted with her.

*Ja, Dieter, but she's so beautiful, why not?*

His first proper look at her in the church had taken his breath away. His attention in the Cathedral had been wholly on the mission as he had crept up stealthily behind her. Carrying her on his shoulder had given him an indication of her form as her breasts bounced against him. No doubt he had hurt her. If he could just peel down her gown and make sure she wasn't bruised. He licked his lips, conjuring a vision of her copious globes in his hands. His *rute* responded.

As he ushered her hurriedly out of the church, he asked himself what he was doing. She would be an encumbrance. Why not simply cut his losses and leave her here? There was something about Blythe Lacey FitzRam he could not relinquish. What would she look like with her hair down, and without the sulky pout she seemed determined to keep on her face?

He resolved to concentrate on the hard reality of the failure of his mission. But his body betrayed him again as Lady Blythe's soft breasts pressed against his back in cadence with the movement of the horse.

# CHAPTER THREE

The mood of the men with whom Blythe rode was sombre. They were keenly aware they had failed in their mission and it had cost their comrades' lives. They rode all day, slowed down by the injured men and, Blythe knew, by her presence in their midst. It was clear from several hushed yet heated exchanges between Dieter and his men that they questioned his bringing her. Did they advocate killing her to rid themselves of the encumbrance?

They camped at night. Every amenity and courtesy was extended to her. Unfortunately, there were no amenities. Her bedraggled dress weighed her down like a stone. She longed for a good tub soak, and privacy. Her braids had come partly undone and she despaired of ever combing her hair again. Her bottom was raw. She could not recall the last time she had ridden so far.

The Black Knight was sensitive to the discomfort of her sore *derrière*, sometimes having her ride before him. She was dismayed and embarrassed by the hard male length pressed against her when the movement of the horse caused unavoidable contact—which was most of the time! He smiled his crooked grin when she eased her body away from his obvious interest. While she had not lain with a man, her mother had enlightened her as to what that particular swelling meant. The thought of lying with this powerful, enigmatic warrior sent a thrill racing up her spine.

Lacking expertise as a healer, she nevertheless did her best to ease the pain of the wounded men. None of the wounds were severe enough to be fatal, but fever could carry off the strongest of men in a trice. Her linen underskirt served to make bandages to stem bleeding, but she had no salve to offer. Her efforts to ease their suffering seemed to soften some of the censure. The sacrifice of her underskirt was a relief in the heat.

The second night they made camp close by a small lake. She looked longingly at the water.

"Do you wish to bathe, my lady?"

Preoccupied with gazing at the shimmering lake, she had not heard her captor approach. The accented voice broke into her reverie and heat suffused her chest and throat. She shook her head.

"No," she said, longing to say *yes*.

He gave her a quizzical look. "With your permission, I intend to avail myself of the lake to cleanse my body and revive my spirit."

He bowed slightly and left her by the campfire. He had spoken to her as if they were friends, equals, intimates—how dare he? He was a brigand who had abducted her. Chivalrous knights were supposed to rescue maidens, not carry them off. Yet his familiarity felt strangely—arousing!

She turned her attention to doing what little she could for the wounded men. It would be a while before the cook had food ready. She was afraid to fall asleep if she sat by the fire. Perhaps she could steal away and at least wash her face in the lake. There was no possibility of removing her clothing surrounded as she was by foreign bandits.

She deliberately strolled away in the opposite direction her captor had taken, hoping to find a secluded spot on the bank.

~ ~ ~

The chill of the water had eased Dieter's anger at the failure of his mission. He prized cleanliness and felt calmer now he had cleansed his body and hair. In an effort to rid himself of his tension, he had walked almost the whole way around the small lake before finally stripping off and plunging in.

He waded to the bank and strode out of the water, raking his wet hair back off his face, trying to recall the words of a ballad about Parsifal he had heard a *minnesinger* perform. As he bent to pick up his drying cloth, a squeal startled him. The song died on his lips. He had thought they had not been pursued, but now he reached for his sword and dagger, bracing to either flee or fight. He peered towards the source of the sound. The woman he had kidnapped stood ten feet away, gaping at him, her mouth open. She had undone the neckline of her gown and rolled up her sleeves. The sight of her bare arms sent blood rushing to his groin.

*Nein, Dieter, not a good idea with this woman. No time to be getting entangled.*

He held the cloth over his erection, embarrassed for her that she had stumbled upon him naked. "Lady Blythe—"

"I thought—I came this way—you had gone the other way—" She was frantically pushing down her sleeves, still staring at him.

It would not be the behaviour of a gentleman to move towards her, yet he wanted to take her in his arms, apologise for her kidnapping, kiss away the fear and embarrassment on her reddened face. A decisive man, his indecision hobbled him. Why had he burdened himself with the complication of Blythe Lacey FitzRam?

Before he could explain that he had walked around the lake, she had turned and fled, leaving him with the problem of what to do with his rock hard arousal.

~~~

Blythe was drowning in a whirling nightmare of trees and lengthening shadows as she staggered back to camp. She should have looked away immediately when she saw the man striding from the lake, water sluicing off his body, his hair dripping wet. The sheer size of him had held her gaze as her mouth fell open.

She paused in her flight to catch her breath, leaning her arm against a tree and resting her head atop it. She closed her eyes, but the image of his broad shoulders, narrow waist, and powerful thighs would not leave her. And his manhood—oh God, who knew they were so big!

His rich, deep voice echoed in her head, though she had not understood the words of his song. Swallowing hard, she hastened to the campfire. She wrapped the blanket set out for her tightly around her shoulders, refusing the roasted hare offered by the cook. She dared not look to the woods from where her captor would soon emerge.

~~~

Blythe was a physical and emotional wreck when they rode into Köln two days later. Neither she nor her Black Knight had uttered a word about the encounter by the lake.

They came to an impressive two-story house. Its stone façade was ornamented with statues of what she supposed were saints. The front wall seemed to soar to the heavens, tapering to a point topped by an ornate crucifix. She had never seen such an elaborately decorated home. Two similar structures stood either side. In the far distance she could see the sun glinting off the Rhine and beyond it the fortified town.

The Black Knight nodded in that direction. "There in Tuitium lurks your friend, Heinrich."

They rode under a curved arch into the courtyard, leaving behind the bustle of the street. She opened her mouth to explain the Emperor was nothing to her, but suddenly a dog barrelled out of the house and leapt at the Black Knight as he dismounted. He bent to accept the joyous welcome of the black and gold dog, laughing and fondling its ears. It licked his face, ran around in circles panting, then licked him again. He fell over as the animal showered him with love and laughed like a small boy as the dog's tail wagged ferociously.

"*Ja, Vormund, ich bin es.*"

When the dog calmed, the Black Knight came to his feet. His face was flushed. It came to her that her tongue was hanging out. Would that she had been the one crawling over him, licking his face, making him laugh. "Your dog loves you," she murmured.

He smiled. Her belly clenched. "*Ja*, Vormund is a good dog. He's our watchdog. His name means—how do you say in English—*Guardian*."

She was surprised. The dog did not look big enough or fierce enough to be a watchdog. She reached out her hand. "He doesn't look threatening."

The dog growled and she withdrew her hand quickly.

Her captor calmed the animal. "He is a Hovawart. They are excellent watchdogs. It will take him a while to get used to you, but then he will protect you with his life."

A while? How long was *a while*? The intensity in the Black Knight's eyes filled her with the fanciful notion that he too would lay down his life for her.

Her knight put his hand on the small of her back and ushered her into the blessed coolness of the house, issuing orders to several servants who appeared as if by magic. He handed her over to a squat little woman with grey hair. "Anna will take you to bathe."

She wished there was something she could hold on to as the opulent surroundings tilted around her at the mention of bathing. Would she ever forget the sight of him emerging from the lake? "But my clothes—I can't—"

He put his hand under her elbow. "Don't worry. Anna will take care of you."

Feeling steadier, she trailed after the little maid, who chatted away in German, not ceasing when Blythe simply shrugged her shoulders wearily in a sign of incomprehension. The woman did not seem taken aback by the sudden arrival of an unkempt Englishwoman.

Anna took her to a well appointed room where she peeled off Blythe's sweat-stained dress, hose and chemise, wrinkling up her nose as she did so. She barked an instruction to one of the other maids who were busily filling the bathtub. The girl left her task and reached up to unpin and unbraid Blythe's hair. She should resist, but longed to have the tight braids gone. Relief surged through her when her hair sprang free and fell to her waist. She was impatient for it to be clean again.

Anna tested the temperature of the water with her elbow before she allowed Blythe to step in. "*Gut!*" she announced, handing Blythe the soap, once she had assisted her into the tub. She swept from the room with a self-satisfied air, shooing out the other maids.

Blythe had never enjoyed a bath more. She lay back in the large tub and soaped her aching body, then dunked her head and washed her hair. Her nipples hardened and she blushed. Thinking of the Black Knight had sent warmth throbbing between her legs and up into her belly. She contracted her muscles, tightening her bottom. The movement sent pain radiating through her, an abrupt reminder of the soreness caused by her journey.

"Stop thinking of him that way!" she chided herself. "He has kidnapped you. You don't even know who he is. Don't show him any weakness. He may intend to sell you."

She leapt to her feet in the tub. "Holy Mother of God! That is what he plans to do!"

Fear washed over her, stealing away the pleasure of the bath.

*Maman, pray for me. Pray for your little girl.*

She would never see her beloved parents again, her fate sealed like those of young women in lurid tales, sold into slavery to satisfy the appetites of eastern potentates.

She sat back down and soaped her face quickly to hide her tears as Anna tapped at the door and entered. She was accompanied by several maids carrying dresses, chemises, hose and shoes. Anna fussed over the laying out of the clothing on the bed, while the maid who had unpinned her hair rinsed it with clean water. She assisted Blythe out of the tub, enveloping her in a luxurious drying cloth. Anna shooed the girl away and took over the drying. Once her body had been scrubbed dry, Blythe examined the dresses, all of fine woven scarlet fabric, reds, whites, blues, and greens. The gowns were not new, but of the best quality. She would be much more comfortable in this wardrobe. The Black Knight had been very generous to his prisoner. How had he arranged all this so quickly? He must have sent word ahead?

She selected a green surcoat dress and a fine linen chemise and the maids helped her dress. Anna's scrubbing with the drying cloth had fortified her and now the maid brushed her long hair until it was almost dry. It felt good to have the tangles out.

Blythe indicated she wanted crown braids, determined to keep the severe style she had worn to deter the men of Heinrich's court. She did not want anything about her appearance to encourage the Black Knight. There was not much she could do about the décolletage of the dresses which she considered much too revealing.

When Blythe was ready, Anna beckoned her through the door, making signs to show she was taking her to eat something. "*Kommen!*"

Blythe was hungry, having eaten only camp food on the journey, and not very much of that, since her stomach had been knotted with fear. She followed Anna willingly. The servant brought her to a large room where the Black Knight sat at an enormous wooden table laden with plates of food and drink. He too had washed away the evidence of their journey, though his eyes betrayed his fatigue.

He evidently favoured black clothing. Tunic, leggings, boots—all the same midnight colour as his long hair, blood red the only relief in the slashed sleeves of his doublet. Now three dogs lay at his feet. Only Vormund got up when his master did. The Rottweiler and the greyhound raised their heads and studied her, their tongues lolling. The greyhound yawned.

Her captor took her hand and brushed his lips to the back of it. "Ah, Lady Blythe, I see you're refreshed." His English was flawless.

Her nipples tingled and pulsating warmth spiralled between her legs. She would have to stop reacting with such wantonness to his touch. She was a woman of nineteen after all, not a silly girl. She bowed slightly to him, withdrawing her hand quickly. "Thank you for the gowns. I am sure I don't know how you managed to find clothing to fit so quickly."

He frowned and seemed uncertain of his answer. Then he smiled his enigmatic smile. "Sit and dine with me. I'm like a starving man after our journey."

~~~

Dieter watched to see if she caught his double meaning, and her blush as she glanced at his groin told him that she did. How to tell her where he had procured the dresses? The lighter gown showed off her figure more than her own unattractive garb. Her hips promised fertility. Her breasts were fuller than his dead wife's, and the fabric strained to contain them. Better not to allow his thoughts to wander in that direction.

His attraction to her puzzled and fascinated him. He should return her to the Imperial court, but for some reason wanted to get to know her. He could not afford to mire himself in domesticity, nor even in a meaningful relationship. His ambition to serve Duke Lothar left no room for that. He had endured a hellish marriage to a mad shrew, and had no intention of reliving such a nightmare again. Besides, he had a son. A young noblewoman would not want to take on the mothering of a child not her own.

He still seethed over the failure of the kidnapping plot, and hoped fervently the Duke would never find out he was involved in the debacle. He did not look forward to meeting with his co-conspirators. They would demand explanations he could not give.

Failure did not sit well with Count Dieter von Wolfenberg, and he had lost good men in the fiasco. How to cut his losses? Mayhap his captive was the child of a wealthy family—very likely since she had been a lady-in-waiting to Matilda. Perhaps there was something to be gained from capturing her after all?

He resolved to put her at ease and garner some useful information at the same time. "Tell me about your family, Lady Blythe."

She looked away, chewing her bottom lip. "My father is Sir Caedmon FitzRam. My mother is Lady Agneta, daughter of Eidwyn Kirkthwaite, my grandfather who was murdered by Scots and their Saxon allies two years before the battle of Alnwick."

"Alnwick?"

She related the details of the historic battle between the Scots and the Normans in the year of our Lord One Thousand and Ninety-three that had left the King of Scotland, Malcolm Canmore, dead on the bloodied field. "It's where my parents met. My mother rescued my father from the battlefield. He had been wounded."

Her voice, now she was calmer, held none of the passion that had washed over him when she was afraid. She was guarding her tongue. He offered her a succulent piece of roasted chicken.

"You like dogs," she said, looking down at the three hounds draped across his feet. "We have dogs at home in Northumbria, but they're not like these dogs of yours. Ours are mastiffs."

All three animals abruptly got up, as if they knew they were the subject of current conversation. Dieter stroked the Rottweiler's head then pummelled the dog's haunches. "This is Löwe, so called because he has the heart of a lion."

The greyhound nuzzled his master's hand. "And this is Schnell, because he is as swift as the wind when he chases hares."

"Will they let me touch them?"

"Perhaps once they get used to you. You told me your father is part Norman, part Saxon?"

She sank her teeth into the meat with relish. Dieter had a sudden urge to jump up and lick the juices from her lips. "Yes," she replied noncommittally.

His eyes fixed on her fingers as she licked the chicken grease from them. He raked his hand through his hair, trying to recall what she had just said. "Is he titled? What lands does he hold?"

"He's the Lord of Shelfhoc Hall in the Welsh Marches."

"But you mentioned a home in the north."

"Yes, Kirkthwaite Hall. It was destroyed as I mentioned, but rebuilt by my—"

She glanced up at him sharply, the fear of giving away too much evident in her narrowed eyes. He decided not to push her. "More chicken?"

She nodded and accepted with a smile. "I am very hungry."

It was the first time he had seen her do anything but sulk. Her beauty stunned him. Why did she insist on pouting and frowning? Why didn't she want him to see her loveliness? "How old are you, *liebling*?"

Her face reddened and she straightened her back, wiping her mouth with her napkin. "A gentleman doesn't ask such questions."

He had been right. She did not understand the endearment he

had used. "But I am no gentleman."

She squirmed in her seat. "I am nineteen."

His mouth fell open, but before he could speak, she rushed on. "I know most young ladies are married by my age, but I wasn't allowed to marry."

Dieter frowned. "Why not?"

"I am in service to her majesty."

Indignation washed over him that such a beauty, made to pleasure a man and bear him sons, had been denied the opportunity. "This seems unfair. Surely you have had many suitors?"

She made a snorting sound. "A lady-in-waiting is considered fair game by many *suitors*, most of whom don't have noble intentions. They're aware we cannot marry."

In a moment of clarity he understood the reasons for her severe hairstyle and pouty face. Here was a desirable woman who had known only the basest instincts of men since leaving the protection of her family. She had learned to defend herself and her heart as best she could. "Did you never wish to marry?"

It was a long while before she answered. "If I ever marry, I would wish for an honourable man like my father. He is kind and loving."

Should he push her? Why did he want to ease the hurts she had been given, to let her know not all men behaved thus? Why would she trust him—he had carried her away. "You have never met such a man?"

"No," she whispered, refusing to look at him.

Löwe lumbered to his feet, waddled over to her and laid his muzzle on her lap.

"He likes you!" Dieter exclaimed, wishing he could lay his head on her tempting thighs and gaze up at her as his dog did. He had a curious yearning for that elegant hand to be stroking and petting him.

# CHAPTER FOUR

The long, hot summer dragged on with no sign of an end to Blythe's captivity. She found it increasingly difficult to be impervious to the Black Knight's charms. For charming he was, and despite the restrictions and difficulties imposed upon Köln by the blockade of the Rhine, he took Blythe to parts of the ancient city founded by the Romans. A maidservant always accompanied them in the stylish carriage he owned. He showed her sections of the Roman city wall and water system, which formerly brought fresh spring water to the ancient city from the Eifel region.

"The name Köln comes from the Roman empress, Agrippina," he explained to her. "The wife of the Emperor Claudius was born on the banks of the Rhine and elevated her "Colonia" to the status of a city in the Fiftieth Year of Our Lord. The Roman road network is still reflected this very day in the layout of the streets."

She tried to remain aloof, though she found the old city fascinating and his company exhilarating. His deep, slightly accented voice soothed her. The light touch of his hand on her back as he assisted her into the carriage caused a tingle that filled her with inexplicable joy. As she descended, his gentle support of her elbow sent desire coiling through her belly. She adopted a habit of taking deep breaths, feigning a desire for fresh air in her lungs. His clean, masculine scent made her salivate.

But he had taken her as his prisoner against her will and she was still afraid he intended to sell her. She did not want to dwell on who might want to buy her and for what purpose. Surely the Black Knight was not a man to commit such a crime? To be safe, she reasoned that if she made herself unattractive she would not be worth selling. Her other inspiration was that she should perhaps suggest he ransom her to her family. Her parents must be frantically worried and would pay willingly. But what amount would he demand?

She kept her face sullen. "It's interesting, thank you for showing me."

~~~

Determined for reasons beyond his comprehension to draw Blythe out of her self-imposed ugliness of face and demeanour, Dieter took her out more and more frequently. She was an intelligent woman who would be interested in knowing how the Romans brought Christianity to Köln, and how the city very soon became the seat of a bishopric. "In the year of our Lord Seven Hundred and Eighty-Five, Charlemagne himself founded the Archbishopric of Köln and bestowed secular powers upon the church dignitaries. The Archbishop of Köln became one of the most powerful feudal lords in the Holy Roman Empire."

She inhaled deeply and yawned. "Hmm."

He was disappointed in her cool demeanour. He was drawn to this woman, had been since their first encounter, but she evidently did not feel the same towards him. It was a blow to his male ego. To her he was simply a guide, whereas he longed to strip off her clothes and make love to her on the floor of the carriage. Her scent filled his nostrils, even when he wasn't with her. She recoiled whenever he touched her, when all he intended was to help her in and out of the carriage. Despite her aloofness, or perhaps because of it, he could not resist increasing the pressure of his hand on her back. He longed to look into those bewitching eyes, but she always avoided his gaze. Having to conceal his seemingly constant arousal from her, and the maidservant, was maddening.

He often watched from the upstairs window as she enjoyed his garden, compelled to spy on her. Then he saw the real Blythe. When she closed her eyes and bent to inhale the fragrance of a flower, his senses reeled. When she beamed a bright smile on his gardener it was all he could do not to run down the stairs and kiss her until she cried for mercy.

She seemed to have no feelings for him, and though he was drawn to her like a moth to a candle's flame, he didn't want his heart burnt to cinders again. His marital experience had left him scarred in more ways than one. His captive lavished her attention on his hounds, not on him. He worried they loved her more than him. They too had fallen under the spell of this enigmatic woman.

Reluctant to alarm her with the progress of plans afoot to rid Köln of the Emperor once and for all, he did not confide the extent of his involvement. He spent a lot of time in clandestine meetings with other supporters of Duke Lothar.

He resolved to concentrate on the military campaign, deciding he may as well go ahead with his plan to ransom her to her family.

~~~

Blythe was aware Dieter hid his actions and political views from her, and suspected his involvement in plans to confront the Emperor. Was it that he didn't trust her? Or was she simply no threat to him, a non-entity he would soon be rid of?

She learned a few words of German by listening to the servants and other members of the household, but refused to speak German to him, feigning incomprehension. If he judged her dim-witted it would lower her value.

The weather cooled as autumn stole over the land. She saw her Black Knight less frequently and when she did he was tense, preoccupied. She sensed he was involved in some sort of imminent military action, and feared for his safety. But she could not tell him of her feelings. She convinced herself it was only fear of what would become of her if aught untoward befell him.

~~~

Something was wrong. Blythe sat bolt upright in her bed, awakened by strident barking. She heard angry voices, urgent shouts. There was a commotion in the garden. Nervously, she approached the window and looked out. The flames of torches danced along the pathways as shadowed figures ran here and there. Soon they congregated in one corner under the apple tree. Peering to see what was happening she caught sight of Vormund. The dog had sunk its teeth into the leg of a man trying to scale the high wall of the garden. He cried out in pain as the dog wrestled him to the ground and clamped its jaws on his arm. Several of the servants surrounded him, two of them holding back the Rottweiler, their hands gripping the dog's studded collar. Then she saw her Black Knight limping towards the group, sword drawn. Fear gripped her heart. Had he been injured? At a word from him, the dog loosed its grip. The servants dragged the man from the garden.

Blythe threw a bed robe over her nightgown and hastened down the stairs, meeting her captor as he limped in the doorway, Schnell at his side. He looked haggard. There was blood on his thigh.

"Stay in your chamber, Blythe. There may still be intruders at large. Don't be afraid. They won't re-enter the house."

She wanted to gather him in her arms, soothe away whatever hurt he had suffered. "What has happened? Who was that man?"

He braced himself against the newel of the banister and sheathed his sword. He hesitated, considering his words. "It seems I have upset someone. They tried to kill me."

She clasped her hands to her mouth. "Kill you? Who?" She moved towards him. "You're hurt."

He held up his hands to reassure her. "It's a flesh wound. Nothing more. I've suffered worse."

Her belly clenched at the thought of this beautiful man being wounded or scarred in any way.

Anna came rushing with linens and bandages and Dieter's valet, Bernhardt, assisted their master to his chamber. Blythe followed up the stairs, unsure as to whether it was appropriate to do so. She longed to help him, to make sure his wound was properly tended. At the door of his chamber she hesitated, watching nervously as the valet helped him onto the bed. "Will you be well, Black Knight?"

He raked his hand through his hair. "*Ja*, Blythe. I will be well. Anna will tend me. I know you are worried. They were probably the Emperor's men. The others will be long gone by now, but we have one of them, thanks to Vormund."

He smiled, but it was a weary smile. "I told you he was a good watchdog. He probably saved my life tonight. Take Schnell with you. You will be safe."

*But will you?*

~~~

His wound healed quickly. The house became an armed camp. No one spoke of the man who had been captured in the garden, and Blythe was afraid to ask.

One day in October her captor took her hand as they dined together. The stirrings of desire his touch never failed to ignite flared again. "Lady Blythe, on the morrow I'll be joining my comrades in an attack against Heinrich's army."

Her heart plummeted. Should she beg him not to go? He would think she had lost her wits. "Why must men always fight and kill each other?"

"*Liebling*," he replied softly, his eyes caressing her quivering lips, "Köln must be freed from the unjust domination of the Emperor. As for us Saxons, well, the conflict has smouldered since the Great Saxon Revolt many, many years ago."

*Liebling? He called me Liebling! Doesn't that mean darling? Perhaps I'm mistaken, and it means something else?*

Dieter was still explaining, brushing his thumb over her knuckles. "Heinrich has made attempts to confiscate Saxon counties as fiefs but has always met obstinate resistance. On the morrow we travel nine miles to Andernach to confront him on the plain."

Blythe was in turmoil. Nine miles! The enemy was a mere nine miles away. She longed to throw her arms around him, beg him not to go, tell him she loved him.

*Love him? Do I love him?*

She did not know his name. He didn't care about her. She was his prisoner.

She wished his thumb was caressing another part of her body instead of her hand. If she looked up at him, he would see the wanton desire in her eyes. "Black Knight, I wish you *Gottes segen* on the morrow. Godspeed."

His eyes widened. He placed his palm against her face. A tear trickled unbidden down her cheek and he wiped it away. "If I don't return from Andernach, be reassured I've sent messengers to your family in England. I'm sure they'll come for you. You're too precious to lose."

Her heart fluttered wildly. She could barely speak as relief swept over her. "My family? You don't intend to sell me? My parents know I'm here?"

He let go of her hand and straightened, a scowl on his face. "Sell you? Is that what you think of me? If your parents don't yet know your whereabouts, I'm confident they soon will."

She did not know what to say, stung by the anger in his voice. "I'm sorry, I—was afraid. I didn't know what you intended to do with me."

"That makes two of us!" he blurted out, shaking his head. He rose from the table, clicked his heels together and bowed. "I'll be gone before you rise so I bid you *auf Weidersehen* now."

She stood to face him, tears flowing freely. "Black Knight, on the morrow you'll leave for war, and I don't yet know your name."

He saw the tears, drew her into an embrace, brushed his lips on hers and breathed, "My name is Dieter, Count von Wolfenberg."

His name was the most wonderful sound she had ever heard. He was a Count! She closed her eyes and opened her mouth to his coaxing tongue. He braced his legs, cupped her bottom and pressed her body gently against him. She felt his desire and thought of what her mother had said about a man and woman joining their bodies. She wanted to crawl all over him, to possess him, to see him naked.

"Dieter," she whispered. "Dieter."

"Blythe, *mein Schatz*, you're so beautiful. I don't want to leave you, but I must."

He pulled away and she felt adrift, frantically trying to remember what *mein Schatz* meant. Was she his *cat*? How could he think her beautiful when she had done her best to present an ugly countenance?

He clicked his heels together again, bowed stiffly, kissed her hand and left.

## CHAPTER FIVE

For the third time the combatants in the conflict between the Holy Roman Emperor and the city of Köln faced each other, this time on the plain of Andernach. Dieter wished he could keep his mind on the business at hand. All he could think of was the bereft look on Blythe's face when he had left her. He had called her *his sweetheart*. Good thing she did not understand German, though sometimes he wondered—

He had left her quickly or he would have torn the clothes from her body and made love to her on the table. He had never wanted a woman as much as he wanted Blythe Lacey FitzRam. But she would never love him. He had frightened her. She thought he was going to sell her. "*Mein Gott*, she would think me capable of that?"

His friend Magnus rode up beside him and they surveyed the mighty host facing them. "What do you think of our chances, Dieter?"

Glad to be distracted from his thoughts of Blythe, he shrugged. "Heinrich has a very strong force, infantry as well as cavalry. Spies tell us he has recruited Franconians, Alemannians, and Bavarians, as well as knights from Burgundy. If he stays true to form, he'll send his dukes to fight the battle, and await the outcome of the conflict at a distance. We number far fewer but cunning and bravery may win the day for us."

Would he see Blythe again? What a fool to have left without telling her of his feelings.

Magnus looked to his left and frowned. "What's the command from Archbishop Frederick? There's a group on the march?"

Dieter rose up in the stirrups to get a better view. Lorraine's forces were indeed galloping towards Heinrich's army. "To throw the enemy off balance a little, he has instructed Duke Henry of Lorraine to rush against their flank."

Magnus struggled to control his skittish horse. "They'll be slaughtered."

"Not if they retreat in time."

A cloud of dust soon gathered on the near horizon. "*Gut!* Duke Henry is retreating, and they are following him. His actions will have unnerved them somewhat. Now, for our part. Count Theodoric and Count Henry of Kessel will attack with us."

Amid a frightful din of trumpets, the opposing armies came together in a bone chilling clash of horses and armour. For a long time the struggle remained undecided. Screams and moans rent the air as heads rolled, severed body parts thudded to the ground and horses stumbled in the gory mud. Men grunted, sweated and bled. Cries of momentary victory were smothered by the onslaught of the next wave of aggressors.

The muscles of Dieter's sword arm were on fire. He was covered in mud and blood, none of it his own, *Gott sei Dank*. Somehow he and Magnus had managed to stay mounted and close to each other. In a brief pause he shouted breathlessly to Magnus. "The Archbishop must send in the Special Force soon, or the day is lost."

As he spoke, a group of young men from Köln, specially chosen for their fighting skills, joined the fray, launching a slashing offensive in a berserker rage. Their wild cries sent chills skittering up and down Dieter's spine.

Magnus too shuddered, but breathed a sigh of relief. "They'll either prevail or die trying."

As expected, the enemy fell back under the crazed onslaught.

Dieter realized the critical importance of the next move. He rallied his men. "We must join Count Theodoric in a direct attack on the disordered enemy."

They cheered and followed him as he galloped into the melee. Though it seemed like hours later, they subjugated the dispirited enemy in a short time. Many of the Emperor's knights were killed or taken prisoner. None of the leaders on the side of Köln were killed or captured except Count Henry of Kessel, a friend of Dieter's, who fell under a horse's hooves and perished.

In the aftermath of the battle, Dieter's heroic leadership was credited with tipping the precarious final balance in favour of Köln's forces. Heinrich had failed to capture the city. He abandoned the siege to return to Mainz and his infant Queen.

~~~

Blythe wandered the halls and chambers of Dieter's home, the three dogs her ever-present companions. "You miss him too, don't you?" she said to Vormund, rubbing his ear. Löwe and Schnell nuzzled for her attention.

She played with the idea of attempting an escape while he was gone. But where would she go? Was it possible to get to Tuitium? What would she find if she did make it there? She had no love of the Emperor, whereas Count Dieter von Wolfenberg—did she want to escape?

*The dogs wouldn't let me go!*

The servants were polite, but they also waited nervously for their master's return. She no longer thought of them as her guards, but doubted they would allow her to leave. She worried about her family. Aidan especially would be bereft at her absence. If only England wasn't so far away. A woman alone would never survive such a journey.

Perhaps if she disguised herself as a nun? But where to procure such a garb? She had heard stories of women who had taken holy orders being raped and murdered. Her own Viking ancestors had not been blameless in that regard.

She had no appetite. Even the garden failed to delight. It seemed there was no recourse but to wait for Dieter's return. But what if he didn't come back? What if he was killed? The thought sent her scurrying to her chamber where she collapsed on the bed, sobbing. The handsome knight of her dreams had come into her life, but he didn't love her, and might never return from Andernach.

## CHAPTER SIX

"Agneta! Aidan! At last! News of Blythe." Caedmon's voice rang through the manor house at Shelfhoc. He clutched a parchment, brandishing it high above his head. "Where is everybody?"

At the age of two score and seven, Caedmon was still an active and virile man, though he suffered from rheumatism in the winter, and his black hair had turned completely gray. He teased Agneta that it was she who kept him young.

Ragna came running. "We were in the Hall. They have found my sister?"

Together they hurried there, bursting through the door with excitement, both shouting at once.

Agneta stood quickly and Caedmon threw his arms around her, laughing. "It's news of Blythe, at last!"

His wife clasped her hands to her mouth as tears trickled down her cheeks. "Blythe," she whispered.

Caedmon knew he was shouting, but couldn't seem to do otherwise. "She's in Cologne! Of all places! I passed through there during my misbegotten journey to the Crusade!"

Aidan had by now jumped up to grab the parchment from his father's hands. "What's she doing there?"

Caedmon slapped his son on the back. "As you see, my boy, she's said to be a *guest* of someone named Count Dieter von Wolfenberg. We're invited to *retrieve* her, which is an odd choice of words. The whole epistle is ambiguous. There is no outright mention of money, but—"

Aidan looked angry. "You mean they want us to pay to free her? Is she a prisoner?"

Caedmon scratched his head. "I'm not sure. Though the letter is in perfect English, it was obviously written by someone whose native tongue isn't English. It's too perfect. I wonder how she came to be a "guest" of this man? The last we heard from our King Henry she was taken forcefully from the cathedral at Mainz when someone tried to kidnap Matilda. Now the abductor wants us to *retrieve* her."

"Will we all go, Father?" asked sixteen year old Edwin.

Caedmon tousled his youngest son's hair. "No Edwin, the Empire can be a dangerous place, but I'll certainly go to *retrieve* my girl."

"And I will accompany you, Father," Aidan said with authority.

Caedmon was about to argue, but it was Aidan's right as Blythe's twin brother to aid in her rescue. His son had been in torment while Blythe was missing.

Ragna folded her arms across her chest and sulked. "I'm never allowed to go anywhere, or do anything."

Edwin snorted. "You do nothing but complain, Ragna. If I'm not allowed to go then you're surely not going. You're only thirteen, and a girl."

Ragna stamped her foot and fled the room. Meanwhile Agneta had slumped into a chair, sobbing. Caedmon went down on one knee at her feet. "At least we know she's safe."

She gripped his hand. "But Caedmon, Cologne is so far away. I feared for you when you journeyed that way before. Poor Blythe, she's so compromised now, no man will want to marry her."

She spoke the truth. Blythe's whereabouts had been unknown for many months and now she had turned up in the hands of a foreign Count. Her reputation would never recover. He grieved for his beautiful, spirited daughter. But she was courageous and had survived whatever ordeal had confronted her. He was determined to bring her home, whatever the cost.

~~~

Caedmon offered his men-at-arms the choice as to whether they wished to accompany him and Aidan. He did not want to take too many men and give the appearance of a belligerent force, but he also wanted the security of armed men about them. He made it clear they were not going for plunder or for gain. It would not be an easy journey, and in all likelihood they would not be home in time for Yuletide. However, he did have contacts along the route from his days on the Crusade.

On a chilly November day Agneta, Edwin and Ragna bid a tearful goodbye to Caedmon and Aidan and a score of Shelfhoc men.

Caedmon kissed his wife deeply. "I've sent a messenger to Baudoin at Ellesmere. He'll get word to Robert. We'll stay at Saint Germain de Montbryce for a day or two after we cross, perhaps gather more men there. Robert will want to help us. I know it's fruitless to tell you not to worry, but remember that Blythe will be with me the next time you see me."

He lowered his voice so only she could hear. "Before you know it, I'll be back in your bed, touching all those places you love me to touch."

Agneta laughed through her tears and blushed, pressing herself against his arousal. "You're going to have an uncomfortable ride, my Lord."

## CHAPTER SEVEN

Blythe awoke early, startled out of her sleep by raised voices outside. Since the capture of Tuitium and the blockade, the streets were often more or less deserted, especially early in the morning, and she wondered what the hubbub was about. She had lain awake for hours worrying about Dieter and had finally succumbed to exhaustion.

"*Sieg! Sieg!*"

She struggled to don her bed robe. "What does that mean? I must find Anna."

She almost bumped into the little maid as she opened the door to her chamber. "Anna, what's happening?"

Anna's cheeks were always two shiny red apples, but now her entire face was beet red and she was breathless with excitement. "Victory for Köln!" she shouted in German. "Victory for Graf Dieter! We've beaten the Emperor! Our brave Köln boys and our courageous Saxons have sent him packing!"

Dancing around, she grabbed Blythe who had understood little, except that Dieter was safe.

The entire household threw itself into preparations for the triumphant return of its hero, their master, who by all accounts filtering up from the streets had played a large part in the victory. Berta, the cook, set off to prepare all the Count's favourite dishes in time for his homecoming. Throughout her stay in his house, Blythe had known the servants respected their master, but now she saw how much they loved him, how proud they were.

She was conflicted. Her heart told her she loved him. Her head told her he had kidnapped her and held her for no reason. His actions had dishonoured her, and she would never be able to marry. No man would want her. He didn't want her, except for his gain. He planned to ransom her to her family. Her heart whispered that she should tell him she loved him. Her head scolded that he would laugh in her face, that he was not the kind of man to fall in love with a woman, especially a foreign woman. He was perhaps a man who might take improper advantage of her confession of love?

She ached for his return to assure herself he was safe. But she longed to see her parents again, hoped her father would come for her, rescue her from this torment. Better to spend her days as a spinster at home with her loving family than here in a foreign land with a man she loved, but could not have.

From an upstairs window, she watched as Dieter and his men rode into the street. She clenched her fists and pressed them to her mouth, uttering a prayer of thanks that Count Dieter Von Wolfenburg had returned unharmed. Pride flooded through her at the sight of the crowds hailing their champion. He sat so tall in the saddle, smiling and acknowledging the accolades with a wave of his hand. To be loved by such a man. Desire flooded through her. She arched her back, ran her hands over the pert nipples of her breasts, then down her belly, bringing them to rest on the aching need between her legs.

She gasped when he glanced up at the window. She stepped back, hoping the thick glass had prevented his seeing her, then hastened down to greet him.

~~~

Dieter was elated by the tremendous welcome Köln had given them, but he was tired. He had thought Blythe might come out to meet him, and was disappointed she had not. He scanned the windows. Was she watching? Did she care he had returned safely? He had thought of nothing else on the journey from Andernach.

The servants mobbed him when he came into the house, bowing and clapping and cheering. Blythe came quietly into the hallway and his mouth fell open. He had never seen her hair unbraided. The auburn tresses fell about her shoulders like liquid amber. His rute swelled at the sight.

He continued to graciously accept the accolades of his servants, hoping none of them would notice his arousal. He wanted desperately to bury his fingers in Blythe's hair, to press her body to his, to kiss her and thrust his tongue into her mouth. She stood motionless, hands clasped tightly in front of her. He sensed her tension and strode over to her. He put his hand over hers.

"Dieter," she murmured shyly, "you've come home safely."

It heartened him to hear her call his house her home. "Yes, Blythe. I've come home—to you." He raised his hand to touch her tresses. "Your hair—" His breath caught in his throat.

He was aware his servants were still milling around, watching curiously, and was glad of it, otherwise he might have done something improper to her at that moment.

He forced himself to move away. "I must excuse myself from your presence, Lady Blythe. It's been a long journey, and I need to bathe."

Her eyes widened and her mouth fell open. She blushed to the roots of her hair. Was she imagining him naked in the tub?

"Of course. Bernhardt has all in readiness, I believe. Perhaps in the dining hall later you can tell me all about your heroic deeds."

He kissed her hand and smiled. "Until then!"

~~~

Aidan FitzRam had accompanied his father to the castle de Montbryce in Normandie many times. Whenever they went there, Caedmon took his son into the crypt where they reflected on the life of Aidan's grandfather, Ram de Montbryce, Earl of Ellesmere and Comte de Montbryce. Though Caedmon was Ram's illegitimate son he had been welcomed wholeheartedly into the Montbryce family, especially by the Earl's wife, Mabelle. The FitzRam family had benefitted immeasurably from the love and legacy left to them. Aidan respected his father's wish to tell and retell the narrative of his relationship with his father and the Montbryce family. Aidan too would pass on the story to his children.

Breaking their journey at Saint Germain took them out of their way. However, it afforded them the chance to visit with Aidan's uncle, his father's half brother, Comte Robert de Montbryce and his wife Dorianne. Robert's five children, Alexandre, Catherine, Marguerite, Laurent and Romain, greeted their visitors enthusiastically. Aidan liked Alexandre. Although much younger than himself, the lad worshipped the ground Aidan walked on, following him everywhere. The older girls were too bossy for his liking, and the other boys too young."

"I wish I could accompany you both," Robert lamented. "I will always be grateful for the sacrifices you made in helping rescue me from imprisonment at the hands of the Duke of Normandie. However, the political situation here is so volatile I cannot be away for too long. Dorianne would have my head in any case if I left her alone with the children."

Caedmon shook his head. "Robert, you and Dorianne have endured long separation in the past. I should never have allowed King Henry to send my daughter to the Empire. Events have proven him incapable of protecting her. This is my duty to uphold. It's my responsibility to rescue Blythe. Mine and Aidan's."

Aidan, who never failed to be amazed at the physical resemblance between his father and his uncle, listened quietly to the conversation between them, and his heart filled with pride. Yet, he was deeply concerned about his twin sister, sensing she faced some sort of crisis that had nothing to do with being kidnapped. He concentrated on sending her positive thoughts.

## CHAPTER EIGHT

The journey to Köln took six days. As they passed through Caen, Caedmon pointed out to Aidan the *Abbaye aux Dames*, where he and Baudoin had found Dorianne and her newborn son, Alexandre, and spirited them to safety at Montbryce. When they passed the great hulk of the castle, Caedmon could barely speak of finding Robert beaten and almost broken in the cells. It seemed like only yesterday, yet ten years had flown since that wretched day.

From Caen they travelled overland without incident to Amiens, through Mons and Maastricht and finally to Köln, where they found a city still in the grip of euphoria over the victory at Andernach. News of Heinrich's humiliation had reached their ears well before they had neared the city.

Caedmon recalled a little of the Germanic languages he had picked up during the Crusade, though it had been twenty years since he had spoken them. They did not know exactly where to find Count Dieter von Wolfenberg, the writer of the letter. To Caedmon's surprise when he enquired, everyone knew where the hero of Andernach lived.

Aidan displayed his impatience with his inability to understand. "What did they say, Father?"

"They speak of this Count as if he's some kind of hero."

They found a field near the Rhine suitable for their camp.

Caedmon and Aidan left most of their men there, taking a handful of their escort to ride to the home of the Count. As they trotted into the courtyard boys appeared to take their horses. They dismounted and strode to the door. Caedmon rapped loudly with his fist, mouth drawn in a tight line, hand on the hilt of his sword. "I am Sir Caedmon FitzRam. I am here with my son Aidan," he shouted in his halting German.

A servant opened the door and bade them enter. It was evident they were expected.

Suddenly Blythe appeared out of nowhere and flung herself into her father's arms, sobbing loudly. Aidan enfolded her from behind in a protective circle and rubbed her back.

"Father—Aidan—I—"

It was Aidan who spoke first. "Blythe, my dear sister, I've worried about you. I've ached with your aches, wept with your sorrows. I'm overjoyed to see you whole. I never doubted you were still alive."

They embraced for many long minutes in silence, simply holding each other, reconnecting, while Caedmon gazed at them, relief sweeping over him. Gradually he became aware of a tall, well-muscled man dressed in black standing at the foot of a staircase. This black-haired devil was the Count, the man responsible for his daughter being in Köln. His first instinct was to walk over and pound him into the ground.

"You are Dieter von Wolfenberg?" he asked abruptly in English.

The man bowed. "I'm he, Sir Caedmon FitzRam. I welcome you and your son to my home. I trust you had a safe journey from England?"

Caedmon noted Dieter's English was flawless. "We've come for my daughter."

"She's here, as you see," Dieter replied, "but I would offer you my hospitality for a few days so Blythe has a chance to prepare for the journey home, and you and your son and your horses can rest after your—"

Aidan interrupted, his voice full of scorn. "We don't need to stay here. We can camp with our men near the Rhine."

Blythe put her hand on Aidan's arm. "Aidan, there is no need to camp with your men. I'm so happy you're here. Please accept Dieter's offer of hospitality so we can all spend time together. I have no wish to camp in a tent."

Aidan looked angrily to his father, who seemed as surprised as he at the way Blythe spoke of the Count. She had called him *Dieter*. It was almost as if—

Caedmon turned to Dieter. "We are obliged to accept your offer of hospitality. We will stay a few days. No doubt we have terms to discuss."

Dieter glanced quickly at Blythe, his lips tightly drawn. "*Gut*! My servants have prepared rooms in anticipation of your stay. Anna will show you the way. If you wish to bathe after your long journey, you have only to let them know. When you are refreshed perhaps we could meet in the gallery. Bernhardt will lead you there."

Caedmon and Aidan nodded and followed the servants. Blythe went with them, arm in arm with Aidan.

~~~

Dieter let out a long, slow breath. The confrontation had gone more smoothly than he could have hoped. He watched Blythe go off with her family, happier than he had ever seen her. He had known when he heard the demand for entry the angry visitor could only be Blythe's father. Dread had filled him. He was not afraid of the man's ire, which was after all justified. But this arrival meant Blythe's departure.

Dieter had entered the hallway in time to see Blythe run to her father's arms. As he watched the tearful reunion he knew that Blythe had been brought up in a loving home, and again he felt terrible remorse for having abducted her. He had brought this family nothing but anguish and still did not understand what had motivated him to bring her to Köln. He suddenly felt bereft, an outsider.

He had seen the expression change on Sir Caedmon's face when the man noticed him. He expected it, understood the anger, and braced his shoulders as the Englishman strode over to where he stood. Though no longer a young man, this grey haired knight was obviously still a force to be reckoned with.

Dieter wished he could put such a smile on Blythe's face. If only she cared for him. He longed to be enfolded in her arms, so he could bury his face in her lovely breasts, make her cry out with joy as he—

He shook his head and leaned heavily on the banister. This had to stop! She would be leaving soon. She did not love him and that was that. He had things to accomplish for his Duke. He pulled himself together and hurried to the kitchens to make sure all was in order for the evening meal.

~~~

Caedmon, Aidan and Blythe clung to each other in the larger of the two adjoining chambers prepared for the men.

"I was sewing when I heard your voice, Papa. I couldn't believe it. I hoped you would come."

Aidan put his hands on her shoulders and looked into her eyes. "Has he harmed you, Blythe?"

She shook her head. "No, Aidan, he's a noble man. He would never harm me."

Caedmon did not understand. "Is he not the person who abducted you?"

Blythe averted her eyes. "Yes, he is, but I was not the intended hostage really. It was part of an unsuccessful plot to kidnap Matilda."

Aidan snorted. "Why didn't he let you go when the plot failed?"

Blythe moved away, fidgeting with the lace of her sleeves. "I don't know, Aidan. At first I thought he planned to sell me into slavery, but I know now he would never do such a thing. So I surmised he would ransom me to my family, and here you are."

Caedmon coughed, not sure what all this meant. "He hasn't asked for a ransom."

His daughter was obviously surprised by this news. "He hasn't? I don't understand."

He put his arm around her shoulders. "Neither do I, daughter. Mayhap after I speak with him things will be clearer. I learned a long time ago not to jump to hasty conclusions. What's all this talk in the streets about him being a hero?"

Blythe smiled broadly. "He *is* a hero, Father."

As she described Dieter's pivotal role in the victory of Köln over the Emperor, Caedmon noticed how glowingly she described the exploits of a man one would think she would hate for what he had inflicted on her. "You seem quite impressed with his bravery."

She blushed and looked away. "Well, he's a brave man. I can't deny that."

Aidan was furious. "Brave men don't kidnap innocent girls."

Blythe seemed at a loss to know how to respond. "Why not summon a bath for each of you to wash off the dust of your travels, and I'll meet you later? I'm so happy you're here. I've missed everyone at home. How are Edwin and Ragna? Is she still a hellion? How is mother?"

She had changed the subject, but Caedmon did not press her. He answered her questions, then bade her leave so he and Aidan could bathe.

"What are you thinking, Father?" Aidan asked after she had left. "Are we going to kill him for what he has done?"

"I'm thinking that if we kill him, the person most likely to be distraught about the deed would be your sister."

~~~

After bathing, Caedmon instructed Aidan to find Blythe and distract her with a walk in the garden. He wanted to confront the Count alone. As the twins strolled arm in arm in the chilly winter air, Aidan was curious about how she had survived her ordeal.

She smiled. "At first it was an ordeal, I agree. But Dieter is a charming and gentle man. He has tried to make me comfortable. He really is a hero, and in truth I'm the one who has made it an ordeal for him."

"I don't understand."

"I've behaved rudely towards him. I've tried to make myself ugly, unattractive to him."

"Why not? He abducted you."

She turned to face him. "Aidan, you're my twin. I know it's no use trying to hide anything from you, but you mustn't tell Father—I was afraid to fall in love with Dieter."

"By the Saints, Blythe!" he retorted angrily. "How could you fall in love with a man who abducted you and kept you against your will for months?"

"I don't know, but I think I do love him. I didn't want to because he's not the kind of man who could ever fall in love, and would probably laugh in my face if I told him I loved him."

Aidan rolled his eyes and threw up his hands. "I'll never understand women! Has he defiled you?"

She punched him hard in the shoulder and he winced. "No, he hasn't! You haven't listened to anything I've said."

~~~

From the upstairs window Dieter watched the exchange between the twins. He saw how comfortable they were with one another, despite the fact they were male and female, and he marvelled at the notion of twins. But they were not in agreement about something, and he wondered what it was. Blythe had punched her brother's shoulder and run off into the house.

However, he did not have time to ponder further. He hastened his pace to the gallery for what he anticipated would be a difficult interview with Sir Caedmon.

The knight awaited him, legs braced, arms crossed over his chest. Dieter noted he had left his sword in his chamber. That boded well. Why did he feel like a naughty boy about to be punished? "Please, sit down, Sir Caedmon."

"I'll remain standing."

For the first time, Dieter noticed something of a Scottish brogue in the knight's speech. Blythe had shared some of her father's story, and he was awed that here stood a man who had endured the People's Crusade and returned home a hero. "May I offer you some refreshment?"

Sir Caedmon shifted his weight and moved closer to Dieter. "Let's not waste time with niceties. You know I want to kill you."

"Yes, I'm aware you feel that way. I would probably feel the same if I was you."

Anger blazed in the Englishman's eyes. "You've dishonoured my daughter."

Dieter was outraged. "Sir Caedmon, I give you my word of honour I have not."

The Englishman stepped closer, fists clenched. "But you've compromised her by keeping her here so long. No woman who has spent so much time alone with a man will be accepted back into society in England. Why did you keep her when you failed to take Matilda? Of what use was she to you?"

Dieter could not look into the man's eyes. "I confess I wish I knew the answer to those questions. I've asked them myself many times. I simply couldn't relinquish her. I had to hold on to her."

"But you've ruined her chances for marriage!" Sir Caedmon shouted.

Dieter shouted back. "I would gladly marry her myself if she didn't hate me so much." The vehemence of his own words astounded him, and Sir Caedmon was obviously taken aback.

"What?" the knight roared.

Unexpectedly, relief washed over Dieter. He had finally admitted the truth of his feelings for Blythe. "I love your daughter,

Sir Caedmon. I realize now I've loved her from the first moment I looked into her eyes in those desperate moments in the cathedral. But she hates me for what I've done to her."

Sir Caedmon snickered. "I know only too well what gazing into hazel eyes can do to a man. She doesn't hate you, Count Dieter."

He glanced up sharply. "What do you mean? How can she not hate me?"

"A woman who hates a man doesn't look at him the way Blythe looks at you. She doesn't speak of him in the way Blythe speaks about you. I haven't seen a woman so much in love with a man since my own sweet Agneta fell head over heels for me!"

Dieter's heart swelled on hearing Caedmon's words, but he seemed to have something stuck in his throat. When he could speak, his voice sounded like someone else's. "You believe she's in love with me?"

"Ask her."

# CHAPTER NINE

Aidan found his father sitting alone, his feet up on a footstool. "I've just had a very strange conversation with Blythe. We have a problem. I'll never understand women. Have you spoken with the Count?"

Caedmon indicated the chair next to him. "Yes. There is no ransom demand. Tell me about this conversation you refer to."

Aidan sat. "I promised Blythe I wouldn't. We've always kept each other's secrets."

Caedmon waited a moment or two. "Did it concern the Count?"

Aidan came to his feet and paced. "Yes—she is—she thinks she is—"

"She thinks she loves him."

Aidan spun around to face his father. "How did you know?"

Caedmon stood and playfully hooked his arm around Aidan's neck. "Ah, my son, I'm much older and wiser than you."

Aidan struggled to free himself from his father's hold. "But aren't you furious? How can she love him? He's a Saxon."

Caedmon released his son, his face sober. "Careful Aidan, don't forget we have Saxon blood in our veins, albeit from different parts of Saxony originally. And never forget the lessons I've tried to teach you about intolerance and hatred."

Aidan gave his sire a sheepish look. "I'm sorry. It's that I can't understand—"

"Aidan, love is often a difficult emotion to understand. Who would imagine for example that a Count from Saxony, living in

Köln would fall in love with our Blythe?"

"He loves her?" Aidan asked incredulously. "By the saints! I swear I'm never going to fall in love. It's too complicated. What are we going to do now?"

"Nothing, except enjoy the Count's hospitality. Come, dinner awaits in the dining hall. It occurs to me that you and I need to have a long conversation."

"About what?"

Caedmon chuckled and tousled his son's hair. "About women, Aidan Branton FitzRam. As my heir you're expected to marry and have children."

Aidan threw his shoulders back and straightened his hair. "I have a lot of time before I need to think about marriage. I'm still one year short of a full score."

Caedmon nudged Aidan towards the dining hall. "That's true, but trust me when I tell you that living with a woman is much more satisfying and joyful if you share love and passion."

Aidan sighed loudly and rolled his eyes. "Father, you and Mother have told us this many times."

Caedmon suddenly realized he did not know if his son was still a virgin. "Yes, Aidan, but you and I have never had a discussion about how to satisfy a woman."

Aidan looked puzzled. "What do you mean 'satisfy'?"

Aidan's deep blush told his Father there was likely a great deal of knowledge he would need to pass on to him. Agneta had made sure their daughters were prepared for marriage, and he regretted now he had not been more direct in such matters with his sons. "I mean in bed, Aidan. Don't worry. We'll talk—it's a long journey home. I'm an expert in these matters! Ask your mother."

~~~

Dieter offered Caedmon the seat at the other end of the oblong dining table from where he sat, and the twins dined facing each other on the sides. Blythe was relieved that her father's anger seemed to have cooled, and the conversation was almost jovial.

"I'm curious, Sir Caedmon," Dieter said, "you're an English knight. Blythe tells me you're part Norman, part Saxon, and yet you speak with an accent reminiscent of Scotland."

"You're right, Count von Wolfenberg, my mother fled to Scotland after the Conquest. I was born there, but returned to live in England when I married my wife."

"Your mother was the Saxon then?"

Caedmon paused only a moment. "Yes, her name was Lady Ascha Bronson. My father was the late Ram de Montbryce, the first Earl of Ellesmere. He fought with William the Conqueror at the Battle of Hastings."

"And that's the reason you bear the name FitzRam, and not Montbryce?"

Blythe feared her father would get annoyed at these personal questions, but Dieter seemed genuinely interested and her father unflustered. What was going on?

"Yes, I have two half brothers—Baudoin, the current Earl of Ellesmere and Robert, the *Comte* de Montbryce in Normandie, and a half sister, Rhoni, Lady MacLachlainn."

They ate in companionable silence for a while before Dieter spoke again. "I've heard things are still unsettled in Normandie?"

The two men chatted on amicably about politics. Dieter told the story of Andernach and shared his strong opinions about the Emperor. Caedmon related the tale of Agneta rescuing him after he fell at the Battle of Alnwick. Aidan and Blythe exchanged curious glances across the table.

After a while Caedmon stifled a yawn. He leaned towards Aidan. "Come, this old man is tired. I can't keep up with you young people any more. Let's retire and enjoy the Count's hospitality. I'm for bed."

"But Father, I thought I would—"

Blythe could have sworn her father winked at Aidan. Her brother abruptly changed his mind.

"You're right. I'm tired. Goodnight, Blythe. Count."

Caedmon kissed Blythe's forehead. "Goodnight, my lovely girl, I've missed you."

"I've missed you too, Father."

~~~

Silence reigned in the room after they left. Blythe twiddled her thumbs nervously. Her hands did not want to be still. She could feel Dieter's eyes on her. "You and my father got along well this evening. I assume you settled on a mutually agreeable ransom for me?"

"I asked for no ransom, Blythe. That's not why I asked your father to come for you."

She looked up from her fidgeting and stared at him. "Why did you ask him?"

He came to his feet and moved to stand behind her. He didn't touch her, but she could feel the warmth of his body. "Because I came to realize I couldn't keep you here any longer, no matter how much I wanted to. If I did you would loathe me more than you do now, and I would find that hard to bear. I knew I had to let you go."

Was he saying what she thought he was saying? "I don't hate you, Dieter. I've tried, and find I can't."

He moved to stand at her side, took hold of her hands and pulled her to her feet. "I wouldn't blame you for hating me. I'm sorry I've hurt you and your family. I couldn't help myself. I want you so badly."

The warmth of his hands travelled into her belly and warred with the chills running up and down her spine. "You want me? For what?"

He put his hands on her waist and drew her to his body. "For my wife, Blythe. I love you. I've loved you from the moment we met. I've denied it, but I can't stand the thought of your leaving here. My life will be empty without you."

She felt the hard evidence of his passion pressed against her and wetness pooled between her legs. Her breasts tingled. Words rushed out of her mouth. "But how can you love me? I've been cold and rude. I was afraid to fall in love with you and pretended to be aloof. If you knew how many times I itched to put my hands on your body and explore every part of you. I've longed to comb my fingers through your beautiful hair, to feel your hands on my body. Dieter, *ich liebe dich*! I love you so much I would die if I had to remain here and not—"

His deep passionate kiss interrupted her. His tongue delved into her mouth and she sucked on it. The sensation sent heat surging from the top of her head to the tips of her toes.

He tore his mouth from hers. They were both panting hard. He took her hand and placed it on the side of his face. "Touch me, Blythe. I've longed for you to caress me. I want to make you my wife in every possible way."

Before she could respond, he put a fingertip to her lips. "I must tell you something before you make your decision."

She had an urge to suck his finger into her mouth, but he looked worried. "What is it?"

"I have a son."

This was not what she expected. If he had a son, it would mean— "A son?"

He went down on one knee, but never took his eyes from her face. "I am a widower, Blythe. My wife died. My son's name is Johann. You need to understand he is my heir."

Her heart went out to the child she had never met. Her mother and father had always been an important part of her life. She could not imagine growing up without a mother. "Oh, Dieter, to be a motherless child. How would he feel about—me?"

He came to his feet. "I might have known your first thought would not be for yourself, but for my child. I love you Blythe Lacey FitzRam. Johann will love you too. Please accept my proposal of marriage."

Her body burned for him. Was this really happening? "Yes, I accept, but my father—"

He hugged her tightly. "I've spoken to your father. I don't foresee a problem."

She laughed. "I wondered why you two were so amicable this evening! You rogue!"

He crushed her to his body, raking his fingers through her hair. "*Ja*, I'm a rogue who carried you away, but you stole my heart with your ugly braids and sullen pouts! I didn't know you spoke any German, and yet you tell me you love me in my language!"

"Dieter, I'm on fire for you. You've awakened feelings in me I've never experienced before. My body aches for you."

He kissed her again. "You're a passionate woman, *mein Schatz*. I hope I'll be able to satisfy your needs."

He flashed his enigmatic smile and rocked his hips against her. "As you can probably tell I would like to do that very thing right now, but I prefer to wait until we're married. I'll speak to Archbishop Frederick on the morrow."

## CHAPTER TEN

Dieter's widowed father and older sister travelled from Wolfenberg, bringing three year old Johann. Blythe fell in love with the child as soon as she saw him. He was a miniature Dieter. The boy seemed overwhelmed and tired after the journey. He clung to his grandfather's leg, wide-eyed, watching the adults greet each other. Vormund licked his face and he laughed as he swiped his sleeve across his mouth. Dieter knelt and held his arms out to his son, but it took a definite push for him to relinquish his grandfather's leg and go into his father's welcoming arms.

Dieter fondled his son's hair. "Don't you remember me, Johann, I'm your Papa? Vormund is glad to see you too, *ja*?"

Johann put his arms around Dieter's neck and hugged his father. "*Ja*, Papa."

Blythe's heart swelled at the love on Dieter's face. He turned Johann to face her, his hands on the boy's shoulders. "Lady Blythe Lacey FitzRam, may I present my only son, Johann Dieter Marius von Wolfenberg."

She wished Dieter had not made the introduction so formal. She desperately wanted the boy to like her. He averted his eyes and shrank away.

His father prodded him forward. "You must make a polite bow, Johann."

The little boy bowed, without looking at her. She fell to her knees and opened her arms. "*Kommen*, Johann. Let me embrace you. We will be great friends."

After a furtive glance at his nodding grandfather, he obeyed. The daunting responsibility of caring for this child swept over her, but it gladdened her that this was another part of Dieter's life she could cherish and protect.

Dieter and his father laughed and Johann went back quickly to his Papa. Dieter hoisted him up on his shoulders and offered his hand to Blythe. "Your nursemaid will take you to bathe, Johann, and then I will show you new toys we have for you."

The boy grinned and nodded and his grandfather took him off to their chambers, leaving Dieter and Blythe alone. He took her hand and led her to the chairs by the hearth. "I hope he likes me," she said.

"He was a little shy, but he'll get over that. He'll come to love you as I do. He will benefit from having brothers and sisters, and I intend to provide him with lots of those."

Blythe smiled at his lecherous grin and blushed. They sat for a while in silence. She wanted to ask about Johann's mother, but was hesitant. Dieter had never revealed anything about her, but the questions had to be asked. "What was his mother's name?"

He glanced up sharply. "I know we must speak of this, Blythe. I want no secrets between us, but it is difficult to talk about. I admit I have put it off."

She rose and went to kneel at his feet, resting her head on his lap. "You don't have to tell me if you don't wish to."

The silence stretched between them. She felt the tension in his body as he stroked her hair. "Her name was Frederika. She was mad."

Blythe raised her head abruptly and looked at him, wishing she had not. Despair haunted his eyes. She gripped his hands and swallowed hard, hating to see him in such pain. "Dieter, my love. What happened to her?"

He inhaled deeply. "Eventually she drowned herself."

Blythe had to sink her teeth into the flesh of her hand to stifle a cry of sorrow and outrage. What this man had endured. "Did she love Johann?"

Dieter shrugged. "I don't think she even knew who he was at the end."

Tears trickled down Blythe's cheek. "Why did you marry her if she was mad?"

He took her face in his hands and wiped away her tears with his thumbs. "We were betrothed when we were children. No one knew then what would befall her. It was an obligation. I did not meet her until the day of our marriage and I sensed then something was wrong, but it was my duty. If I'd known the extent of her madness, I would not have married her, but the die was cast once we were wed. I never loved her, Blythe. You are the only woman I have ever loved."

She put her hands over his. "And you are the only man I have ever loved, ever will love. Your child is my child."

He came to his feet and helped her rise, pulling her into his embrace. "I never expected to find a love like ours, *liebling*."

"Nor I."

~~~

Caedmon FitzRam walked proudly into the Old Cathedral in Köln with his magnificent daughter on his arm. She looked radiant and his heart was filled with joy that she had found someone with whom she could share love and passion. He was sorry Agneta could not be there. However, Dieter had sent messengers to Saint Germain, and Robert would send the message on by way of the regular relays the Montbryces used. He was confident it was the quickest way to get the happy news of Blythe's betrothal and marriage to his family in England.

He laughed as he thought of his precocious daughter, Ragna. She would be mortified not to be present at her sister's wedding and would ask him thousands of questions. He studied his eldest daughter, trying to memorise the details of the occasion, for he well recognised Aidan would be useless in this.

Blythe's blue silk dress, edged along the hem with ermine, fell gracefully from the high waist, banded with a wide sash of the same silk, which emphasized the swell of her breasts. He noted with satisfaction that she was indeed her mother's daughter. The bodice had long sleeves and a cerise coloured cowl plunged from her shoulders to the high waistline. As she walked she lifted the edge, revealing a cerise coloured underskirt and dainty shoes tied around the ankles.

Dieter had given her an amber necklace as a betrothal gift and she wore it proudly now. On her head she bore a circlet headdress, beribboned with cerise ribbons, and a shimmering veil. Caedmon closed his eyes and his thoughts drifted back to his own wedding in the fledgling abbey at Alnwick. Though not a wealthy man then, he had been just as consumed with love for Agneta as Dieter seemed to be for Blythe.

The Count wore a long sleeved black tunic of fine wool, black leggings and black boots. White ribbon adorned the black hilt of his sword, and a long white cloak, worn off the shoulders, fell almost to his feet. It struck Caedmon he had never seen his son-by-marriage in anything other than black clothing.

Johann acted as his father's page and was dressed in garb identical to his father's.

Caedmon smiled. He would be able to report to Ragna that it was indeed a magnificent wedding. He relished teasing her mercilessly about it. In that regard, Aidan would be the perfect ally.

~~~

Archbishop Frederick conducted the lengthy ceremony. As he settled into the second quarter hour of his homily, Blythe's mind wandered over what Dieter had told her about the cathedral in which she knelt. Christian buildings had existed on the site since the fourth century. Her thoughts flew back to the coronation ceremony in Mainz. It seemed long ago and far away. How unhappy she had been then.

She longed for the nuptial ceremony to be over, the banquet to be done. It had been a fortnight of restraint that had stretched both hers and Dieter's patience. She wanted to get on with discovering the passions her mother had hinted at. She thirsted to see Dieter naked and he had told her he dreamed every night of running his hands through her auburn hair while she lay beneath him.

Aidan did not speak German, and he shifted restlessly in his pew. He was still cool towards Dieter and she suspected it was difficult for him to accept his twin would be far away.

Her father didn't miss his cue when asked to place the coins symbolic of her dowry on the Bible. Caedmon had endowed her with one of his Sussex estates and a substantial sum of money. Dieter had presented her with an estate he owned in Saxony.

It would soon be Yuletide and the cathedral was chilly. Incense hung in the air as if frozen in place. Her toes were freezing. Dieter noticed her shiver and tightened his grip on her hand, smiling his enigmatic smile. His warmth filled her with longing. Would anyone notice if she kissed his hand? She willed the Archbishop to cease speaking.

Finally, the rites were completed and everyone processed out of the cathedral. Dieter and Aidan lifted Blythe by the forearms so her feet would not touch the slippery path. Anna draped a warm fur around her shoulders and Dieter shrugged into a wolfskin coat held out for him by Bernhardt. Laughing, they were bundled into a horse-drawn sleigh and tucked in. Köln had experienced an unusual December snowfall. Dieter kissed her deeply as the driver cajoled the horse into a trot and headed for his house.

"*Ich liebe dich*, Blythe," he whispered, caressing the side of her face and gazing into her eyes. "I love you, my wife. You're so beautiful."

The love she saw in those blue depths humbled her. "I love you too, *Schwarze ritter*."

He enveloped her in his arms, pulling her to him and tucked her cold hands inside his coat, warming them with his body. She felt the firm muscles of his chest.

She shivered. "My feet are so cold."

"Not far now, *liebling*, and then I'll warm your feet. In fact I hope it won't be long before I'm warming your whole body."

She shivered again, but not from the cold.

~~~

Blythe was delighted to see throngs of cheering crowds assembled to greet the hero of Andernach and his bride as they arrived home. He assisted her from the sleigh, taking a moment to kiss her, to the delight of the crowd. He waved, picked her up and carried her over the threshold of his house.

"*Willkommen, Gräfin* von Wolfenberg, welcome to your home, my Countess."

She kissed him and rubbed her cold nose against his. They laughed. He sat her on a chair and rubbed her feet, until she stopped shivering. How could his hands be so comfortingly warm when they had been outside in the frigid air?

Excited servants scurried here and there, looking important. As the guests arrived they were ushered into the dining room, and Dieter and Blythe took their places at the head table, accompanied by Caedmon, Aidan, her father-by-marriage, Dieter's sister, and Johann. Shy at first, the little boy had quickly responded to the loving attention Blythe had heaped on him. She was enjoying getting to know Dieter's modest father and sister who were proud of Dieter and treated her like a queen.

Indeed she felt like royalty as the festivities commenced. Their guests were happy for them, and she almost burst into tears when her father winked and smiled. How she loved him. He had been the rock of their family, and she felt privileged to be the daughter of such a loving man. She knew many young women at Henry's court who had no relationship with their fathers.

To have her twin there was a boon beyond measure. She caught him gazing at her thoughtfully several times and wondered what his true feelings were. She leaned in to whisper to him as the food was being served. "Aidan, you know you'll always be the most important man in my life?"

He smiled back, clasping her hand. "No, but I don't object to being the third most important, after Dieter and Father."

Caedmon rose to toast his daughter and her new husband. Dieter's father came close to tears expressing his sentiments in his toast.

Dieter embraced him, and then proposed a toast of his own to his bride. "I'm the most fortunate of men. I am today the husband of the beautiful Blythe. My bride is a woman of incredible courage and fortitude. Though she's not of our homeland, she has embraced our culture and our customs. She's a woman I'm proud to call my wife. Please drink to the long life and health of my bride, Blythe Lacey von Wolfenberg."

Voices echoed the toast and tankards banged loudly on tables. Blythe rose to respond. "*Graf* Dieter Von Wolfenberg is a man any woman would be proud to have as a husband. But he has given his life to me, and I'm humbled by his gift. I am doubly lucky that I have two new men in my life, Dieter and his handsome son, Johann." She fluttered her eyelashes at him and smiled. "*Meine damen und herren*, drink to the long life of my husband, Count Dieter von Wolfenberg, the hero of Andernach."

Again the toast was echoed and loudly cheered. Johann grinned, though he looked like he might fall asleep any second. His father tousled his hair and whispered something in his ear. He came to Blythe and kissed her cheek. She hugged him, her heart full.

The servants waited at tables and served plentiful vegetables, including cabbage, carrots, onions, beets and garlic. Kippers made from herring caught in the North Sea were a delicacy appreciated by the guests, and Blythe was secretly pleased she had long ago coaxed Trésor, the cook at Ellesmere Castle, into sharing the secret Montbryce recipe for trout. As soon as the guests tasted the delicate flesh she saw their amazement. Praise ran high for the roasted swan and peafowl. Beer and wine flowed freely, and by the time the *krapfen*—fried pastries with sweet fillings—were served, everyone was well into their cups—everyone except Dieter and Blythe whose intoxication came from heated glances exchanged between them. Johann had fallen asleep and been taken to his chamber by his nursemaid.

Dieter squeezed Blythe's hand and leaned close. "I fear the Archbishop is so far gone he may collapse before he has blessed our marriage bed. Let's adjourn to our chamber."

He rose and announced to the guests, "My bride and I will await you in our matrimonial chamber."

Cheers and guffaws broke out.

When they reached their chamber, Dieter gave her a conspiratorial wink and urged her into bed fully clothed. She hesitated. "Wait! Let me take off your cloak."

She raised her shaking hands to the ornate clasps holding his white cloak in place and unhooked them. The cloak fell to the floor and pooled at his feet. He put his hands on her waist and growled. "Maybe we'll lock the door and dispense with the blessing."

To her surprise an answering growl emerged from her throat as he brushed his lips over hers, lifted her on to the bed, and tucked the bed linens up to her neck. Then he climbed in beside her after pulling off his boots and tossing them against the wall.

Five minutes later their giggles were interrupted by the solemn entrance of the tipsy Archbishop, leaning heavily on his crosier, his mitre askew on his bald head. A crowd of well-wishers gathered behind him as he intoned God's blessings on the marriage bed.

They tried to be serious, holding hands beneath the covers, and burst out laughing when the last of the group left. Blythe sobered a little at the wistful expressions on the faces of her father and brother.

The newlyweds flung the bed linens aside and stood facing each other, hand in hand, breathless, still fully clothed. "Dieter," Blythe said at last, "I want to take off all your clothes. I want to see my Black Knight naked. I've dreamt of it for so long."

He undid the topmost fastening of his tunic then held out his arms to her in a gesture of submission. She grasped the hem of his tunic and slowly, tantalizingly, raised it over his head as he held his arms in the air. She tossed the garment aside then smoothed her hands lovingly over his shoulders and arms.

"Raise your arms again," she commanded. He obliged and she touched the black hair of his underarms, inhaling the scent of him. "Silky," she whispered as a bolt of longing shot through her. His eyes never left her face.

*He wants to see my reaction to his body.*

She laid her cheek against the black hair on his chest, gasping at its softness. Her fingertips ran over the muscles of his broad chest, her thumbs grazing his nipples. He shuddered and she paused to gaze into his smouldering eyes.

He stood with his legs braced. She lowered her eyes to look at his manhood, straining against the wool of his leggings. This man's most private part would soon be revealed to her once more. She had longed for it since the stolen glimpse at the lake, but now she hesitated, a little afraid.

She untied the bindings, hooked her thumbs into the waistband and slowly peeled the garment from his body. Her hair brushed against his swollen phallus, covered now only by his linen braies. He growled deep in his throat and laid his hands gently on her shoulders. She helped him free one foot then the other from the leggings. His toes were long, the nails beautifully manicured. Her breasts swelled, the linen of her chemise chafing the hardened nipples.

"Untie my braies," he whispered.

His seductive voice touched the core of her being. She did as he asked and removed the last piece of clothing covering his body. She rose and looked upon him in his nakedness. He stood before her proudly, his eyes burning into hers. What she had not seen in the twilight by the lake was a thin scar that ran from his navel to his groin. The blade had come dangerously close to his manhood.

He held out his hands. "Do you like what you see?"

She licked her lips, scarcely able to breathe. She traced the length of his erect manhood with one fingertip, wanting to remember this moment forever. "Dieter, you're magnificent. It's been worth the wait."

She touched the faint scar. "This isn't where the Emperor's would-be assassin wounded you."

He lifted her hand and kissed it. "*Nein,* that is a memento from Frederika."

Bile rose in Blythe's throat. "She did this to you?"

"She wanted to unman me."

Blythe did the only thing she could think of to ease the pain a madwoman had inflicted upon him. She licked the other woman's mark, trying to erase it from his body. "Make love to me, Dieter. Make me a woman."

He took her hand and placed it firmly on his shaft. "You're already a woman, Blythe. This night I'll make you *my* woman."

His elegant hands disrobed her quickly and the blue and cerise silk lay in a puddle at her feet. She felt the heat of his burning gaze.

He placed her hands on his sex. "Touch me again, Blythe, put your hands on me."

"Your skin is soft, Dieter," she murmured. "You're so—large—and full."

"Move your hands," he whispered, breathing hard and grazing his chin against her face. "You know what's going to happen soon, *liebling*? You know we'll join our bodies?"

"Yes, Dieter, I know. My mother prepared me for this night. It's only that—I didn't realize a man's—"

He put a forefinger on her lips. "Hush, sweetheart. I'll ready you. It might be painful the first time, but you're a passionate woman, you'll triumph over the discomfort. You'll carry us both to ecstasy."

He lifted her back onto his big feather bed.

Her body was on fire. She responded to the urge to have this man possess her, opening her legs as his mouth found her nipples and suckled. His lazy fingers trailed down her stomach. Spasms tore through her as he caressed her most intimate folds. She fell under his spell, murmuring his name over and over.

"Blythe, my Blythe," he whispered, "I've longed to possess you, longed to make you mine. I need to come inside you now. Are you ready to welcome me?"

"Now, Dieter, now, now, now."

He knelt between her legs, nudged them further and guided his manhood into her.

"Look into my eyes, Blythe," he commanded as he thrust home.

She could not tear her gaze away from his as the pain came and went, but the urge went on—and on—and on, until finally the climax came. He cried out with her as waves of pleasure swept over them. Blythe sent a silent prayer of thanks to her mother, who had been right all along.

~~~

Dieter watched his wife sleep. He had never ached so unbearably for a woman. It had been difficult enough concealing his rock hard erections when he thought Blythe would never care for him. Now he seemed to have no control at all over his *rute*.

Blythe's sensuous innocence sent his senses reeling every time he looked at her. The desire in her eyes had promised and delivered a physical joining that exceeded all expectations, and his expectations had been high. He was proud of his body. He was a man of action, a warrior. Women were attracted to him, and he enjoyed their company, but Frederika had stolen from him any desire to remarry. The prospect he had been given another chance and found a deep love made him giddy.

Yet, as he had stood under Blythe's burning gaze in their marriage chamber, he had unexpectedly felt unsure. Despite her passionate nature, she was an innocent. Would his size frighten her? Would he please her?

Subjecting himself to her slow undressing had been a torture that inflamed him more, the scent of her female arousal filling his nostrils. It was her right to know about the scar. He shuddered at the memory of how close Fredericka had come to making him a eunuch. But Blythe's reaction had been to lick him. He had almost lost control, dragged her to the bed, fallen atop her and plunged into her depths like a wild thing.

He recalled his anger over the botched kidnapping, but now knew God had smiled on him that day. This woman had come into his life, a woman who ran her fingertips over his body, over his maleness, savouring her exploration of him. What a contradiction she was—naive, yet knowing. Her mother had prepared her for their union and he sent a silent prayer of thanks to the mother-by-marriage he had never met. What a fortunate man Sir Caedmon was! Dieter's bride had not been fearful. The gleam in her eyes had betrayed her joyful anticipation. How many new brides insisted on undressing their husbands first! He had never before basked in the glow of such admiration.

The whisper of the silk gown sliding off her body had fanned the flames burning in his loins. He had dreamed of her breasts, of her body, but nothing had prepared him for the sight of her lovely nakedness.

He rejoiced at the memory of the warm wetness of her intimate folds on his fingers. The ecstasy on her face when she had released humbled him. She had been tight when he slid into her, but as their gazes locked he had watched passion triumph over pain, her contractions pulsating on him when she released again. When his seed had erupted inside her, the breath had rushed from his lungs. He hoped Blythe's father had not heard his loud cry of euphoria.

~~~

Caedmon and Aidan wanted to be home in time for Yuletide, and departed almost immediately. Blythe clung to them for a long while before they mounted. She might never see them again. Aidan could not speak. Caedmon clasped Dieter's hand. "I'm entrusting to you the life of my daughter. Take good care of her."

Dieter's father and sister returned to Saxony, taking Johann. He would be safer there until the conflict with Heinrich was over once and for all. The newly-weds celebrated Yuletide alone, completely immersed in their new found delight in each other's bodies. They celebrated the Pagan tradition of burning the Yule log, lying naked before the hearth. He sang for her the ballad of Parsifal he had been singing at the lake when she had stumbled upon him naked. They laughed at the memory.

For Yuletide dinner they dined on traditional roasted goose and Humble pie made from the heart, liver and brains of a deer. Blythe taught the cook how to make mincemeat tarts. The servants entertained them with a *trope*, chanting in dialogue the story of the nativity and the Holy Family. Dieter offered a toast of thanks to all his servants, wishing them health and happiness for the coming year. They returned the wishes.

However, everyone in Köln acknowledged that the problems of the Empire's domination remained unresolved and that a confrontation still loomed between Duke Lothar of Saxony, Dieter's overlord, and the Emperor.

~~~

Throughout the month of January in the year of our Lord One Thousand One Hundred and Fifteen, Dieter was kept busy organizing soldiers who would fight in the ongoing conflict with the Imperial Army. Though Emperor Heinrich had tried to bring Duke Lothar to heel, the Saxon continued to intrigue against him, and Dieter was the undisputed leader of the opposing forces in Köln. Lothar intended to be Emperor.

Emboldened by their success at Andernach, the rebel forces

decided to mount an all out attack. Blythe found all this talk of war and intrigue very unsettling, especially when Dieter told her the Imperial army was well to the east of Köln, and his men would likely have to ride several days to join forces with Duke Lothar.

At the end of the month the confirmation came that they would be riding to join the Duke in Mansfeld, a four day journey. Dieter spent many days preparing his armour and weapons, Blythe watching him sadly. She was proud of his prowess as a warrior and his reputation as a hero, but fearful of what might happen to him. She had just found him and couldn't bear the thought of losing him. The day he left, bundled in his huge wolfskin coat to keep out the chill, she clung to him. Tearful servants gathered to see him off.

"Don't worry, Blythe," he whispered in her ear. "This is something I have to do. I'll return safely. Nothing can keep me away from you for long."

"We'll be waiting for you," she murmured, trying not to cry.

He held her away from him. "We?"

She nodded. "Your son and I."

He hugged her ferociously and buried his face in her neck. "You're with child? You didn't tell me."

"I wasn't sure—but now I think it is so. I didn't want to distract you from your mission."

He placed his hands on her belly. "You'll never be a distraction. You're my life, but life will be better for all Saxons, including this little one, once we get rid of Heinrich."

"*Auf Weidersehen*, my love."

"*Auf Weidersehen*, Blythe. Take good care of my son until I return."

He kissed her deeply, mounted his stallion and rode out to join his assembled forces.

~~~

Their route took them through the village of Brilon situated high in the hills on the upper reaches of the river Möhne. The town lay between the Arnsberg Forest to the west and Lake Diemel to the south-east.

From there they went on to the hill town of Warburg where they stayed in the Old Town in the Diemel Valley. Nordhausen at the southern edge of the rugged Harz Mountains was their next camp, where they went to Mass at the Cathedral of the Holy Cross. Dieter prayed for the success of their campaign and for his wife and unborn child at home. He had called Köln home for some time. He loved the city and his house there, but he would eventually take his family home to his own estates in Wolfenberg.

Finally they passed south east of the River Harz, through Sangerhausen and on to Mansfeld, where Lothar waited.

Five days later the forces of the Emperor commanded by Hoyer of Mansfeld gathered at Welfesholz to await the united Saxon troops led by Duke Lothar. Before the battle, Hoyer put his fist through a stone and proclaimed to his men the certainty of a victory over the enemy.

The armies clashed in a long and bloody battle. The fight ended in the total destruction of the imperial army and Hoyer's death. Heinrich took flight. Duke Lothar had broken Imperial power in Saxony. He was now the most powerful noble in Saxony and the wealthiest prince in all of northern Germany.

The battle had lasted several days and Dieter and his men were exhausted. He had lost a number of them and took charge of finding and burying their bodies. Some had to have limbs removed. The piteous moans of the wounded drifted across the camp and the stench of death filled the air. Dieter was sickened by it and longed to return home. He resolved to be done with war now that Lothar had been victorious. He would return to Wolfenberg with Blythe and take care of the lands Lothar had given him to rule over as *Graf*.

At the end of February he was free to return to Köln. He had sent messengers ahead and as he rode into the courtyard Blythe came out to meet him. His heart and his *rute* soared at the sight of her. He was exhausted, but his beautiful and passionate wife would soon restore his energy.

~~~

In the autumn of that year Blythe and Dieter welcomed their son, Lothar Caedmon von Wolfenberg into the world. *Graf* Dieter von Wolfenberg paraded around the house firmly holding his baby son belly down on his hip, much to the delight of all the devoted servants and seemingly Lothar himself. Johann rode on his father's back, laughing and giggling.

When the babe wailed his demands, Blythe took him to her breast. "This child is going to be ruined if you keep on this way."

Johann wandered off to play with his toys. Dieter loved to watch her feed his son. Contentment washed over him. Blythe loved the manor house in Wolfenberg as much as he did. He had another healthy boy. After Lothar's birth, he had strutted around the house like a madman, proudly showing everyone his son's maleness. The midwife had trailed after him, objecting loudly. If it was possible, he loved his wife even more after the birth of their child. "You were born to be a mother, Blythe. You're radiant."

She gazed at her son. "I'm not sure yet whom he favours. Perhaps when he grows hair we'll have a better idea! He has your blue eyes, though my mother told me a baby's eyes sometimes change colour."

"I hope his will change to the colour of yours. Sometimes I think they're brown, sometimes green. You're a woman of mystery!"

His arousal grew as he stared at his family. He ran his hand over his son's head and then let his fingers trail over his wife's swollen breast. "Perhaps when you're done with Lothar you can see to my needs? I know I can't enter you yet, but there are other ways to—"

He looked at her speculatively, hoping she would not be shocked. He should have known better!

Her eyes twinkled and a suggestive grin lit up her face. "Dieter, you know I'll always be ready to meet your needs in whatever way I can!"

# SWEET TASTE OF LOVE

*My son, eat honey, because it is good,
and the honeycomb, which is sweet to taste.
So shall the knowledge of wisdom be to your soul.
When you have found it, then there shall be a reward.*
*~Proverbs 24:13/14*

For Jane Lockie McIntyre Kincaid
*~a true Scot*

## PROLOGUE

*The Narrow Sea,
25th day of November, 1120 A.D.*

The doomed vessel splintered on the jagged rocks of Quilleboeuf, tossing screaming revellers into the snarling sea. Caedmon grabbed Agneta when he felt the first shuddering groan of the floundering ship, but she was torn from his arms as they plunged into the dark, frigid depths.

"Agneta!" he shouted as he surfaced, gasping for air, tasting salt. "Agneta!"

Heads bobbed, arms flailed, people screamed in the seething darkness, but where was his wife? A cold wave swamped him and something struck the back of his head. He had a fleeting recollection of the bloody battlefield at Alnwick where he had been severely wounded thirty years before. Agneta had rescued him, nursed him back to health.

Dazed and panting for breath, he groped for whatever had hit him and clung to it. It was part of the broken ship.

"Agneta!" he shouted again, shoving his hair off his face, peering into the darkness. She must not die alone.

He recognised her choking cough. Her illness had robbed her of breath before this. "Agneta!"

"Caed...!"

He caught sight of her just before her head disappeared beneath the waves. Clinging to the wreckage, he struck out with one arm. Fewer heads were visible now, many drunken victims claimed by the sea.

He exclaimed with relief when she struggled back to the surface. Where had she found the strength? Willing his numbed legs to kick, he threw one arm around her ribs and dragged her to the wreckage. The heavy winter cloak twisted around her frail body worked against him. Her hair covered her face and she shivered uncontrollably.

She took in great gulps of air. "I want to die with you, Caedmon. I'm—cold!"

He held her tightly, smoothing back her hair, but every wave forced the now grey strands over her face.

He tried to keep his fear for her out of his voice as his numbed hands sought to free the ties of her cloak from around her neck. "Hold tightly to me and the wreckage."

She clamped a death grip on his shoulders, gasping for breath. "Caedmon—we are going—to die!"

Another swell hit them. He coughed, the salt stinging his nose. "No, we are not! Hold on to me! I have you. I'll never—let you go."

Cold seeped into his bones. How long could he hold on? With a last desperate surge of strength, he clenched his jaw and forced Agneta against the wreckage. He covered her body, locking his arms around the wood. Lungs afire, his legs would no longer tread water.

They drifted, clinging to the flimsy piece of splintered wood. The current carried them away from the rock where *La Blanche Nef* had run aground. Soon there was only silence. He prayed they were being carried to shore, but had no sense of how long they had drifted. The salt water blurred his vision.

"Agneta! Stay awake. We will—be rescued."

"I cannot, Caedmon—I'm freezing. I want to sleep."

"No! Talk to me! Stay awake."

"I love you—Caedmon—there's no better place to die—than in your arms. Hold me. Hold me fast. Death has stalked me for many a month."

Her words tore at his heart, but she was right. Better to die together. There would be no rescue. He thought of his children and bade them a silent farewell, heartbroken that he would never see them again. He had done his best to be a good father, to set them on the right path. Agneta had, after six years, finally insisted on making the long journey to Saxony to meet her son-by-marriage and Blythe's three children. She had seen for herself how happy their daughter was with Dieter. Praise be to God he and Agneta had taken their children's place on this voyage home.

His sons and daughter had given up the coveted chance to sail aboard the luxurious White Ship with the other young people, knowing their mother was unwell. It was an uncharacteristic self-sacrifice on the part of his wilful daughter that had saved their lives. Ragna had talked of nothing else but accompanying the Crown Prince and his retinue. Aidan, Edwin and Ragna would not die with the hundreds of other doomed noblemen and women aboard the Aetheling's famed vessel. They were safely aboard an older, less comfortable longboat.

The knowledge brought him peace. He and Agneta had lived long, happy lives. It was fitting they should die instead of their children. He prayed the captain of their ship was not a drunken sot like the White Ship's commander. He'd had a bad feeling about the voyage from the moment they had embarked.

Caedmon wondered fleetingly if the heir to the English throne had been lost. Last he had seen of William, he was frantically trying to haul people into the only lifeboat. Pray God he had survived. King Henry would be devastated at the loss of his only son. And what of England, if the succession were put in jeopardy?

That could not be Caedmon's concern now. He thanked God he and Agneta would die together. He would not have lived long without her. "I love you, Agneta. Thank you for the love and passion we have shared."

She pressed her cold lips to his, loosened her grip on his shoulders and put her arms around his neck. "Caedmon."

"Agneta," he rasped in reply, drifting into sleep. When he awoke, his beloved had slipped from life. He kissed her. "Even in death you are beautiful, my Agneta."

He tipped his head back to look at the stars, then let go of the debris. He had come close to drowning twice before, once in the River Dee and again in the Balkans during the Crusade. It was meant to be. Holding Agneta to his body for the last time, he allowed the icy waters to carry them to the resurrection in which they firmly believed.

## CHAPTER ONE
*Lindisfarne Abbey, Holy Island, Northumbria*
*Two Months Later.*

Ragna pinched her lips together. "Your decision is ridiculous, Aidan. I have no intention of entering a nunnery."

Aidan FitzRam inhaled deeply. Arguing with his sister was never easy. She was used to getting her own way. His sullen-faced younger brother leaned against the wall. Neither sibling was happy with his choice. He pulled the rough cowl away from his neck. "No one expects you to. It is my decision to enter the monastery. It is my fault mother and father died in the White Ship disaster. I must atone."

Ragna stamped her foot. "But you will chafe at the monastic life."

Aidan rolled his eyes. "That's why it's an atonement. Lindisfarne Abbey is dedicated to St. Aidan. I was meant to live my life on Holy Island."

His sister threw her hands in the air, then pointed an accusing finger. "Mother would be devastated by this, Aidan. It was not your fault nor mine nor Edwin's that our parents drowned with Prince William and the flower of English nobility. Don't you see their deaths gave us a chance to live? Our parents never intended you to be a monk. You're the heir to Kirkthwaite Manor and Shelfhoc Hall, not to mention the Sussex estates. You must sire sons."

Aidan chewed his bottom lip. "I am responsible for their deaths. It was I who suggested they take our places. Edwin can have whichever hall he wants. I'll cede my right to the remaining property in favour of your husband, or Blythe's husband or their sons."

Edwin raked his fingers through his hair, then rubbed the back of his neck. He drew a breath, looked at his sister, turned on his heel and left.

Ragna shook her head vigorously as she paced. "I'm not married, nor do I intend to wed. Dieter won't want either English property. You have no right. You can see how Edwin feels. *Godemite!*"

Aidan stuffed his hands into the sleeves of his robe, digging his fingers into his forearms. "I have every right, and you shouldn't blaspheme. It's not ladylike."

Ragna snorted.

Aidan sighed. "You can live at Kirkthwaite or Shelfhoc, married or not. I intend to remain here and devote my life to God. Now go!"

A tear trickled down Ragna's cheek. "You're four and twenty. You have a lifetime ahead of you. Blythe will never forgive me. I cannot leave you here, Aidan."

He put his hands on her shoulders and kissed her forehead. "You have no choice."

She tore away from him and rested her forehead against the stone wall of her brother's dormitory. "If you will not take up your rightful place for me, then do it for England. Your country needs strong barons now the succession is in jeopardy. You were born to follow in Father's footsteps."

Aidan shook his head and held out his arms, wondering what he had eaten earlier to make his belly churn. "Try to understand, Ragna. I must do this. Please leave now. Kiss me before you go. Give me your blessing."

She whirled around, gritted her teeth and stormed out, slamming the door.

Aidan's shoulders tightened further. He fell to his knees, praying for fortitude to bear the lonely years ahead. He missed his father's guidance. Caedmon FitzRam had been the rock of the family. Was Ragna right? Was he avoiding his responsibilities by becoming a religious? Or was the devil tempting him away from his vocation? He had heard the call when he learned the devastating news. He must atone. Their deaths were his fault. He should have died instead.

~~~

Ragna was forced to pause in her flight from the confines of Lindisfarne. Edwin had ridden off alone in the direction of Kirkthwaite. She was distraught and feared she might fall from her horse. She instructed the captain of her guard to halt his men. "I cannot leave Aidan there, Leofric."

Leofric Deacon took hold of her steed's reins with his good hand. "Caedmon and I endured many difficulties together, Ragna. I mourn his loss. Aidan is seeking his way, as your father did when he joined Peter the Hermit's Crusade before you were born. You must have faith he will find it."

She blinked away tears and accepted the kerchief he offered, covering her face. Since the awful news had come she had cried a great deal, something she had done rarely before. Where was the courage that had earned her the nickname *Wild Viking Princess*?

This lifelong friend of her father's was always positive, despite the cruel disfigurements suffered in the Battle of Alnwick long ago. She blew her nose. "We must cling to the hope he will come to his senses, Leofric. I need him. Blythe is far away in Germany. I feel bereft. Why can he not see he is leaving me alone with the immense responsibilities of father's holdings? Edwin is not strong. He would make a better monk."

"Aidan sees nothing now but his own grieving guilt. Never fear, Ragna. You're not alone. The Montbryces will help you and I'm still here, though no longer a young man."

Ragna smiled bitterly as she looked sadly at Leofric's bald head, his skin withered over his missing ear and eye. He was alone now, Coventina having died two years before, devoted to her beloved Leofric to the last. Ragna would miss his steadfast support when he too was gone.

It was true her father's powerful paternal family would help her, but she had never felt so alone. Anger at Aidan's selfishness burned in her heart.

## CHAPTER TWO
*Northumbria, April, 1121 A.D.*

Nolana Kyncade squeezed her eyes tight shut. How long could she hold her breath underwater? Was that the echo of horses' hooves still crossing the stone bridge above her, or the thudding of her own heart?

She must evade her stepfather's men. The dastard intended to marry her to Baron Grouchet, a man two score years her senior. The auld bugger needed an heir, his only son having gone down with the White Ship. Her stepfather wanted the coin the Norman would pay for her, and to be rid of the stepdaughter who chafed under his leash. What had her dead mother seen in the man?

She had run, her only plan to escape to a place of sanctuary until—until what? She had fled without coin, without even a dagger. Her stepfather made sure she never had access to either. He was a man who kept tight control of his purse and his armoury. The future looked bleak. Why did men have the right to make all the decisions for a woman? Perhaps the novitiate would be a solution. Then she wouldn't worry about men ruling her life ever again.

A religious life would also mean abandoning her dreams of a family and children. She loved children, but not if they were fathered by a decrepit sot.

Her lungs bursting, she broke the surface and gulped in great breaths of air. Birds chirped. Leaves rustled. Water dripped from her nose and streamed from her hair. No sound of horses. She pressed her elbows into her ribs in an effort to stop the uncontrollable trembling that shook her.

She had to move, but her legs seemed frozen in place in the icy water. She was rooted to the spot. She managed to pull off her *playd*, struggling to wring out the water. Spluttering, she peeled the ringlets back off her face and, after several unsuccessful attempts, scrambled up the bank. She had already walked for most of the day, leaving Berwick behind once she had crossed into England. There was no chance of refuge in Scotland. No border clan would challenge her powerful stepfather.

It would soon be dark. She scanned the seemingly endless expanse of moorland, teeth chattering, looking for any sign of life. She must stop whimpering and find shelter. Was that a wisp of smoke off in the distance? Perhaps a croft? They might take pity and allow her to stay for a night.

The hem of her sodden *léine* felt like it was weighted with lead as she slogged over the moor to the tiny cottage she now spied. Though she hugged the wet *playd* to her body, it offered little warmth. The smell of wet wool assailed her nostrils as she clutched it beneath her chin. Darkness had fallen by the time she balled her fist to pound on the door, frozen to the bone. "Shelter, for the love of God, I beg shelter."

The door scraped open a crack and Nolana had to cling to the frame to avoid collapsing into the cottage. She opened her mouth but no sound came out. The wizened face of an auld woman appeared, a long stemmed wooden pipe clenched in her teeth. "Be gone. Want no borderers 'ere."

Nolana took a deep breath, hoping her voice would return. "I'm not a borderer. I'm soaked to the skin and will surely freeze to death if you don't take pity."

The old woman hesitated, chewing the stem of the pipe, then dragged the door open and motioned Nolana inside. "They was 'ere looking for ye."

Nolana tensed and hesitated on the threshold. "For me?"

The woman grabbed her arm and pulled her inside. "Aye. Don't play the innocent wi' me. Armed men they were, asking after a young lass."

Nolana decided it was best not to lie. She was close to succumbing to exhaustion and needed this woman's help. "They are my stepfather's men. I've run away. I eluded them by ducking in the burn."

The old woman looked her up and down. "Takes a brave lass to do such a thing. I've a spare shift. Take off yer wet clothes, dearie. They'll dry by the fire. I lack company. Gets lonely up 'ere on these moors."

Nolana peeled off the wet garments and accepted the homespun shift. It was like a shroud, but its enveloping roughness brought warmth to her skin. The woman spread her wet clothing by the hearth.

Nolana thanked her. "I'm sorry, I don't know your name."

The crone sucked on her pipe once more then took it from her mouth. "Folks call me Jennet."

Nolana hugged the shift to her breasts, and rubbed her arms, chasing away the chill. "Thank you, Jennet. I'm Nolana Kyncade."

"Y'are a Scot then?"

There was no point giving her full Gaelic name. Her father, having sired no sons, had named her his *champion*, but the language had been forbidden her for so long she had forgotten it. "My stepfather's lands are in the Scottish lowlands. I'm from further north, closer to the Highlands. I came south with my mother when she wed my stepfather."

Jennet shrugged and took another draw on her pipe. "Now, yer mother's dead, and ye hate yer stepfather?"

Nolana smiled ruefully. "Aye. He wants to wed me off to an auld man."

Why was she confiding in this woman? Perhaps the pleasant odour of the pipe smoke had soothed her.

Jennet laughed. "Ye dinna want to wed an auld man. 'Twas my fate for many a year! Thank God the bugger's dead now, nigh on five and ten year sin'."

Nolana inhaled the scented smoke. "What's in your pipe, Jennet? It smells good."

Jennet pursed her lips and blew out more smoke, wafting it towards Nolana, mischief in her eyes. "Aye. 'Tis me own blend. Mostly red clover, rose hips and a touch of a secret ingredient."

Nolana smiled, but could barely keep her eyes open. "Secret ingredient?"

Jennet put a fingertip to her lips, looked around furtively and whispered, "Honey."

Nolana arched her brows, but had to stifle a yawn. "I'm sorry. I walked a long way today."

Jennet pointed to a pallet by the hearth. "Sleep now. I'll wake ye in the morn."

"But where will you sleep?"

Jennet tapped her pipe on the stones of the hearth and curled a finger inside the bowl as she blew into it. "I've a pallet in the loft. Heat rises. You need the hearth more than I do. I bid ye goodnight."

Nolana accepted the pallet and drew the meagre blanket over her. "Goodnight, Jennet."

She drifted into a fitful sleep haunted by visions of a life behind convent walls.

# CHAPTER THREE

Nolana woke to the comforting aroma of baking. For a moment she was back in her father's manor house in the Carnsith Fells. She remembered clambering out of bed as a child and hastening to the kitchens where Cook had crusty rolls to break her fast.

It was pointless to dwell on those days. They were gone. Her stepfather had razed the manor when he had wed her mother. "No use leaving an old house empty," he had declared. "You'll be living in the lowlands. Why pay these people to keep up a manor if you don't live in it?"

*These people*, who had taken care of her since her birth, were thrown out, rendered destitute. No amount of protest on her mother's part would change his mind. She soon gave up the fight, and Nolana watched the only home she had ever known go up in flames. She hated men, and the weakness of her mother who so feared being alone she had succumbed to the dictates of this arrogant male monster.

He had driven her to an early grave after the birth of their son, Nolana's half brother, Ingram. Nolana had no doubt he had beaten her mother. He deemed it his right. She swore never to be subject to the commands of a man.

Jennet's voice broke into her reflections. "Yer awake. Barm cake?"

Nolana accepted the warm roll and gratefully sank her teeth into the fluffy bread, relishing the barmy taste. She swallowed and licked her lips. "Good, Jennet. This is the best bread I've ever tasted."

Jennet chuckled. "That's because yer starving, lass. Try the goat's milk."

They ate together in companionable silence. Nolana sensed there was something Jennet wanted to say, but she waited.

"Have ye thought on where ye'll go next?"

Nolana shook her head. "I suppose there's nothing for it but a nunnery. I've heard Lindisfarne Abbey is not far from here."

Jennet spat into the hearth. "Lindisfarne is good for naught but the mead they make. The convent is no life for a pretty girl such as thee. Ye can stay 'ere a while. Like I said, I need company."

Nolana wandered over to see if her garments were dry. "It's kind of you, Jennet, but I'll be forced to make some decisions soon."

Jennet poured water from a ewer into a bowl. "Abide wi' me a bit, lassie, while ye decide. Wash off the dust of the journey and get thyself dressed."

~~~

Nolana stayed with Jennet for a sennight. She gathered peat for the fire, tended goats and collected eggs, staying close to the cottage. She loved the wild beauty of the moor—the stunted oaks that clung to life on the windswept horizon, the coarse tufts of cottongrass, the craggy outcroppings of time-blackened rock. Here they were on the edge of the moor. In the far distance, behind the cottage, away from the sea, lay the forbidding peaks of the Bens. Nolana's gaze wandered there often when the mists cleared—it reminded her of home.

At night they talked of Nolana's dilemma. Jennet did her best to dissuade her from the nunnery, but offered no other solution.

"Perhaps I should live in a lonely cottage up on the moor, tending my goats and hens."

Jennet spat into the fire, her usual sign of disgust. "Bah! That's no life for a young lass. You should be married, with bairns."

Nolana wiped her runny nose and stared at her hands. She had wanted children, a fine husband. Now—

"Tell thee what," Jennet offered, "ye'll journey with me into Beal market Tuesday next. The monks'll be there selling their mead. They'll bring honey too. Ye can mayhap ask their advice, though they don't mix much with folks. Too high and mighty."

## CHAPTER FOUR

The monotony of monastic life grated on Aidan. The same thing happened at the same time every endless day. He had grown up in a noisy household full of love, laughter and argument. In the Abbey he was drowning in silence.

The rough wool habit irritated his sensitive skin. Had it ever been washed? He was not the first monk to wear the odious garment. Decay lingered in its folds.

His mother's table had provided rich and satisfying victuals. Abbey food was tasteless and there wasn't enough to satisfy a bird, let alone his robust appetite.

He chafed at the pettiness of those superior to him who demanded his obedience in everything. While Aidan had never been the hellion his sister was, he was the eldest son of a proud man, a hero of the First Crusade. He was heir to wealthy properties, descendent of a noble Norman family. He was not used to obeying imbeciles. He had clenched his fists so often his palms bore the imprint of his fingernails.

The FitzRams prized cleanliness, but here he was forced to wait a sennight between baths. The stench of his body disgusted him. Bathing for the postulants consisted of standing naked while older monks tossed icy cold water at them, taking what he considered perverse pleasure in the act. It reminded him of the treatment his uncle Robert de Montbryce had received in Duke Curthose's cells. He longed for a good tub soak.

They had denied him his name. Now he was Brother Christian. It seemed a slight to the murdered uncle for whom he had been named. He had protested, citing the dedication of Lindisfarne to St. Aidan, only to be rebuked for the sin of pride for comparing himself to a saint.

Though no longer a virgin, he had never been a man to pursue women. He wanted someday to find a woman to love as his father had loved his Agneta—as Dieter loved Blythe. Thoughts of his twin sister brought to mind the journey home from her wedding in Cologne six years before. What a green lad he had been then. It seemed to suddenly occur to Sir Caedmon FitzRam that he had not passed on to his son his knowledge of how to please a woman in bed. Aidan had been astonished and somewhat embarrassed by the apparent sexual prowess of his father—something he had never given any mind to before. He had a new respect for his sire after that—and for his mother!

Once they were back in England it was as if women were aware Aidan had this new knowledge. He became the object of constant female attention. Was it something a man exuded?

The reality of never again making love to a woman saddened him. When he thought on it, his shaft responded, despite his best efforts to quell his arousal. He prayed for strength not to succumb to the needs of the flesh, but he was weak.

Judging by the muffled gasps and groans in the dormitory at night he would wager he was not the only monk seeking solace at his own hand. He had been at Lindisfarne four months; how was he to survive a lifetime? Ragna had been right. Sometimes he thought he might have fallen ill. His chest felt tight and his head ached constantly.

He recalled his mother's tales of her time as a novice in Alnwick Abbey—she had hated the repetition. He was his mother's son.

Memories of her brought a lump to his throat. He had to be stronger. He was being tempted from his calling. God expected him to atone. He would do it. He would put aside thoughts of returning to Kirkthwaite. Ragna would manage without him. She had Leofric Deacon to help her, and their Montbryce uncles and cousins would do what was necessary. He readily admitted Edwin would be of little help to his sister. He was too shy, too otherworldly.

*My brother would make a better monk.*

The one thing Aidan did enjoy was his involvement in the making of mead. At least he was doing something, not praying and chanting all day and all night.

He had not been allowed access to the recipe, though he had

caught a glimpse of the vellum embossed with brown ink. Some of the monks who had been at Lindisfarne for years had not been trusted with the full knowledge. But he had been shown how to gather the honey, and how to separate it from the wax. He had been limited to the hives in the hollowed out tree trunks the monks had devised, but soon the task would begin in earnest when the *skeps* were destroyed and opened.

He had spent many hours making new conical beehives to replace the ones they would tear apart. His hands bore deep scratches from the blackberry briars used to bind together the coiled straw. Removing bramble thorns and splicing the briars was a newly acquired skill. He had learned how to fasten the *ekes* to the bottom of the skeps to give the bees more room to make honey. Brother Tristan, the Cellarer, had even whispered the secret name of the barm. "We call it *godisgood*, Brother Christian, *godisgood*, because without its God-given properties, we would have no mead."

He was confident he was being groomed. Perhaps if he worked hard to earn the Abbot's trust, he might become a mead maker and hold on to his sanity. He would embark on this goal when he accompanied the Abbot and two other monks to Beal market Tuesday next. At least he would be outside these oppressive walls for a short time. Perhaps then his headache would ease.

~~~

"Remember, Brother Christian, detachment—at all times detachment. We are venturing into the world, where temptation abounds."

Aidan resisted the urge to roll his eyes. They were off to the market in the village of Beal. How much temptation lurked there? Did the elderly Abbot know what temptation was? How long had he been incarcerated within the abbey? "Yes, Father Abbot. I'll be careful."

The Abbot tapped his forefinger against his lips. "Best not to speak to the young women there."

Ah—such was the temptation the Abbot feared. It would not do to lose a young postulant to the sins of the flesh. Aidan was confident there would be no village wench buxom enough to tempt the son of a noble family.

He was charged with loading mead and honey into the oxcart. It was a warm spring day and by the time he was done, his skin prickled. He longed to strip off the hated habit and plunge into a cool lake.

He climbed into the back of the cart, swearing under his breath when a spile from the rough planking drove into his thumb. He sucked it, wanting to whine like a child.

The Abbot and two other brothers climbed into the cart and they set off. The slow progress lulled Aidan to sleep as the cart lurched over the rutted sands to Beal. The tide swept over the causeway twice a day, cutting the island off from the mainland.

He awoke disoriented when the Abbot reined the ox to a halt. This was not the way to impress, falling asleep on the way to market. He stumbled out of the cart, his skin itchy, his thumb throbbing. He lifted the first *rundlet* to his shoulder.

The Abbot pointed. "Carry it to the stall over there. Careful now. Not much of last year's mead left. This is the best. It has aged for a twelvemonth. Don't want to spill any of our liquid gold."

*That's all I need!*

The Abbot scurried over to brush dirt off their allotted stall, leaving Aidan and the other monks to heft the *rundlets* and flagons. He had explained to Aidan that most of their revenue would come from sales by the tumbler, but wealthier folk might purchase a flagon. Though Aidan had been to markets in Northumbria before, he had never been to Beal. Judging by the bustle of activity around them early in the day it promised to be an enjoyable experience. If only he was wearing something other than his robe.

~~~

The afternoon sun was warm, but Nolana kept her face and hair shrouded beneath her *playd*. She and Jennet had been of the same mind that her stepfather's men might come to the market. No doubt they sought her still. Her flame red hair would draw them like bees to the honey pot.

Despite the heat, she was glad to be out in the open for a while, not caged like a miscreant. She had done nothing wrong, her only fault a longing for respect and happiness. She stayed close to Jennet, enjoying the sights, sounds and smells of the market. It reminded her of home, of the Fells. These were simple folk, plying their wares, trying to make a living, to feed their families.

Jennet pressed something into her palm. "Take these. I'm off to ply our goat cheese yonder."

Nolana opened her hand to reveal the coins. "I cannot, this is too generous. You have little—"

Jennet curled Nolana's fingers around the coins and pushed back her hand. She pointed to a stall where brightly coloured ribbons fluttered in the sea breeze. "Nay, happy I am if ye'll use it to buy thesel' a bit o' frippery from yon mon. I'm too owd for such, but thee—"

Nolana swallowed hard. This auld Englishwoman she barely knew treated her like a daughter. She pecked a kiss on Jennet's cheek. "I'll take but a moment." Tucking the coins away, she wandered over to the haberdashery merchant, her step a little lighter.

# CHAPTER FIVE

Aidan was ready to collapse with fatigue. He had never been a lethargic man. His mother had often complained he had too much energy. He and Blythe had on occasion led their parents a merry dance when they were growing up. What he wouldn't give now for a scolding glance from his mother.

He raked his fingers through his hair and leaned back against the wooden frame of the stall, brushing away the horseflies drawn by the honey. What would it be like to be tonsured? His hair had always been long, dark like his father's.

Memories of his parents filled his head. A lifetime would not be enough to atone for the manner of their deaths. Their bodies had never been recovered. His father's long-held desire to be interred alongside his father in the crypt at Montbryce would not be fulfilled.

A shuddering breath caught in his throat. He eyed the jars of mead, estimating how much longer they would remain in the crowded marketplace. His sandaled feet were caked with dust, his throat bone dry. Idly wondering how he might filch a sip of the precious mead without the Abbot noticing, he closed his eyes, absorbing the sounds of commerce around him.

A fly buzzed in his face. He swatted at it and forced one eye open. A young woman was making her way to the haberdashery stall. At least, he thought she was a young woman. How odd to be shrouded by a *playd* on such a warm day. But her bearing and figure bespoke a young person. He stood up straight to get a better view. Her garb indicated she was a Scot, but not a lowlander, and not a person of low birth. Her *léine* had been dyed saffron. She reached out to finger the coloured ribbons hanging from the crossbeam, glancing around furtively, drawing the brown *playd* further over her head.

*She's afraid of something—or someone.*

His gut clenched—and then she turned and seemed to look directly at him. Her obvious nervousness did nothing to detract from her loveliness. His mouth fell open. She turned back to the stall, reaching up to point to a particular ribbon. The merchant handed it to her. She raised her arms. The *playd* fell to her shoulders, revealing the flame red bounty of her hair. Aidan's breath caught in his throat. For once he was glad of the shapeless robe—his erection was a rod of iron.

She replaced the shawl quickly and paid for the ribbon. Four or five armed men came into view, sauntering through the market. He did not recognize the devise they bore on their tunics. The woman lowered her head, turned away and hastened in the direction of the stall selling mead.

*Jesu! She's coming this way!*

~~~

There was only one place Nolana might find safety. The tall young monk she had espied must be from Lindisfarne. He had long hair—a postulant—but that was of no consequence. There were four monks, one of them elderly and seemingly in charge, the Abbot perhaps. She would beg sanctuary if the men pursued her. Though they were not on sanctified ground, surely holy men would not allow her to be dragged off.

The postulant looked nervous. He wiped his hands on his robe, backing away from her. She dared not steal a glance to see what her pursuers were doing, but the young monk was looking beyond her. Suddenly he lurched forward, a tumbler in his hand. "Mead—mistress?" he stammered, his eyes still on the men.

Then he looked at her. A spasm of desire snaked through her for the first time in her life. How could those beguiling blue eyes and long black lashes belong to a man who had given his life to God? He was handsome too, and tall, though in need of a bath. She tried not to wrinkle her nose. He had sensed she wished to evade the men. The question in her eyes asked if they were still there. He smiled and the tingling in her breasts became intense. Heat surged in her body. What was she thinking? This man was a monk. She gripped the edge of the stall.

He leaned towards her and whispered, "They're gone."

Before she could stammer her thanks, the older monk suddenly appeared at the postulant's side, elbowing him out of the way. "Get thee gone, mistress, if you don't intend to purchase."

She experienced a moment of panic. The younger man was poised to retaliate. He glared at the older monk, his jaw and fists clenched, but then turned and fled into the crowd.

She looked back at the monk whose self-important air convinced her he was the Abbot of Lindisfarne. She had hoped to confide in him, seek advice or sanctuary. A cold chill swept over her. Compassion would not be one of this man's strengths. She opened her mouth, but no sound came out.

He shook his fist. "Be gone, I say."

Afraid his raised voice might attract unwanted attention, she turned to leave. Someone grasped her elbow and panic returned, until she heard Jennet's voice. "Why are ye shouting at my niece, ye scurvy monk? She came to get my honey from thee."

The Abbot spluttered his apology, but his eyes betrayed his annoyance. "A thousand pardons, Jennet. Here is your pot."

Jennet paid the Abbot, linked her arm in Nolana's and escorted her *niece* away from the stall. "We'll walk slowly, so's not to arouse interest."

Nolana did not recall much of the long walk back to the cottage and only took a deep breath once she was safely inside its walls.

~~~

From the shadow of the market cross Aidan watched the two women walk away, desperately trying to control his breathing. He had looked into the depths of green eyes and seen fear. An overwhelming desire to protect this unknown young woman had swept over him, but the pompous Abbot had shoved him out of the way. The man was lucky Aidan hadn't slain him with his sword—but he no longer had a sword, was no longer a man of action.

He sank to the ground, his back sliding down the cool stone of the obelisk. Was this another test of his resolve? How many temptations would be thrust before him? His shaft still throbbed mercilessly, and there was no hope of relief here in the crowded market. He had never believed in love at first sight, though his father had often boasted of being smitten the moment he set eyes on Agneta. Aidan recalled how disdainful he had been of Blythe and Dieter and their instant attraction to one another. What had transpired here? Why did he want to pursue the women, throw his arms around the green-eyed beauty and make her his?

He raked his hands through his hair. What was he thinking? It was obvious she had been disgusted by the odour of his body—who wouldn't be—it disgusted him. The way he had stammered—she likely considered him an imbecile, cast off by his family and hidden away in a monastery.

The Abbot's voice roused him from his stupor. They were loading the cart. Wearily he came to his feet and trudged back to help. No doubt he would receive a stern lecture once they regained the Abbey.

~~~

Nolana fretted for two sennights. Safety lay in the Fells. Her father's people would take her in, protect her. But such a journey would be impossible alone, and there was no home to return to.

Jennet told her to stay as long as she wished, but what future was there in such a life? She would live in fear of discovery. Her stepfather was too close.

It seemed the Abbey was her only hope, but the elderly monk had put the fear of God in her in the wrong way. Then there was the young postulant. She couldn't get him out of her thoughts.

What was the attraction? He was woefully in need of a bath and a shave, though she sensed he was aware and ashamed of it. Why had she wanted to run her hand over the stubble of his beard? She daydreamed of shaving him, something she had never done for any man. The notion filled her thoughts, resulting in a puzzling pool of moisture between her legs and an embarrassing new habit of drooling.

She was a stranger to him, but he had risked the displeasure of his Abbot to assist her, quickly sensing the danger.

Despite his unkempt appearance, she had been struck immediately by his male beauty. And those eyes—why would he shut himself up in a monastery? His bearing bespoke a man made to sire children—virile, strong, capable—a man who had spent many an hour in training fields, practising swordplay. He had spoken only four words to her, but his manner of speech indicated he was of noble blood. What was he doing on the Holy Island of Lindisfarne?

Her preoccupation annoyed her. What did it matter to her if a handsome young man closed himself off from the world? What was he atoning for? She resolved to stop obsessing about him and decide what action to take to resolve her own problems.

But at night she dreamed of him, of long muscular legs entwined with hers, of strong arms wrapped around her. She felt stirrings of longing she had never felt before in unmentionable places and awoke each morning with her hand where it should not be.

Nolana was confused and ashamed.

## CHAPTER SIX

"I grow weary of the wait, Maknab. I'm not a young man. Time is of the essence."

Neyll Maknab resisted the urge to take Baron Grouchet by the scruff of his scrawny neck and point out he was the one who was weary—weary of the auld man's constant harping and weary of chasing his wilful stepdaughter. When he caught her—and he had no doubt he would—he would make her rue the day she had led him on this merry dance.

He straightened the cuffs of his doublet. "She is in Northumbria, I am sure of it. We will find her and you shall have your bride."

Grouchet spat. "Bah! Northumbria is vast. She might be anywhere. You haven't had any success. Perhaps I should look elsewhere. I want an obedient woman."

It was a threat the fool had made before, and Neyll determined not to rise to the bait. Though he desperately needed the coin, he must not let Grouchet know it. "She will obey you, Baron, if I have to thrash it into her."

Grouchet spluttered. "Sir, I am capable of disciplining my own wife. Would not be the first time."

Neyll bowed his head. "Of course. I didn't mean to imply—"

The baron waved his hand in dismissal and slumped into a chair. "Think on it no further. I am anxious to have her wedded and bedded. I must have an heir."

"And you shall. Nolana has few options open to her. She might think to flee north, but who will accompany her there? No lowland

Scot will risk my wrath by aiding her. She has only the Church to fall back on. I have instructed my men to watch the villages near the Holy Island of Lindisfarne. My gut tells me that's where she'll be found."

The baron did not reply. To Neyll's disgust the auld fool had fallen asleep.

~~~

Aidan feared he was going mad. Perhaps the grief of his parents' death had been too much? No matter what he was doing—praying, reading, chanting, eating, collecting honey, washing clay vessels—no matter where he was—indoors, outdoors—whether on his feet, his knees, his backside or his bed—the memory of those auburn curls wouldn't leave him. If perchance he thought of aught else, it was the green eyes.

Why did she fear those men? Who was she? She was a Scot, for God's sake. His family had a long standing mistrust of lowland Scots. His Kirkthwaite grandparents had died at the hands of marauding Scots, along with Aidan's namesake.

It was a test—a supreme test he must not fail. He would be rid of his preoccupation with this woman, whom he would likely never see again. He was sure the Abbot would not permit him to go into Beal for the next market after the dressing down he had received, admonishing him not to fall prey to the temptations of the flesh.

The desire that spiralled through Aidan whenever he conjured an image of the young woman was more torture than temptation. He prayed for guidance. It did no good. She filled his thoughts.

He wished Ragna and Edwin would come to visit. He would charge one of them with finding the woman, seeing to her safety. But the Abbot had probably forbidden it, and the perceptive Ragna would know instantly there was something wrong.

How were they managing the estate without him? His uncle, Baudoin de Montbryce, the Earl of Ellesmere, would take care of any problems at Shelfhoc Hall, situated as it was not far from his own castle at Ellesmere in the Welsh Marches. Kirkthwaite Hall, close to the Scottish borderlands, needed a strong hand, and Edwin—well—

And what of the Sussex manors their grandfather had left to his illegitimate son, Aidan's father?

God would provide. Aidan had been called to serve Him. But it was hard not to be concerned.

~~~

Nolana fidgeted with her *playd*. "Nay, Jennet, I cannot accompany you to the market again."

Jennet drew heavily on her pipe and blew out the smoke slowly. "Ye must. The Church is yer only choice now, lass. Ye must speak with the Abbot of Lindisfarne. I'll put in a good word for ye."

Nolana paced, fingers clenched in her hair. "But my stepfather's men. They may still be there."

Jennet blew smoke rings. "Nay, they be long gone. 'Tis safe now. It saddens me, but the church is yer only chance, lass."

Nolana chewed her lip. "But there is no convent at Lindisfarne."

Jennet nodded. "No, but the Abbey is a cell of Durham Cathedral. The Abbot will get you there safely."

Nolana hugged her arms tightly around her breasts. If she had to be a nun, at least there would have been some solace in being close to the young postulant. God would surely punish her for these impure thoughts. This was no time to be dreaming about a man, especially one impossible to attain. Perhaps that was the attraction. He was no threat. She hoped he would not be at the market, though at the same time she longed to see him again.

# CHAPTER SEVEN

Aidan was pleased the Abbot had grudgingly allowed him to come to the market a second time. At least he was in the fresh air, among people, and his headaches had eased of late. He had striven to suppress the persistent desire to see the green eyed girl again, convinced the chances of her being at the market were nonexistent. She was fleeing someone and would be long gone by now. He prayed she had evaded the men who pursued her. He shuddered, hefting the last of the mead from under the canvas in the back of the wagon. The Abbot had instructed him to leave it there until they needed it, to keep it cool.

He hoisted the cask to his shoulder and turned. Suddenly, the girl who filled his thoughts was there in front of him, breathless, frantic, looking over her shoulder. His mouth fell open. Their eyes met. She stopped dead. Without a second thought, he lowered the mead and gestured to her to climb under the canvas. She didn't hesitate, lifting her skirts. He glimpsed bare ankles. Blood rushed to his groin. She struggled into the cart and he put his hand to her elbow. A tingling jolt ran up his fingers and into his arm. She turned to him, wild-eyed.

*She felt it too!*

"Quickly," he rasped, "under the canvas. I'll distract them."

She crawled into the hiding place and he straightened the edges, ensuring she was covered. His heartbeat thundered in his ears. He picked up the cask, poised to hoist it onto his shoulder, when the men appeared. They were breathing heavily. One of them, sweat pouring from his brow, strode to Aidan's side. "Good brother, hast seen a young lass, red hair?"

This man was definitely a Scot, a borderer. Aidan assumed the pose of an imbecilic monk. "A lass? Nay, I've seen no lass."

One of the other men snickered. "Yon mon wouldn't know a lass if he saw one. Let's go. She can't have gone far."

They hastened off. The canvas moved slightly. "Stay where you are. They may come back. I'll deliver this mead to the Abbot then return. Don't move."

He walked away slowly, then turned back. He had to know, in case she decided to flee. "What is your name?"

"Nolana," she whispered. "Nolana Kyncade."

He mouthed her name. *Nolana.* It was the most beautiful name he had ever heard. He hurried off back to the stall, berating himself for his weakness, and frantically plotting how to get her to safety.

~~~

Despite the heat of the day and the stuffy confines of the canvas cover, Nolana could not stop shivering. She had gaped in disbelief after stumbling upon the monk, the same man she hadn't stopped dreaming about from the moment she had first seen him. Was the hand of Fate at work here? She had been careless, believing the Maknab men would have given up the chase. As soon as she had espied them across the field, dread had filled her. She would be caught. There was no hope.

Now she lay hidden, fear thudding in her throat, but feeling strangely safe. The monk had not hesitated to aid her. His commanding voice instructing her to hide had been a lifeline rescuing her from drowning. This was no mewling monk without a brain. Here was a decisive man of action. Her body warmed and she felt her face flush at the recollection of the things she had dreamed of doing with him. What a sinner she was.

Sounds came to her from the market, but no sign of her trackers. Perhaps she should flee? But her monk had told her to stay where she was. How would he get her to safety? Strange she somehow trusted he would. But he was a monk—not even a monk, a postulant, without authority. One against many if the men reappeared. She did not believe the Abbot would be on her side if they were challenged.

Her breathing slowed. Her eyelids grew heavy. She curled up under the canvas and dozed.

"Nolana."

She opened her eyes and squinted when a shaft of late afternoon sunlight crept under the edge of the canvas. Her monk peered at her, his face full of concern. "Are you all right?"

She yawned and stretched. "I fell asleep." She remembered where she was and why. "I must go. It should be safe now."

He lowered the canvas, then raised it again. "No, they are still about, idling by the market cross, flirting with women from the village. They seem to know them by name. They've been here a while, waiting for you."

"And I walked right into their trap. I'll never be safe."

He looked into her eyes. "I'll make sure you're safe from them, Nolana."

She frowned. "But I'm a stranger to you. I don't know your name."

Her monk hesitated. "I am Brother Christian."

She was strangely disappointed. "Brother Christian," she whispered.

"But my real name is Aidan."

His name was Aidan. At last she could call him by name. "I planned to seek sanctuary today, Aidan. I have no choice but to enter a nunnery."

A wave of revulsion hit him. He knew what it was to be shut away and could not abide the vision of this beauty enduring the same fate. It had been his choice to leave the world. She would be forced. "No. I won't permit it."

Her mouth fell open and he instantly regretted his outburst. "I mean, no, believe me you don't want to spend your life locked away in a convent. You're too beautiful."

Suddenly he heard the Abbot's voice nearby. He lowered the canvas. "Hush. Be still. We will be loading the empty vessels soon for the return to the abbey. Stay hidden. Don't make a sound."

Nolana protested. "But I can't go there."

"It's your only chance."

He turned to face the Abbot, his heart beating wildly. What was he doing? How was he to smuggle a maiden into the monastery, and what was he planning to do with her once he got her there?

He had no answer to these questions. He had to help her get away from those men. Great evil would befall her if they caught her. It came to him that if he got her to the abbey, the Abbot would be unable to force her return once the tide came in.

The Abbot's face was sour as he eyed the cart. "What took you so long, Brother Christian?"

Aidan took the empty container from his Superior. "I apologise, Father Abbot, I was dallying, enjoying the pleasant afternoon sunshine. Let me help you."

He carefully placed the cask up against the bundle of canvas, then reached to take a second one from another brother. Gradually he built a protective wall separating Nolana from the men once they climbed into the cart.

As they pulled away from the market he caught site of the old woman who had accompanied Nolana. She was obviously searching for her. Their eyes met. He hoped she understood his silent signal.

## CHAPTER EIGHT

*Beautiful.* Her monk had said she was beautiful, though she didn't feel like a thing of beauty, curled up under the heavy canvas in a smelly oxcart. The calm that had lulled her to sleep had fled, to be replaced by dread and uncertainty. This was madness. What was Aidan thinking? What would the Abbot do when she was discovered?

Again she cursed a world where men made the rules and women were forced into impossible situations. Once more she was at the mercy of men, and on Holy Island she would be surrounded by them. The odour of unwashed male bodies swept over her, mingling with the smell of mead. Bile rose in her throat. No doubt she didn't smell too fresh either after the afternoon she had endured. She hoped none of the men in the cart had a good sense of smell. Would monks know the scent of a female? It was at once humorous and terrifying to ponder.

There was no conversation among the men. Perhaps they weren't allowed to speak to each other. If she had to endure a vow of silence she would die. She prayed she would not be sent to a convent with such a rule.

A voice startled her. "We've almost left it too late thanks to your dawdling, Brother Christian. The tide is coming in already. We'll barely make it to the island."

"*Mea culpa*, Father Abbot. Again I apologise."

Aidan's voice! How safe it made her feel, despite the note of sarcasm in his words.

A short while later the cart rumbled to a halt. She held her breath. The cart lurched as the men descended. Now she would be discovered.

His voice was strong, full of authority. "A word, Father Abbot."

"What is it, Brother Christian? I'm tired and have yet to see to—"

"There is a woman in the oxcart."

Nolana pressed the back of her hand to her mouth to stifle a giggle, imagining the look of confusion and consternation on the old cleric's face.

"A woman?" The Abbot was choking. Was Aidan biting back the impulse to laugh? *Aidan.* How right his name sounded. It was as if she had known him forever, like a brother. Nay, the feelings that assailed her in Aidan's presence had naught to do with brotherly love.

Her monk cleared his throat. He *was* trying not to laugh! "Yes. She requested sanctuary. I granted it."

Silence. Had the Abbot died of an apoplexy brought on by shock?

"You—you granted sanctuary?"

"I did. You may castigate me later, Father, but she is no doubt suffocating under the canvas while we stand here."

Suddenly the canvas covering was whipped away. Nolana blinked and struggled slowly to her feet, legs cramped and stiff. Three monks gaped. In the rapidly waning light the Abbot's contorted face glowed red. Aidan had a trace of a smile on his face. He offered his hand.

She walked to the edge of the cart. He reached up, put his hands at her waist and lifted her down. She took hold of his shoulders. It was the first time she had put her hands on him. She remembered the jolt that had travelled up her arm when he had helped her into the cart in those desperate moments in the field. The warmth of his hands seeped into her ribs and pooled in her breasts. His robe felt rough, but his shoulders were broad and muscular. They belonged to a knight, a warrior. How did he bear the rough robe against his skin? He grinned, reassuring her, and desire spiralled in her most intimate place.

"I have two sisters, one of them my twin. I am used to helping maidens alight from conveyances."

The Abbot snorted and waved a dismissive gesture to the other gaping monks. "Be gone, back to your dormitory and prepare for supper. There is naught of interest to you here."

They scurried off, heads bowed.

The Abbot steepled his hands under his hooked nose and sniffed, as if some distasteful odour had assailed his nostrils. "Now, Brother Christian, who is this woman?"

How typical, Nolana thought, that he did not address her directly. She took a step forward. "I am Nolana Kyncade, daughter of Laird Ian Kyncade, late of Turaid Kyncade in—"

The Abbot turned his head slowly and looked at her as if she were a maggot. "You're a Scot."

She gathered the *playd* around her shoulders and stiffened her backbone. "I am a Highlander. I seek sanctuary from the cruelty of my stepfather."

He scoffed. "And who might he be?"

Nolana felt a twinge of fear. "Neyll Maknab."

The Abbot's mouth fell open. "Maknab? He's your stepfather? What is this cruelty you speak of?"

Her discomfort grew—a man would not understand. "He wishes to marry me to an auld man."

The Abbot looked scathingly at Aidan and pointed a boney finger at Nolana. "You've brought this wench here because she cannot obey her father's wishes in the matter of marriage?"

Aidan shifted his weight, looking sheepish. The smile had left his face. "She was fleeing, afraid, she asked for sanctuary. I did not know from what."

Oh God. He was of the same mind. She might have known. Aidan too would believe she should have obeyed her stepfather.

She fell to her knees and grasped the hem of the Abbot's robe. "My intended betrothed will beat me. He is a cruel man, as is my stepfather. I wish to become a nun. I beg you for sanctuary."

The Abbot was clearly uncomfortable. "Get thee to the refectory, Brother Christian. I'll deal with you later. I must see Mistress Kyncade to a private cell and ensure she doesn't come into contact with—"

She was to be a prisoner. Aidan walked away, fists clenched, broad shoulders rigid, his mouth tightly drawn. The forbidding walls of the abbey soon swallowed him up.

*Don't leave me.*

She had never felt so alone.

~~~

Filled with conflicting emotions, Aidan had no idea what he was eating. Maknab! Why hadn't he recognised the devise on the men's tunics? Nolana was Maknab's stepdaughter. It was a widely held belief at Kirkthwaite Hall, and in the nearby village of Bolton, that it was Maknabs who had attacked and destroyed the manor long ago. They had slaughtered Aidan's grandparents and uncles in the process.

Though Aidan's own father had unwittingly abetted in the destruction, he had never confirmed or denied it was the Maknabs with whom the Saxon refugees had allied themselves. It was a topic Caedmon FitzRam had wanted left in the past. He had been of the belief at the time the holding belonged to Normans, whom he then considered his mortal enemies—before he learned he was the son of a Norman.

Aidan swallowed hard, afraid the food might come back up his throat—Nolana Kyncade beaten and forced into a marriage she dreaded. He lay his hands flat on the trestle table, palms down. His fingers still tingled with the memory of holding her body. She was lightness itself, and he had wanted to twirl her around in the air, throw her over his shoulder and carry her off to bed—his bed.

He must convince the Abbot to grant her asylum. But he could not allow her to become a nun. Religious life would destroy her. She was spirited, brave, warm, a woman born to love a man. The thought filled his lonely heart with unbearable yearning.

## CHAPTER NINE

Nolana believed the hand of God had stirred up the gale that lashed Holy Island for three days after her arrival. The weather had been unseasonably warm and now it seemed the heavens had unleashed their pent up fury. Nothing moved on or off the island.

She had been confined to a small cell. Food was brought, but all she saw of the men who delivered it was the top of their tonsured heads, their eyes fixed on the tray. Obviously they had been given strict instructions. It was difficult to be sure, but she believed a different monk came each time. She longed for Aidan to be the bearer of food, but he would never be allowed contact with her. She prayed he had not been too severely punished for his compassion.

She paced the few steps the cell allowed, hugging the *playd* tightly to her, trying to keep warm. She was given no books to read. The Abbot no doubt believed her illiterate—a woman and a Scot. How little these Northumbrians knew of the windswept Fells and the people who dwelled there.

Her anger over her fate intensified at the sound of the windblown surf hurtling itself at the ancient stone walls. She had been shut away in this tiny hole because she was a woman who had dared want a voice in her own fate. She was given no news of what the Abbot intended to do with her. Whatever it was, it would not be good. Either he would ship her off to a nunnery, or summon her stepfather. She was helpless, like the midges struggling to free themselves from the spider web above her pallet.

On the third day of her imprisonment, late in the day, the Abbot rapped on the door and shouted. "The storm has abated and I have sent a message to the Bishop in Durham. No doubt he will send an escort to take you to the convent. In the meantime, you must earn your keep. The monthly laundry takes place on the morrow—you will assist with the bucking. Someone will come to collect you at dawn."

Nolana slept fitfully that night. It was more than she had hoped for, and she was to be allowed a reprieve from this box, albeit that she would be steeping linens in lye. Pray God she might at least catch a glimpse of Aidan.

~~~

Aidan was relieved the Abbot had allowed him to continue his work with the bees. He had assumed it a lost cause during the hour long lecture in the *misericord* on the subject of the sins of the flesh and the follies of rash decisions.

The diatribe had included the Abbot's utter disbelief that any woman should question the edicts of a man. She should be soundly beaten in that event. Aidan deemed it fortunate Ragna was not present.

He thought of his father and the respect he had always shown their mother. No one had judged him less of a man for it. Nor would anyone have dared suggest that Caedmon FitzRam was not master in his own house, but he didn't have to be a tyrant to be such. The same had been true of Aidan's grandfather, Ram de Montbryce, despite his being a powerful Norman Earl, a hero of the Battle of Hastings.

It seemed to Aidan that women responded better to kind words and love than to threats and brutality.

He had served his penance—five hours on his knees in the chapel, five hours spent with his thoughts on nothing besides Nolana Kyncade.

Prevented from tending the outdoor hives during the storm, he looked forward to visiting them. There had not been much activity in the manmade *skeps* sheltered in the recessed bee boles in the south wall and covered with protective straw hackles. Likely the bees would be out and about again today.

Their industry inspired him. Free to fly abroad, they never failed to return to their hive. Sad that by the time the *skeps* were broken open the bees would be dead, killed by sulphur smoke. Fervent prayers would be sent heavenward for the repopulation of the new *skeps* by new colonies, and the process would begin again.

Aidan sensed great excitement among the monks. The first day of breaking open the *skeps* signalled a new beginning, a harbinger of summer that surely must follow the late spring ritual. Taking honey in the spring allowed the bees a chance to replenish over the summer.

Honey would be jarred, new beeswax candles and writing tablets made, and best of all, fresh mead fermented. There would be projects to keep him busy, a respite from the monotony of winter.

The band of brothers selected for the task helped each other don the masks that would protect them from bee stings. Aidan's round wooden mask didn't feel particularly secure after another brother had fastened the ties behind his head. Hopefully his cowl would help deter the bees. Brother Tristan, who seemed to have taken a liking to Aidan, told him they would make two kinds of mead with the fresh honey—ordinary *meth* for the common folk and *metheglin* for the nobility. Aidan suspected some of the latter would find its way into the hands of the Abbot and his cronies.

"What's the difference?"

Brother Tristan put a finger to his chapped lips and looked around. "Lavender, and sometimes rosemary," he whispered with a conspiratorial wink.

They made their way first to the hives in the tree trunk hollows. Brother Tristan deemed it a safer place for the postulants to start. They had already had some experience collecting small amounts of honey. These bees would not be killed, but the smoke from smouldering cow dung heaped in a clay shell would lull them into gorging on honey.

Aidan was glad of two things. Firstly, he had not been charged with collecting the dung. What's more, he was to scoop out the honey and not hold the hot shell from whence the obnoxious odour emerged. Tall as he was, Aidan would be obliged to stand on tiptoe in order to reach inside the hives since the trees were cut at a height out of reach of animals.

Everything went as planned. They had collected honey and wax from a dozen hives. Thankfully no one had been stung, and the masks had stayed in place. The smoke had worked its magic. The thick linen bindings protecting Aidan's hands were saturated with honey.

But his back ached. He had been too long on his knees on the stone floor of the chapel. Bending in an unnatural position to scoop out the liquid gold, poised to react if things went awry, had also taken its toll. He prized fitness and worked hard at keeping in good fettle, now it seemed his body was weak. Sweat poured down the back of his neck and trickled into his eyes as he laboured in the sun, the cowl over his head. The mask prevented him wiping his brow.

Only one hive left.

"Keep the smoke going," Brother Tristan urged the postulant holding the clay shell. Aidan suspected the young man was in an even worse state, contending as he was with the acrid reek of the cow dung under his nose and the heat of the clay shell in his hands. He took one hand off the shell to fan the dwindling smoke towards Aidan. His intention was probably to blow on the dung. He inhaled deeply, but his breath caught and he coughed—and coughed—then hacked and hacked. Aidan was afraid the youth might choke. In his panic, the lad dropped the clay shell to grasp at his mask.

Aidan reached out to grab his hand. "Don't take it off! You'll get stung."

Too late. The young man wrenched off his mask and was stung instantly. As he screamed and lashed out, his hand caught the edge of Aidan's mask. It slipped askew on his wet face. Aidan reached up to right it with his honey soaked hands. The bees had become agitated with the commotion and without the smoke to subdue them they swarmed Aidan's hands.

He reflected later that the unexpected intensity of the stings must have been what caused him to panic. How else to explain why he had ripped off his mask and rubbed his eyes? If the stings on his hands were painful, they were pinpricks compared to the unbearable fire consuming his face. He fell to his knees, aware only of a deafening roar, yet somehow he heard the calm voice of Brother Tristan warning the others not to run.

Within minutes Aidan was being carried inside the walls of the abbey. A few bees still buzzed around him, but they disappeared quickly. His eyes were sealed shut, his hands on fire.

Brother Tristan remained in calm control. "Take him to the Infirmary."

Trembling uncontrollably and gasping for air, Aidan vomited. Choking was the last thing he remembered before darkness engulfed him.

## CHAPTER TEN

Nolana had spent most of the day stirring the cauldron which Brother Thomas used to steep the linens in lye. The Laundry was set off the Kitchens, since fires weren't permitted anywhere else in the Abbey.

She felt like a limp rag. The steam had dampened her clothing and she had long ago discarded the *playd*. Her *léine* clung to her and sweat trickled between her breasts and down her back.

To her dismay, several monks passing in and out of the kitchens gave her more than a cursory glance, then cast their eyes down and scurried off, faces red. No matter the clothing, her ample breasts were difficult to conceal. Maknab's table had offered meagre sustenance, yet her breasts continued to grow.

Her thick hair was heavy with moisture. Ironically, her throat was bone dry. She had been offered nothing to eat or drink. How good a tumbler of mead and a spoonful of honey would taste. She was a slave, longing for the blessed coolness of her hateful little cell.

After interminable stirring, she had to heave the sodden cloth out of the vat and transfer it to another cauldron of cold water to rinse. Fortunately, two burly monks came to haul the rinsed linens to the drying racks after they had wrung as much water as possible from them.

Another monk was responsible for keeping the fire going, but when the new wood was added, billowing smoke brought tears to her eyes. Crackling sparks flew, sometimes stinging her raw hands.

Late in the afternoon, Brother Thomas waddled over, laden

with another pile of linens. "Surely not more?" she rasped.

He dropped the pile next to her. "No, these are clean. Take them to the Infirmary."

*Escape!*

Would the Abbot approve of her wandering the passageways? She had no intention of raising the question to Brother Thomas. Taking a deep breath, she reached for her *playd* and stooped to pick up the heavy pile. "I don't know where—"

He strode away, muttering directions. "Stay there and make yourself useful. We're done here."

She stepped out of the Laundry, relishing the fresh air of the cloister. It was a warm afternoon, but the air felt cool on her damp hair and clothing. Thank goodness for the *playd*.

She made her way through the silent corridors and hallways, relieved not to bump into any of the monks. Where was everyone? She paused before a large wooden door. This must be the Infirmary. She had followed Brother Thomas's instructions exactly. The linen pile was getting heavy. She leaned her back against the door and pushed. It creaked open and she peered inside.

There were six raised pallets in the room, two of which had shapeless mounds atop them, covered with linens. Another monk, standing next to one of the pallets, pressed a finger to his lips and beckoned her. "I'll show you where to place them," he whispered. Since he showed no surprise at the presence of a woman, she surmised everyone in the abbey must by now know of her existence.

She followed and swayed nervously as he reached for each linen in turn and placed them into an armoire. Her knees were ready to buckle and exhaustion swept over her. Should she ask for a salve for her hands?

Suddenly a gaggle of noisy, agitated monks burst through the door, some of them swatting at bees that followed them. They were carrying another monk who appeared to be in a stupor, his hands wrapped in something. The shapeless mounds craned curious necks. The monk assisting her rushed to investigate the commotion, barking instructions. They lay the unfortunate on one of the pallets and she caught sight of his face. Her heart stopped. She dropped the linens. "Aidan."

She thought she had screamed his name, but no one paid attention to her. Silently she cowered by the huge armoire. His face was destroyed, beautiful eyes swollen shut. They took a dagger to his hands and sliced off the wrappings. She bit her knuckle and choked back a sob. His elegant hands resembled the ham hocks that hung in her stepfather's smokehouse.

"We must remove the stings first," a monk said. She gulped air. She wanted to flee, but stood rooted to the spot. If she remained silent, perhaps they would not notice her presence. Aidan needed her. She couldn't leave him in this state.

Another monk had been stung, though not as badly as Aidan. They were tending him. He was sobbing, taking blame for what had happened. A choking desire to kill him rose up in her throat. The stench of burnt dung hung in the air. She was going to be sick.

"Take off his robe," the Infirmarian ordered. "Fetch the ointment."

She leaned on the armoire, transfixed, while they stripped Aidan. She ought to leave, but how to do so without being seen? If they discovered her—her limbs were frozen in place, eyes fixed on her monk.

His pale body was a sharp contrast to the redness of his hands and face. But he was a beautifully made man—not what one would expect for a monk. What was she thinking! She had never seen any man naked before, and had no idea what to expect. His body was different from hers. Where she was round and soft, he was hard and well muscled. Where she was small, he was big and broad. Her arms and legs were short and shapely, his long and corded. He had hair on his body, as she did, but in different places, and he had something nestled at the top of his thighs she didn't have. She should look away.

Aidan moaned, jolting her back to reality. They draped linens over him, obscuring his body from her view. She was relieved and disappointed. She had wanted to run her hands over him, feel the planes and angles of his body, soothe him, bring him comfort. He had done much for her, she was powerless do anything in return.

"The garlic in the ointment will soothe the pain," one of the monks said.

"Aye! Works every time," another agreed. "Lucky for Brother Christian this happened here at Lindisfarne where we know about bee stings."

*Lucky?* Again the urge to strike out rose in her breast. Aidan felt no pain now, but he surely would when he recovered his wits.

"But this is bad." The monk spoke in a barely audible whisper. "He might lose his sight. We'll pray diligently for him, and for the wretch who caused the accident. He feels responsible."

*As he should!*

Unable to stand any longer, Nolana slipped to the floor beside the armoire. Gradually, everyone but the Infirmarian left. Darkness fell, plunging the room into deep shadow. A lone candle flickered beside Aidan's pallet, casting him in a strange glow. The mounds snored. She huddled in the *playd*, mouthing a mantra learned at her mother's knee.

*Let all be well, let all be well, let all be well.*

Her eyelids drooped.

~~~

"Water."

Nolana's head jerked up. Where was she? Had she heard a voice?

"Water."

*Aidan.*

A snake coiled in her belly. She peered around the side of the armoire. All was in darkness. The candle by Aidan's palette had burned out, but in a shaft of moonlight she discerned the outline of the Infirmarian slumped in a chair in a far corner. She crept to Aidan's side and looked at him. His eyes were still swollen shut. He licked his lips. "Water."

She espied a pitcher next to one of the sleeping mounds. Silently she tiptoed to it and inhaled. It was ale and would have to suffice. Returning to Aidan's side, she held the pitcher to his lips. He gagged at first then slurped greedily, his head falling back to the palette when he had slaked his thirst. She put her chapped hand on his forehead.

He inhaled sharply. "Nolana?"

She withdrew her hand as if she had been burned. How did he know she was there? She hadn't uttered a word.

"Nolana?"

Something had lodged in her throat. "Aye, Aidan. I'm here."

"Bees," he whispered. "The bees. Wasn't their fault."

She touched his forehead again, tears streaming. "I know. Drink another sip."

He held up his hands. "I cannot hold anything. My hands—"

"I'll hold it for you."

He accepted more ale, drinking greedily. She spied the salve they had used to soothe his pain. Scooping out a portion, she carefully dabbed it on his swollen flesh. It smelled of garlic, and something else—urine? "I am afraid to hurt you. My hands are rough."

He moved his head, his lips a tight line. "You have the touch of an angel. You cannot hurt me."

She smoothed ointment across his eyebrows, but was afraid to apply it to his eyes. "I wish I could see you," he rasped. "The sight of you would heal me instantly. I see you often in my dreams. My neck pains me, am I stung there?"

She put both hands on his neck and smoothed them down the length of it, pressing her thumbs to the soft place below his Adam's apple. "I cannot feel anything."

"I feel something."

She blushed to see the linens tent at his groin and hastily withdrew her hands.

"Don't stop. Your touch soothes me."

She stole a glance at the still sleeping Infirmarian and put her hands back on Aidan, gently pressing her fingers into his neck and shoulders. She kissed his forehead. He raised his head to press his lips against her breast, inhaling deeply. Driven by a need she had never felt before, she let her hands wander over the muscles of his chest, savouring the silkiness of the faint dusting of black hair.

"Climb into bed with me," he urged.

She pulled back, alarmed. "You're delirious, Aidan. You don't know what you're saying. You're lying on a pallet in the Infirmary."

He clamped both arms around her waist. "Nay, my sweet love, we're at Kirkthwaite, in the lord's chamber. On the morrow we'll sleep late."

Kirkthwaite? This man was the lord of Kirkthwaite? How often she had listened in disgust to the auld men of the Maknab clan boast of their murderous rampage at Kirkthwaite thirty years before. They claimed to have destroyed the manor. This man was lord there? What was he doing in a monastery?

She had to get away, but didn't want to alarm him. She lay his arms down gently, careful not to touch his hands. "Hush, Aidan. Rest now. I must go. If they catch me here—"

She pecked a kiss on his forehead. His brow was fevered.

"Don't leave me," he whispered faintly. "I need you." A deep breath shuddered through him and soon he was snoring softly.

Sniffing away the tears, she pulled the still damp *playd* over her head and crept from the Infirmary. She had longed to be more than a chattel in a man's eyes. But Aidan was a monk. The bitter irony of it all.

## CHAPTER ELEVEN

"*Godemite*, Aidan!"

Aidan forced his eyes open a crack. The swelling had lessened and shapes were discernible without much pain if he peered through his lashes. Relief washed over him. "Ragna!" he rasped.

"Edwin is here too."

Edwin's face floated into his field of vision. "Edwin, thank God you've come."

He closed his eyes.

"Look what they've done to you, brother. You are coming home to Kirkthwaite now."

He shook his head slightly, instantly regretting the movement. "No, Ragna. I want you to do something for me."

"I'll not take no for an answer, Aidan."

He took a deep breath, imagining his sister with her hands on her hips, petulant chin thrust out. "Listen. I cannot talk for long, you must listen, for once."

He heard his sister's snort, but Edwin asked, "What is it, Aidan?"

"There is a woman here. Her name is—"

Ragna snorted again. "You're delirious. This is a monastery. I'm the only woman here."

He opened his eyes just as Edwin pushed Ragna out of the way, none too gently. "Go on," Edwin said.

"Nolana Kyncade sought sanctuary here from her stepfather. The Abbot is sending her to a nunnery in Durham. You must prevent it. Take her to Kirkthwaite. Keep her safe there."

Ragna sulked at the foot of his pallet, arms folded across her chest.

Edwin shook his head. "But who is this woman, and on whose authority are we to do this?"

Aidan's head was pounding. "She's a Scot—"

Ragna stamped her foot. "A Scot?"

Edwin turned to her. "Ragna, hold your tongue. Can't you see he is in pain and trying to tell us something important?"

Ragna's mouth fell open.

*Well, well. Edwin has found his backbone.*

"Thank you, Edwin. This woman is not suited to religious life. You must safeguard her at Kirkthwaite. Her stepfather may pursue her and force her into an abusive marriage."

Ragna stopped pouting. "What father would do that? Who is he?"

Should he tell them? They would find out soon enough. "Neyll Maknab."

Both siblings gasped, but said nothing, then Ragna asked, "Where are they keeping her?"

"I don't know. She has come secretly to see me twice while I've lain here, but yesterday she didn't come. You'll speak to the Abbot and force him to give her the choice. I must be assured she is safe."

Edwin saluted. "It will be done." He hurried from the Infirmary.

Ragna leaned close to Aidan's ear. "What is this woman to you?"

How to explain what he did not understand? He swallowed hard. "She's a young woman in trouble, Ragna. I want to help her."

His sister put her hand on his forehead. "I had better assist Edwin. I can be more forceful."

Aidan chuckled. "I don't know, he seems to have found some courage. Did he actually salute me?"

Ragna shrugged and left, but in minutes she and Edwin returned, both agitated. "She's gone already."

Aidan's heart plummeted. "What?"

"The escort from Durham took her yesterday."

Aidan struggled to sit up. He reached out his still swollen hand and gripped his brother's arm. Edwin's eyes widened in surprise. "Edwin, you must pursue them. Take a contingent of our men-at-arms and go after them. They must not reach Durham. Promise me!"

Ragna put her hands on Aidan's shoulders. "Calm yourself. We will do your bidding and see her safely delivered to Kirkthwaite. You must rest and get well. Then we'll speak of your return home."

Aidan had no strength left to argue. He collapsed onto the bolster and closed his eyes. "Thank you. Go quickly."

~~~

Nolana's heart ached that she had been denied the opportunity to say farewell to Aidan. She had finagled only one other visit to the Infirmary, narrowly avoiding getting caught applying salve to his hands. He was in greater pain and seemed to have no recollection of his suggestion she share his bed at Kirkthwaite, proving her suspicion he had been delirious. She was relieved. There was no future for their relationship. But her heart raced at the image of them abed together, limbs entangled.

The escort from Durham consisted of two elderly nuns in a wagon accompanied by five mounted guards. They had brought a novice's habit, and she was forced to leave behind her *playd* and *léine*, her last links to her roots. Sister Magdalena stuffed Nolana's hair into the confining coif, remarking that it would be an easier matter once they reached the mother house in Durham where they would crop it short. A leaden weight settled on her heart. It was her mother's weakness that had brought her to this. She would never forgive her. She should be relieved she would be shut away, protected from men—but Aidan, oh God, Aidan.

She rode in the back of the wagon. The nuns ignored her. The two guards riding behind ogled and smirked, elbowing each other in the ribs. The procession navigated the causeway and turned south to Durham. After a mile or two they entered Fenwick Wood. It was eerily silent. No birdsong. No creatures stirring. The horses grew nervous and a sour taste rose in Nolana's mouth. She held her breath and scanned the thick wood for an avenue of escape.

They rounded a bend. Her mouth fell open. In the middle of the track cowered Jennet, shoulders hunched. A burly giant bearing the Maknab devise on his tunic held the back of the old woman's neck. Nolana's blood turned to ice in her veins.

The guards reined in their horses. Their leader addressed the giant. "You there. Make way. We are emissaries of the Bishop of Durham. These women are under his protection."

Nolana did not see the silent arrow that pierced the man's heart until he grunted. His body slipped from the horse and thudded to the ground. Sister Magdalena screamed in outrage, and the remaining guards fled into the forest. Nolana gripped the sides of the wagon when Neyll Maknab sauntered out of the wood. The giant had forced Jennet to her knees. Nolana stood up in the wagon, hoping her icy fear didn't show. "Let her go. She's just an auld woman."

"I didn't mean to tell, I didn't," Jennet wailed.

Neyll smirked. "She was most forthcoming concerning you and your whereabouts. It took little persuasion."

Nolana climbed out of the wagon and knelt by Jennet, pushing away the giant's hand. She put her arms around the sobbing woman. "You're a brute, Neyll Maknab. You prey on defenceless women."

Nyell strolled over to her and fingered her veil. Sister Magdalena made a sound of protest but he silenced her with a look. "Nonsense. I am the soul of generosity. Instead of killing these women, I intend to let them go on their merry way, without you of course, daughter." He jerked his thumb in the direction of Durham.

Without a moment's hesitation, Sister Magdalena urged the horse forward. The wagon pulled away. Nolana watched them go as she came to her feet. "I am not your daughter. My father was a noble man. You are not."

Neyll smacked her across the face. She reeled and stumbled into Jennet. "Noble or not, I am the man who holds sway over you and you will obey me. Your precious crone had best be gone, before I change my mind."

Jennet looked pityingly at Nolana then scurried off into the trees.

A Maknab man held the reins of the dead guard's horse. Neyll took her hand and dragged her to the animal. "Mount, Nolana. And don't think to escape. I am done chasing you. My patience is at an end. Next time you run I will kill you."

Nolana clung to the pommel and the stolen horse was led north towards the border.

~~~

She sensed the moment they crossed into the Lowlands. The tension left Neyll's shoulders. Here he was feared and he feared no man. It took but a day to reach his tower stronghold at Kolbrand's Path, but to Nolana it might have been a journey to the other side of the world.

The habit chafed her thighs and bottom and by the time they arrived she was sore and exhausted. The hated stone towerhouse loomed before her in the fading light. The crashing waves of the North Sea hurled themselves against the outer ramparts of the fortification. She had been elated to escape this wretched place where she had known nothing but unhappiness. She shivered. What punishment did her stepfather plan? She hoped the aged Baron, her intended betrothed, was not in residence.

They passed over the ditch and through the wooden palisades. Someone lifted her from the horse. Her knees buckled when her feet hit the ground and she leaned against the animal.

Neyll came up beside her. "Take her to the tower."

Her feet never touched the ground as two men lifted her by the arms and bustled her off to the chamber at the top of the tower. They dumped her on the pallet bed and withdrew. She heard the bar drop into place. Too exhausted to cry, she curled up and fell asleep.

## CHAPTER TWELVE

The Infirmarian allowed Aidan out of bed. The swelling around his eyes had improved considerably and he was enjoying a stroll with Ragna in the Abbey garden. His sight had not been affected by the stings. Hopefully his hands would soon be back to normal. He walked arm in arm with his sister. It felt good.

They had never been close. Aidan and Blythe were—well, they were twins. Ragna was several years younger than he was, and she had always been independent—a hellion. Everyone in their family called her *the Wild Viking Princess*, saying she took after their Danish ancestors.

She must have sensed what he was feeling. "It's good to walk with you like this, Aidan. You and I have never been friends."

He smoothed his hand over hers. "But we love each other just the same."

A tear trickled down her cheek. "We can do no less as the children of Caedmon and Agneta FitzRam."

He took a deep breath. "May God have mercy on their souls."

Ragna snorted. "If they aren't welcome in Heaven, there is no hope for the rest of us."

He squeezed her hand and they continued their stroll.

"Tell me about Nolana Kyncade."

Aidan pulled up sharply. "There's nothing to tell."

Ragna punched his shoulder, reminding him of when Blythe had done the same thing years ago in a garden in Germany. "You aren't hiding your feelings for her very well, Aidan. Why don't you admit you're in love with her?"

Aidan walked on, studying his feet, then turned to face her. "I made a commitment to God, Ragna. How can I renege? Nolana is God's way of testing my mettle."

Ragna opened her mouth to reply, but her gaze fell on Edwin, who was hastening towards them, escorted by a monk. "It's Edwin."

Aidan turned quickly. Edwin's face plainly showed his consternation. Dread threatened to rob Aidan of his tenuous balance. "Tell me."

Edwin took a deep breath. "We followed them, but in Fenwick Wood we came upon the body of one of the Bishop's guards, an arrow through his heart."

Aidan had to sit down. He clung to Ragna. "Nolana?"

Edwin looked ready to burst into tears. "I've failed you, brother. There was no sign of her, but the tracks led in the opposite direction. We followed them to Berwick, but lost the trail."

Aidan shook his head and put his hand on his brother's shoulder. "It's no matter. I know where they've gone. Her stepfather has her. You aren't the one who has failed, Edwin. That dubious honour falls to me. I'm not my father's son."

Ragna punched him again. "Now you've gone too far, Aidan. Father was proud of you. You are more like him than you know. Make a decision. What are you going to do?"

Aidan squared his shoulders and smiled. "What I should have done days ago. Save the life of the woman I love."

Ragna whooped. "Now you're acting like a FitzRam."

~~~

Nolana gazed down at the sea, forehead resting on the rusted iron bar across the window slit. Why had someone long ago deemed it necessary to secure such a small and impossibly high opening? She licked her parched lips, tasting salt. Laughing gulls soared and danced on the stiff breeze. Compared to the vastness of the ocean, she was a mere nothing. Was it for this she had been born—humiliation, cruelty and despair? Surely life should hold more promise? But as long as men ruled, women would suffer. The only compassionate man she had ever met, ever loved, was a monk—out of reach.

*Loved?* Did she love Aidan? No man had ever made her body

ache in unmentionable places before. Even thinking of him now in these dire circumstances, moisture pooled between her legs and her breasts tingled. Perhaps she was going mad? Would the Baron want to marry a madwoman?

She shrugged. Her fate was sealed. Grouchet would not care, provided she was fertile.

## CHAPTER THIRTEEN

Nolana did not partake of the victuals Maknab had provided for her wedding feast. It was more than likely she would vomit before the night was out. Her wedding night. She flinched when the decrepit sot who was now her husband pinched her breast yet again after taking a swig of ale. He had already imbibed far more than he ought. She prayed he might succumb to a drunken stupor before they got to the bridal chamber. Revulsion filled her whenever she looked at him.

For the first time since arriving back in Neyll's keep, she was to be allowed to sleep somewhere other than in the tower chamber. She had eaten little food in the intervening sennight and her belly rebelled at the sight of the sumptuous feast laid on by her stepfather. Grouchet must have paid him well for her body.

The ceremony in the Maknab chapel was a farce. The priest ignored her protestations that she was unwilling. He knew from whence came his stipend. After a patronising nod and a pat on the head, he droned out the nuptial rites. Grouchet swayed on his feet and belched several times, rheumy eyes fixed on her breasts. His breath nearly felled her when he claimed his husbandly kiss. He reeked of decay.

If she could put her hands on a dagger, she would dispatch the Baron, Neyll and then her miserable self. Her stepfather had made sure she had no access to escape or weapons, only allowing her to bathe and change clothes on the morning of her wedding.

He strutted around the Hall, the consummate host, accepting the congratulations of his fawning guests on the marriage of his stepdaughter to an English baron, a Norman nobleman no less. What a fortuitous alliance. Perhaps she might be sick before she reached the bridal chamber.

Her thoughts constantly drifted to Aidan, but she forced them away. What was the use? She must think of him as Brother Christian—he was lost to her, as she was to him. He was a monk, committed to a life of religious devotion. He wouldn't leave the monastery for her, a woman he barely knew. It was unlikely he felt the same intense stirrings she did. He had invited her to share his bed. Of course he had been delirious with pain—

It suddenly occurred to her this was Tuesday. Brother Christian would be at the market in Beal, plying his mead and honey. Would he think of her? The memory of his strong body and knee-buckling smile never left her. The bile rose in her throat again.

One of Neyll's men strode in and whispered in his laird's ear. Neyll grimaced, then glanced over to her and smirked. He waved a dismissive hand and the man hastened from the Hall.

Neyll drained a goblet of wine then came lazily to his feet. Nolana didn't trust the evil glint in his eye. He sauntered over to the centre of the dais, calling for his goblet to be refilled. He didn't demand attention, but it came immediately. A hush fell over the gathering. Nolana's heart beat wildly. She glanced over at Grouchet. He had passed out.

"Gentlemen and ladies, and dear daughter Nolana, Baroness Grouchet, it appears we are to be favoured by a guest from the famed Abbey of Lindisfarne, a monk no less."

A murmur of surprise rippled through the crowd. Nolana gripped the edge of the table as the room spun around her. No! Not Aidan, not here, not now. He could not witness her humiliation.

All eyes turned to the entrance as a monk entered, accompanied by another well-dressed young man. They were obviously brothers, despite the difference in their garb. A one-eyed man walked behind them. Nolana prayed that Aidan would not look at her. Why was he here?

"Welcome to you, Brother. We are honoured. Welcome to the wedding feast of my daughter."

~~~

Aidan hesitated only a moment before his still swollen hand went to the hilt of the sword he no longer wore. He had come too late. He looked quickly at Edwin. "Do nothing untoward, brother," he whispered. "We are among enemies."

Should he scan the crowd, look for her? He dreaded the pain he would see in her eyes. He had failed once again to protect someone for whom he cared deeply.

He bowed to Neyll. "Thank you for your welcome, Laird Maknab. I am Brother Christian from Lindisfarne Abbey."

Neyll coughed loudly. "A postulant, I see."

Edwin tensed beside him, but Aidan strove to remain calm. "I am indeed a postulant, but Lady Nolana was enjoying the sanctuary of my Abbey and our Abbot grew concerned when she did not arrive safely in Durham. The discovery of the body of one of her guards increased our alarm. I am charged with ensuring her safety. Most of the older monks are not fit enough to journey here in search of her."

It was not an outright lie—there was some truth in his words. The Abbot had been distraught, fearful of the ire of the Bishop of Durham. Neyll need not know Aidan was not on an errand for the Abbot, who had harangued him interminably when he had told him he was leaving the Abbey.

"You'll be sorry," were the old monk's parting words.

In the end, Aidan had bowed and walked away. It was one of the hardest things he had ever done—a foreswearing of the vow made to his parents to atone for their deaths.

He and Edwin had sent Ragna back to Kirkthwaite with some of the men, then ridden hard to Kolbrand's Path, seat of the Maknab. He was grateful for the steadfast presence of his father's old friend, Leofric, who had sniffed away an embarrassed tear when he had embraced Aidan outside the monastery. Leofric's disfigurement rendered him a fearsome sight, sometimes useful when confronting adversaries.

Aidan's gut clenched when his eyes fell on Nolana. She was pale and thin, her eyes downcast. Despair haunted her face. Her gown was ill fitting. His heart went out to her—a bride should look radiant on her wedding day. He itched to throttle the monster in whose Hall he stood.

Neyll's voice intruded. "You can see, Brother, that Nolana is safe and sound, enjoying her wedding feast with her new husband."

Aidan's eyes followed Maknab's gesture. An obese elderly man sat with his chin slumped to his chest, his legs splayed. The horror of Nolana's fate struck him full force. His own sense of loss made him want to weep for her and for himself. He should have listened to his heart when he first set eyes on her.

Leofric coughed. Neyll seemed to notice him for the first time. "What devise is this your man wears upon his tunic?"

Aidan squared his shoulders. "We are FitzRams."

He paused. Having let his enemy know he was dealing with a Norman family, he deemed it useful to impart the full weight of his identity. "The FitzRams of Kirkthwaite Hall."

His words were repeated around the Hall in hushed murmurs of disbelief. Maknab widened his stance, arched his brows, but said nothing. Aidan was sure in that moment that the rumours of Maknab involvement in the massacre of his grandparents were true. He glanced back at Nolana. Their eyes met. Was there a glint of admiration in those green depths?

He looked back at Maknab. "We shall make it our concern that Lady Nolana enjoys continued good health. Thank you for your hospitality."

Without bowing, they turned and left.

Aidan held on to his despair and anger until they were safely away from Kolbrand's Path. When they were sure they had not been pursued, he dismounted, doubled over and retched. Edwin stood beside him, his hand on his brother's shoulder. Leofric kept watch, holding the horses' reins.

It was he who spoke first. "Let's get you back to Kirkthwaite, Aidan. You'll feel better once you've bathed and are in your own clothes. We'll tend your hands, then decide what to do."

Aidan shook his head. "There is naught we can do. I have failed her."

Leofric gripped his arm with his good hand and shook him. "Do not lose hope. If it's meant to be, we'll find a way to rescue her."

"Aye, by God!" Edwin shouted, raising his fist and surprising them both.

## CHAPTER FOURTEEN

No amount of prodding or poking would rouse the Baron. Neyll was none too happy as he watched his men labour to carry the man to his chamber. He leaned over Nolana menacingly. "Seems you have a reprieve for this night, daughter, but you cannot long escape the inevitable. You will bear that fool an heir."

Nolana gritted her teeth. "Or you won't get full payment?"

He raised his hand to strike her then hesitated. "Take care, Nolana."

She smirked at him. "It won't be easy for you, will it Neyll, now I'm under the protection of my *husband*?"

He clenched his fists. "Don't be too sure. Get to your chamber."

A cold chill settled in Nolana's bones as she slowly mounted the steps to her bridal chamber, her thoughts filled with images of Aidan. She prayed her husband had not regained his wits. Considering the amount of ale he had drunk, she wouldn't be surprised if he slept for a sennight.

She slipped into the chamber. Grouchet lay on the bed, snoring loudly, his mouth agape. Someone had wrestled him out of his clothing and into a nightshirt. She was relieved Maknab had provided no maidservant for her, no doubt thinking her husband would be the one to remove her clothes. She settled into a chair in a shadowed corner and tucked her knees to her chin. Over and over, Aidan's proud words echoed in her mind. *The FitzRams of Kirkthwaite Hall*. Had he come at the behest of the Abbot? Did she dare hope he had left the monastery to find and claim her for his own?

What did it matter? She was doomed. But she would cherish the memory of his presence, a humble monk refusing to be intimidated by her stepfather. But he wasn't a humble monk. He was a proud nobleman, as she had suspected. She would never forget the look of anguish on his face when he learned she was married. If he had left the religious life for her, would he now lay blame at her door? Why was he in the monastery anyway?

These questions plagued her fitful sleep. When she woke at dawn, the Baron snored on. She had spent her wedding night with her loathsome husband, but was still a virgin. She sat bolt upright, trembling at the boldness of an idea creeping into her mind. The Baron's eating dagger was still tucked into its scabbard on the table beside the bed.

Killing him would take her to the gallows, and she doubted she would have the fortitude to commit murder. But if he believed he had claimed his marital rights perhaps he would leave her in peace for a while.

She tiptoed over to the table and withdrew the dagger, willing the trembling in her hand to stop lest she drop it.

*Let all be well.*

She slowly peeled back the linens on one side of the bed, poked the point of the blade into the pad of her thumb and squeezed. She smeared the oozing bubble of blood on the sheets.

*Let all be well.*

She held her breath when the Baron stirred, licking his lips. When he stilled, she wiped the dagger on the linens and placed it back in the scabbard.

She must disrobe to ensure the success of the trick. Frantically she struggled out of her gown and lay beside him in her *léine*, smearing another drop of blood on her thigh. She let out her breath. The Baron's eyes flew open. She stuck her thumb in her mouth. He turned his head to look at her, raking his gaze over her breasts. He reached over to fondle one.

*Pray to God I look like a woman who's been bedded.*

"Good morn, wife."

She took her thumb from her mouth and forced a smile, hoping she was fluttering her eyelashes in the correct manner. "Good morn, husband."

He grinned, but then looked down at his own body. "Good God, so randy I didn't take off me nightshirt."

Nolana's heart was beating wildly and she felt her face redden. "You were anxious, my lord."

He looked at her curiously. Would he believe her? He would punish her severely if he discovered she had tricked him. Suddenly he reached over and yanked up her *léine* to peer at her most private place. He traced a fat finger over the blood smeared on her thigh. She stifled a gasp. He smiled then pushed her over to reveal the bloodied sheet. He patted his groin. "Hah! I may be getting up in years, but the old shaft still works, eh?"

She pulled her *léine* back down, avoiding his gaze, glad she hadn't been obliged to look upon the *old shaft*. She doubted his body would be as pleasing to behold as Aidan's—but she must stop thinking on that. "Aye, my lord. It works, and I am rather sore this morn."

*Forgive me, Lord.*

He put his finger under her chin. "I'll leave you be so you can heal quickly. Mayhap I've already planted the seed of my heir?"

"Mayhap, my lord."

*Let all be well.*

~~~

Neyll eyed them warily when the Baron escorted his bride to the Hall to break their fast. Her husband was unsteady on his feet and bade her fill his trencher from the servery. He sat down heavily beside Neyll, boasting of his marital prowess with suggestive gestures.

*Men are such arrogant fools.*

She must not get too confident. It was a reprieve only. The sentence had not been revoked. Neither man rose when she approached the table and took a seat. She hoped she was blushing and looked sufficiently ravished as Neyll raked his eyes over her.

The Baron sliced off a chunk of cold mutton with his dagger. Nolana held her breath, unable to take her eyes off the weapon. He stuffed the meat into his mouth, then spoke, stopping only to swallow. "Off to England today—not a long journey—make it by nightfall—take my bride home—"

Neyll protested, offering his hospitality, reminding the Baron of his *obligation*. Grouchet was adamant. "If you want the coin, Maknab, you'll have to come to England for it. I don't wander around Scotland with large sums of money on my person."

He took a long swig of ale, belched and came to his feet. He grasped her elbow, apparently unaware she had eaten nothing. "Come along."

Nolana was happy to be escaping Maknab's clutches, but fearful of being taken to a remote English manor. Would she ever see the heather covered hills of the Fells again?

## CHAPTER FIFTEEN

Aidan had to admit he was content to be home. Ragna fussed over him. He wondered how long that would last! She seemed determined to sate his appetite, but he didn't object. It was good to have a full stomach again. His hands were healing well.

He had overindulged in bathing too, ordering a tub every day and luxuriating in the joy of being clean. Leofric jested he was in danger of washing himself away.

He could not wash away the memory of Nolana's anguished face. Whenever he remembered his first sight of her at the market his cock hardened. He had never ached for a woman as he ached for her, though they had barely spoken ten words to each other. Was he bewitched?

She was now beyond his reach. He may as well have stayed in the monastery. Such thoughts brought on more feelings of guilt. He had forsworn his pledge to atone. However, the notion of returning to Lindisfarne filled him with dread. He could never don the hated robe again. He was too fond of fine raiment and the way they made him feel. Why had he believed he could be a monk?

He wandered around the house, remembering many happy times spent with his parents and siblings. One day he summoned enough courage to enter his parents' chamber, undisturbed since their deaths. His hand fell upon the journal his father had kept during the Crusade. Parts of it had been read to them over and over when they were children—they knew it by heart. He clutched the worn and tattered book to his chest, grief rising in his throat.

The house was quiet. Ragna was napping and Edwin had gone out. He settled into a chair and unfastened the bindings. The parchment was brittle, the ink faded after five and twenty years, but the sight of his father's firm hand relating the horrors he had survived reduced him to tears. He sobbed uncontrollably until he could sob no more. Curling up, he hugged the book to his chest.

When he woke the light was fading. It was supper time and Ragna would be wondering where he was. Somehow he felt better. It came to him he had never wept since receiving news of the shipwreck.

They had endured endless days of hoping his parents might have survived somehow. Then came the bitter despair as the unavoidable truth had sunk in. A Yuletide of unbearable grief. Aidan had shouldered the responsibility of consoling Ragna and Edwin, sending messages to Blythe and Dieter in Saxony, and to the Montbryces in the Marches and Normandie. He was the eldest son. He had needed to be strong.

The codex had fallen open to an entry which described a dream. Worn out and wandering in Asia Minor, Caedmon FitzRam had not known if he would ever see his Agneta again, and was unaware she had borne him twins.

The rumours about Xerigordon are enough to make the hairs on the back of my head stand up—except I have no hair. I remember the first time I saw Agneta's beautiful hair. It was very short! What a bittersweet memory. I ache for her, in my heart and my loins.

I've had a recurring dream. I ride up to a castle. Agneta is there, but she's been transformed into a tree—a beautiful lush green tree. She smiles at me as I approach, and then I hear a sound. It's birdsong. I frown, not knowing where the sound comes from. Agneta slowly raises her arms and they become branches. I look up at the branches, and see two birds nesting.

I wish I could fathom what the dream signifies. I asked a Romany, but all he was interested in was my coin. He mumbled something about the castle foretelling great wealth. That surely can't be true. Maybe I didn't understand his language properly.

Though Aidan knew the passage well, its full meaning struck him for the first time. "Blythe and I were the two birds. Ragna was right. I am part of the heritage of this family. It is my responsibility to carry on the line."

He felt a sudden intimate connection with his father he had never felt before, despite their bond. Caedmon had ached for a woman, as Aidan ached for Nolana. He didn't recall his father reading out that part! If only his story could end happily too.

*Happily?* Caedmon and Agneta FitzRam had drowned! But they had lived happy lives with each other and their children. His father and mother would have given thanks that their deaths had saved the lives of their children. The family was painfully aware his mother's days were numbered in any case. Aidan's suggestion they sail on *La Blanche Nef* had not forfeited his parents' lives. It had saved his own and his siblings' lives. There was nothing to atone for in that. It was the fault of the drunken captain of the ship that it had foundered and sunk.

An enormous weight lifted from his shoulders. He tied the bindings, clutched the book to his breast once more, kissed it and returned it to its proper place. He resolved to move into his parents' chamber, feeling certain it was what they would have wanted.

## CHAPTER SIXTEEN

The Baron was too fat to sit a horse and chose instead to ride with Nolana in the wagon. At first she dreaded the journey, but he soon fell asleep and they arrived at his estate without incident as the sun was setting.

They partook of a small supper. Nolana was unnerved by the pitying looks of the household staff—did they know something she didn't? It was evident they feared their master.

She pecked at her food, though she had eaten little for days. Would he leave her be, as promised, or expect her to fulfill her marital duty now she was in his house? She feared promises meant naught to him.

He leaned into her. "Not hungry, I see. Too anxious to enjoy another romp, eh?"

She smiled weakly. "I am still sore, especially after the long journey in the wagon."

He chuckled. "Don't worry, I'll make it better. Come."

Her belly churned. Time to accept her fate. Aidan was not about to come charging through the gate on a magnificent steed. She allowed the Baron to lead her by the elbow to their chamber where he summoned a maidservant to assist her. "I'll go for one last nightcap while you prepare."

He had already drunk several tankards of ale with his supper. How did he remain standing? The timid maid helped her undress and gave her a pretty shift. It was of fine quality, but not new. Should she ask? "Whose—"

"The mistress before you. She died." The woman bobbed a

curtsey and left.

Nolana climbed into bed and pulled the linens up to her chin. She would soon be forced to surrender her maidenhead to a brute she did not love. Why had she expected more? It was the fate of many women. She wondered if her mother had felt anything for Neyll Maknab. If she had not—

Grouchet stumbled into the chamber, already in his nightshirt. At least she had been spared the spectacle of watching him undress. He staggered to the bed and lay down heavily, thumping his chest with his fist. "A bit winded—the steps."

He lay on his back for a while and Nolana listened to his laboured breathing. Only his death could save her now, but he wheezed on.

*God forgive me for wishing him dead.*

He scrambled onto his hands and knees, succeeding after three tries. "Now, the memory of last night's romp escapes me. Let me see your delectable little body again, my sweet. He pulled her shift up roughly, exposing her. He licked his lips and reached to pull his nightshirt over his head. She couldn't avoid looking at his maleness. Thanks be to the saints his head was covered momentarily. She might have laughed had she not been so afraid. She stared in fascination at what hung between his legs—a wrinkled prune topped by something the size and shape of a crooked thumb. From what she understood of the marital act, it involved the male member being inserted into the female's body. She wasn't sure how that might work in this case. Perhaps there was more to come.

He tossed away his nightshirt, enfolded his member in a beefy hand and shuffled to loom over her, breathing heavily. She trembled uncontrollably, despite the heat of a hearty fire in the grate. He moved his hand rapidly on his shaft, now peeking out in apparent surprise from the end of his fist. Bile rose in her throat.

His face was as red as the blood garnet of the signet ring bobbing up and down before her. Sweat poured from his brow. He braced himself with his free hand beside her head. "Only a short while now, my sweet," he rasped. "Spread your legs."

*Mammie!* The name died in her throat. What good would calling for her mother do? She obeyed him with a whimper and squeezed her eyes shut, setting her jaw. With a grunt, he collapsed onto her, forcing the breath from her lungs. She bit her tongue and tasted blood, bracing for penetration.

He lay absolutely still. She waited, holding her breath. Why wasn't he moving? Surely there was more to it than this? Had he fallen asleep? She was afraid to move. It was good if he slept, except she might suffocate.

She squirmed and tapped his shoulder. "My lord, I cannot breathe."

There was no response. She poked more forcefully, struggling to be free, digging her heels into the mattress. It was then she became aware of what was missing—the sound of his laboured breathing. A fierce trembling took hold and dread filled her belly. Could it be she lay trapped beneath a corpse? Had her wish to see him dead come to fruition? Had she cursed him? Would God punish her for this? The chamber spun around her. She fisted her hands and pummeled the sides of his body.

She didn't know how much time had passed before the weight was dragged away. Frantic voices shouted. A woman cooed and clucked. Nolana's nakedness was covered with something warm but rough, and she was carried from the chamber, screaming uncontrollably.

## CHAPTER SEVENTEEN

The shock and undeniable relief of her husband's death kept Nolana abed for a day. She stared into nothingness most of the time, unable to shed a tear. She called on the memory of Aidan's smiling face as a lifeline whenever the horror of what had happened threatened to drown her.

She did not want to set eyes on the Baron again, but it was expected she help prepare him for burial. The servants struggled mightily to dress Grouchet in his knightly finery, their noses wrinkled. She came close to giggling on occasion, sinking her teeth in the flesh of her hand to restrain her nervous laughter. He looked ridiculous, but rituals had to be observed.

It was a relief to have the ceremony over. She inhaled deeply as she climbed the stone steps out of the crypt, shrugging off the niggling feeling of guilt that she had wished him dead, and now he was. It was evident she was now looked upon as a woman who seduced men to their deaths. If only they knew the truth.

Her emotions were in knots. She was free of the Baron and was now his only heir, which meant she was a woman of wealth and property. But her stepfather would expect his due. He believed Grouchet had bedded her, thanks to her own chicanery. It was only a matter of time before he learned of the Baron's demise and her vulnerability as a woman alone.

Aidan FitzRam too would believe the Baron had taken her maidenhead. He wouldn't want her. He had probably gone back to the monastery.

Safety from Maknab lay in the north, but she would never make it there alone and a cohort of Northumbrian guards from her husband's demesne would be of no help. She could not expect it of them.

The atmosphere in the castle was one of relief. The Baron had not endeared himself to his household. They fawned over Nolana. She had done the impossible—slain the dragon. Maknab would not hesitate to spill their blood.

Though they treated her with respect, these people were strangers to Nolana. She felt isolated. She needed a friend. Aidan had been her friend. He had been willing to aid her though she was a stranger. He might no longer want her, but he was the kind of man who would honour a friendship.

She was not sure where Kirkthwaite Hall was located, but it was in Northumbria and someone in the castle would know. She prayed Aidan was there and had not returned to Lindisfarne.

~~~

One of Kirkthwaite's men-at-arms rushed into the Hall as the family gathered for the midday meal. Leofric came to his feet immediately. The man bowed to his captain. "There is a troop of armed men outside the rampart. They request entry."

Leofric glanced at Aidan, who had come to stand beside him, before he turned back to the soldier. "Whose devise do they bear?"

"Grouchet."

Aidan felt a coil of apprehension in his gut. Why would the Baron's men come to Kirkthwaite? "Do they appear to be belligerents?"

The man shook his head. "No, my lord, they are a lady's escort."

*She's fled to me.*

He looked over to Ragna, who had leapt to her feet, her mouth open—apparently speechless for once. Edwin grinned from ear to ear. Aidan did not stop to think of the implications of such an action on Nolana's part—her husband would surely pursue her—but the only thing that mattered was she had fled to him. "Allow them entry. I myself will accompany you. Come, Leofric."

The minutes he stood waiting in the bailey were the longest of Aidan's life. Perhaps it wasn't Nolana. Who else might it be? Was life with the Baron so unbearable she had run away? He would kill the Baron if a hair of her head had been harmed.

She rode into the courtyard, but didn't smile when she saw him.

His shaft soared at the sight of her, but his heart fell. He reached to put his hands on her waist to help her dismount. It seemed long ago when he had helped her down from the wagon in the grounds of the Abbey. Then she had worn simple Highland garments, and he had been garbed as a monk. Now she was dressed like a lady and he wore the clothing of a nobleman. He hoped when he opened his mouth, words would emerge. "Baroness Grouchet," he croaked, regretting it instantly.

She put her hands on his shoulders, her green eyes showing surprise at his attire. "Please don't call me that, Aidan."

Her breasts grazed against him as she slid from the horse, silk skirts whispering against the leather of the saddle. He wanted to press her against him and kiss her, but she was another man's wife. He couldn't take his hands off her. "Nolana," he whispered.

Leofric cleared his throat. Edwin rushed forward, grabbed Nolana's hand and kissed it. Ragna appeared out of nowhere and threw her arms around Nolana, who seemed flummoxed by this affection from strangers.

Aidan wished he was the one embracing her. "You'll smother our guest, Ragna. This is my sister, Nolana. And you've already met Edwin, and Leofric."

Was there nothing better to say? She must judge him a cold fish. He took a deep breath and squared his shoulders. "Welcome to Kirkthwaite Hall. Please, come inside. We were sitting down to eat. You must join us. Your escort is welcome also."

He had wanted to show his elation that she was entering his home, take her to his parents' chamber, now his, and ask her to share it with him.

She turned to give instructions to her captain. Aidan noted the authority in her voice and the man's deference. Being a Baroness suited her. Gone was the fear and uncertainty. But what had replaced it? There was no smile, no innocence. Disappointment flooded him.

She allowed him to take her hand to escort her inside, but did not look at him. "I was afraid you might have returned to the monastery, but I see—"

He tightened his hold on her hand. "I will never go back there. The monastic life isn't for me. I doubt if they would have me anyway."

Was it his imagination or had her hand become warmer?

Suddenly she halted and turned to look at him. He had thought the fear gone, but it still lurked in the green depths. "Before you welcome me into your home, I must tell you I am again seeking sanctuary."

He took hold of both her hands. "Nolana, I will do anything I can to protect you, but you are another man's wife. The law of the Church won't allow me—"

She gripped his hands. "He's dead, Aidan. Dead. I wished him dead, and now he is."

She sobbed and swayed against him.

She had killed him. He would lose her to the gallows. "Dead? Your husband?"

Everyone had come to a halt around them, listening, mouths agape. He waved them away. Ragna pouted, but Edwin dragged her off.

Aidan felt the softness of Nolana's breasts pressed against him. He had dreamt of fondling her, longed to put his lips on her nipples and suckle. His knees threatened to give way. His arousal throbbed and tingled. She was a rag doll in his arms. She must be exhausted, but he had to know. "How did he die?"

A deep breath shuddered through her. "I cannot tell you, not yet."

He took hold of her shoulders and held her apart. "Look at me, Nolana, tell me you didn't—"

She looked at him sharply and pulled away. "You believe I killed him? You judge me capable of such a deed?"

Relief and apprehension swept over him. "No, but sometimes when a person is— "

She shook her head vehemently. "He was an old man, Aidan. He suffered an apoplexy and died. I was not responsible."

She might still be his! He scooped her up in his arms. "I will take you to a chamber where you can rest. Then we'll talk. I'm not sure why you need sanctuary if Grouchet is dead?"

She leaned her head against his chest. "Maknab will want his due."

Old resentments welled up in Aidan's gut. "Maknab?"

"Grouchet paid him only part of what he demanded. The remainder was due once I'd been bedded. It was dangerous to remain at Grouchet Castle alone. I didn't know where else to go."

Pain snaked through Aidan. The beast had deflowered his

lovely Nolana. What had he expected? She was the man's wife. She might be carrying the Grouchet heir. He kissed the top of her head, savouring the scent of rosemary in her hair. "I'm glad you came here. I will protect you."

She had fallen asleep by the time he laid her on the bed that had until so recently been his.

## CHAPTER EIGHTEEN

Maknab bristled. He had made the tiresome journey to Grouchet anxious to collect his due, only to learn of the Baron's demise. "What do you mean, dead?" he demanded of the stable boy who cowered before him.

The boy avoided his glare. "The Baron died—of a fit. We buried him a sennight since."

Maknab narrowed his eyes. "And where, pray, is the Baroness?"

The boy edged away. "Gone, my lord—but I don't know where."

Neyll grabbed the urchin by the throat. "If you're lying—"

The boys eyes widened in terror. "She took men-at-arms with her. I swear I don't—"

Maknab tossed him to the ground and he scrambled away.

Where had she fled? He could plunder the riches Grouchet had no doubt amassed, but how much sweeter it would be to see Nolana cower in terror before him, hear her beg. He had endured years with her simpering mother when what he truly wanted was the red haired bitch who had never shown anything but disdain and contempt for him—he grew hard at the thought of bending her to his will.

Suddenly it came to him. The tightness in his chest eased. Adjusting his *playd*, he turned to his burly henchman. "She's gone to Kirkthwaite. She thinks the erstwhile monk will protect her. We'll see about that. Time to finish what my grandfather began. I'll rid the earth of Kirkthwaite Hall once and for all."

~~~

Kirkthwaite was ringed by a rampart and ditch, but it was not a castle and Aidan worried they might not withstand a full scale assault. While he had a goodly number of men-at-arms, they may not be enough. It was too late to send to Ellesmere Castle or to Shelfhoc Hall in the Marches for reinforcements. By the time they arrived, Kirkthwaite might lie once more in ruins, its inhabitants butchered by Maknabs. He was determined not to let such a horror happen.

He did not want to worry them unduly when he called his siblings together to discuss their defence. Edwin spoke first after hearing Aidan's concerns. "What we need are more defenders and more weapons."

Aidan nodded, rubbing the heel of his hand along his chin. Had his brother suddenly grown taller?

Edwin continued. "The villagers have as much reason to fend off the Maknab as we do. They laid waste to the cottages in Bolton and killed many of the inhabitants there, not only here at Kirkthwaite. I wager they'd be willing to come to our aid. If Maknab attacks us he's likely to destroy the village again."

Aidan stopped rubbing his chin, then slapped his brother on the back. "*Godemite*, Edwin, you're right. They may only be armed with pitchforks and shovels, but they have heart. They'll be safer within the rampart anyway. Go! See to it. I leave it in your hands."

Edwin hurried off, his head held high. "Our quiet baby brother is growing up," Ragna said.

Aidan laughed. "He's older than you are, Ragna."

"Yes, but it has never seemed so. Will we be safe, Aidan? I'm a little afraid."

Aidan put his arm around his sister. "I'm sorry I've brought this trouble here. Perhaps I should take Nolana away—"

She leapt to her feet. "No! I will not be a party to that. You love her, Aidan, and she loves you. Do not cast her out."

"You believe Nolana loves me?"

Ragna cradled his face in her hands. "Of course she does. Talk to her."

~~~

Aidan found Nolana gazing at the many FitzRam family mementoes hanging on the gallery walls. It had been one of his mother's favourite pastimes, particularly as her illness worsened. A lump rose in his throat and he inhaled sharply. His mother would have loved Nolana.

She turned to look at him. Sadness still haunted her eyes. She pointed to a small ceremonial dagger. "This is intriguing."

Aidan was stunned. Of all the trophies on display, she had chosen the one his mother valued most. He took it down from its mounting and stroked his hand over the ornate handle. "It belonged to my mother. Her Danish grandfather carved it. She believed the Viking depicted there was him."

He handed it to her and she accepted it carefully, examining the craftsmanship. "It's an object of great worth, I'm sure."

Aidan took a deep breath. How to explain the dagger, its role in his mother's journey? "It has a long and significant history. It saved my mother's life."

Nolana handed back the dagger. "Is she still alive, Aidan? I would love to meet her."

He had to pause before replying. "No, she died. Both my parents are dead." He turned away to replace the dagger so she wouldn't see his agony. He felt the warmth of her hand on his back. "I know what it is to lose both parents, Aidan. I feel your pain."

Words stuck in his throat. He leaned his forehead against the lime-washed wooden panelling.

She rubbed his back. "Your grief is still fresh, isn't it? How long ago did they die?"

He turned to face her and choked out the words. "A few months. They drowned—in the White Ship disaster."

She gasped and her hands went to her mouth. She squeezed her eyes tight shut and shook her head. "Oh, Aidan."

He brushed away a tear rolling unbidden down his cheek. He cleared his throat and squared his shoulders. "I'm sorry, Nolana. Grown men don't cry."

She reached for his hand. "A man who cannot cry isn't a man. Grief is nothing to be ashamed of. You loved them a great deal, didn't you?"

He could only nod his head. If he opened his mouth he would blurt out the truth of why they were aboard the White Ship.

She took both his hands and drew him to the chairs. "Sit with me, Aidan. Tell me the dagger's history."

Gradually his pain eased as he recounted how Agneta's mother had taken her own life with the dagger in despair after the slaughter of her husband and sons. "Ragna was named for her, Edwin for my murdered grandfather. I was given the names of my mother's slain brothers, Aidan and Branton."

"But you said the weapon saved your mother's life."

He swallowed hard. He wanted to share his family's history with her, but it was hard. He would be obliged to reveal his father's role in the destruction and the Maknab involvement. "When my father discovered he was the illegitimate son of a Norman Earl, he despised himself."

Nolana's eyes widened. Aidan continued. "Aye! He had believed he was the son of a Saxon warrior killed at Hastings. Listen to me. *Aye*! It was one of my father's favourite expressions. He was born in Scotland—his mother fled there after the Conquest."

Nolana smiled. "Your father was a Scot?"

"Ironic, isn't it? He grew up in Scotland and whenever I hear you speak, I'm reminded of his brogue. Anyway, he wouldn't accept he was the embodiment of everything he had despised his whole life. He went off on the First Crusade, unaware my mother was expecting a child—a child that turned out to be twins. Blythe and I. In her despair, my mother sought to take her life with the dagger, but somehow the carving called to her, told her to seek help from my Norman grandfather, which she did."

He came to his feet, went back to the dagger and traced his fingers over the carving of the Viking. "My mother wanted Blythe to have this after her death. It was made for a woman's hand. But my twin lives in Saxony, so here it remains for the moment."

"Mayhap one day you'll take it to her."

Aidan shrugged. "Not me, I'll be too busy taking care of the FitzRam properties to go wandering over Saxony."

Nolana came to stand beside him. "I heard of the great losses of the White Ship, but I never thought to meet anyone who had lost a loved one. It was rumoured only young people died with the Aetheling."

Aidan took a deep breath. "My parents were aboard that ship at my suggestion. Ragna, Edwin and I were supposed to sail with William's party. My mother was dying. I thought she would have a better crossing on the opulent *Blanche Nef*. I was the one who should have died."

Suddenly Nolana knew why Aidan was in the monastery. "You became a monk to atone."

He remained silent.

Her heartbeat drummed in her ears. "And now you've forsworn your vow because of me. I'm sorry, Aidan. I must leave. You need not deny your vocation because of me."

He took her hands. "No, Nolana. I believed God had called me to atone. I was wrong. Like my father, I didn't know how to handle the shock. I wasn't a good monk. Indeed, I hated the monastic life. My father had to endure the horrors of the Crusade before he came to recognize who he was. You are my Crusade—my test. You've made me see who and what I am."

She looked into his eyes. "And what are you?"

He put his hands on her shoulders. "A man in love."

Nolana did not know how to react to his declaration. She had sworn never to put her life in a man's hands. She despised men. A man had died trying to bed her, an experience that filled her with immense shame and guilt. The mere thought of it robbed her of breath. She had wished him dead. How would she lie with another man without recalling that nightmare?

She hated England and the Lowlands because of all that had happened there. Maknab still pursued her and would harm Aidan's family. His clan had already wrought enough damage on them, something she was sure Aidan was not aware of. She ached to return to her beloved Fells.

But another ache rose as the warmth of Aidan's hands seeped into her shoulders. He bent to brush his lips on hers—her breasts tingled. He laved his tongue over her lower lip. The tingle became an insistent prickle that hardened her nipples against the fabric of her *léine*. He coaxed her mouth open and pressed his lips more firmly, sucking her tongue into his warm mouth. A sound emerged from deep in her throat she had never made before.

She entwined her arms around his neck, twirling her fingers in his hair. He growled, put his hands on her waist and drew her body against his. She felt his hard male length pressed against her most intimate place. Here was no Baron Grouchet. An image of Aidan lying naked in the Infirmary leapt into her mind. Desire spiralled up her spine and settled at the apex of her thighs. She was on fire, hot and wet, out of control.

Nothing good would come of this. She broke away.

He frowned. "What's wrong, Nolana? I know you feel the same way."

She glanced up at the dagger. If only she had some talisman to guide her, help her sort out her feelings. "No, Aidan. I cannot. There are things you don't understand about me. You hardly know me."

He cradled her face in his big hands. She longed to give her life over to his protection, draw on his strength. "The moment I saw you in the market at Beal, I knew you. I should have listened to my heart then."

"But you were a monk!"

He chuckled and pressed his arousal against her, nuzzling her neck. "I was trying to be, but my body sent me a different message. Give yourself over to me, Nolana. I will protect you with my life."

She tore away from him and paced, her fingertips pressed to her forehead. "I don't want another death on my hands. One man has already—" She stopped abruptly. She had come close to blurting out the awful truth.

Aidan put his hands on the back of her neck and kneaded his fingers into her flesh. "You are no more guilty of causing Grouchet's death than I am of bringing about my parents' demise."

The burden became intolerable. His strong fingers were igniting flames in her body, sending icy heat from the top of her head to the tips of her toes. A sob escaped her constricted throat. "He died in our marriage bed, lying on top of me. I feared I would suffocate."

Aidan gathered her in his embrace and cradled her as she wept. When she calmed, he kissed the top of her head. "I don't love you any less because your beast of a husband died in the manner he did. I ache for the pain it has caused you. He was an old man. When our bodies join, there'll be a *little death*, but you'll love it."

Her mouth fell open. She should protest, not truly understanding the husky words that had sent shivers to her core, but he smiled and put his finger to her lips. "We must speak of other things first. Ragna, Edwin, Leofric and I have been planning the defences if and when Maknab attacks."

She took a deep breath. "It's not right that you are risking everything for my sake."

He shook his head. "Nolana, this has little to do with you and more to do with history."

Relief swept over her. "You know?"

"Aye, we've suspected it was Maknabs who destroyed our home

and killed my kin."

Icy dread filled her heart. "Neyll will stop at nothing. His clan has long boasted of the killings at Kirkthwaite. But they claim the manor house was totally destroyed."

"It was. My Norman grandfather arranged for it to be rebuilt, for my mother's sake. This isn't the original house. We've traditionally spent part of the year here and part at Shelfhoc, in the Welsh Marches. That house belonged to my Saxon grandmother, Lady Ascha Woolgar. It was my father's birthright."

"Neyll will be incensed, if he isn't already."

"We're ready for him. My father kept a well-trained troop of men here given our proximity to the border. It won't be the first time we've fought off brigands. The villagers will aid us. They suffered at Maknab hands too. It has taken two generations, but we'll avenge my family at last."

~~~

Aidan was reasonably confident, but could not be certain of success against Maknab without knowing how many men rode with the Borderer. He did not want Nolana to be aware of his doubts.

"Don't worry," Edwin kept saying, "I've seen to everything we planned."

Where had this confident new Edwin been hiding? Too bad his father had not lived to see the transformation. His brother seemed to be everywhere at once: overseeing the preparation of weapons, training with the men, practising swordplay and defence moves, inspecting the rampart, reassuring villagers. It felt good to have his brother at his side in this endeavour, and Leofric too had expressed his appreciation of Edwin's boundless energy.

Ragna had thrown herself into preparing bandages, readying salves, organizing a makeshift infirmary in the Hall, teaching maidservants to tie tourniquets, lining up pails of water and ewers of ale. Nolana assisted her and the two women worked well together. Aidan had never known his sister to willingly accept anyone's suggestions, yet now she deferred to Nolana seemingly without rancour.

The pallets readied for the wounded reminded him sharply of the pain he had endured after the bees swarmed him. Nolana had come to him then, at considerable risk, and done what she could to ease his torment. He was sure she loved him. He had to get her to admit it. What was she afraid of?

He wished he could erase the memory of the Baron's death. How terrified she must have been. A vision of the old man ravishing her plagued him. He had dreamt of being the one to possess her first. They would never share that intimate joy.

How would he feel if she was with child? Was it possible to love the spawn of a dissolute monster such as Grouchet? Nolana would love her own child, even if she had loathed the father. Aidan would love any child of Nolana's.

The Barons' death had made her a wealthy woman and any son she might carry now would be heir to Grouchet's holdings. But he suspected she had no love for the Baron's castle. She was a Scot.

Of course! That was part of her reluctance. She missed her own country. Aidan had never travelled to the north, but had heard tell of its wild beauty. How to compete? She didn't want to live in England, or in the Lowlands, and Aidan certainly could not live in a remote part of Scotland. His responsibilities as the head of the FitzRam family made it impossible.

But he resolved to see her safely delivered there if she did indeed want to return. It would break his heart, but he counted her happiness above all else.

## CHAPTER NINETEEN

An outrider careened into the bailey. "Beacon's bin lit, my lord," he told Leofric. "Maknab's bin sighted."
"How many?"
"Dunno. Didn't see 'em mesel'. Jus' the beacon."
Leofric slapped him on the back. "Good man. There are victuals in the kitchens."
Aidan and Edwin strode into the bailey and Leofric gave them the news.
Aidan turned to Edwin. "Our revenge is at hand. Gather the men and get them out to the rampart now."
Edwin reached out his hand. "I won't fail you, Aidan. I know in the past—"
Aidan grasped his hand. "This is the present, Edwin. We'll not dwell on the past."
Edwin swallowed hard and looked at his feet. "I'd hoped—never mind—we'll be fine without them. I for one am prepared to fight to the death to defend this place."
He hurried off, leaving Aidan to wonder what it was Edwin had hoped. No time to be concerned about that. He ran to the Hall. Nolana and Ragna had organised the women of the household and all was in readiness. Ragna came to embrace him. "Go with God, Aidan. You will prevail. I have every confidence."
He was tempted to ask her who she was, but the sight of Nolana wiping away tears distracted him. He went to embrace her and she clung to him. The feel of her body pressed against him gave him courage.

"Aidan, there is much I want to say to you. I owe you my life—"

"Hush, Nolana," he said softly. "Let me hold you. We'll talk when I return."

He kissed her deeply. "I love you, Nolana. I will not allow Maknab to win. I must go." He strode from the Hall, not looking forward to riding his horse with a stubborn erection.

~~~

Edwin had seen to the widening and deepening of the ditch in front of the rampart. Aidan stood atop the wooden palisade and looked back towards the house. At the time of the massacre, Kirthwaite Hall had been woefully defenceless. Things would be different this time. He closed his eyes, imagining the terror of that fateful day. His mother, then a young girl, had hidden in an abandoned barn and watched the slaughter of her father and brothers. His own father had unwittingly aided the Scots in the destruction of the manor house, believing it belonged to Normans. What strange twists and turns life sometimes took.

"Maknabs! Devil take 'em!" came the cry. Suddenly men could be seen scrambling through the ditch. A volley of rocks rained down from the rampart. Some fell under the onslaught. The rest retreated and all was still.

"Be ready!" Leofric bellowed. "They'll come again—in greater numbers. That was a test."

The light was fading. Aidan fretted. "He's waited until we cannot see them approach. We should have had flares."

"Light the torches," Edwin yelled. Within minutes, light flooded the ditch, revealing huddled figures in dark *playds* edging their way to the rampart. Aidan looked at his younger brother in amazement. "Well done, Edwin. I should have thought of that."

Edwin winked. "Father's idea, actually. He mentioned it often."

*Really? What was I doing? Evidently not listening.*

Leofric gave the command. "Barrage!"

Again rocks rained down and the figures either fell or retreated.

"Where did we get these rocks?" Aidan asked.

Leofric shrugged. "Edwin's had the villagers out on the moors, collecting."

The next wave of lowlanders did not come surreptitiously. They swarmed over the rise screaming like souls possessed. Maknab was not amongst them. Where was the devil?

"Bowmen!" Edwin shouted. Arrows flew, striking many of the invaders, but still more came on, some too close to the rampart. "Bowmen!" Edwin yelled again, and the scene repeated itself. Aidan felt useless. Edwin was protecting their home singlehandedly.

~~~

Nolana paced, biting her nails. The only casualty brought to the infirmary was a villager who had been burned lighting a flare. Ragna was tending him. He had told them of the assaults on the ditch and rampart. "They ain't got to the rampart," he reassured them. "Young Master Edwin done a right proper job of defence."

Still she worried. What if Aidan were killed? A lead weight settled on her heart. If they defeated Maknab, people would die in the victory. Aidan had lit a fire in her belly. She loved him fiercely. Why had she tried to deny it? He was not like the other men she had known. He would never use or abuse her. She would be safe with him.

She returned to the villager. "What of Sir Aidan? How does he fare?"

The man looked up at her. "Don't rightly know. I didn't see him, but there was no hue and cry of his death, so I suppose—"

*No hue and cry of his death!*

If he died she would do more than cry, she would scream until she went mad. Just as she would go mad living in the Fells without him. Her happiness depended on him. She wanted to run out to the rampart and throw her arms around him. She touched Ragna's arm. "I must go to him."

Ragna grasped her wrist. "Nay, I'll not allow it, Nolana."

"I must tell him I love him."

"He already knows."

She threw herself into Ragna's embrace. "He might die, Ragna. I've been a fool. I want nothing more than Aidan."

Ragna stroked her back. "He'll come back, Nolana. I know he will. He loves you. He'll not allow Maknab to destroy what our parents strove to build. Neither will Edwin and neither will Leofric."

Nolana choked back the lump in her throat.

Suddenly, the doors crashed open and injured men were carried in. "The rampart's breached," one man yelled. "Hand to hand now on the palisade."

Nolana rushed to aid the wounded, trying to control the fear that swept over her at the sight of their injuries. *You are a true Scot, used to hardship. Where is your courage? Has Neyll purged it? Nay, I'll not let the scurvy Maknab reduce me to a whimpering fool afraid of her own shadow.*

Reassured Ragna and her women had the situation in hand, she ran to the gallery, yanked the Danish dagger from its mounting and ran out into the courtyard. There were lights on the rampart in the distance. Part seemed to be on fire. She ran towards it.

*Let all be well.*

Halfway to her goal, she encountered a ring of men, villagers and men-at-arms, armed to the teeth. "Stop, lass," one of them called. It was Leofric. "Ye cannot go out there. Stay behind us. We're the next line of defence. If they break through yon rampart, they'll come this way."

It would be useless to defy them. She was one woman against many men. He was right. She would bide with them, and await her chance to help the man she loved. Smoke burned her nostrils and made her eyes watery. Weapons clashed out on the ramparts.

*Let all be well.*

She peered beyond the ring of defenders. A seething mass of men shouted, fought, swung, hacked, screamed and cursed.

"Hold," Leofric commanded, his mutilated hand held high in the air.

The melee came closer. Were the Scots gaining the upper hand?

"Hold," Leofric menaced, his hand still raised.

She peered through the darkness and caught sight of Edwin. He was a man possessed, slashing and slicing at anything moving near him. But where was Aidan?

The swirling mass came closer. "Nowwwww!" Leofric roared, lowering his hand and charging full tilt, his sword held high.

The defenders surged forward, farmers with pitchforks, woodsmen with axes, knights with swords. They hurled themselves at the attackers. Nolana did not want to watch, but her eyes were fixed on the snarling, angry conflict.

Then she saw him. All sound ceased. Aidan and Neyll exchanged sword blows like the wooden knights on strings she had seen children play with in the market. Pull the string, one knight thrusts; pull the other, his opponent parries. She held her breath and crept forward, crouching close to the ground, the dagger still clutched in her hand.

Out of nowhere, a group of mounted knights burst on the scene, hacking at the *playd* clad attackers. Bloodcurdling screams rent the air. One of the knights yelled a war cry in Latin and brandished his sword. The lowlanders fled. The heavenly host had ridden to the rescue of Kirkthwaite Hall.

Still crouched, frozen in confusion, Nolana glanced back to where she had last seen Aidan. Only Maknab stood there now, swaying on his feet, his sword bloodied. A body lay at his feet.

*All is not well.*

Filled with screaming rage, she tightened her grip on the dagger and rushed at Maknab. Bloodlust clouded her vision. She would kill him, or die trying. He turned and smirked, raising his sword. The smirk left his face and he looked down in apparent disbelief at the dagger embedded in his chest.

She looked at her shaking hand. It still held the Danish dagger. She looked back at Maknab. Edwin stood with his foot on the laird's chest, wiping a dagger on his *playd*.

She fainted.

## CHAPTER TWENTY

Nolana startled awake, smoke stinging her nostrils. She gulped in air, then felt an urgent need to expel it in a loud scream. "Aaaaaaidannnn?"

Strong hands took hold of her shoulders. Her body knew the feel of those hands. "Hush, Nolana, it's all right. I'm here."

She grasped a hand and held it to her face. It held the scent of Aidan, but she had seen him lying dead at the hand of Maknab. Someone stroked her hair, cooing soft words. She swallowed hard, opened her eyes and looked around. She lay atop one of the pallets in the Hall. Aidan leaned over her, one hand smoothing hair off her face, the other arm swathed in bandages up to his shoulder.

She struggled to sit up. "What—?"

He pushed her down gently. "Don't try to get up. All is well. We won. Maknab is dead. Edwin finished the job for me."

"I remember. I thought you were dead and I hadn't told you—please forgive me."

He kissed her forehead. "There is nothing to forgive."

She closed her eyes, trying to sort out the images. "Those men, horses—"

"I'll let Edwin explain."

She hadn't noticed Aidan's brother standing nearby. He came to the side of her pallet. "Tell her," Aidan said.

"It was my uncle, Baudoin de Montbryce, with his sons and a party of their knights—from Ellesmere."

This did not make sense. "In the Marches?"

Aidan chuckled. "Aye. They made it here in three days."

Nolana looked at both brothers. Edwin seemed pleased with himself. "I don't understand. How did they know you needed them?"

Edwin grinned. "I sent a bird to Shelfhoc with word to ride to Ellesmere for help."

Aidan raked his good hand through his hair. "It was so bloody simple and obvious, I can't believe I didn't think of it. We use pigeons regularly to send messages to Shelfhoc."

Edwin laughed and punched Aidan's good shoulder. "You were preoccupied with other things." He looked pointedly at Nolana, winked and walked away.

Aidan shook his head. "Who would have believed my timid brother Edwin would be the one to save us?"

"But you're hurt, Aidan."

He shrugged. "Baudoin's arrival took me by surprise. I let my guard down for a moment and Maknab managed to slash my shoulder. Apparently, your maniacal attack distracted him sufficiently that Edwin felled him with a dagger through the heart."

She smiled. "Maniacal? Are you saying I'm a mad woman?"

He kissed her. "Mad for me, I hope."

She blushed and nodded.

"This arm is something of an impediment, otherwise I would put both arms around you and ask you to be my wife, Nolana Kyncade."

She rose and knelt on the pallet so they were eye to eye, reached out and put both arms around him. "I have two good arms, and I say yes to your proposal, Sir Aidan Branton FitzRam."

He smiled and seemed about to kiss her, but then—"Are you sure you want to live in England, Nolana? You miss your homeland."

She sighed. "I love the Fells, but I wouldn't be happy there without you. And Maknab razed my father's towerhouse."

He kissed her deeply, holding her firmly round the waist with his one good hand, savouring the softness of her breasts against his chest. They clung together for a long while. He didn't want the moment to end, but became aware of several curious figures watching them. "Come, Baudoin wants to meet you, but don't be too friendly with my handsome cousins."

~~~

As they walked to the courtyard, Aidan's hand resting

possessively on the small of her back, Nolana savoured a contentment she had not experienced since childhood. She felt safe at last, as though she were back in her father's care. This strong, gentle man would be true to his word.

    She confided to Aidan that she had never met an Earl before. He reassured her. "Baudoin isn't haughty like some Norman earls. He and my father weren't just half brothers, they were friends."

    When she caught sight of his cousins, her eyes widened. Gallien and Etienne de Montbryce were indeed handsome young men. Tall, broad shouldered and well muscled, they were replicas of their father, Baudoin, the Earl of Ellesmere, who stood beside them. Though the Norman had lived half a century he was still an attractive man. His greying hair had probably once been as inky black as his sons'.

    She made to curtsey when Aidan introduced her, but Baudoin took her hand and kissed it, as did his sons. They exchanged polite pleasantries and discovered Gallien and Nolana had been born in the same year. Both were nineteen, Etienne two years younger.

    Aidan shook his uncle's hand. "I can't possibly express my relief at your presence here. You and your men made the decisive difference in this battle. Thank you."

    Baudoin put a hand on his shoulder. "I didn't hesitate once we received Edwin's message. Your father was a great man, Aidan. You know he saved my life in Florence. You are family and Montbryces stand with family. I was immensely saddened by the news of your parents' drowning. I thank the saints every day neither of my sons was aboard the fated White Ship. We are one of the few Anglo-Norman families that did not lose a son or daughter. It doesn't bode well for the future of this country or for Normandie. You heard tell there was only one survivor?"

    Aidan nodded his head. "Aye, a butcher from Rouen, who'd gone aboard to collect a debt! According to him, Prince William survived and was hauled into a smaller boat, but he ordered it turned around when he heard his half sister's pleas for help."

    Baudoin shook his head. "*Oui*, then so many scrambled onto the rescue boat that it too sank. William's cousin, Stephen, must be offering many prayers of thanks that he stepped off the boat just before it sailed."

    Edwin had joined them. "Rather like what happened to us. We changed places with our parents, because of mother's illness.

Aidan's suggestion saved us."

Aidan shrugged, relieved to finally accept that painful truth without feeling guilt. "Edwin, you're the one who saved us this time. Thank you. You have proven yourself a capable warrior. I cede to you Shelfhoc Hall to oversee as yours. I cannot adequately take care of both Halls and the Sussex estates."

Edwin clasped his hand and the brothers embraced. "Thank you, Aidan, I love Shelfhoc Hall."

Baudoin slapped Edwin on the back. "Good! You'll be close to us in the Marches, nephew. Now, where's that wilful niece of mine?"

Aidan chuckled. "Believe it or not, Ragna has taken charge of running the household."

Nolana gasped. "I was supposed to be helping her." She hastened away.

The men watched her go.

Gallien rubbed his chin. "If I was a few years older, Cousin Aidan, you'd have a fight on your hands for Nolana. She's beautiful."

Aidan wagged a finger at his cousin. "If you so much as look at her with too much interest, I'll have your hide. She is mine."

Baudoin laughed. "She is lovely, Aidan. I'm anxious to hear her story, and what you intend with her. Her brogue reminds me of your father. Is she a Scot?"

"Aye, from the north. My intention is honourable, uncle. She is to be my wife."

Baudoin stretched his arms over Edwin and Aidan's shoulders. "Good! It hasn't been easy for your family, but this is the way your parents would have wanted it. If you had drowned, they would have been devastated. But, we are still alive, and I for one am hungry. I smell an enticing aroma coming from the kitchens. I see my sons have already followed their noses. There'll be no food left if we don't go quickly."

## CHAPTER TWENTY-ONE

Baudoin de Montbryce and Caedmon FitzRam had been half brothers, but the resemblance was so striking most people believed they were full brothers. Aidan therefore found it appropriate that his uncle was still at Kirkthwaite when he married Nolana. His presence was a comfort.

Aidan's shoulder wound was healing well and Ragna had allowed the bandages to be removed. She embraced the task of preparing for the wedding with great glee. In her usual whirlwind manner, she created a flurry of activity in every corner of the manor house. Cook was schooled in the exact dishes to be served. Seamstresses from the village were employed to create new gowns, and she threatened them with dire consequences if her instructions were not followed. Servants were tasked with sweeping and cleaning the manor and woe betide anyone who appeared at the celebration with a tunic that was anything but pristine. All the while she oversaw the care of the wounded.

She soon had Gallien and Etienne at her beck and call, which amused their father greatly. He told Aidan, "They're not used to being bullied by a female. They have two sisters, of course, but Fleurie and Isabelle are timid. Ragna's got these two wrapped around her little finger."

Aidan smiled. "That's Ragna, our Wild Viking Princess. She certainly is the one who most exhibits our Danish ancestry. Can't you envision her at the prow of a longboat? Mayhap she should have the ceremonial dagger, rather than Blythe."

Edwin was delighted to be Aidan's second. In short order he

had the men-at-arms cleaning their uniforms and weapons. He arranged for the village priest from Bolton to conduct the ceremony, and somehow managed to fill the small church with fresh flowers. He selected which of Aidan's doublets, leggings and boots he judged suitable for the rites. He aided Leofric with the burial of the dead.

It rather amused and comforted Aidan. Caedmon and Agneta would be proud of all their offspring. Their deaths had brought their children closer.

He shared his thoughts with Nolana on the eve of their wedding. They had fled Ragna's frenzied activities and found the gallery deserted. She stood in front of the hearty fire, rubbing her arms. He came up behind her and pulled her back against him, his arms crossed under her breasts. The warm weight of them felt delicious. He had been determined not to become too aroused in anticipation of the morrow, but it was useless. He was sure she could feel his hard need pressed against her bottom. "Let me warm you."

She leaned her head back against his good shoulder. "I'm not cold, only nervous."

He kissed her neck, delighted to feel her tremble. He was sure his betrothed was a passionate woman. She had endured a terrible agony in her first marriage bed and he was determined to erase that memory. He would use every one of his father's seductive suggestions to bring her pleasure. He couldn't imagine there'd been anything pleasant in the Baron's lovemaking efforts. "Everything will go to plan. No one would dare let any detail go awry with Ragna breathing down their neck."

She pulled away from him. "I'm not worried about the arrangements. This will be the most organized wedding in history!"

A knot of fear coiled in Aidan's breast. She was still afraid. He thought he had slain her demons—the Baron and Maknab were dead, and she had admitted she would not be happy without him in Scotland—but something held her in its thrall. He turned her to face him. "Tell me, Nolana. What is it that haunts you?"

She closed her eyes and shook her head. "I envy your love of your mother, Aidan."

This he had not expected. He remained silent, hoping she would confide in him.

"I came to despise my mother. Her weakness was the cause of

my torment."

He held her close, fingering her hair. "I don't understand."

"My mother didn't love Maknab, but she allowed him to control her life, and mine, because she didn't want to be alone. She needed the support of a man so badly, it killed her, and almost cost me my life. I need you, Aidan, but I'm afraid to surrender myself to you."

Aidan took a deep breath, hoping his words would not alienate her. "I am not Maknab, and you are not your mother. I never met her, and I don't know what drove her to him, but I do know what grief can do. I shut myself up in a monastery. Don't judge your mother too harshly, Nolana. My grandmother took her own life and at the time my mother hated her for it, but she came to understand the power of grief and despair. Maknab sought to exploit your mother. That's not why I want you. I love you. You're essential to my happiness."

Nolana inhaled sharply and rocked her head in her hands. "But you might die!"

He took hold of her shoulders. "Death comes to us all—"

"No!" she shouted. "I mean in our marriage bed. You teased me about a *little death*, but I don't see the humour. My husband died trying to enter me. I am a sinner and God cursed my marriage bed because I wished for my husband's death."

Aidan's mouth fell open.

*Trying*, she'd said.

He took another deep breath, his thoughts in turmoil. He suddenly sensed how fragile this young woman was. "Listen to me carefully, Nolana. You've not had the benefit of a mother to enlighten you about marriage and what happens between a man and a woman."

She wrenched away from him. "I know only too well. I was wed to a monster. I hated his touch."

He pulled her back. "Do you have the same feelings when I touch you?"

Tears flowed freely down her blushing cheeks. "No. My feelings for you are different. I ache for you."

He kissed her forehead, humbled and exhilarated to be the man initiating his beautiful Nolana into these intimacies. "My sweet, it's the ache of desire that leads to the *little death*. The joining of a man and a woman can be wonderful. It transports a person to another world. You die a little death. You're out of your earthly body for a few glorious moments and you enter heaven."

She clung to the front of his doublet and lay her forehead against his chest. He put his hand on the back of her neck. She was warmer than a few moments before. "Our joining won't be the same as the one you endured with Grouchet."

She glanced up at him, confusion in her eyes. "Grouchet didn't—you believe—no! He never joined his body to mine. He died trying."

Aidan wished the drumming in his ears would cease, then realized it was his heart. He dared not open his mouth lest a tiny squeak emerge. He wanted to laugh, cry, scream, shout. Instead, full of hope, he murmured, "You're still a virgin?"

She looked at him strangely. "Of course, I thought you understood that. Were it otherwise, you wouldn't want me for wife."

The enormity of her innocence struck him full force, but he had to be forthright. "Nolana, it wouldn't matter to me if you'd been taken by a whole army of men, I would still want you for my wife,"—she wriggled to get free—"but I cannot tell you how elated I am I will be your first love. I promise it will be memorable. In a good way!"

She gave up her struggles and leaned into him. "Forgive me, Aidan. I am unversed in the ways of good men. Please, be patient."

If they weren't getting married on the morrow, he would have torn the clothes from her body and claimed her on the planked floor of the gallery his mother loved so well. He cleared his throat, hoping the throbbing need he pressed against her would not alarm her. How to know what horrors had transpired in the misbegotten matrimonial bed of the Baron?

Perhaps a taste of what was to happen in their marriage bed might be in order, just to reassure her. He took her hand and placed it on his arousal. She startled, but did not take her hand away. "This is for you, Nolana. On the morrow, we'll join our bodies and I will bury myself deep inside you, making us one."

She nodded, her breathing ragged, but kept her hand still. "Feel me, Nolana, feel what you do to me. I grow hard at your touch."

Slowly, her fingers pressed against his shaft. Tingles spiralled up his spine. Perhaps this wasn't such a good idea. The morrow seemed a long time off. He cupped her breasts in his hands, rubbing his thumb over the erect nipples. She moaned. He bent to lick each nipple in turn through the fabric of her gown. The pressure of her fingers increased. She murmured his name.

# CHAPTER TWENTY-TWO

Nolana woke before dawn on the day of her wedding, still murmuring Aidan's name. She had felt bereft the night before when he had curtailed their intimacies, but it had been difficult for him too. She had wanted to wrestle him to the floor and tear off his clothes, put her hands on his flesh.

Aidan inflamed her. The memory of his lips on her breasts made her mouth go dry. Wetness flooded her most intimate place when she recalled the feel of his hard male length in her hand and remembered the desire in his eyes. She stretched languidly, purring like a lazy cat. Yawning, she sat up and lifted her breasts, fingering her pointed nipples, remembering Aidan lying naked in the Infirmary.

When Maknab and Grouchet ogled her she felt nothing but revulsion. The loving lust in Aidan's warm blue gaze made her knees go weak and filled her with an urge to tear off her clothes and press his lips to her breast. This was what it was to desire a man. She ran her fingers through the snarls in her hair. Had her mother ached with the same feelings for her father? She had been devastated by his death. Perhaps Aidan was right. The grief and loneliness had been too much to bear. It had driven her to Maknab.

Suddenly, Ragna flew into the chamber. "Come along, no lolling in bed today. We've much to do."

With a happy sigh, Nolana surrendered to the ministrations of her soon to be sister-by-marriage. It would be good to have a sister. Marriage to Aidan was providing her with a family as well as a husband, and, if God wished it, they would have children of their own. Life was good.

~~~

As he witnessed his nephew's wedding, Baudoin de Montbryce's memory went back to his own marriage to Carys, two score years before. He and his brother Robert had married the same day, in a double ceremony. His wife and daughters would be disappointed they were missing these festivities. How blessed he had been in his choice of a wife.

It had been a challenge to convince his parents he should wed the daughter of his father's arch enemy, and he had whooped for joy when her father, Rhodri, had unexpectedly agreed to the marriage. Thanks be to God he had persevered, sure of his love for Carys.

He prayed Aidan and Nolana would discover the same ecstasy and joy he had enjoyed with Carys. Judging by their inability to keep their hands off each other, the carnal side of the marriage would proceed well.

The family often jested it was the curse of the Montbryce men to be in love with their wives, unlike most noblemen of their acquaintance. Perhaps the curse would carry over to the FitzRams!

He leaned over to Gallien, kneeling beside him. "If only my brother Caedmon were here to see this. He would be proud of his children."

Gallien smiled. "Mayhap he is here. *Tante* Agneta too. Don't you feel them?"

Baudoin looked towards the altar where Aidan and Nolana knelt, swearing their vows. Suddenly, a sparrow flew down from a beam and circled the interior of the church, causing many to look up as it flew overhead. It returned to the beam, where another sparrow roosted.

Aidan glanced up at the beam then turned to look at his uncle over his shoulder. Baudoin well knew the dream Caedmon had recorded in his codex, having accompanied his half brother back from the Crusade. He smiled at Aidan and nodded, then turned to his eldest son. "You may be right, Gallien. You may be right."

The rites proceeded. Aidan and Nolana were pronounced man and wife. He was about to claim his husband's kiss, when the door banged open and a gust of wind swept a whirl of dust into the church. Necks craned as all eyes turned to see who had caused such a disturbance.

A tall, bearded man stood in the doorway, his legs braced. His garb bespoke a lowland Scot. A collective gasp echoed off the stone walls. The sparrows abandoned their nest. Nolana fainted in Aidan's arms. Baudoin leapt to his feet, cursing that his sword, along with that of every man present, lay at Kirkthwaite Hall. He stood nose to nose with the newcomer. "Who are you? What is the meaning of this intrusion?"

The young man glowered. "I'm Ingram Maknab, son of Neyll."

# CHAPTER TWENTY-THREE

Aidan lifted Nolana as his kinsmen rushed to the door of the church to confront the uninvited guest. They were unarmed, but would fight with any means at their disposal to protect their own.

Ragna tore off her wimple and fanned Nolana. His wife stirred in his arms and opened her eyes. She seemed disoriented for a moment but then gasped, "Ingram!"

He tightened his grip on her. "All is well. He's being dealt with."

She wriggled out of his arms. "They mustn't hurt him, Aidan. He's not his father. He's a good man."

He looked to the door of the church. Ingram held his hands out before him, no weapon in evidence. "Nolana," he called out to her, "tell them I come in peace."

She swept down the aisle, elbowed her way through the defenders, and embraced the Scot. Aidan's gut clenched with jealousy. Who was this man? He strode to her side, pulled her away from the lowlander. "You're holding my bride, intruding on my wedding."

The Scot bowed. "I am not here to intrude. I'm happy to see Nolana wed. I come to claim my father's body. It's only right he be interred at Kolbrand's Path. I am laird now. It's time we put an end to the bad blood that has existed here for nigh on thirty years. My father allowed old hatreds and greed to rule him. He was a hard man to live with—Nolana can attest to that. I often bore the brunt of his anger, until he banished me."

Nolana nodded in Aidan's embrace. "He's my half brother."

Ingram continued. "I came to pledge friendship. Bloodshed and revenge benefit no one. Let what was in the past remain in the past."

Aidan stared at him. Was he sincere? Nolana's happy smile reassured him this man was to be trusted. He reached out his hand to the Scot. "Enter, Ingram Maknab. I was about to kiss my bride."

He bent to kiss her, intending it to be gentle, but the highs and lows of the past hour and the exhilaration of the moment got the better of him and he kissed her fiercely, delving his tongue into her mouth. Everyone whooped their approval as Nolana's face reddened and she clung to Aidan, returning his kiss.

It was as well Edwin had insisted Aidan wear a long doublet for the ceremony.

~~~

Aidan closed and barred the door of his chamber after firmly ushering out the last of the well-wishers. He had made it quite clear he would take care of preparing his wife for bed without their aid. He turned to look at his bride. "If you'd licked the chicken juices off your fingers one more time I'd have taken you right there on the table."

Nolana giggled, dipped her finger in her tumbler of mead and stuck it in her mouth, sending more arrows of desire to Aidan's core. "Surely not in front of everyone, husband."

Aidan took hold of her wrists. "Beware, Nolana, you can only tease a man so far."

She blushed and cast down her eyes. "I'm sorry, Aidan, I didn't mean to tease you."

He was contrite. He hadn't meant to make her feel a wanton, something Nolana definitely was not. His intention was to make this night memorable and he had started off on the wrong foot. He drained his own mead, then licked her fingers. "Sticky!"

She smiled shyly.

He drew her into his arms. "May I help you undress, my lady?"

She looked at him nervously and nodded. Her hands fidgeted with the belt of her surcoat. He gently brushed them away. "Let me."

He undid the decorative knot Ragna had fashioned in the twisted gold thread and brushed his lips against her belly as the belt fell to the wolfskin rug. She was breathing more rapidly as she put her hands on his head. He smiled. "We won't do anything you don't wish to do this night. Can I remove your shoes?"

He licked his lips. What would she think if she could read his thoughts as he imagined his tongue delving into her moist folds?

She nodded mutely. He drew her over to sit on the bed. He knelt and removed one shoe, then massaged the sole of her foot, digging his thumbs into her flesh. She leaned back on her elbows while he repeated the painstaking process with the other foot.

"Aidan," she breathed.

Her pose accentuated the thrust of her lovely breasts. He might have to make greater haste. He ran his fingers lightly over the soles of her feet. She giggled. "I'm ticklish."

By now he was a hungry wolf. When had his appetite become overwhelming? He had never wanted a woman so badly.

Slowly he lifted her skirts until they were over her knees. He untied the bows securing her stockings and removed them, kissing each toe in turn. He ran his fingertips over her calves. Her skin was smooth as silk. "I hope my hands aren't too rough," he whispered.

"Perfect," came the murmured reply. She was lying flat on her back now, legs parted slightly.

He leaned forward and smoothed his hands the length of her thighs, pushing the fabric far enough that he caught a glimpse of his goal. She must not feel invaded. He licked each thigh, starting at her knee and going as far as he dare. She entangled her fingers in her hair. Her hips rose off the bed as she stretched languidly.

"Aidan," she purred.

His need was pressing. "Sit up and I'll take off your surcoat and *léine*. I want to see your body."

She obeyed as he lifted the garments over her head and outstretched arms. The glint of passion he saw in her eyes sent more blood rushing to his groin. She crossed her arms over her breasts. "I've never been completely naked in front of a man."

How could that be? She and the Baron had spent *two* nights together. He had expired on the second night. What had happened the first night? He had to know, had to be sure.

She reluctantly told him how she had duped the drunken sot, shyly showing him where she had smeared the blood on her thigh. He bade her lay back, knelt between her legs and kissed her there, his eyes on her pink jewel and the golden curls of her mons. He eased her legs apart, turning onto his side, his weight on his forearm. He gently placed his thumbs on her most intimate place and opened her nether lips. "He never touched you here?"

She shook her head vigorously. Aidan fought to control the urge to leap up on the bed and beat his chest. "Do you like it?"

The shake turned to a nod. "It sends strange feelings through my body."

*Godemite!*

He carefully slid one finger inside her, hooking it slightly as his father had indicated, feeling the inner flesh respond to his touch. God! She was warm and wet. She whimpered and lifted her head to look at him.

"Don't be afraid. I love you."

"As I love you. I was born to love you, Aidan."

He had longed to hear her say the words and relief washed over him. Caution be damned. He needed to taste her. He put his lips to her womanhood and licked her juices, swirling his tongue over her swelling nub.

"Aidan." There was a hint of uncertainty in her voice and in her eyes.

"I want to taste your honey. You are so sweet."

As she watched him, mewling sounds emerged from her throat. He delved his tongue into her and she called out, crushing the bed linens in her hands, her hips lifting from the bed. He grasped her hips and held on, sucking and licking until she screamed her fulfillment.

He had yet to touch her breasts and she had released. Life with Nolana held promise.

He rested his head on her mons while her wits slowly returned and her breathing slowed. "Was that my little death?" she whispered.

He chuckled. "The first of many."

She sat up. "You've seen me. Now I want to see you. Again."

His elation turned to puzzlement. "Again?"

She blushed and smiled. "I've seen you naked before."

He searched his memory. "Where? When?"

"I'll never tell."

She screeched when he lunged for her. "You should never have told me you're ticklish."

She gasped for breath and laughed as he tickled her belly. "Pax! Pax! In the Infirmary," she finally admitted. "I hid and watched the monks disrobe you. I was there when they brought you in from the hives."

Panting, he stared at his naked wife's beautiful breasts. He wagged his finger at her. "Wanton woman! And did you like what you saw?"

Her face reddened more and she bit her lip. "It was the finest male body I'd ever seen."

He preened, then it came to him what she had said. There was a gleam in her eye. "But you'd never seen—"

She giggled. He sat on the edge of the bed, tore off his leggings, hose and braies and came to his feet beside the bed. She stopped giggling and gasped when she laid eyes on his manhood, rigid against his belly. "Aha! As I thought, wench. You didn't see me to my best advantage then!"

~~~

Nolana wanted to laugh with him at his jest, but her throat had gone strangely dry. The Baron and Aidan were indeed very different. But how might such a thing fit inside a woman, inside her?

He must have sensed her fear. He put her hand on his shaft. "Don't be afraid. I know I am big, but we've already eased the way and I'll go slowly. Move your hand on me, like you did before."

She obeyed, hoping she was doing it correctly. He sucked in a sharp breath. His shaft looked powerful, yet delicate and sensitive. The silkiness of his skin awed her. She had an urge to run her tongue from root to tip. What would he think of that?

"I'd love it if you did," he murmured. She hadn't spoken out loud. Her wanton open-mouthed gaping and the way she had licked her lips must have betrayed her desire. She bent to swirl her tongue over the swollen end of his shaft, then sucked him into her mouth. He groaned, raked his hands through her hair and rocked his hips slowly. "I can't hold on much longer, Nolana. But this is sweet torture. I am at your mercy."

The power she held as a woman struck Nolana for the first time. Giving herself to this man did not mean she had lost control. She had gained more. Power could be a destructive thing. Maknab was a testament to that truth, but she and Aidan would never use the sway they held over each other to destroy. He might dominate her as the male, but he would do it to bring her pleasure, not pain.

Aidan withdrew his shaft from her mouth, cupped her face and kissed her lips, then her nipples. He suckled each hardened tip in turn, grazing them lightly with his teeth. She moaned and arched her back, cradling his head to her breasts. He carefully slid a finger inside her. "You're still warm and wet. Are you ready for me?" His eyes betrayed his need. His shaft looked painfully engorged. But he had asked, not taken. "I'm ready, my love."

He settled her on her back and opened her legs wide. His hand guiding his shaft, he dipped into her opening and slid inside in one thrust, never taking his eyes from hers. She tried not to grimace at the stab of pain that arrowed into her core, but he kept thrusting and the discomfort eased. "The pain will pass, Nolana. I cannot stop now."

She gripped his shoulders, then his thighs. His body felt firm and vital. As the urgency of his thrusts increased, so did the warm tingling inside her, tantalizing, building, promising then fading, promising then fading, then mounting to an unbearable—suddenly she was tumbling into an abyss of soaring bliss, her cries mingling with Aidan's primal shout as his essence filled her.

He collapsed onto her, breathing heavily. Her fists clenched. Panic threatened when she feared she might suffocate beneath him, but then she calmed, relishing his warm weight on her. He stirred and came up on his elbows. "Sorry, too heavy."

She pulled him back, curling her arms around his shoulders, trailing kisses along his neck. "No, I can bear your weight."

# EPILOGUE

Ingram Maknab returned to Kolbrand's Path with Neyll's body. The Maknabs and FitzRams forged an alliance that brokered an end to many a bloody feud in the volatile borderlands between England and Scotland.

Gallien de Montbryce eventually inherited the title Third Earl of Ellesmere. Edwin took ownership of Shelfhoc Manor in the Welsh Marches and maintained a strong relationship with his cousins. The Montbryces and FitzRams worked to bring prosperity to the region.

Kirkthwaite Hall became famous throughout Northumbria for the quality of its mead and honey, which were rumoured to rival Lindisfarne. Aidan got used to being stung by bees, and taught his children to treat them with healthy respect. Aidan and Nolana FitzRam sired twelve children. Three sons and three daughters grew to adulthood. Nolana never returned to the Carnsith Fells.

Ragna? Who could predict what a Wild Viking Princess might do?

# MEDIEVAL MEAD RECIPE
## (from "Tractatus de magnete et operationibus eius")

Translation follows, but it's fun to try to decipher the language first!

ffor to make mede. Tak .i. galoun of fyne hony and to þat .4. galouns of water and hete þat water til it be as lengh þanne dissolue þe hony in þe water. thanne set hem ouer þe fier & let hem boyle and ever scomme it as longe as any filthe rysith þer on. and þanne tak it doun of þe fier and let it kole in oþer vesselle til it be as kold as melk whan it komith from þe koow. than tak drestis of þe fynest ale or elles berme and kast in to þe water & þe hony. and stere al wel to gedre but ferst loke er þu put þy berme in. that þe water with þe hony be put in a fayr stonde & þanne put in þy berme or elles þi drestis for þat is best & stere wel to gedre/ and ley straw or elles clothis a bowte þe vessel & a boue gif þe wedir be kolde and so let it stande .3. dayes & .3. nygthis gif þe wedir be kold And gif it be hoot wedir .i. day and .1. nyght is a nogh at þe fulle But ever after .i. hour or .2. at þe moste a say þer of and gif þu wilt have it swete tak it þe sonere from þe drestis & gif þu wilt have it scharpe let it stand þe lenger þer with. Thanne draw it from þe drestis as cler as þu may in to an oþer vessel clene & let it stonde .1. nyght or .2. & þanne draw it in to an oþer clene vessel & serve it forth.

For to make mead. Take 1 gallon of fine honey and to that 4 gallons of water and heat that water till it be as long. Then dissolve the honey in the water, then set them over the fire and let them boil and ever scum it as long as any filth rises thereon.

Then take it down off the fire and let it cool in another vessel till it be as cold as milk when it comes from the cow. Then take lees from the finest ale or else barm (yeast) and cast it into the water and honey and stir all well together, but first look before putting your yeast in that the water with the honey be put in a clean tub and then put in your yeast or else the lees for that is best and stir well together.

Lay straw or else cloths about the vessel and above if the weather is cold and so let it stand 3 days and 3 nights if the weather is cold. And if it is hot weather, 1 day and 1 night is enough at the full. But ever after 1 hour or 2 at the most assay thereof and if you will have it sweet take it the sooner from the lees and if you will have it sharp let it stand the longer therewith.

Then draw it from the lees as clear as you may into another vessel clean and let it stand 1 night or 2 and then draw it into another clean vessel and serve it forth.

# WILD VIKING PRINCESS

*"Maybe some women aren't meant to be tamed.*
*Maybe they just need to run free*
*till they find someone just as wild to run with them."*
~Sex and the City

Dedicated to Vikings and their descendants

## PROLOGUE

*Strand Island, Denmark,*
*February, 1124 AD*

Reider Torfinnsen swayed on unsteady legs, gaping in disbelief. He clutched a half-empty tankard, his innards twisted in knots. His father lay dead at his feet, Gorm's dagger in his back. Torfinn was dead before his body slumped to the wooden floor, but he had not uttered a sound. The simple gold circlet, symbol of his kingship, had slipped from his head to clatter against the boards.

Reider had imbibed too much ale, but this was supposed to be his betrothal feast—a man about to wed was expected to get drunk. Belatedly, he thought to save Margit from whatever further treachery his step-brother planned. He dropped the tankard, spilling its contents, and reached for his dagger. It was wrenched away and strong arms forced him to grovel before his father's body. A knee pressed heavily into his back.

A voice dripping sarcasm penetrated his pounding head. "Now a real man will rule here, and I will be his consort."

Reider looked up, narrowing his bleary eyes. Margit? He blinked, not believing the sight before him. Why was his betrothed's arm draped over Gorm's shoulder, her breasts rubbing against him? Gorm sneered triumphantly, tightening his grip around Margit's waist. They shared a brazen kiss, then the usurper bent to retrieve his dagger. He turned Torfinn's body over with his booted foot, picked up the crown and pouted when it proved to be too big.

Reider dared not look at his father's beloved face, now contorted in a grimace of shock. He swallowed the bitter truth that the assassins had planned carefully. He wasn't the only one well into his cups. His father's entire royal guard lay dead around him. The stench of blood filled Reider's nostrils. Armed thugs—he recognized them as his step-brother's cronies—had herded the loyal subjects of Strand against the wall of the Great Hall. Few had brought weapons to the festivities and those who were armed had been quickly disarmed. Women sobbed quietly in the protecting embrace of their husbands, men whose scowling faces betrayed their outrage and powerlessness.

Sobering quickly, Reider struggled to be free of Gorm's henchmen. Words stuck in his throat, so great was his heartbroken rage. "He was your father, Gorm. He loved you."

Gorm smirked, the crown of Strand perched askew atop his head, and spat out a chewed fingernail. "He was my step father. You are the son he loved. Now I will have what was to be yours. Get him out of my Hall."

They dragged Reider out into the frigid night and along the beach. The crunch of boots on pebbles sounded his death knell. He felt the cold bite of a dagger at his throat and swallowed hard, waiting for the end. He would not cry out. For his father's sake he would die well.

Suddenly there was a scuffle. He vaguely heard voices barking urgent commands. His captors slumped to the ground beside him with a grunt. Strong arms hooked his armpits, and he was half carried, half dragged, unable to make his legs work. The wet warmth trickling down his thighs was strangely comforting. He must still be alive if he had pissed himself. Hurled into a longboat, he hit his head on the decking and succumbed to oblivion.

~~~

He came to his senses at dawn, braced against the crosswale. A blanket covered him, but the wool smelled damp and the wind bit into his flesh like a whetted knife. He peered over the side. There was no sign of land.

His friend and comrade, Kjartan Eldarsen, stood at the tiller, his tight jaw and tense stance confirming that the grizzly events of the night before had been real. Reider put his hand to his neck. It had been bound with linen, but his body stank of urine and the sweat of fear. A thirst for revenge welled up in his throat. He quickly closed his eyes and leaned over the side to retch, pressing a hand to the binding.

Kjartan beckoned another shipmate to take the tiller, then strode over to Reider, bracing his legs to the movement of the boat. He put his hand on Reider's back. "Retching won't help your wound. Not like a master mariner to be seasick."

Reider wiped his mouth and looked up at his friend. Kjartan's gray eyes held a glimmer of amusement and Reider smiled ruefully. He opened his mouth to agree, but no sound came out. Kjartan frowned as Reider struggled to speak, his heart racing. His friend again put a reassuring hand on his shoulder. "Don't worry. They intended to cut your throat. Rest your voice. It will return."

Reider came to his feet on shaky legs, hugging the blanket around his shoulders against the biting wind. He touched his pounding head and winced when he discovered a goose egg over his eyebrow. As if the hangover wasn't enough! Grief and anger clouded his thoughts and made him dizzy. He clutched the side of the boat. Though he stood beside Kjartan, if he'd had a voice, he would have been obliged to shout over the wind and the snap of the full sail. His thoughts were in turmoil.

Gorm's treachery against a man who loved him like his own son cut deep, but Margit's actions were unfathomable. If she had married him, the rightful heir, she would have ruled anyway, in time. He had been content for his father's sake to agree to the arranged marriage with the chieftain's daughter from Heide. She had hidden her cunning nature well.

Kjartan shrugged one shoulder, his face sour. He divined his friend's thoughts. "I've often said women are not to be trusted."

Reider shook his head, embarrassed to admit to his confirmed bachelor friend that he had fancied Margit in love with him. All the while she had thirsted for Gorm!

He would swear off women and ply the trade routes with Kjartan. Never marrying would mean no heirs, but what did it matter now Gorm had stolen the peaceful island principality off the Danish coast?

*Nej!* He could not turn his back. He must avenge his father's death and regain his birthright.

Kjartan's voice broke into his thoughts. "We head for Husembro. We can hide in the cove. It will give us time to plan."

Reider felt guilty he had lain in a stupor while his friend and ally effected their escape. He mouthed a question. "Pursuit?"

Kjartan shook his head, a mischievous glint in his eye. "I made sure they couldn't follow."

Reider put his hand on his comrade's shoulder, and drew him into his embrace. He wanted Kjartan to know how grateful he was.

His friend only nodded, but a loud cheer erupted from the crew. Reider turned to look at the men who had helped save his life. He thrust his fist into the air, struggling to yell a battle cry. Blood rushed to his head. His feet felt like lead weights. His belly churned. He prayed he would not retch again.

The men exchanged confused glances, then Kjartan led the rallying call. "For Strand," he bellowed, raising his fist.

"For Strand," the men echoed.

"For Torfinn!"

"For Torfinn!"

"For Prince Reider!"

"For our prince!"

Reider could only bow his head in acknowledgement, overwhelmed by their loyalty. Would he prove to be worthy of their trust and confidence? The future loomed full of dark uncertainty. The daunting task of ridding Strand of a cruel usurper was his, and he was poorly prepared. Why had he not taken his responsibilities more seriously? He had thought his father would live forever.

He and Kjartan stood together for a long while in silence as the boat skimmed the waves. Reider swore under his breath never to trust a woman again. Were it not for Kjartan and his men, he too would be sailing a stone ship to Valhalla.

# CHAPTER ONE
*Kirkthwaite Hall, Northumbria, England,
March 1124 A.D.*

Ragna FitzRam stamped her foot, brandishing her sister's letter under her brother's nose. "I intend to go, Aidan, and you cannot stop me. Blythe thinks it's a wonderful idea and is anxious for my visit. We haven't seen each other since our parents' deaths."

Aidan tried vainly to interrupt Ragna's tirade as she carried on. "It is our duty to deliver to Blythe the ceremonial dagger our mother wanted her to inherit."

Aidan stopped pacing. It was a wonder he had not worn a groove in the floor of the gallery after years of fruitless arguments with his stubborn younger sister. He took a deep breath. "That's an excuse, Ragna."

Another stamp of the foot. "No!"

Aidan held up his hand, hoping to silence her, though it was unlikely. "It is out of the question for you to undertake such a journey without either myself or Edwin accompanying you."

Ragna snorted, her face red, blue eyes bulging. "But you will never go back to Saxony. You're too busy administering the FitzRam estates—and making babies with Nolana."

Aidan had always considered himself a patient man, but he pointed a warning finger. "You go too far, sister. Don't forget it was you who urged me to sire children when you were trying to convince me to leave the monastery."

Ragna ignored him, putting her hands on her hips. "Edwin is

busy with Shelfhoc Hall. He won't accompany me. I've equipped my own escort."

Perhaps he had misheard? "What! Mercenaries?"

Ragna held up her hands, palms facing him, as if to ward off any further objections. "Everything is arranged. I don't want to take protection away from Kirkthwaite. We will sail from Newcastle to Hamburg, and Dieter has arranged a Saxon escort from Hamburg to Wolfenberg."

Evidently their brother-by-marriage was part of this scheme. Aidan took a step towards his sister, tempted to throttle her. "What?"

For the first time, some of the defiance left Ragna's face. "I will not cross the Narrow Sea."

Aidan held his tongue. Sailing from the south coast of England to Normandie would be too painful—it would open the still raw wound of their parents' drowning four years before in the White Ship disaster. It was a painful truth. Distance had denied the sisters a chance to grieve together. He took a deep breath and put his arm around her shoulder. She remained stiff, refusing to yield. "Ragna—"

She pulled away. "Aidan, you think of me as a little girl, but I am a woman of three and twenty. I never intend to marry and I want to live my life my way. You and Nolana have little Ingram and Symon, and no doubt more children to come. I want to go to Blythe, give her the dagger. It's what Mother would have wanted."

Aidan could not recall ever winning an argument with her, and wasn't likely to win this one. "I'll consider it—if I'm assured you have a well armed escort."

Ragna flew into his arms. "Thank you, Aidan. Don't worry, I'll return safely in a few months and resume my life as doting spinster aunt to your handsome children. And I'll take Thor with me."

Aidan might have known she would want to take the hound. Thor had been her constant companion since their uncle, Baudoin de Montbryce, had given her the *alaunt gentil* puppy three years ago. As he stroked her back, he had to admit that life at Kirkthwaite Hall did not offer Ragna much excitement. He was usually immersed in the day to day workings of their fledgling mead-making endeavour, and their two infant sons took up most of Nolana's time.

Did he want his sister to stay at Kirkthwaite for his own soul?

To keep her safe? To protect the FitzRam family from the possibility of another devastating loss? He had to allow her to go, but what a waste it would be if his beautiful, spirited hellion of a sister never married. He chuckled inwardly. It would take a patient man to tame their *Wild Viking Princess*. Ragna chafed at the nickname, but it had stuck since childhood and suited her well. No one in the family looked or acted more like a descendant of Danes than Ragna, and none of her siblings had Ragna's fair hair. Their Danish grandmother had died before any of them were born, but Aidan suspected Ragna looked exactly like the woman for whom she had been named.

## CHAPTER TWO

Aidan accompanied Ragna to the Newcastle docks with an escort from Kirkthwaite Hall. He intended to interrogate the leader of the mercenaries she had hired, hoping to find a flaw in their credentials. He squared his shoulders and approached the young warrior. "Who recommended you to my sister?"

The man replied without hesitation. "The Earl of Ellesmere."

Aidan looked at him in disbelief, feeling his face redden. "My uncle Baudoin?"

"*Oui*, milord."

Aidan stole a glance at his sister, who had a look of innocent satisfaction on her face. The vixen had laid a trap for him! Why had he not had the foresight to ask how she had known of the mercenaries before they left home? He had forgotten how manipulative she could be.

He tried to find fault with the ship and its captain, but both garnered excellent references from anyone he consulted.

Reluctantly, he agreed to allow Ragna's trunks to be loaded on to the cog. "Are you absolutely sure you want to make this journey?" he asked her. "I have a bad feeling."

"You know I have to, Aidan. Don't worry. Thor will protect me. You're simply feeling protective of me. I will be back before you know I am gone. And Captain Philion's men will see me safely to Hamburg. I will give Blythe your love."

She waved an imperious hand towards the vessel. "What can happen aboard such a fine ship?"

He did not want to mention that the ship that had sunk four year before, taking their parents' lives, had been a cog. In that instance, the captain's drunkenness had been the main cause of the catastrophe. No reason to think the *Nordique* would meet the same fate as *La Blanche Nef.*

He pointed to their mother's dagger tucked into a scabbard on her hip. "Wouldn't it be safer to pack that in one of your trunks?"

She patted the weapon. "No, I want to keep it with me. It will be my lucky talisman."

He escorted her on board and inspected the tented area that had been set up for the passenger. He checked the food supplies with the ship's victualler. He inspected once again the weaponry and credentials of every one of the ten mercenaries. He went over every detail of the voyage with Philion, though he understood nothing of charts and tides.

Ragna became impatient. "Aidan, I am embarking on this voyage, no matter how much you try to delay it. I am the only passenger. Are you not yet reassured I will be safe?"

Aidan could not shake his foreboding, though he had to agree his sister seemed to have thought of everything. She had even garbed herself as a young man for greater safety.

He put his hands on her shoulders. "I will never forgive myself if something happens to you."

She covered his hands with hers. "Nothing will happen, Aidan. It's only a three day voyage. You are being too cautious."

Aidan shrugged. "One of us in the family has to be. It's a characteristic you have never been known for, sister. I see nothing will dissuade you. Kiss me goodbye. Send us a message once you arrive."

Ragna surprised him by hugging him tightly and kissing him on both cheeks. "Of course I will. Take good care of Nolana and your handsome sons while I am away. Keep those babies away from your bees."

Despite his concerns, Aidan laughed. "I will. Believe me, I remember only too well the pain of bee stings."

The moment of shared laughter made him feel better. Ragna would be perfectly safe. He wished her *Godspeed*, then disembarked.

He sat atop his horse, watching from the dock as the *Nordique* pulled away with its precious cargo. He raised his hand in a farewell salute, perturbed by the look of fearful apprehension on his sister's face.

~~~

The wind-whipped sand stung Reider's eyes as he struggled in the driving rain to replace the broken rope. They had been lucky. The majority of the moorings had held and they had not lost either longboat to the storm tide—yet.

The elements raged with a wild fury the like of which he had never seen before, though he had lived his life on the sea. His heart had raced more than once with the gut-wrenching terror that came with being at the mercy of a turbulent sea, and shuddered for anyone caught in this storm. Its sudden intensity had taken everyone by surprise.

His boats strained at their moorings, but he feared they would not remain undamaged, even in the shelter of their hidden cove. There was already wet sand in the hull of the one he had secured. Too much would sink it. The crew would start repairs at the first sign of a break in the weather. It was vital their boats always be ready.

A voice came on the wind. "Reider!"

He straightened his shoulders and peered into the darkness, icy rain pelting his face, his fingers numb. It was Kjartan. Perhaps his friend needed help with the other boat?

Satisfied the newly secured ropes would hold, he rammed his hands back into his sealskin mittens and set off across the sodden sand to assist his comrade.

Kjartan stood ready to greet him. "All secure here, let's walk back together. This wind is enough to sweep a man away. I'll hold on to you and you hold on to me!" He linked his arm playfully in Reider's.

They struggled up the beach to the lodge like two drunken fools. Kjartan grabbed the nape of Reider's neck and squeezed. "Good to see a smile on your face, my friend, instead of your usual scowl."

Reider shrugged him off and stopped smiling. As they made their way to the lodge, he became lost in thoughts of treachery and vengeance, grieving for his father. He and Kjartan were soaked to the skin and panting hard when they ducked under the shelter of the low overhang in front of the wooden structure. Kjartan pulled off his sealskin hood and shook the rain from it. "What a storm!"

Reider stooped to unlace his wet boots, but Kjartan grasped his arm. "What's that? Out there." He pointed out to sea. Reider squinted. The moon's glow had transformed the driving rain to an impenetrable screen of silver. He shook his head. Kjartan pointed again. "There. See. In the waves."

Reider still saw nothing, but Kjartan was known to have exceptional eyesight, so he peered again.

*Af Odin! It's a ship. Surely Gorm would not pursue us in this storm? He'd have to be mad.*

He indicated he had seen the ship.

Kjartan shoved his hood back on. "It's not a Danish ship."

The vessel was barely visible. How could Kjartan tell what kind of ship it was? The man had the eyes of an eagle.

Kjartan stepped away from the overhang and called to Reider over his shoulder. "Get the men. Whoever is out there won't survive this storm if we don't help them. They are trying to make it to the shelter of our cove."

Mindful of the unwritten law that men of the sea go without pause to the aid of those in peril on the waves, Reider strode into the lodge, grabbed the metal rod suspended from the tocsin by a strip of leather, and struck the triangular alarm repeatedly.

The men sprang to their feet, and within minutes had donned their foul weather gear. They followed Reider to the cove. Kjartan stood at the tiller. "Untie the moorings," he yelled. "We'll take this boat out. Someone get the sand out of the bottom, or none of us will survive. I need only one skeleton crew."

Not one man withdrew. Kjartan barked out the names of the men who would accompany him. They scrambled aboard, grabbing oars and manning their positions. Reider shoved the boat off and leapt aboard, almost missing his footing as the boat rocked wildly in the swell.

Soon they were rowing hard to reach the distressed boat, muscles bulging with the strain, faces tense. The spray quickly had them drenched. Reider braced his legs at the prow, clinging on for dear life, praying the stout rope around his waist would be enough to secure him. The boat pitched and rolled.

As they neared the other boat, Reider saw that Kjartan had been right. The stricken vessel was not Danish—Norman perhaps? Wherever they had come from, they were being tossed like a cork on the snarling sea. They had lost their sail and steering oar by the look of it. The efforts of the few remaining oarsmen were getting them nowhere. She was a large boat, larger than the one that had come to her rescue.

The Danes came as close as they dared, but near enough to see the grim desperation on exhausted faces turn to open mouthed surprise when they espied the Danish longboat. Huddled figures clung to the mast, but any shelter had long since been lost to the wind.

Widening his stance, Reider cupped his hands to his mouth to urge them to jump into the sea, but no sound emerged. Frustrated, he made a wide beckoning motion, but heads shook in disbelief.

*It's your only chance.*

Suddenly, a figure moved away from the others clinging to the mast, climbed unsteadily onto the side of the stricken ship and leapt into the water. A boy! He clutched something to his chest, but lost his grip on whatever it was when he hit the water.

Every head turned to watch the lad flail his arms, trying in vain to make headway towards the smaller boat. He seemed determined not to give up, though stark fear was etched on his face. It was evident he was not a swimmer and would likely drown, dragged under the waves by heavy furs.

Reider looked back at Kjartan struggling to hold the tiller with the help of another crewman. The plucky youth was the only one with the courage to jump. Reider would not let him drown. He took a deep breath, offered up a prayer to *Aegir*, and dove in.

The impact of the icy water took his breath away when he resurfaced. The swells towered over him. He kicked his legs, treading water. Timbers creaked and moaned as the boats battled wind and waves. Then came another sound borne on the wind—the yelping of a dog! He caught sight of it nearby, swimming in circles, barking frantically. Suddenly, the boy's head bobbed back to the surface next to the animal.

Reider sucked in another deep breath, swam to the boy and clamped his arm around his ribs, surprised to feel a flotation device strapped around his upper body. Reider had heard of sailors wearing inflatable animal skins when they went to sea. Much good it had done! The boy was unresponsive. Reider waved his free arm and his crew hauled him back with his prize. The hound paddled after them, disappearing beneath the waves several times.

After two harrowing attempts, Reider managed to hand the boy off to a shipmate. He heaved his own body back on board with difficulty, barely able to make his frozen limbs work. Leaning over the side precariously, he reached down and hooked his numbed fingers into the exhausted dog's studded collar. The creature was nearly done for. He put his other hand on the dog's rump and hauled it up to the boat with what little strength remained. He braced himself with the squirming dog against his chest, then tossed it, hoping someone would catch it. He collapsed to his knees and coughed till he choked. Lungs afire, he gulped air.

Several men from the stricken vessel were now in the water, swimming to the Danish boat, doubtlessly emboldened by the heroic rescue they had witnessed.

Suddenly, a swell lifted the battered cog, held it suspended, then turned it upside down. The Danes could do nothing to aid the men trapped beneath. The exhausted swimmers were dragged one by one into the Danish boat.

Reider caught sight of the doomed ship's name, barely visible and upside down. He squinted. *Nordique?*

Shivering, Reider signalled to Kjartan to take them back. They had saved as many as they could. His friend nodded grimly, his clenched jaw showing the strain of the battle against the elements.

# CHAPTER THREE

The exhausted Danes moored the boat in the hidden cove. Though the storm's rage had weakened, it had been an ordeal getting back safely. The shivering survivors cowered together in the stern.

The lad lay like a corpse, on his side, in a pool of water in the bottom of the boat. The shivering dog had curled up next to him. The animal growled when Reider leaned over to listen for signs of life.

*Ja*! The courageous urchin was still breathing, barely. Reider scooped him up and carried him off the boat and up to the lodge as fast as his frozen legs would allow. The black dog shook the water from his pelt, then raced to follow, barking furiously.

Reider had to get the lad out of his wet clothing. Suddenly the frail body shuddered and the youth retched sea water over Reider's parka. His head fell back with a groan and Reider was struck by his fine features. Too feminine—a pretty boy. Typical foreigner! Reider rolled his eyes—*udlændinge!*

He kicked open the door, bracing to keep his balance, and hastened to his pallet. They had built this lodge after their frantic flight from Gorm. It was a simple structure, oak wall posts held together with tie beams, but Reider's and Kjartan's status afforded them a privacy curtain for their sleeping alcove. It was a bare-bones existence, but it was warm and provided shelter from the elements, except when the thatched roof leaked!

Reider dropped to his knees and deposited the boy on the dirt floor. No use getting the straw mattress wet. He intended to remove the youth's clothing then put him to bed, get him warm. The shivering dog took up a position at the end of the pallet, barking without surcease, though it looked close to dropping from exhaustion. Reider held up a hand, hoping the animal understood he was trying to help his master. The dog calmed and slumped to the floor, its head on its front paws, whimpering. Reider breathed a sigh of relief.

He stripped off his own wet clothes and tugged on a dry pair of braies from his sea chest. He rubbed his hands together, blowing on his frozen fingers. When some of the feeling had returned, he set about untangling the knotted ties of the boy's hood. Frustrated, he finally yanked it off, surprised to see a tight skullcap beneath, evidently another peculiar foreign habit. He pulled. Long hair tumbled out, twisted in sodden rattails. Reider gasped. A strange fashion for a boy to have such a long mane! Reider's shoulder length hair was much the same blonde colour, but this lad's—it must go to his waist!

One of the boy's boots had been lost. Reider pulled off the other and rubbed the small, white feet hard. A strange discomfort crept into his belly. The feet were—appealing? He had swallowed too much seawater, a truth borne out by the raw fire in his chest.

He pulled at the bindings of the long furs. They were thick and heavy. It was a miracle they hadn't dragged the wretch to the bottom of the sea. Whoever this was, his family was not poor. The idea of ransom flitted into Reider's head.

He pulled the boy's body against his chest with one arm, intending to ease the furs off his shoulders with the other. His breath caught in his throat. Alarm surged through him. What the—? He remembered the softness above the boy's ribs. To his consternation, a tingling stirred his *pik*.

Only the saturated tunic and leggings remained, but the truth of the *lad's* gender as *his* chest heaved could no longer be denied. Reider licked his lips, certain that when he removed the tunic he would see a magnificent pair of female breasts.

With trembling hands he undid the belt. The dog growled, raising its head. Reider rubbed its wet ears and noticed a scabbard on the *boy's* hip. He unfastened it and eased out a small dagger. It was old and beautifully crafted, a Viking carved intricately into its handle.

Beyond his alcove he heard sounds of the other men being fed and warmed and given dry clothing. Soon Kjartan and the others would come to see how the *boy* fared. He must get rid of the wet clothing.

He grasped the hem of the tunic, took a deep breath, squeezed his eyes tight shut and peeled it over the *boy's* head. The dog came to its feet, barking loudly. Reider squinted one eye open, then blinked rapidly. His heretofore mildly interested *pik* stood to attention. He stared incredulously, filled with an urge to swirl his tongue over the pert pink nipples bared to his view. Margit's breasts were ample, but these, these were—perfect.

He combed his hand through his hair, suddenly aware it was still wet. Cold chilled his bones, though his body was suddenly a raging inferno. Quickly he raised the girl's hips and eased off the leggings. He could not look away from the golden curls at the top of her long legs. His gaze raked over her naked body, her beauty making him ache.

He grabbed a drying cloth, hesitated a moment, gripping the material tightly, then draped it over her. Carefully, he rubbed her shoulders, then her long arms, then her flat belly. He took a deep breath before patting her breasts dry, easing them up to dab the delicate skin beneath. He fisted the cloth then rubbed her thighs, knees and shins. When he tossed the wet linen into the corner, the dog ran over to sniff it, but then returned quickly to his mistress's side.

Reider gazed at the girl. He clenched and unclenched his fists, itching to touch her. His mouth was bone dry, every muscle in his body tight. He shook out his hands, put them to his face to make sure they had warmed, then spread his fingers and touched her thighs. He pressed the tips lightly into her flesh, relieved to feel warmth returning to her limbs. If he pressed a little harder with his thumbs, he could ease her legs apart and perhaps catch a glimpse of—

She tossed her head and moaned, hugging her arms to her breasts as she turned onto her side. He withdrew, feeling like a naughty child caught misbehaving. He lost his balance and groaned at the sight of her perfect round bottom. The dog whimpered.

Gritting his teeth, Reider lifted the girl onto his bed, fanning her wet hair to hang off the pallet. He piled blankets and furs on top of her. The dog stopped whimpering and crawled to curl up at his mistress's feet. Reider retrieved the drying cloth and rubbed it over the animal. It turned liquid eyes to him. "*God hund,*" he mouthed, hoping the animal would understand.

Panting hard, Reider stood and looked down at his guest. Who was this foolhardy woman who jumped into raging seas holding a dog, and carried a Danish dagger?

After wiping the weapon dry, he put it back in its scabbard. He grabbed dry clothing, all the wet raiment, and the scabbard, then left for the sanctuary of Kjartan's alcove, relieved his burdens at least hid his raging arousal. The dog watched him leave.

## CHAPTER FOUR

Kjartan sat on his pallet, lazily rubbing his wet hair with a linen cloth. He watched Reider dump the sodden clothing on the dirt floor with ill disguised irritation. "Why are you filling my space with your wet things?"

He glanced at Reider's groin. "What's got you all excited? Aren't you exhausted like the rest of us?"

Reider tightened his smile, wiped off his chest and pulled a dry tunic over his head, knotting the belt tight. He snorted and pointed in the direction of his alcove with his thumb, shaking his head.

The sneer left Kjartan's face. "What?"

Reider cupped his hands and put them to his chest, lifting imaginary breasts.

*The lad's a girl.*

Kjartan laughed incredulously, then grimaced as his fingers snagged through his tangled hair. "Are you sure?"

Reider bristled, and indicated the size of the breasts he had uncovered.

*I may not know much about women, but I do know what breasts are.*

Kjartan drew his knees up and wrapped his arms around his bent legs. "What amazing news! The way she jumped fearlessly, with a dog in her arms. A woman, you say?"

Reider slumped down beside his friend and pulled on his leggings, forcing his still hard erection into the confines of the soft sealskin. He held up his hands in bewilderment.

*What am I to do with her?*

Kjartan burst out laughing. "Only you would ask that question, my friend. Take her to bed. Judging by your *upset*, I assume she is comely?"

Reider jumped to his feet, shaking his head vigorously, spattering Kjartan with droplets of water.

Kjartan grabbed his arm. "Hey! Hold on, I didn't mention marriage. Make her your *thrall*. Then you can bed her at your whim and not worry. She'll be your slave."

Reider raked his hand through his wet hair, then wiped it on his tunic. He retrieved the scabbard, intending to shove it in the waistband of his leggings. Instead he drew the dagger and handed it to Kjartan. His friend turned the weapon over several times, examining the handle carefully. "It's the girl's?"

Reider nodded.

Kjartan traced his finger over the Viking. "This is definitely Danish, a woman's dagger, and if I'm not mistaken it was carved somewhere along this coast. It's old. I've seen something similar before, but where? How did she come by it?"

Reider took back the dagger and shrugged, making a sign that the woman was still asleep.

Kjartan came to his feet. "You've left her alone?"

Reider reassured his friend by pointing to her wet clothing, which he picked up, along with his own, intending to spread them on the drying lines strung around the central hearth. He regretted sharing the information. Kjartan's guffaws followed him as he completed his task. He hurried to his own alcove, arousing the curiosity of the men.

~~~

Torgrim Jakobsen hovered outside Reider's alcove. "Sounds like the lad's feverish, my lord. Cryin' out like a girl."

Reider hunched his shoulders and gripped the curtain, but did not open it, unwilling to share his discovery. He nodded his thanks to Torgrim and sent him on his way.

He waited until the seaman shuffled off before opening the curtain a crack and sidling in. Relief and agitation washed over him when he looked at his *guest*. Thanks be to *Freyja* that Torgrim had not seen her. She had thrown off the blankets and furs and writhed on his bed, completely exposed. The hound watched his mistress, but did not make a sound. He turned mournful eyes to Reider.

The arousal Reider had successfully calmed roared anew, but the girl's pallor disturbed him. He knelt and touched the back of his fingers to her cheek. She was too hot, though she shivered alarmingly.

She shoved the blankets off again and again, tossing her head back and forth. He stayed in a kneeling position beside the pallet at first, but then had to lie alongside her, his arm keeping the covers in place. The salty smell of the sea clung to her damp hair.

The storm raged on outside, the wind whistling through the wattle and daub walls. Loose timbers banged. Water dripped from gaps in the thatch. His eyes became heavy, and he dozed fitfully, exhausted by the rescue and his concern for her.

*Concern? Why should I care? She's only a woman, a foreigner to boot.*

The dog fell asleep, sprawled at the foot of the pallet.

~~~

"I'm—cold."

It was a mere whisper, but it woke Reider. The dog's ears pricked up. It yawned and came slowly to its feet, looking first at its mistress, then at Reider.

*English.* She had spoken in English. He and Kjartan had traded with the English. He knew something of their language.

How to warm her? He was chilled without blankets or furs, the memory of the icy water washing over him. He made a decision, stripped off his tunic and crawled under the furs. Apart from the dog, his body provided the only warmth. He drew her back against his chest, careful to put his hand on his own thigh. He had never taken a woman against her will and would not take advantage of one in the throes of a fever. Nor did he wish to rile the dog, who seemed to sense Reider meant the girl no harm.

He willed his arousal to abate, longing to cup her breasts and thrust inside this beautiful woman whose bottom rested on his shaft. Good thing he had not removed his leggings. The touch of her bare skin on his *pik* might have undone his resolve completely.

Exhaustion released him from his torment.

## CHAPTER FIVE

*F*ather, mother, pray for me!
Your little girl is coming to you...
Narrow Sea...
A Viking...at the prow of a boat...
Beckoning... jump into the sea...
Jump...
A Viking...
He will deliver me and Thor...
Farewell, brothers... sister...
Don't weep for me...
I am safe in the arms of my Viking.

Reider understood little of the foreign ramblings of the girl as the fever tormented her sleep in the night. He thought she called to her parents, and recognized *Viking* and *Thor*, but the rest was incomprehensible.

At dawn he smoothed her hair off her face. She was still warm, but the fever seemed to have abated and she slept peacefully. She was beautiful despite her ordeal—high cheekbones, proud nose, fine features—like a princess. He didn't know her name, so he would call her *prinsessen*. Why not? He had been a prince, before Gorm's treachery had stolen his birthright.

He heard the sounds of the crew preparing to break their fast. Normally he would be up before them. Men respected a leader who did not stay too long abed, something he remembered his father had often told him.

He was reluctant to leave the girl, though he could not say why that was. He lay on his side watching her, his arm crooked to support his head. She was a mystery, a woman who had the look of a Dane, but spoke English, who dressed like a male, but was very much a female. Why was she in the North Sea in the worst storm in living memory, with a loyal dog!

Perhaps Kjartan was right. He should make her his thrall and she would live with him as his slave. *Freyja* knew he wanted her body! But this woman was no slave and he doubted she would accept such a life willingly. He had no wish to live with a woman who hated him, having narrowly escaped that fate with Margit. He did not want to be the object of this woman's hatred.

The quality of her clothing and the dog's collar indicated she was from a wealthy family. Ransom was probably a better option, but then he would have to give her up. He rolled onto his back with an exasperated sigh, pressing his palms against his temples. She stirred beside him and he sat up quickly. He should put his tunic back on. She might be alarmed if—

~~~

The ear-shattering shriek that pierced the air when her long lashes fluttered open brought men rushing to his aid. The dog leapt up and barked furiously, baring its teeth. Reider stumbled off the pallet and slid through the curtain, careful not to reveal her. He reassured his crew over the noise of her cries and the barking. Kjartan was calmly helping himself to smoked *laks* and bread, a smirk on his face.

Hastily, Reider re-entered his alcove. His *prinsessen* stood in the far corner of the cubicle, back rigid, a fur clutched to her nakedness. Anger, not fear, twisted her lovely face. She would claw his eyes out if given the chance. The dog stood defiantly in defense, growling. Reider held out his hands, palms facing her, in what he hoped was a calming gesture.

She touched her hand to the dog's head. "Be quiet, Thor."

Why did she call on Thor, God of Thunder? At least her sultry voice had calmed the dog.

She snarled at him. "Where is my dagger?"

He shook his head and stepped away.

She scowled at him, evidently angry he did not understand. She clenched her fist and made a thrusting movement. "Where is my dagger?"

He pointed to the dagger at his waist.

Her eyes blazed as she held out her hand. "Give me my dagger."

He shook his head, thinking he had never seen eyes the colour of a summer sky before.

She stamped her foot, took a deep breath and pointed to the fur clutched to her breast. "Where are my clothes?"

This he understood. He arched his brows and raised a finger, hoping she comprehended he wanted her to wait. He left the alcove to retrieve her tunic and leggings drying by the hearth, with his own clothes. He grabbed his tunic and shoved it over his head.

A glimmer of relief showed in her eyes when he returned. She pointed to the pallet. "Put it there."

He tossed it down and stepped back.

"My furs?" she demanded.

This word he understood from his trading days. He pointed beyond the alcove.

She glared at him, then waved a dismissive hand. "Go! I cannot dress in front of you."

He went to stand outside the curtain, arms folded, wondering why he allowed this woman to give him orders as if he were a thrall.

Thirty curious faces glanced in his direction.

"You have to tell them," Kjartan said loudly.

His friend was right. He nodded his permission.

Kjartan informed the men. "The lad we saved is a woman."

The chewing stopped while they considered this new information. Judging by the loud laughter that followed, Reider's plight was of great amusement.

*No doubt they think I bedded her. Perhaps she thinks the same.*

He hurried over to the trestle table, tore off a chunk of bread and loaded it with salmon. Maybe food would improve matters. His *prinsessen* must be hungry. He noticed the handful of other shipwreck survivors huddled together, blankets around their shoulders, fear and uncertainty written on their faces.

Several of his crew elbowed each other knowingly, watching him hasten back to his alcove with his peace offering.

## CHAPTER SIX

Having donned her rumpled tunic and leggings with some difficulty, Ragna threw a blanket around her shoulders and sat cross legged on the pallet. She pressed her arms into her ribs to stop the trembling that shook her, and put her hands on Thor's head. The dog whined, nuzzling into her.

The last thing she remembered was her leap into the sea. It seemed like a nightmare. She did not know why she had jumped, other than that the longboat was obviously the only hope for the people aboard the doomed vessel.

She vaguely remembered the tall Viking at the prow, beckoning. Was he the man in whose bed she had awakened? Had they slept together? Had he—? She didn't feel violated or sore and there seemed to be no blood in evidence. But the sight of his broad naked chest when she woke had sent tremors spiralling through her. She had seen male torsos while treating the wounded during Maknab's siege of her home years ago, but this man was—massive.

She must control her fear. He must not think her weak. He did not have the look of a cruel man. His eyes were gentle, a soft brown.

*Godemite!* He must have undressed her, seen her naked! No wonder he looked at her that way. She would have to be on her guard. If only she had her dagger. It was imperative she retrieve it. The weapon held too much significance for her family for it to be lost to a Viking barbarian. It had once saved her mother's life. It was her duty to deliver the heirloom to Blythe, the eldest daughter.

She heard a polite cough and assumed it was her Viking. At

least he had manners enough to warn of his presence. "Enter," she said, as confidently as she could, hoping he would not detect the tremor in her voice.

He came into the alcove, grinning broadly, his big hands full of bread. Her belly turned over, but she put the upset down to a lack of food. The corners of her mouth edged up.

He held out bread, then looked at the pallet, pointing to himself with his thumb, his brows arched. She edged back to the wall, pulling Thor closer. The Dane sat down cross legged facing her. For a big man he moved gracefully. But why did he not speak? She noticed a pink scar across his throat.

He again offered bread with what looked like fish spread on top. She accepted. Their fingertips touched for an instant and a spark passed between them, causing her to glance up at him sharply.

He laughed and his face reddened. He had noticed it too, but seemed more surprised by the sound of his own laughter! It sent a flush flooding across her chest.

He bit into his own portion and chewed heartily, gesturing for her to do the same.

She broke off part of the bread and fed it to Thor. The dog carried it to the corner, then gobbled it down. Ragna nibbled the food. It was delicious. Smoked fish of some sort. How curious to eat fish to break one's fast.

"Good," she murmured, taking another bite.

Thor came back for more. The man held out bread. Thor sniffed it warily, then took it from his hand. The Viking smiled broadly.

What was the strange sensation his smile caused in her belly?

~~~

As the woman ate, her hair kept falling over her face and she became impatient, pushing it back. Reider pointed to the braided leather headband he wore around his forehead, then to the chest where he kept a spare one, then at her. Warily, she watched him come to his feet. He leaned over to retrieve the headband, then moved to put it around her head. She shrank back and put up her hands in defense, dropping her food.

He backed away, disappointed she had not allowed him to touch her beautiful hair. She was not as brave as she wanted him to believe, but he admired her courage. She was in essence a captive and captives were of necessity enslaved. That would be the fate of the other survivors, especially here where they had no thralls to serve them. Why not command her to do his bidding, to be his slave? She would have died but for him. She should be grateful.

Instead he held out the headband. She pointed again to the pallet and he placed it there, between them. Never taking her blue eyes off him, she leaned forward to retrieve it, smoothed back her hair and fastened it around her forehead. "Thank you," she murmured.

An uncomfortable silence followed. She probably wondered why he did not speak. Eyeing the dagger, she pointed. "My dagger?"

Once more he shook his head, pointing to himself.

That made her angry. She fisted her hand and thumped her chest, her fascinating eyes unexpectedly welling tears. "No, dagger mine! My family's."

The hound growled menacingly.

Evidently this weapon was of great importance to her family. She must know he could not return a blade she might use against him. She pushed away the remaining food and turned away from him, burying her nose in the dog's coat.

His *prinsessen* had dismissed him!

## CHAPTER SEVEN

Sooner or later Reider would have to allow the woman out of the alcove. What would he do when he went out fishing or working on the boats, or in the forge—tie her up?

The crew would wonder why he hid her away. He wondered too. For some reason he was reluctant to share this maiden. His *pik* hardened, for he suspected this intriguing woman was a virgin.

He brought Kjartan into the alcove with him, clearing his throat as he entered. She turned cold eyes to look at him, like a queen would look at a commoner. He coughed again, glad of the long tunic he wore, and indicated his friend.

She frowned when Kjartan held out his hand. "My name is Kjartan Eldarsen."

Visible relief swept over her face as she grasped his hand. "Charrtan? You speak English!"

He chuckled, a glint in his eye. "Not well, but a few words. May I introduce my friend, Reider Torfinnsen. Reider apologizes that he has lost his voice—a wound." He drew his finger across his throat. "Also, we thought you were a boy."

Confusion showed on her face when Reider took her hand and kissed it, astonishing himself. "Rider Torvinson," she whispered.

Kjartan shifted his weight. "We do not know your name, my lady."

She looked into Reider's eyes, her gaze sending blood rushing to his already aching loins. "My name is Ragna."

She bent down to pat the dog. "And this is Thor."

*Thor?*

His mouth fell open. She bore a Danish name! His name on her sensuous lips sounded heroic, noble. He wanted her throaty voice to repeat his name over and over. It reminded him that he was still a prince, despite Gorm's treachery. He had allowed his stepbrother's betrayal to intimidate him. Some of his hopelessness left him.

"Ragna," he whispered hoarsely, a lump in his dry throat making his voice sound like someone else's.

Kjartan let out a whoop of elation. "*Ja!* my friend. I told you your voice would return."

Ragna looked nervously from one to the other, but hesitantly smiled her approval of his pronunciation. "Yes, Ragna FitzRam."

Reider recognized her name as a Norman patronymic. The doomed boat was probably Norman. He stared at her, afraid that if he spoke again a squeak would emerge. Finally he managed, "You bear a Danish name, *Prinsessen* Ragna."

She scowled at him and pursed her lips. "My grandmother was Danish. I was named for her."

Uncertain as to the reason for her sudden change of humour, he signaled Kjartan. He wanted his friend to explain that they were about to introduce her to the crew.

She took a deep breath. "I am ready."

He held out his hand and was surprised at the firmness of her grip. Her heat travelled up his arm. Annoyance surged in his gut when Kjartan took her other hand, but he smiled to reassure her and opened the curtain.

~~~

Ragna had not wanted to take Reider's hand, but she felt alone in this strange place, despite Thor's presence. The tall, blond Viking seemed friendly. His smile melted her fears. Was he trustworthy? She had awakened in his bed, but was confident he had put her there for warmth, rather than to ravish her.

What manner of man was he? His chamber was a cubicle in a crude shed that was a far cry from the opulent English manors she had grown up in. He was a sailor, probably a fisherman, a man beneath her rank. Yet she was drawn to him. Her name had apparently been the first word he had spoken for who knows how long.

Most men engendered a feeling of exasperation in her, they were so malleable. This Rider wouldn't be as easy to cajole as most men were. Strangely, the thought excited her. Perhaps she had swallowed too much seawater.

She stepped through the curtain, Thor on her heels. The first thing that struck her as her eyes darted cautiously around the chamber was the lack of decoration. No trophies of war hung on the bare boards; no tapestries adorned the walls; no rugs warmed the floors; no banners wafted in the warm air that rose from the crude hearth.

The ill-shaven, well-muscled men who stared at her evidently shared the sleeping spaces along the outer wall. They had no privacy curtain. These were the brave souls who had risked their lives to save hers. Did they live here—together? The air was heavy with the smell of wet clothing and male bodies.

Reider cleared his throat. "Men of Strand—"

The men gawked, then cheered loudly. Thor barked. Ragna bent to calm him.

Reider smiled broadly, nodding his acceptance of the good wishes. These men obviously held him in high regard. Then he turned to her. "Men of Strand, I present to you Ragna FisRam."

It was close enough. She smiled tentatively. Her name seemed to surprise them. Several licked their lips. Some returned her smile, others elbowed their neighbour. She pulled the blanket more tightly around her shoulders and clutched Thor's collar.

Reider squeezed her hand. "You will afford our guest the respect she is due."

Whatever he had said surprised some of them further. She turned to Kjartan, putting her hand atop his. "Please thank these men for saving me, and my dog."

He translated and many smiled back. "We were glad to do our part, but it was Reider who saved you."

She looked at her Viking. She suddenly knew that if he had not beckoned, she would never have jumped into the sea. She had trusted him to save her and he had, at the risk of his own life. She felt a bond with this man that she had never felt with anyone outside her family. It alarmed her. She inclined her head slightly and murmured, "Thank you, Rider."

His face reddened and he took her hand from Kjartan's. "Kjartan is my second in command. These men are our loyal crew."

Ragna looked round again and became uncomfortably aware

that she was the only woman in the large chamber. She scanned the recesses. Were the women hiding there?

Her gaze fell upon a man she recognized, Captain Philion, the fool who had put their lives in jeopardy by deciding to ride out the storm. He had evidently abandoned ship after her leap of faith. Clad in a simple tunic, he ladled food into bowls from a large cauldron hung over the hearth. Scowling, he carried them to one of the trestle tables where he set them down in front of the foreigners. He cast a look of resentment at her and a shiver went up her spine. Another man, the young leader of the mercenaries she had hired, served other crew members.

Something stuck in her throat. Sweat broke out on her brow. She suddenly felt light-headed. After cheating death, these men had been forced into servitude. Was this the fate that awaited her? Her blood turned to ice. It was more likely she would be delivered into a different kind of servitude. The smiling politeness of Rider and Chartan was meant to lull her into acceptance of her fate, a woman alone with a crew of rough men. But she would not yield. There was a reason her family called her their Wild Viking Princess.

# CHAPTER EIGHT

For the second day in a row, his dismay increasing, Count Dieter von Wolfenberg watched ship after ship limp into the port of Hamburg. Their crews told harrowing tales of the worst storm in living memory. Many blessed their good fortune at finding shelter along the coast to wait out the gale. Men of Christian persuasion crossed themselves in benediction for any unlucky soul caught in the sea's fury.

Dieter's apprehension grew each time the ship he had travelled from Saxony to meet failed to appear. It carried his sister-by-marriage, Ragna FitzRam. He dreaded bringing the news to his wife that her sister had been lost at sea. Blythe had barely recovered from the grief of her parents' loss in the White Ship disaster four years before. She had miscarried twice since.

Unsure how long they might have to wait, he had sent his men off with Magnus Braunschweig. He was confident his old friend would take care of finding a suitable place to pitch camp. Dieter scoured the docks, going from ship to ship, enquiring about a Norman cog. His search yielded nothing, until he chanced upon a captain who had picked up a survivor of a capsized cog. The man had not lived long after his rescue, but had told a tale of his ship turning over after a Danish longboat had come to their aid. Trapped under the ship, he had clung onto the drifting wreck for hours.

Dieter doubted this was Ragna's boat. Why would it be close to Danish shores, unless it had been blown a long way off course? "Did the wretch say which port they had sailed from?"

The sailor drew hard on his wooden pipe. "Newcastle."

Wreathed in foul-smelling smoke, Dieter rubbed his fingers against the stubble of his chin, nervous to ask the next question. "Did he say aught of the Danish boat rescuing anyone?"

The captain sucked on his pipe again and blew out an impressive array of smoke rings. "In his delirium, he raved about a madwoman with a dog jumping into the waves to swim to the longboat."

If any woman had the courage to leap into the swells of a raging sea, it was Ragna, and she would never leave her beloved hound behind. Despite the lump in his throat, Dieter asked, "Did he say if this woman reached the longboat?"

The man hacked up phlegm and spat it out. "He thought a few of his fellow crew made it to the rescue boat, though he pitied those that did."

A cold chill settled in Dieter's spine. He suspected he knew the reason. "Pitied?"

"It's well known the Danes have always forced captives into servitude. It's not likely they'll be any more humane to those they saved from a watery grave."

Dieter thought sadly of his sister-by-marriage. He had only met her once, four years ago after the birth of his daughter, Sophia. Ragna was beautiful, opinionated and stubborn. Blythe had told him the FitzRam family's nickname for her. Now she was probably in the hands of Vikings.

Slavery would destroy a woman of Ragna's temperament. It was his duty to do something, now convinced that this story of a woman jumping into the sea was Ragna's tale. He discussed with the seaman the likely places where the cog might have capsized, then hastened off to lay plans with Magnus for a search. Blythe would expect no less.

## CHAPTER NINE

Ragna pushed away the half eaten trencher of fish. She should eat, but her appetite had fled. The men among whom she had lived for two days had maintained their friendly demeanour and made no attempt to force her into any compromising situations. They had erected a crude wooden screen around the spring where the men bathed. The frigid water had left her teeth chattering for a long time afterwards, but she prized cleanliness and appreciated the privacy.

She had slept in Reider's bed, but he had remained on the hard floor beside his pallet, never touching her. The strange disappointment she felt at his distance irritated her. Was it because Thor lay on the other side, or did the Viking not want to touch her? She had lain awake, studying his features while he slept.

He was a handsome man. Male beauty was something she had never given any thought to, though she had known many attractive men. They had left her indifferent. This broad-shouldered Dane stirred unwelcome sensations in strange places.

Her fingers itched to reach out and trace his proud nose, touch his long blond hair, trail her finger along the thin line of golden curls that began at his bronzed chest and worked its way down. Would the hair feel soft, or wiry?

Her thoughts shocked and disturbed her. Agneta FitzRam had made sure her daughters were aware of what took place between a man and his wife in the marriage bed, and had often insisted that they would immediately recognize their true love.

Were these new feelings the sensations her mother had spoken of? Ragna had dismissed her mother's beliefs, though her parents had been deeply in love. Blythe had confided she had known the moment she met Dieter that he was her soul mate. Nolana often jested that Aidan had made her go weak in the knees when she first met him, though he was a monk then! But true love was for others, not for Ragna.

It frustrated her that she knew nothing of this Viking. What was he doing here, living a bare-bones existence, seemingly miles from anywhere? It was obvious from their demeanour and language that he and Kjartan were not simple peasants. Why were there no women? And why had he called her *princess*? Perhaps she had misunderstood. He had barely been able to talk then.

His voice, deeper now, scattered her thoughts. "Do you not like *hellefisk*?"

Kjartan and Reider's limited knowledge of English had enabled them to communicate and she had tried a few words of Danish, hoping to please her ancestors.

She replied, partly in his tongue and partly in her own, nodding her head, but indicating with her spread palms she had eaten enough. "Yes, I like fish, but I am not hungry." How to explain her discomfort at the icy stares of her fellow survivors, serving food to their new masters?

She hesitated, then asked, "Why do you eat only fish? Do you not farm, or trade foodstuffs with other communities?"

Reider looked to Kjartan, then seemed to chose his words carefully. "This is not our home. We live here and survive off the bounty of the sea until we can return to our rightful place."

Something passed between the two men, something they were reluctant to tell her. What did he mean, *rightful*? Was that what he had said? She took a deep breath. "And your women? They are at your home?"

Again the two men exchanged careful glances. Reider clenched his jaw and bitterness stole into his warm brown eyes. He rose abruptly and stalked out of the hall.

Her mouth fell open and dismay flooded her heart. She felt her face redden.

Kjartan put his hand on hers. "Do not be offended. He is not angry with you. We do not know what to expect when we return home."

She frowned. "How long have you been away?"

Kjartan considered his answer. "One month."

She was stranded with men who had been without the company of women for a month. She would have to tread warily, but caution had never been her strength.

Kjartan scratched his forehead. "*Ja*, we have lived here one month, or maybe a little more. We built this lodge for shelter. Our home is grander than this, but—"

He looked toward the door through which his friend had left. "We have lost much, Ragna, but the tale is not mine to tell. It is for Reider to tell you, if he wishes."

She looked wistfully at the door. "But will he tell me, Kjartan?"

The Dane shrugged. "He does not trust women. Neither do I."

~~~

Reider tied and retied the mooring rope, though he knew it to be secure. His innards were in knots. This woman confused him. Her mere presence hardened his *pik*. He wanted her, but this was a time to give his attention to their plans for regaining his birthright.

Since the rescue, he and Kjartan had not discussed their ideas once. After their flight, they had often talked long into the night, recalling the legend of Amleth and how he had avenged his father's murder. Reider had rejected the notion of feigning witlessness as Amleth had done. Gorm would not be fooled by such a plan.

Before Ragna's arrival, Reider spent every spare hour sharpening weapons. A well prepared arsenal was essential. He had not been near the forge since her advent.

He still knew little about her, and why should he want to? Yet he did. His determination to swear off women had lasted one month! Was it because he had not set eyes on a woman in that time? Should he reveal anything of himself to her? He ached to tell her of his father's death, of Gorm's treachery and Margit's betrayal. She must wonder why they lived here in this lonely place. Kjartan would not tell the story. It would be for Reider to do so.

If he told her, she might think less of him. He had failed to see the treachery brewing in his midst, and it had cost his father's life. Reider, the great Prince of Strand, brought low by a scheming woman. Now he lay each night on the hard packed earth beside his pallet, his sleepless thoughts full of how to impress the woman in his bed, beneath his furs.

Why not just take her? Why did her opinion of him matter? He inhaled deeply, filling his lungs with the smell of the sea. An unexpected noise behind him caused him to whirl around, dagger in hand. Ragna backed away nervously.

He sheathed his weapon. "I didn't hear you approach. You should be more careful."

She fixed her gaze on the pebbles. "I am sorry."

He wanted to reach for her hand, to reassure her, sorry he had alarmed her. She shivered and pulled her fur closer, looking over her shoulder. Did she seek Kjartan?

She looked back at him. "*Fortæl mig.*"

Kjartan must have given her the Danish words. She wanted to hear his story. He shook his head. "Not here." He pointed to the lodge. "Inside."

## CHAPTER TEN

Reider ushered Ragna into his alcove, his hand on the small of her back. She teetered on the edge of some precipice from which there would be no return, but could not turn away.

He brought in two crude wooden stools. "Sit."

She obeyed, envisaging her reaction if either of her brothers had spoken to her in the same manner.

Thor sat on his haunches beside her. Reider straddled the other stool. Water dripped somewhere. Her gaze fixed on his powerful thighs. One leg twitched nervously. He clamped his wind-bronzed hands on his knees, stilling the movement. She dragged her attention to his mouth, startled that he had already started to speak, his brown eyes full of sadness.

"—dead at my feet."

She gulped. What had he said? She stared at him, open-mouthed. "I don't understand."

The twitching began anew. "It is indeed difficult to understand. I gaped in disbelief. My step-brother's dagger in my father's back."

Her heart went out to him. She knew what it was to lose a beloved parent, but murder? She touched his hand, feeling his warmth. "I am sorry. Your step-brother?"

Thor lurched forward and licked their joined hands.

Reider's jaw clenched, but he patted Thor's head. "Gorm. He rules in my stead."

*Rules?* What did he mean? She decided to say nothing, hoping he would confide more. She wished fervently that she spoke his language. He seemed hesitant. There was something he did not want to tell her. The distracting leak in the thatch seemed to have worsened. Did they fix the leaks, or just wait until the rain stopped? Why was she filled with a desire to know him? Perhaps if she spoke of her parents—but to share her grief with a stranger? She tapped the side of her leg and Thor came to sit beside her again.

She took a deep breath. "My parents—" She swallowed hard and removed her hand from Reider's. Had she ever spoken of the tragedy to anyone outside her family?

All she could hear was the incessant dripping of water. Someone needed to stop that leak.

"My parents drowned together—in the White Ship disaster."

Reider shifted his attention to her mouth. "I have heard of this disaster. Hundreds of Anglo-Norman nobles perished in the Narrow Sea."

She rocked back and forth on the stool, eyes closed, too distraught to continue. Thor rested his muzzle on her lap, whining.

Reider reached for her hand and cradled it. "You loved them."

She squeezed her eyes closed, hoping to stem the tears. Ragna FitzRam did not cry. But Reider wiped away a tear with his thumb. "I feel your heartbreak."

She could no longer hold back the guilt. The sound of the water dripping in the adjoining chamber drummed in her ears. She tore her hand from his and crossed her arms over her breasts. "It should have been me," she wailed. "I was to board that ship, not them."

Reider fell to his knees before her and took hold of her hands. Thor lay down beside her. "You cannot blame yourself for that. I do not know why you were not aboard and they were, but I am sure you did not cause the ship to sink."

Relief washed over her. How many times had she told her brother Aidan the same thing years ago? He had come to terms with it, but she knew in that moment that she never had. With a few heartfelt words, this man she barely knew had cleansed her of guilt she had carried for years.

She opened her eyes. His were filled with compassion for her in the midst of his own grief. How typical that she would be so immersed in herself that she would ignore the feelings of others. A floodgate broke within her. She took a deep breath. "Tell me of your father."

Reider told her tales of his childhood, of growing up the only son of a powerful, loving man, of his father's second marriage after his mother died, and of his relationship with Gorm, the stepbrother who would murder his father. "I never suspected his treachery," he said softly. Still on his knees, his head had dropped to her lap. She stroked his hair, truly feeling the pain of another for the first time in her life.

Suddenly, he stiffened and withdrew to his stool, startling Thor. It was like being drenched with ice cold water. "What is it, Reider?"

He did not meet her gaze. "Nothing. Now you know the story and why we are here, and why we must reclaim our birthright, the kingdom that is rightfully mine."

"Kingdom?"

His voice had lost its resonance. "Strand is a Danish principality. I am my father's legitimate heir. I must fight for what I have lost. I cannot afford to be distracted."

He came to his feet and left abruptly. Thor barked, cocked his head and looked up at his mistress, apparently as confused as she.

The dripping had ceased.

~~~

Reider cursed himself for turning away from Ragna. She had confided things to him that he suspected she had never shared with anyone, and had not scorned him for his shortcomings as a prince.

Thanks be to Thor someone had stopped the irritating dripping of water that had played on his nerves while they had talked.

He scrubbed his face with his hands, digging his nails into the roots of his hair. He was a Prince, but sometimes he wished he was not of noble blood. Perhaps then life would be simpler and he could enjoy Ragna, make her part of his life. But Gorm's treachery had left him with nothing to offer any woman.

Ragna would not be content to live her life as the wife of a landless fugitive.

*Wife?* Where had that thought come from? Did he trust her enough to marry her? It was probably a moot question. He suspected Ragna would never yield to any man.

When he had regained his kingdom he would help her continue her journey. He resolved to avoid her as much as possible. There was no future for them together.

# CHAPTER ELEVEN

Ragna saw little of Reider and Kjartan over the next sennight. Her Viking came deep in the night to sleep beside her, but rose each morning before dawn. She knew he had been there. His scent lingered in the disheveled furs and blankets she held to her nose when she straightened them each morning.

Something was afoot. The crew was restless, working on the boats or in the forge most of the day. The thralls were conscripted to assist with the labour. The stockpile of sharpened swords, axes and daggers grew. Food was provided on the trestle tables each day. Men came in, took their portion and left.

Her thoughts turned to her family. Would Dieter search for her, or would he think her lost to the waves when her ship did not arrive in Hamburg? Blythe would be bereft. Her sister had not fully accepted the deaths of their parents. Aidan would blame himself. Guilt had driven him to become a monk after their parents' deaths.

But what were the chances of Dieter finding her where Reider's enemies had not tracked him? What did Reider intend to do with her when he left? She had no doubt they planned to leave, and soon. Would she be abandoned here, alone, with no means of escape? Or would she be taken with them on their quest for justice?

Given a choice she would prefer the latter, though it would take her further away from rescue. The possibility of Reider's leaving and never seeing him again filled her with dread. She saw only glimpses of him during the day, but never stopped thinking about him.

Her preoccupation and the lack of activity annoyed her. Ragna thrived on action. She sometimes wished she had been made a thrall; at least they had things to do. To alleviate her boredom, she often walked to the water's edge, looking out to sea, wondering if Dieter searched or if hope had been abandoned.

One morning she and Thor walked further along the beach than usual, away from the cove. She inhaled the salty smell of the sea, watching the waves rush to shore. She heard the crunch of boots on pebbles and knew it was Reider by the icy heat on the nape of her neck. He stood behind her. She longed to lean back against him and feel his powerful arms wrap around her.

*I could stay in this lonely place forever, if he was with me.*

The astonishing thought set her teeth on edge. Shivering, she crossed her arms over her breasts.

Thor wagged his tail vigorously and jumped up on Reider. Even her dog loved him. Reider rubbed Thor's ears, then took off his parka and put it around her shoulders. "Are you cold?"

She gathered the garment tightly under her chin, inhaling the scent she recognized as uniquely his. Did he know her scent? Did he feel anything for her? "No, I am not cold."

He put his hands on her shoulders and turned her to face him. He had pulled his hair into a tight braid, ready to face his enemies. To her dismay, tears rolled down her cheeks. She had not cried since the devastating news of her parents' deaths, and never for a man. She had been determined not to show her vulnerability to this man in particular, yet the tears flowed. She closed her eyes.

He drew her to him and his warmth seeped into her. She lay her head against his chest, feeling, for the first time in her life, the hard swell of a man's arousal pressed to her body. Her mother had been right. It did strange things to a woman's insides.

He took a deep breath and stroked his hand over her hair. "It is time. We are leaving."

His rich voice rippled over her. What did he mean? Would he take her with him? She glanced up sharply to look into his guarded eyes, and knew he would not. Frowning, she gritted her teeth and pulled away from him. "You are not taking me with you?"

He held her fast. "I do not want to leave you here, but where I go is full of danger. We sail first to the neighbouring principality. They were my father's allies. We have already sent messengers. We hope they will help us, but things change. You will have Thor with you, and I will leave two of my crew here, and the thralls."

A hot burst of anger welled up inside her. She rubbed the back of her neck, then put both hands on his chest and shoved him away. "They are not thralls. They are free men you have forced into servitude. They hate me because I am still free." She strode away, resentful that she was not free either. He had somehow enslaved her in a fascination with him.

He caught up to her and grasped her elbow, pulling her back. "I know you are angry, but I must regain my kingdom and avenge my father's death. If not for my own sake, then for my people. Gorm and his consort will not be good rulers."

The way he spat the word *consort* gave her pause. "His consort?"

Reider's spine stiffened and he fisted his hands at his side. "I have no wish to speak of her."

Hatred contorted his fair face. A certainty settled in her heart. "She is the reason you do not trust women."

He turned away, picking up a pebble and hurling it into the waves. Thor plunged into the water in pursuit. Reider murmured something she did not hear. She moved closer. "I'm sorry, I didn't—"

He turned abruptly, his face a mask of pain. "Margit was my betrothed."

He picked up a handful of pebbles and threw them one after the other in rapid succession.

This man she had come to care for had suffered the worst kind of betrayal. She should tread carefully, but out came, "Did you love her?"

*Why don't you think before opening your mouth?*

He whirled around and her breath caught in her throat. "Love? There is no place in my heart for love, Ragna."

~~~

Ragna's knees trembled. It was like a kick in the belly. But she would not allow him to best her. She took his parka from her shoulders and thrust it at him. "Will you return here for us after you win back your precious kingdom, or will you forget Ragna FitzRam and leave us to die?"

He accepted the parka, but threw it down. He put his hands on her waist, drew her to his body and brushed his lips against hers. Wanton sensations arrowed to her core and she put her arms around his neck. He pressed his warm, coaxing tongue to the seam of her lips. She allowed him entry with a groan of longing. He swirled his tongue over her teeth and delved deep. She sucked on him rhythmically, feeling his hard arousal again pressed to the place between her legs where warmth flooded. Wave after wave of intense desire broke on the shore of her heart. She thrust her breasts forward, burning for his touch.

Suddenly he tore their bodies apart, his breathing ragged, a look of intense longing on his face. She swayed, drowning in cold frustration.

He stooped to pick up the parka. "I could never forget you, *prinsessen* Ragna FitzRam."

He untied his leather headband, then slipped hers from her head and replaced it with his own. It still held the warmth of his body. He clenched her headband in his fist, put it to his nose and inhaled deeply, then strode away.

Buffeted by the wind, she watched his broad back until he was out of sight. A tidal wave of grief threatened to swamp her. She had never surrendered any part of her heart to a man, now he was leaving. He might never return.

She did not know how long she had remained on the shore, watching the waves without seeing them. When the two longboats came around the headland, Reider stood with Kjartan in the stern, his hand raised in salute.

Thor barked frantically. She held on to her resolve not to wave back, but when the boats were specks on the horizon, she raised her hand. "Please come back," she whispered to the wind. She had not even wished him Godspeed.

~~~

Reider watched until Ragna and her beloved dog were barely visible. Would he ever again run his hands through the beautiful tresses that billowed in the wind like a golden banner? He did not expect her to return his salute. She was too stubborn. He had never met such a wilful woman, but her wild nature excited him. She would be a challenging mate for some man.

The thought of another bedding her filled him with anger, but he had nothing to offer her, certainly not his heart. Margit had destroyed it. He suspected Ragna would expect nothing less of her mate than his whole heart. She was not a woman of half measures, probably because of her Danish blood!

Despite his determination to avoid her, he had been inexplicably unable to stay away from his alcove at night. He had made sure she did not know he slept beside her, stealing into the small space late into the night and leaving before she awoke. It had been torture not to reach out and touch her as she slumbered.

He touched his fingers to his bottom lip, remembering the taste and smell of her—spicy like her nature. He had not intended to kiss her. He had kissed women before, but nothing had prepared him for Ragna's kiss. Her groan of longing had inflamed him even beyond the rock-hard erection that arose whenever he was near her. It was the kiss of a passionate woman, but an innocent one. He suspected she had never kissed a man. Her warmth as she sucked his tongue and thrust her breasts had sent desire crashing through him. It had taken considerable control not to take her on the shore.

He removed her leather headband from his tunic, inhaled her lingering scent and fastened it around his head.

His heart leapt into his throat when she suddenly raised her hand in salute.

"I will come back for you, Ragna, my *prinsessen*."

~~~

Once the boats had disappeared beyond the horizon, Ragna knelt to hug Thor, then wandered slowly back to whatever awaited her at the lodge. The dog whimpered as he kept pace with his mistress. She patted his haunches. "You too feel his absence already, don't you, my loyal friend?"

She took her time, stooping occasionally to throw a pebble or two into the waves. Thor gave up chasing them, discouraged when there was nothing to retrieve.

When she pushed open the heavy door of the lodge, her eyes widened. The thralls were dressed in their own clothing. One of the Danes explained Reider had freed them at her request.

Needing to be alone to come to terms with this new revelation and her feelings of loss, she hastened to the alcove. Atop Reider's pallet lay her mother's dagger, still in its sheath. She grabbed the precious weapon and held it to her breast. Unable to stem the tide of tears any longer, she fell on to the bed and sobbed until exhaustion took hold. Thor curled up beside her, whimpering.

# CHAPTER TWELVE

After days of planning and consulting with locals, Dieter and Magnus came to the conclusion it would be impossible to search the marshy coastline on horseback. They would have to obtain a boat, and a crew, since neither they nor their men were mariners. Local seamen would be familiar with tides and the lay of the land.

In their quest for a boat, they heard reports of a brutal massacre on the island principality of Strand. Speculation was rampant that the heir apparent might have escaped. Dieter paid little attention, preoccupied with fears for Ragna.

Magnus secured a boat and crew, mostly Saxons with some Danes. Their captain demanded what Dieter considered a high price, but Magnus pointed out they may have to go as far as Strand, and that might prove dangerous in the present situation.

The Danish captain, Ivar Sigurdsen, took charge of obtaining and loading provisions aboard the *knarr*. Dieter and his men embarked from the dock in Hamburg, having stabled their horses at a reputable farm.

Dieter was apprehensive. He was not a sailor, and had never been on a boat, except to travel from time to time along the Rhine.

They sailed down the Elbe. He found his sea legs and thought it might not be too bad. Once they reached the open sea, uncontrollable retching left him exhausted. Many of his men suffered the same affliction, much to the amusement of the seasoned crew.

They took their time, carefully exploring the shoreline. Dieter appreciated the captain's knowledge of the area and admitted that he and Magnus could not have undertaken this search alone. He did not hold out much hope of finding Ragna.

As they scoured the miles of coastline, he tried to keep his attention off the movement of the waves. His disordered thoughts drifted to the tale of the flight of the heir of Strand, then to his recollection of the story of the heroic rescue undertaken by the Danish longboat. Were the two events connected somehow? Could the Viking who had come to the rescue of the Norman cog be the Prince of Strand?

If Ragna lived, was she caught up in a dangerous struggle for power? It was reassuring that the crew Magnus had hired was aware there might be conflict ahead and would enter the fray if necessary. If Ragna had been enslaved, they would likely have a fight on their hands to free her.

Dieter did not fear conflict. Hailed as a hero of the battle of Andernach, he had played a significant role in the victory of Köln against the Holy Roman Emperor. But he was glad to have a strong militia with him.

Sigurdsen docked at a village or settlement each evening, and it became apparent he was known and welcomed along the coast. The talk around the campfires turned to the massacre. There was general agreement the Prince of Strand would join forces with a neighbouring principality in an attack to regain his birthright. There seemed to be no further doubt that the prince had survived the massacre.

Dieter asked Sigurdsen's opinion. "If this prince did escape, where would he have gone?"

"Husembro."

The man had not hesitated. "You seem sure of that."

Ivar shrugged. "It is the logical place. An inlet with hidden coves, but not far from Strand."

Dieter gazed out at the black waters, whitecaps still visible in the moonlight. "How long to get there, if we go directly, without searching the shore on the way?"

Ivar took off his woolen cap and scratched his head. "You think the woman you seek is with Prince Reider?"

Dieter felt a pang of doubt. This shrewd seaman probably judged him naive to rely on a hunch. He swallowed hard. "I do."

Ivar laughed and slapped him on the back. "Me too."

"You do?"

Ivar lay back to gaze at the stars, his hands behind his head. "Prince Reider is exactly the kind of man who would go out in a storm to save another boat. And if anyone would be likely to jump into a roiling sea to save another person, it would be him."

Dieter craned his neck to look at the stars. "You know him then?"

"I do, and I know his step-brother, Gorm, who now rules in his place." He sat up and spat. "Never did trust the man."

## CHAPTER THIRTEEN

Margit slapped the thrall hard across the face. "Ouch! Be more careful with the comb."

Olve scrambled to her feet and retrieved the whalebone comb from the floor, her face reddened with the imprint of her mistress's hand.

It gave Margit satisfaction that the thrall trembled as she tried once more to unsnarl the thick curly tangles. She was in a mood to make others suffer. As usual, Gorm had left her bed during the night after satisfying his own needs, leaving her wanting. It amazed her that such a well-endowed man knew nothing about a woman's pleasure. He had not been persuaded to marry her, though she had tried every ploy in her arsenal to convince him.

The comb snagged again. Margit screeched, leaned back in her chair and kicked the child hard in her swollen belly. The thrall cried out and doubled over, crawling out of the chamber when Margit sent her packing. "Send another thrall, one who is not so careless."

That should take care of the wretch who had stupidly gotten with child, probably Gorm's.

Margit seethed as she paced back and forth, tugging the comb through her black hair. Gorm's smell still clung to her. He treated her no better than a thrall. Worse, because he would kill her if she lay with another man. He seemed to have forgotten that without her help he would not be sitting on the throne of Strand.

He gave her no say in the judgments he rendered, did not allow her a seat on the dais beside him. She would have been better off marrying Reider. She cupped her breasts, remembering with a shiver how Reider's big hands had fondled them. She barred the door, took a deep breath and brushed her palms over her hard nipples, frustrated that she would have to once again take care of her own needs.

~~~

Reider choked on his response when Dagfinn Alfredsen embraced him, uttering words of condolence he knew were heartfelt. His father and Dagfinn had been friends and allies for many years. The two neighbouring principalities had supported each other for generations. The Hall in which they stood had witnessed many marriages between the two peoples.

Dagfinn looked him in the eye. "I never trusted your stepbrother."

Resentment stuck in Reider's throat. "Was I blind? Why did everyone else see his treacherous nature, but I didn't?"

The older man put his hands on Reider's shoulders. "Because, my boy, you see the good in people, but sometimes you are blind to their faults. Your father was the same. He became so determined to make a strategic marriage with Gorm's mother, he failed to see the son's greed. It cost him his life."

Reider let out a long breath. "My life too, had it not been for Kjartan."

Dagfinn shook Kjartan's hand and embraced him. "Welcome, Kjartan. Your cousins are anxious to renew acquaintance. It's been too long since you visited your family here."

Kjartan smiled. "I agree, and it is to my shame that it is tragedy that brings me here this time. With your permission I will seek them out."

Dagfinn slapped him on the back. "Go now. Bring them."

Reider watched his friend leave, envious of Kjartan's extended family. Dagfinn eyed him curiously. "What of Margit?"

A worm coiled in Reider's bowels. "She betrayed me. Her betrayal cut deeper than Gorm's. I will never trust a woman again."

But as he swore, his thoughts went to Ragna. He sensed she cared for him. Would she betray him, if he trusted her with his heart?

A thrall approached with tankards of ale for Reider and his men. Others brought victuals. "Sit! Enjoy our meagre fare," Dagfinn declared.

Reider gazed at the haunch of venison and inhaled deeply. "My lord, we have dined on naught but fish for a month. This is ambrosia."

Dagfinn chuckled. "Eat then! We'll fill our bellies and talk of how we might defeat this murderous usurper."

They sat down to feast. Kjartan entered the Hall with uncles, aunts and cousins in tow. He had not seen them for several years, and their boisterous joy was evident. He reintroduced Reider to two female cousins, little girls when Reider had last seen them. Now they were alluring young women. Reider winked at his friend.

"Never mind that," Kjartan said with a shrug. "I have something to show you."

He placed a cloth-covered bundle on the table and carefully unfolded the wrapping to reveal a small dagger. Reider's mouth fell open. How had Ragna's dagger come to be here? He frowned and glanced up sharply at Kjartan. "How—?"

His friend picked up the dagger and handed it to him. "Almost identical, wouldn't you say?"

Reider accepted the weapon and ran his fingers over the intricately carved Viking on the handle. Emotions warred within him. The same artisan had carved this dagger and Ragna's. "Where did you get this?"

Kjartan pointed to one of his cousins. "It belongs to Dagfrid, my beautiful cousin. It is a family heirloom passed down from generations ago, but only to the women. It was made for a woman's hand. When I saw Ragna's, I knew I'd seen something similar before."

Reider's thoughts were in a whirl. "But this means—"

His comrade finished the thought for him. "Ragna and I are somehow of the same blood. Probably second or third cousins many times removed. We may have shared a grandfather four generations ago."

Anger crept into Reider's soul. "She lied then. She must have known."

Kjartan took the weapon from him and wrapped it in its covering. "Lied? How could she know? Do you think she arranged the storm so her boat would be blown off course and she could leap into your life and mine? Be reasonable, Reider. Take care that grief and hatred do not make you doubt everyone. Ragna has never given us cause to believe her a liar. She is an honourable woman. Fate has brought her back to the land of her ancestors. She is one of us."

## CHAPTER FOURTEEN

Ivar coaxed his boat slowly into the mouth of Husembro cove before dawn, admonishing everyone on board to remain silent. They had anchored off shore overnight. Dieter's heart throbbed in his ears. He had lain awake, listening to the creaking of the ship's timbers as it floated in the mercifully calm sea. Unlikely as it was that he would find Ragna here, hope surged within him. He had to cling to it.

The weak rays of the rising sun barely penetrated the fog on the water. He peered into it. Was there a crude shelter tucked into the forest beyond the beach? He tapped Ivar's shoulder and pointed.

"Looks like a lodge," Ivar whispered. "Not been there long I'd say. Might be we are on the right track, but I don't see any boats. That concerns me. We'll wait until there is more light before we make a move."

As the *knarr* rocked in the waves, Dieter's belly turned over. He did not want to be seasick now of all times. He took a deep breath and concentrated on the barely visible shoreline, looking for movement.

"There!" Ivar pointed. "Men on the beach."

Dieter made out two or three dark figures. One of them lit a fire. A woman emerged from the building, accompanied by a black dog. She was bundled in furs, but there was no mistaking the banner of blonde hair. The fog lifted as though her arrival had heralded the sun, and excitement bubbled up in his throat. He gripped Ivar's arm. "It's her."

Ivar narrowed his eyes. "We must be careful. We cannot assume she is with friends, but there seems to be only a handful of men. However, we do not know how many are inside the lodge. We'll approach slowly and I'll hail them. I still see no boats."

Timbers creaked as the *knarr* strained closer to the shore. The noise caught the attention of those on the beach. The men drew daggers. One of them motioned the woman to return to the lodge. She seemed ready to obey, but then turned to look out to sea, shielding her eyes.

Dieter chuckled. "Definitely Ragna." He waved and shouted her name.

~~~

Emerging from the lodge, Ragna inhaled the damp air, dreading another day with no word from Reider and his men. She had lost track of how many days they had been gone. Where were they now? Had they persuaded their old allies to help them?

The men left to guard her were friendly and the freed thralls treated her with respect, grateful for her part in their liberation, but she was still the only woman among them. How long would she be safe? They were vulnerable here. She sensed it, though the Danes doubted Gorm would attack, especially with the persistent fog.

Suddenly, Torgrim drew his dagger and ordered her back to the lodge. A boat had pulled into the cove. She shielded her eyes to determine the threat. As the fog lifted she saw that it was not a longboat.

Someone waved. She narrowed her eyes and gasped. "Dieter?" she whispered. She had not seen her brother-by-marriage for several years, but was sure it was he waving frantically. Then she heard his voice on the wind. "Ragna!"

Relief surged over her. "Dieter has come to our rescue, Thor." She would not be marooned on this lonely shore. She would see her family again. Waving both hands high over her head, she jumped up and down. Thor ran round in circles, barking loudly. "Dieeeeterrr!" she bellowed, running into the waves. Torgrim ran after her, trying to pull her back. "No, no, Torgrim, it's all right. It's Dieter. I know him. Put away your weapons."

Her excitement spread to the other survivors and they too waved their arms, shouting and beckoning for the ship to come into shore.

Dieter leapt into the waist high water and strode towards the beach. Ragna waded out to meet him and collapsed into his outstretched arms. "You came," she sobbed. "You didn't give up."

Dieter grinned broadly, hugging her tight. "Ragna! I am relieved to find you."

Laughing, they waded out of the water, Thor leaping in the

waves and chasing his own tail. Dieter's hand went to the hilt of his dagger when he saw the Danes with their weapons drawn, but Ragna reassured him. "We are safe with them. They were left here to protect me."

The shipwreck survivors mobbed Dieter, shaking his hand and thanking him.

Ivar's crew came ashore and introductions were made. The Danes knew Ivar and obviously felt comfortable with him. They too became swept up in the celebration. Ragna had not given any thought to how isolated and vulnerable they too must have felt. They had been left behind because of her, when they would rather have gone to fight with their leader, their prince.

The newcomers were welcomed into the lodge and invited to break their fast. Dieter was given dry clothing and his apparel strung on the drying line. Everyone shared their story. Ragna shuddered when she told Dieter of jumping into the sea.

He laughed. "I heard the tale, and I knew that if anyone had the courage to leap into the sea, it was Ragna FitzRam."

Ragna was astonished that her fate had hinged on the ramblings of a dying survivor of the wreck. The newcomers learned the details of Reider's betrayal, and that he and Kjartan had gone to regain Reider's birthright.

Like the Danes, Ivar also believed Dagfinn Alfredsen would fight with Reider. "He's a good man. Murder of a rightful ruler would not sit well with him."

~~~

The thought occurred to Ragna that Ivar might be a good source of information. "Captain Ivar, tell me about Margit."

The seaman looked at her curiously. "You speak of Margit Hansdatter?"

Ragna felt her face flush. "I do not know her name. She was Reider's betrothed," she murmured, hoping her nervousness was not obvious.

Ivar drew on his pipe. "Margit came from Heide as an arranged bride for Reider. She is a beautiful woman..."

Ragna's heart fell.

"...on the outside. But I always thought her devious."

Torgrim snorted his agreement, spat into the hearth and said something in Danish. Ivar explained. "She betrayed Reider with Gorm."

*No wonder Reider mistrusts women.*

Dieter came to his feet. "You can stop worrying. We will be on our way as early as the morrow. Ivar will take us back to Hamburg."

Ragna should have been elated, but her thoughts were full of Reider. To never see him again, and not know what happened to him?

## CHAPTER FIFTEEN

A hue and cry went up early the next morning. Longboats had been sighted entering the cove.

"Gorm's henchmen!" Torgrim shouted breathlessly, running by Ragna on his way out of the lodge. She had lain awake for hours, clutching Reider's headband, and finally risen before dawn.

Dieter had slept in Kjartan's alcove, but was already up and dressed. He issued curt orders to his men and Ivar rallied his sailors. They left and Ragna followed.

"Stay here, with Thor," Dieter ordered.

She stamped her foot. "I can fight. I have my dagger."

Her Saxon brother-by-marriage held up his hand. "*Nein*, Ragna. I insist. Blythe would never forgive me if anything happened to you at this juncture."

She sat down heavily on a bench, pouting as she listened to the sound of boots running across pebbles. Soon she heard metal clanging on metal, strident shouting, cries of pain. She paced back and forth, anxious to know what transpired outside. Thor followed her movements, cocking his head.

The minutes stretched interminably and her frustration grew. When the clamour lessened, she tightened her grip on her dagger and crept to the door, inching it open. The conflict seemed to be over. Dieter and Ivar stood at the water's edge looking out to sea, unharmed. Dieter still had his sword drawn. One of the enemy longboats had pulled away from the shore, apparently fleeing. Bodies lay on the bloodied pebbles of the beach.

Without warning, a burly Dane barreled through the door, knocking her to the floor. Blood poured from a gash across his forehead. She squealed as the dagger fell from her hand. Her heart in her throat, she scrambled away from the attacker, screaming loudly. A glimmer of hope surfaced when she heard Dieter shout her name, but died when the Dane stooped to pick up her weapon. Surely she would not be robbed of life by her mother's dagger?

With a menacing growl, Thor leapt at the intruder, sinking his teeth into the giant's leg. The Dane howled and fell to the floor. Then he kicked Thor hard with his other foot, sending the dog careening against the wall with a loud whimper.

It was too much. Ragna came to her feet, and rushed at the intruder, waving her arms. Her loud shrieks evidently took him by surprise. He staggered to his feet and ran out, shoving Dieter to the ground when he collided with him. He ran into the waves in pursuit of his fleeing comrades. Thor followed hard on his heels. Ragna ran after him, but Dieter restrained her.

"He has my mother's dagger," she wailed.

Dieter held fast, breathing heavily. "Your life is more important, sister."

She fell to her knees, keening the loss. The cold pebbles jarred her bones. "He will likely drown, taking my dagger with him to the bottom of the sea."

He pulled her back to her feet and held her tightly as she sobbed. "We prevailed against them. That's the important thing. Your fellow shipwreck survivors fought well, as did the Danes on our side. Gorm's men suffered considerable losses. I am only sorry some of them escaped to limp back to their leader. But we have one of their boats."

Ragna scanned the shoreline, breathing a sigh of relief when Thor emerged from the sea, apparently uninjured. Her hero shook the water from his pelt and raced to her side.

## CHAPTER SIXTEEN

Roar Knutsen was relieved to be back in Strand. It had taken his last reserve of strength to reach the fleeing longboat. His comrades had hauled him aboard with great difficulty. Had they been rowing away at full power he would never have made it. His head wound had bled like the devil, even after the long while he had spent in the water. He would bear the scar for the rest of his life, a reminder of the failed expedition. The puncture wounds in his leg were deep and painful.

Glad though he was to be home, he did not look forward to the dressing down they would surely receive from Gorm. Margit's rage would be intolerable. Roar regretted ever agreeing, while in the throes of a drunken stupor, to help Gorm take the throne. His rule had benefited no one, least of all the men who had aided him. Gorm had listened to Margit's treacherous flattery and believed it, but he was no leader of men.

The raid on Reider's hideout had been ill advised, but Gorm would not be dissuaded. Roar thought bitterly of the lifelong friends he had lost in the battle at Husembro, and Reider and most of his men had not been there in any case. The only thing Roar had to show for the foray, beside the wounds, was a handsome carved dagger, though it was too small for his hand.

He and his companions came wearily to their feet in the Hall when Gorm swept in with Margit on his arm. He escorted her to a seat, climbed the step to the dais and sat on the throne. He sprawled in the elaborately carved chair for several minutes, chewing his fingernails, scowling at the assembly. Roar's nervousness increased. The head wound burned, pain gnawed his leg.

"Knutsen!" Gorm finally bellowed.

Roar came forward and went down on one knee. "My lord Gorm."

Gorm leaned forward. "How many times must I remind you?

It's Prince Gorm."

Filled with disgust, coupled with an urge to snicker, Roar touched his hand to his heart. Did the fool not realize the crown he wore was too big for his head, in more ways than one? "A thousand pardons, my lord Prince."

Gorm squirmed, digging his stunted fingernails into the arms of the throne. "Explain your failure to deliver Reider Torfinnsen to me. You have returned with far fewer men than you took with you."

Roar itched to tell the arrogant nobody that Reider had not been at the encampment, that everyone had deemed it a fool's errand, but he thought better of it. Gorm had no interest in anything he had to say. An uncomfortable silence hung in the air.

Suddenly Gorm leapt to his feet, waving a dismissive hand at Roar. "Can no one track Reider Torfinnsen for me? Must I do everything myself? Get out of my sight."

Roar stood and backed away, breathing a sigh of relief. When he turned, Margit's malevolent glare had his gut plummeting back to his feet. She would not let him off so lightly.

Gorm strode out of the Hall, accompanied by several minions for whom Roar had no respect. Margit came to her feet and beckoned, raking her cold eyes over him, stripping him bare. She fluttered her eyelashes. "Attend me in my chamber, Roar."

She left, a round-shouldered female thrall following in her wake. He was sure the girl had been pregnant the last time he had seen her. But he couldn't be concerned with that. He had his own worries. If Gorm caught him in Margit's chamber, he was a dead man.

~~~

Margit smirked. She had grown to womanhood in Heide, surrounded by burly warriors, full of their own bravado, afraid of nothing—except a woman who knew how to manipulate them. It amused her that Roar Knutsen, fearless giant, stood before her now, licking his lips, looking around nervously, shifting his weight. What would he do if she put a firm grip on his manhood?

She took a step forward, her eyes locked on his groin. She glanced up at his face, pleased to see sweat beading on his forehead. She opened her mouth, intending to taunt him, but her gaze fell upon a dagger tucked into his belt. She reached for it. He closed his eyes and looked as though he might swoon. She yanked the dagger from his belt. "What is this?"

His eyes flew open in alarm then settled on the dagger. He let out a sigh of relief. "A dagger," he stammered.

She touched the tip of the blade to the end of his nose, sniggering when he went cross-eyed. "I know it's a dagger, fool. It's a woman's dagger. Why do you have it?"

She ran her fingers over the intricate carving, recognizing the worth of the old weapon. She had never seen the like before, though the figure carved on the hilt was definitely a Viking.

Roar squirmed. "I captured it. In the raid."

Margit scoffed. "From a woman?"

His eager answer shocked her. "*Ja!*"

A woman at Reider's encampment? She chewed her lip as jealousy gnawed at her. "A woman at Husembro? Who was she? Describe her."

Roar shook his head, eyeing the dagger. "I know not. She was hidden in a lodge and I stumbled over her. I thought there was a chance Reider might be hiding inside. She was a blonde. Long hair down to her waist. I had to flee before I had a chance to kill her. She had a mean dog. A man came to her rescue and our boat had pulled away—" His voice trailed off.

*Coward!*

"—he was not a Dane."

This captured her attention. "Not a Dane?"

Roar sweated still. "He was not dressed like a Dane, and Ivar Sigurdsen was with them. We were outmanned."

She waved her hand in dismissal. "Be gone. You sicken me."

He turned to leave, then had the temerity to look back at the dagger, a question in his eyes. She smirked. "*Nej*, Roar. The dagger is mine now."

## CHAPTER SEVENTEEN

After long deliberation, Dagfinn's battle plan was deemed the most likely to succeed. The best time to attack Gorm was at night. Not only would darkness provide cover, most of the drunkards and malcontents who had supported the usurper would be well into their cups by nightfall.

Sailing at night was risky, and a frontal attack from the sea fraught with dangers. Gorm and his cronies would be on the watch. Instead, Dagfinn proposed they sail in daylight to the opposite side of Strand, trek overland, wait until nightfall and attack from the rear.

Though the rocky leeward side of the island provided few landing places, one of Reider's farms had a small dock they could use.

Kjartan was concerned that if their overland attack failed, they would have no means of escape by sea.

Reider rubbed his chin. "You are right, my friend, but I think Dagfinn's plan offers the best chance of success."

Kjartan scratched his head. "I agree. Every proposal has risks. I'll prepare the men."

Reider and Dagfinn shook hands, and his father's ally slapped him on the back. "The gods will favour us, Reider. We are fighting for justice and honour. Gorm has no honour. My commanders will ready our men. It is fitting we should help you regain your birthright."

Reider embraced his neighbour, swallowing the lump in his throat. "Thank you, my lord."

~~~

Reider and Kjartan were left with little to do while Dagfinn's men prepared the fleet. They and their crew were outfitted with armour and weapons. Reider was glad to have his hand on an axe once again. It was his favourite weapon but he was out of practice.

He and Kjartan had spent an hour in mock combat. Muscles Reider had not used for a while were already aching.

"How fortunate we are to have such an ally, Kjartan," he said as they paused for refreshment, marvelling at the number of boats and men Dagfinn had committed to the fight.

Kjartan sheathed the dagger, his weapon of choice. "Indeed, but he and your father were friends, as well as allies. He knows you would do the same for him if needs be."

Both men wiped the sweat from their brows and bare torsos, then resumed their practice.

It felt good to be engaged in hard physical exercise again. They had trained during their exile, but now there was purpose to it, a feeling it was real. Vengeance was within reach.

Though the prospect filled Reider with more determination than ever, something was missing. Would vengeance be enough? What then? Strand would need a strong ruler. Was he equal to the task? With Ragna he could be.

Preoccupied with this startling thought, he swung at Kjartan, but his friend nimbly sidestepped and Reider stumbled forward.

Kjartan sheathed his weapon and bent at the waist. He put his hands on his knees, catching his breath. "Your thoughts are elsewhere, my friend. I could have plunged my dagger to the hilt in your gut. Could it be you are thinking of Ragna?"

Reider opened his mouth to deny it, but Kjartan knew him too well. "She has crept into my thoughts a time or two," he conceded.

Kjartan grunted. "Hah! A time or two? You are besotted with the woman."

Reider took another practice swing with the axe. "Is it that obvious?"

Kjartan put his hands on his hips. "It pains me to say this, but Ragna has almost restored even my faith in women. She is a rare jewel. Forgive me, my Prince, but you would be a fool to drive her away."

~~~

Two days later, as the fleet approached Reider's remote farm, it seemed the gods were not on their side. The waters were choppy and the early morning rain came down in sheets. The dock was small. It had not been used for years and some of the timbers were rotten. One boat holed on the jagged rocks and the men aboard had to swim for shore in the chilly water. Two drowned, weighed down by their armour.

Each boat in turn disembarked its warriors at the dock, then anchored further out with a skeleton crew. Eventually three hundred tired men were safely landed, soaked to the skin. The sun came out and steam rose off their wet gear as they marched the mile to the farm. Once they had dried their weapons, they would rest until late afternoon then begin the trek to the Great Ringhouse.

Reider, Kjartan, Dagfinn and his commanders gathered in the tiny farmhouse, welcomed heartily by the tenant farmer and his wife and children.

Dagfinn chuckled, watching the farmer's wife bow and scrape as she scurried to provide her unexpected noble guests with refreshment. "They are proud you have chosen their little abode to launch your offensive."

"They are good tenants who take care of the land," Reider murmured, smiling as he too watched the farmer's five urchins, all miniatures of the very pregnant farmwife. He had never thought much about siring children, but now he felt a yearning to hold a child of his own, Ragna's child.

"They have naught good to say about Gorm's rule," Kjartan added.

They reviewed their plans, then settled down to rest. The farmer took his family off to the barn, insisting Reider sleep in his bed. The deer hide curtain provided some privacy to the little niche. He wiped the last of the rain from the lamellar cuirass Dagfinn had given him, stripped it off and flopped onto the pallet. Hands behind his head, he gazed up into the rafters, stretching his legs. The woodsy scent of the cooking fire smouldering in the hearth teased his nostrils.

No doubt the farmer and his wife made love quietly here so as not to wake their children. His *pik* stirred at the thought of Ragna. How he wished she was in his arms, here in this simple little house with its sturdy oaken timbers and planked walls, joining with him to make beautiful blonde babies.

He dozed fitfully for an hour or so, the task ahead weighing heavily on his mind. The clothing that had dried on his body earlier in the day felt stiff and uncomfortable. Impatient, he rose, put his armour back on, then went to find Kjartan. In short order the invading force was ready to begin the trek. At first the terrain was rocky and hilly, but levelled off as they approached the main village.

~~~

Twilight descended as Reider and Dagfinn's men dug into their hiding places just beyond the outlying ring houses.

Kjartan returned from scouting the area. "Gorm has no guards in place on this side of the village. He never did think past his nose."

Reider shrugged one shoulder, tightening his grip on the handle of his *stridsøkse,* running his finger lightly over the blade of the axe. "He'll regret that."

There was a sudden commotion. One of Dagfinn's men appeared, dragging a villager by the scruff of the neck. "We caught this wretch spying on us," he declared gruffly, throwing the peasant at Reider's feet.

The man turned fearful eyes to Reider, then came to his knees. "My lord Reider! Is it you? Praise be to our Lord Jesus Christ that you have come."

He touched his fingertips to his forehead and made the Sign of the Crucifixion across his body. "We have prayed for your return. Gorm is an agent of the devil who takes everything and gives nothing in return."

He quickly surveyed Reider's men crouched in the ditch. "You have many warriors to aid you, but be assured the villagers will also come to your aid. We may have only pitchforks and shovels, but we will fight for you. Your cause is righteous."

Reider put a hand on the man's shoulder. "What is your name?"

"Kristian, my prince."

Reider extended a hand. "Get off your knees, Kristian. I want you to scout the Great Hall and the dock. Find someone to help you if you wish. Come back with news of how many men we can expect, where Gorm is, anything you deem useful. Be careful. Do not give yourself away."

Kristian kissed Reider's hand, nodded and scrambled away.

Dagfinn's man bristled. "How do you know you can trust him? He may sound the alarm."

Reider shook his head. "Did you not hear his name and his oath? He is a Christian. Gorm has never embraced that religion and indeed has always done his best to make life difficult for its adherents. Our friend will be glad to see the last of Gorm."

Time passed slowly as they waited for Kristian's return. From the raucous noises that drifted to their ears from the village, it appeared drinking was already well underway in the main Ringhouse that housed the Great Hall. Reider gritted his teeth and stood to shake out the cramped muscles in his legs. Last time he had been in the Great Hall—

Kristian slid into the ditch, panting hard, wild-eyed. "The Usurper is not in the Great Hall. Roar Knutsen and the rest of the survivors of the rout at Husembro are there, drinking heavily and wenching."

Reider held up his hand, a chill marching up his spine. "Rout at Husembro?"

Kristian's head bobbed up and down with excitement. "Gorm sent a raiding force to attack you in Husembro, but they were routed by a large force of men. Few returned, many of them wounded."

A large force of men? Who had been at Husembro? Had some other wandering band of marauders taken Husembro and defended it against Gorm's men? He pressed his fingertips to his forehead. If anything had happened to Ragna—

Kjartan's voice broke into his thoughts. "What of the dock?"

"Just a few men, but they too have imbibed a quantity of ale."

Reider gripped his axe. "And Margit? Did she and Gorm marry?"

Kristian snorted and crossed himself again. "*Nej*! Gorm's fair consort is not in the Great Hall either. The two are rarely together. She looks at him with murder in her eyes."

Reider put his hand on Kristian's shoulder. "I owe you a great debt, Kristian. We will do all we can to restore justice to our homeland. Go now. Prepare your neighbours."

Kristian nodded and slipped away.

Reider turned to Kjartan and Dagfinn's man. "Pass the word. We will allow Kristian time to marshal the villagers. Watch for my signal to advance."

Reider stared at the moon, his thoughts still on Ragna. Was *Màni* watching over her as he made his way across the night sky? When the silver orb had moved what he judged to be a sufficient distance, Reider gave the signal and the invaders advanced through the village. Men armed with pitchforks, shovels, and scythes stole silently out of the small ringhouses and formed a rear guard.

To a man, the army paused, weapons raised, for Dagfinn to invoke Thor's blessings before he dispatched a contingent to the dock. The main body rushed to the Great Hall, weapons in hand, every man echoing Reider's hoarse battle cry.

"For Strand."

## CHAPTER EIGHTEEN

Fear gnawed at Gorm as he paced his chamber. Where was Reider? He had been confident that the raiding party he sent to Husembro would locate and kill his rival. Wherever his hated step-brother was, Gorm did not doubt he plotted revenge and must be disposed of before he convinced Dagfinn Alfredsen to join the conflict.

Thanks to Kjartan Eldarsen, Strand's legitimate heir had escaped. Gorm's inept henchmen had been incapable of carrying out an assassination. He had taken care of Torfinn, but his men had let Reider slip through their fingers. Margit had harangued him incessantly about it. The woman had such a bloodlust. It sickened him. He dared not fall asleep in her presence. How could he have believed her avowals of undying love?

Loud shouts interrupted his thoughts. He threw open the door and strode into the hallway. Sounds of conflict reached his ears from the Great Hall, yet there had been no alarm sounded from the docks. He gripped the hilt of his dagger and commanded his guards to accompany him.

When he reached the Hall, his question was finally answered. Reider, armed with a *stridsøkse,* fought with Roar Knutsen. The older man was flagging under the onslaught of Reider's axe. Gorm thought to turn and run. But to where? If Reider had not attacked by sea, he had come overland—no chance of escape there. Gorm had not foreseen the necessity of protecting his flank.

Dagfinn had indeed come to the aid of his old ally, bringing a large force with him. Gorm espied Kjartan Eldarsen retrieving a dagger from the body at his feet. Frustration choked him. Here was the source of many of his problems. He drew his own blade and rushed towards the man who had foiled his plans. Kjartan turned to face him and smirked, infuriating Gorm.

Suddenly, Reider was beside Kjartan. "He is mine, old friend."

Gorm swiveled his head. Roar's bloodied body lay slumped

against the wall. Reider was a formidable force with an axe, but Gorm would hold the advantage if he rattled his step-brother's temper, set him on edge. He returned his glare to Reider. "So, brother, it comes down to you and me."

To his dismay, Reider remained calm. "You are no brother of mine, Gorm. Do you intend to fight me alone, or will you need your guards to help you?"

Irritated, Gorm waved off his henchmen who were soon fending off other attackers. Reider and Gorm circled warily, assessing each other's weaknesses. Gorm wished he had thought to grab his axe.

~~~

Margit heard the commotion in the Great Hall. Reider had come and would seek to kill her. Dread filled her heart, but the conflict drew her like a moth to the flame. She crept into the Hall and pressed close to the rough wooden wall. Keeping to the shadows, she grasped the stolen dagger firmly behind her back. If she had to die on this godforsaken island, she would not die alone.

Reider's invading force had overwhelmed Gorm's men. Margit was not surprised, especially when she caught sight of a man she did not recognize, though from his bearing she knew he must be Dagfinn Alfredsen.

Kjartan Eldarsen and another man held everyone at bay as they watched Gorm and Reider engage in a battle to the death. She grunted involuntarily. Gorm had already slashed Reider's forearm.

The two warriors grappled. Reider held firm to the wrist of Gorm's dagger hand. Gorm's free hand was clamped over Reider's on the handle of the axe. Reider twisted his leg around Gorm's and her lover fell to the planked floor, but he rolled to his feet, dagger still in hand. Sweat poured from his furrowed brow. The crown had slipped sideways over his ear. Growling, he pushed it back. Margit could smell his fear.

Reider took a swipe with his axe, narrowly missing his step-brother's head. Gorm thrust with his dagger, but Reider stepped back nimbly.

To Margit's eyes, Reider looked different, more mature, calmer, though he faced a skilled warrior in Gorm. It would complicate matters, but she hoped Reider would triumph. He was the better man. She had grown to hate Gorm. He was weak.

Reider never took his eyes off Gorm's. He had the look of a

man confident of victory. He elbowed his opponent hard in the ribs, knocking him off balance. Gorm staggered to his knees, but recovered quickly.

The two men circled again. Gorm lunged, but Reider stepped aside and Gorm stumbled forward. Reider whirled and struck his step-brother on the back of the head with the heel of his axe. Gorm yelped in pain, but remained on his feet, swaying slightly. He glared at Reider and spat.

Reider licked his thumb and drew it down the blade of his axe, a glint in his eye. Gorm hunched his shoulders and wiped the sweat from his brow with the back of his hand. The ill-fitting crown fell to the floor and rolled to rest at Reider's feet.

Reider smiled. Desire coiled in Margit's core. What a fool she had been. She tightened her grip on the dagger. Might there be a way to save herself? She lunged forward out of the shadows and buried the weapon to the hilt in Gorm's back. Blood spurted from his mouth and he fell like a giant tree hewn by the woodcutters, dead at Reider's feet.

~~~

Reider stared in bewilderment at the dagger in Gorm's back, incensed the traitor had not died at his hand. Had Margit truly killed him? Did the treachery of this woman know no bounds? The look of wide-eyed disbelief on Gorm's face brought to mind how astonished Reider must have looked the night of the massacre. But the most difficult thing to comprehend was how Ragna's dagger came to be lodged in Gorm's back. Reider's heart lurched. Ragna would not have parted with the dagger willingly.

Kjartan grabbed Margit and pulled her away, kicking and screaming. Reider drew the dagger from Gorm's body, wiped it on his step-brother's tunic and examined it carefully. Kjartan gave the screeching Margit over to two comrades and strode to Reider's side. "Is it Ragna's?"

Reider shook his head, the cold certainty seeping into his belly that he had left Ragna vulnerable at Husembro. Was she dead? Loss and loneliness swept over him. "Can it be your cousin's?"

Kjartan examined the hilt carefully. "*Nej*, it's Ragna's."

Reider walked over to Margit, determined to hold on to his temper, despite the dread rising in his throat. What role had this treacherous bitch played in Ragna's demise? He brandished the dagger under her nose. "Where did you get this?"

She struggled to be free of the grip of his comrades. "Reider, forgive me. I was a fool. It is you I love." He tucked Ragna's precious possession into his belt and fisted his hands, resisting the urge to strike Margit across the face. This creature knew nothing of love. "What have you done with the woman the dagger belongs to?"

~~~

Recognition of the truth dawned. Now Margit understood the new Reider. He loved another—the blonde woman from whom Roar had stolen the dagger. She shoved her hair back out of her eyes and folded her arms across her breasts. Her belly burned. "She is safe."

Reider took hold of her shoulders and shook her. "Where is she?"

Margit gritted her teeth. "Instruct these fools to release me and I will tell you."

Reider nodded to the men. Margit rubbed her upper arms and looked coyly at Reider. "The woman you seek will be released, unharmed—on one condition."

Reider scoffed. "You are in no position to bargain, Margit."

Margit laughed. The fire had spread to her chest. "Oh, but I am. What is this woman to you, Reider? You seem concerned. Her life is in my hands. One word from me—"

Reider glared at her. "You sicken me, Margit. What is it you want?"

She looked him straight in the eye. "To be your wife."

Reider's mouth fell open and he looked at her with such hatred she feared he might kill her on the spot. Would her gamble pay off?

Reider pointed to Gorm's body. "Any man married to you would never sleep, Margit. You might stab him in the back."

She sidled up to him, putting her hand on his arm. "I would never dream of killing a man who kept me satisfied. You can be that man."

He cringed and pulled away. "Take this woman to a cell. Be careful with her. She is dangerous and cunning."

Margit grasped his arm again. "Surely you will not imprison your betrothed?"

He shrugged her off. "Take her."

She remained defiant as they dragged her away. "Remember, one word from me—"

## CHAPTER NINETEEN

Her unease growing, Ragna sat on a flat rock near the docks and watched Captain Ivar's men prepare the *knarr* for the return journey to Hamburg. Thor's muzzle rested on her knee. She stroked the loyal dog's back dispiritedly. The other survivors were in high spirits, looking forward to getting back to their lives before the shipwreck. Dieter was buoyant, obviously relieved to be taking Blythe's sister to safety.

Why did she feel bereft? She had lost the treasured dagger, for which she would never forgive herself. But something else tugged at her. She looked over to the Danish longboats where Reider's comrades were loading their own provisions in preparation for the voyage home. They planned to follow Reider to the principality of their ally and hopefully from there to Strand. If Reider's attack had been unsuccessful, they would do what they could. If it had succeeded, they would be happy to return to the only home they had known.

Had Reider regained his rightful place as ruler of his people? Did he ever think of her?

What ailed her? A boat stood ready to deliver her to her anxious sister. She would be free, safe in the hands of a skilled captain and a worthy brother-by-marriage. Yet she could not be rid of the conviction that she should be going in the other direction—to Strand. Reider needed her.

It was folly. He had uttered no words of love, had asserted there was no room in his heart for love. They had exchanged headbands—what kind of love token was that?

*Love?* Did she love this exiled Viking prince? Was she meant to be his princess? She took off the braided headband and inhaled the scent of his maleness and the salty smell of the sea. She caressed the inside with the pad of her thumb.

Dieter strode up from the shore, beaming, holding out his hand.

"Are you ready?"

She rubbed Thor's ears, came to her feet and took a deep breath. "I cannot go with you, Dieter. I'm sorry."

He stopped abruptly, his grin turning to a frown. "I do not understand. You want to remain here?"

She took hold of his hands, but looked at her feet. "No, Dieter. I must go to Reider's aid."

He squeezed her hands and smiled. "Ah! Now I understand! The Viking princess is in love."

She glared at him, annoyed at his jest, but he was serious. "I cannot explain it, Dieter, and it makes me angry to admit it, but I must go to him."

Dieter put his arm around her shoulder. "You have always charted a bolder course, Ragna. You do not need to explain it to me. I am the man who kidnapped your sister more or less by mistake, then refused to give her up. I knew she was meant to be mine, and look at us now! Married ten years, with three children, four if you count my son by my first marriage."

She clasped his hand. "Thank you, Dieter. I will go with the Danes. Tell Blythe I am sorry."

Dieter put his hands on her shoulders. "Ragna, if you think I will allow you to go to Strand alone, you are mistaken. My men and I will accompany you, and it won't take much persuasion for Captain Ivar to come with us. He has expressed great anger at what happened to Reider's father, for whom he had great respect. I will speak with him."

~~~

The *knarr* and the longboats set sail the next day. Ivar and his men had been eager to go. Ragna's fellow survivors had balked. They wanted to return home. Strangely enough it was Captain Philion who had changed their minds. "We owe our lives to Reider Torfinnsen and Kjartan Eldarsen. We would be dead men if it were not for them."

"But they enslaved us," the young mercenary protested.

"You are free men again, thanks to Ragna FitzRam. Will you turn your back on her now?"

Ivar had suggested the naysayers remain at Husembro and wait to be picked up on the return journey, but in the end they had agreed to sail together.

They followed the Danes to Dagfinn's territory. As luck would have it, they put into the jetty as Dagfinn was returning home. Ragna caught sight of Kjartan aboard one of the incoming longboats. Where was Reider? Dread pooled in the pit of her belly. She waved and called Kjartan's name. He jerked up his head and raised his hand to shield his eyes. He seemed surprised to see her, and raised both arms to wave back.

When the boats were moored he ran along the dock and threw his arms around her. "Ragna! You're safe! We were on our way to Husembro to see how you fared."

Thor barked his pleasure at Kjartan's arrival, wagging his tail.

Kjartan squeezed Ragna tightly. She could barely breathe. "It's good you are pleased to see me, but—"

He released her and laughed, but a frown creased his brow. "Pleased! You have no idea. I've much to tell you."

He knelt to pet Thor who rolled over on his back, tongue lolling, legs in the air. Kjartan rubbed his belly.

Dieter and Dagfinn had both hastened to the jetty where she and Kjartan stood and introductions were made and explanations shared. As the men shook hands and Dagfinn formally welcomed the visitors to his land, Ragna tapped her foot impatiently. "Where is Reider?"

Kjartan put his hands on her shoulders. "He is well. He has regained the principality for us, with Dagfinn's help. Gorm is dead. Margit killed him"

This did not make sense. "But I thought—"

Kjartan looked away. "She is a devious woman."

She narrowed her eyes. "*Is*? She still lives?"

Kjartan hesitated, scratching his cheek. "*Ja!* And in one week, she and Reider are supposed to wed."

Dieter came to Ragna's aid as her knees buckled. He grasped her elbow and put an arm around her shoulders. "I have you, sister. Don't assume the worst."

Anger boiled in her heart, the heart she had been ready to give to Reider. Now he was promised to the treacherous woman who had betrayed him. "Obviously, Dieter, Prince Reider does not need our help. It was a mistake to come here. On the morrow we'll sail for Hamburg."

Kjartan held up both hands. "Wait! You do not understand, Ragna. He consented to marry her because he believed she held you captive."

Ragna frowned. "Me?"

Kjartan took a deep breath and proffered his hand. "Where to begin the tale? Come, sit with me in the Hall and I will tell it to you."

~~~

That Ragna was a cousin, albeit far removed, elated Kjartan. That she had decided to come to Reider's aid instead of sailing safely to Hamburg filled him with happiness for his friend. But Margit's lies held Reider in her web. He had feigned a willingness to wed the treacherous schemer if he thought it would save Ragna's life. Ragna was a determined young woman, known for her stubbornness. It was important she understand Reider's decision. Kjartan bade her sit, but she refused.

"Margit killed Gorm with your dagger."

Ragna gasped. "I don't understand. How did she get it? It was stolen from me by one of the men who attacked us at Husembro."

Kjartan looked at Dieter for an explanation. "We repelled them easily. They were probably not expecting a large force. The burly giant who stole Ragna's dagger swam out to reach the escaping longboat, after Thor bit his leg. We assumed he drowned."

"Evidently not. It may have been Roar Knutsen. Reider wounded him in the battle, but he looked as though he had been in a recent fight, limping badly. He may not survive. Margit already had the dagger. She killed Gorm and threw herself on Reider's mercy. Upon seeing his reaction to the dagger, she must have realized how much he cared for you. Roar may have been the one to reveal your existence. Margit used Reider's concern to her advantage, leading us to believe she had you imprisoned and held sway over your life."

Ragna chewed her nails, something he had never seen her do before. "Reider was concerned for me?"

Kjartan took her hand. "What Reider feels for you is more than concern."

Ragna slumped into a chair. "But he is to wed Margit."

"He will not wed her if he knows you are safe."

She came to her feet. "Then we have no time to waste."

Kjartan chuckled. "Ragna, you are the perfect mate for Reider. But there is more I need to tell you. Sit down. You will not believe the next part."

Ragna pouted, and sat huffily. He beckoned to a young woman

seated at a table near them. She came to her feet and approached them, holding a bundle, which she placed in front of Ragna. Ragna frowned and looked inquiringly at Kjartan. "Open it," he said.

She squared her shoulders and opened the cloth wrapping, gasping at the object she beheld. "My dagger—wait—no, it isn't mine! But it looks—" She glanced up sharply at Kjartan.

He put his hand on the girl's shoulder. "Ragna, may I present my cousin, Dagfrid. This dagger is hers."

Ragna's frown showed her confusion. "But it is identical to mine. It's as if the same person carved the hilt."

He held out his hand. "Exactly, cousin."

Dieter interrupted. "You mean to say the same person did carve them? That you and Dagfrid and Ragna share an ancestor?"

Kjartan did not expect to be emotional, but as he took hold of Ragna's hands, he choked on the lump in his throat. "Ragna, I believe, four generations ago, we shared a grandfather."

Ragna sat open-mouthed, running her fingers over the carving of the Viking. She looked from Dieter, nodding with an amused look on his face, to Dagfrid, beaming a big smile, to Kjartan. Then she too smiled broadly and leapt into Kjartan's arms. "This is wonderful. We knew our roots on my mother's side were Danish, but I never expected to meet any of my relatives. When I set sail, I did not intend to visit Denmark."

Kjartan hugged her. "Fate sometimes has a way of making things happen that we do not plan."

Dieter pumped Kjartan's hand. "I suppose we are vaguely related too! I am married to Ragna's sister, Blythe."

Ragna turned to Dagfrid and embraced her. "Cousin," she rasped.

Wiping away tears, she asked Kjartan, "But where is my dagger now?"

"Reider keeps it with him."

## CHAPTER TWENTY

While he waited for the guards to bring Margit from her cell, Reider settled into his father's throne and brooded, his hand resting on the hilt of Ragna's dagger. He seethed with dread, longing to hold Ragna and be assured of her safety, frustrated by his feeling of powerlessness.

In the custody of two of his men, Margit burst into the Hall, dishevelled, dirty, and toweringly furious. The stink of the gaol clung to her. "This is no way to treat the woman you are to wed, Reider Torfinnsen."

Reider tightened his grip on the dagger, itching to thrust it into Margit's heart. Did she indeed hold Ragna captive, or was it a ploy to manipulate him? He dare not take a chance with Ragna's life. If Roar Knutsen survived his wounds and the fever that ravaged him, Reider might extract the truth. Margit was unaware that Roar still lived.

Reider missed Kjartan's counsel, but it had been imperative that his friend go to Husembro to determine what had happened there. He had to be wary with Margit, had to make her believe he would indeed marry her. His heart belonged to another, a woman who might never give herself over to a man, but he knew he would not live long if he wed Margit.

He forced a smile. "Are the guards not taking adequate care of you, Margit? Do you not have food, and warmth?"

She sneered at him, scratching her head as though it itched unbearably. "You will free me now, or the woman will die."

The frenzied glint in her eye gave him pause. Margit's thirst for power had pushed her into madness. He would need to be wary. "If you kill her, you and I will never wed. What assurances do I have that you will not murder her after you and I are married?"

She sidled up to the throne, and put her hands on his thighs, leaning forward to emphasize her cleavage. "I give you my word."

.der snorted and removed her hands. "The word of a woman ıas betrayed every man who ever trusted her? I will not agree ɦe ceremony unless you guarantee her freedom."

Margit put her hands on her hips and paced. "Hah! Then you will kill me and turn to her."

Reider shook his head. He would not take the life of this pathetic creature, but neither would he allow her to harm another soul. "I give you my word not to have you executed. You know me as a man who honours his promises. Now, what is my guarantee?"

She glared at him.

Would she relent?

He returned her stare.

Margit thrust out her chin. "I cannot reveal where she is."

He leapt to his feet and strode over to her, anger and frustration rising in his throat, his nose inches from hers. "Because you do not have her. You are lying."

She spat in his face.

Disgust rose in his throat. He wiped his cheek and ordered the guards to take her away. She screamed obscenities as they dragged her out.

His innards in knots, Reider went to see if Roar still lived.

~~~

The giant's fever had left him, but he lay rigid on his pallet. His eyes were closed, his pallor ashen. The thrall who tended him, one of his concubines, shook her head. Roar was dying.

"Has he spoken?"

She kept her eyes downcast. "A few words."

"What did he say?"

"He is in pain, my lord prince. His words make no sense."

Reider looked at the once-mighty warrior. Had this brute slain Ragna? Or imprisoned her? He had to know. He turned to the thrall. "Leave us!"

She bowed and obeyed at once.

He leaned close to Roar's ear and whispered his name.

The giant's eyes flickered open.

"You know who I am, Roar?"

The giant nodded. "My lord Reider," he rasped.

"You are dying, Roar."

Knutsen nodded and swallowed hard.

"Will you enter Valhalla, Roar, or will the guilt of your misdeeds consign you to *Hel?*"

Roar's eyes opened wide. "My lord Reider, I regret my part in your father's murder. It was a mistake to support Gorm. I beg your forgiveness."

Reider grasped Roar's cold hand. "I accept your confession."

The tension eased out of Roar's body. Reider watched him for a short while, then put his hand on the man's festering shoulder and pressed gently. "You are not free yet, Roar. What have you done with the blonde woman from Husembro?"

Roar winced. "Blonde? Nothing! I swear. I took her dagger, but I did not kill her."

"You left her there?"

The giant licked his lips, breathing hard. "I had to escape. Her vicious hound sank its teeth in my leg. I do not know what happened to her."

Reider smirked. Thor, a vicious hound? The plucky dog had evidently saved Ragna. He eased the pressure on Roar's shoulder. "And you gave her dagger to Margit?"

Roar snorted. "Not willingly."

Reider gave the dying man ale to sip, holding it to his parched lips. "Is there anything else you wish to tell me?"

Roar clutched Reider's hand. "You will be a good ruler, my prince."

They were his last words.

## CHAPTER TWENTY-ONE

"Strand ahead!" Ivar shouted from the prow, Thor barking at his side. The Danes in the accompanying longboats yelled in jubilation and lifted their hands in salute. The noise caught the attention of men on the beach, who waved back.

Ragna gripped the side of the *knarr* with one hand. Dieter held the other. He kept silent, for which she was grateful. She had always been strong, but now she worried she would cry like a baby if Reider had indeed wed Margit. Perhaps it was fanciful to believe he cared for her, a wilful Englishwoman. A Danish prince would no doubt be expected to marry into another powerful Danish family.

The beauty of Reider's homeland took her breath away. To one side the land was completely flat and green as far as the eye could see. Sheep dotted the landscape. To the other, the beach soon rose to become grass-tufted dunes. Beyond loomed soft blue hills, dotted with forests and farms. Her fur hood slipped to her shoulders and the wind whipped her hair over her face. She loosed her grip on the rough wood to smooth it back. Fingering the braided headband, she tossed her head and looked back to the beach.

Reider stood on the shore, legs braced. His hand was raised in a welcoming salute, his long hair flying free in the breeze, her headband around his forehead.

He had come to greet her! Her breasts tingled and she stifled the urge to giggle like a child, feeling her face redden. What would Dieter think? Her brother-by-marriage squeezed her hand. She looked up at him. He was smiling. She returned the smile and raised her hand to wave to the man waiting for her.

As the *knarr* came into shore, Reider waded out into the shallows, arms outstretched. Her dagger was tucked into his belt. She laughed, climbed onto the side and leapt into his arms. "My

Viking beckons again and I can do naught but jump into his welcoming embrace."

He too laughed and staggered backwards when Thor leapt from the boat. Reider cradled her, carrying them to the shore. "Must I always be saving you and your hound from the sea?"

She reached up to finger the headband, then put her palm to the side of his face. "I seem compelled to leap into your arms, Reider."

Once they reached the beach, Thor jumped from her lap, wagging his tail furiously. Reider set her back on her feet, put his hands on her waist and pressed her to his body. "You came to me," he rasped, then kissed her with a hungry intensity.

She felt his hard male length against her belly and her heartbeat pulsed between her legs. Kjartan and Dieter had both disembarked from their vessels and they led the good natured cheering. Ragna had forgotten she and Reider were not alone.

~~~

Reider made a mock bow to his audience, and offered Ragna his arm. She introduced him to Dieter and told of his role in her rescue. Everyone walked in the direction of the Great Hall, but Reider pulled her aside and escorted her to his private lodge.

She had followed him to Strand! He had recognised Ivar's boat as one that could have carried her to safety, but she had chosen to come to him.

Kjartan was right. He would be a fool to let her go. He kissed her again, inhaling the spicy scent he had missed. Ragna aroused him like no woman before. His heart had skipped a beat when he realized she was aboard the incoming boat. The moment the wind had whipped her hair over her face, his *pik* had turned to granite. He coaxed her lips with his tongue. "Open for me, Ragna," he whispered.

She parted her lips and he delved his tongue deep inside the warmth of her mouth. She tasted salty. Jealousy had surged in him at the sight of her holding another man's hand on the boat. He cupped her bottom and ran his tongue over her teeth. The deep groan that emerged from her throat betrayed her longing. She had ached for him as he had ached for her. Did his *prinsessen* love him?

Suddenly, she pulled away, pushing her hands against his chest, pouting. "You said you would come back for me, Reider, but I have been forced to search you out. You left me at the mercy of your step-brother's men. Had it not been for Dieter and Ivar—"

*Life with Ragna will never be dull!*

He put his forefinger to her lips. "I know. In hindsight, I should have taken you to Dagfinn, but my desire for revenge and justice clouded my thoughts. I doubted everyone. Forgive me. When I was told of the battle at Husembro, my heart broke."

She frowned. "Your heart? You have no room in your heart for me. You told me so."

He put his hands over hers. "After Margit's betrayal I thought never to trust a woman again. Anger consumed me. That was before I met you. You are direct and forthright, and you inflame me as no woman ever has. I would trust you with my life, and my heart."

She blinked and inhaled sharply. "You would entrust your heart to me?"

He pressed her hand against his chest. "I already have. Can you not feel it beating for you? I want you to be my wife, Ragna, my *prinsessen*. It isn't the life you've been used to, but—"

Now she put a silencing finger to his lips. "But what of Margit? Kjartan told me you were supposed to marry her."

"I wanted her to believe that, because I didn't know if she had captured you. I had to ensure your safety, but I would never have married her. It's you I love."

"You love me? How can you love me? I am stubborn, and wilful, everyone says so. You will think this amusing, but my family has always called me their Wild Viking Princess."

He was convinced then that Fate had brought this incredible woman to his side. "It is obvious to me you were destined to be mine. You truly are a Viking, of Kjartan's lineage, and you will rule with me as my *prinsessen*. It's fitting I called you by that name from the moment I met you. Be my bride, Ragna. I want to live my life with you."

~~~

From the tips of her toes to the top of her head, Ragna's body burned for the man who stood before her. Agneta FitzRam had been right. Love conquered all. If someone had foretold that Ragna would marry a Danish prince who ruled a remote principality on the shores of the North Sea, she would have laughed in their face. Where was the excitement in that? Now she knew it was where she wanted to be, where she had to be.

"I wish my mother and father had met you, Reider. My mother often told me I would know when I met my soul mate. She was right. When you beckoned me to jump into the sea, I obeyed without thinking. My heart knew you were my destiny."

Reider cradled her face in his hands. "You will marry me?"

She put her hands over his and smiled. "My parents would have approved of you, and I am confident my brother-by-marriage will give his consent on behalf of my older brother, Aidan."

Then she winked at him. "But I would have said yes anyway, with or without their approval. I love you, Reider Torfinnsen."

~~~

Reider whooped loudly, scooped her up and strode to the Great Hall, where a large crowd had assembled. Kjartan was introducing Dieter to everyone, and Ivar was renewing old acquaintances. Heads turned when Reider kicked open the door. "People of Strand, greet your future *Prinsessen*. Ragna FitzRam is to be my wife."

A moment of utter silence ensued. A lump stuck in her throat. They disapproved of his marrying a foreigner. Then a rousing cheer went up and she breathed a sigh of relief. They spent the next hour accepting hugs and handshakes of congratulations.

At length, Ragna got a chance to speak privately with Dieter. "I am sorry Reider made the announcement without consulting you, Dieter. I suppose my visit to Blythe will have to wait a little longer."

He shrugged and kissed her forehead. "Be truthful, Ragna, my opinion would have made no difference. But for what it's worth, I approve. And you won't be too far away from Wolfenberg here in Strand. No treacherous sea crossing; just a short cruise to Hamburg, and then overland."

She hugged him. "Thank you, Dieter. No wonder Blythe loves you. And thank you for coming to my rescue. Just one more favour."

He arched his brows. "Of course."

"I'll be writing to Aidan, to explain. Perhaps a letter from you would help reassure him?"

Dieter chuckled. "It would be my pleasure. He'll have a difficult time believing the story."

Ragna laughed. "But he'll be excited to hear of our Danish ancestors. I plan to learn of Kjartan's family's history."

Reider joined them and put his arm possessively around Ragna's shoulders. "I apologise, Count Dieter, that I have not welcomed you properly to our lands, and thanked you for saving Ragna's life. I hope you will stay for our wedding."

Ragna clapped her hands together. "Yes, please stay, Dieter, then you can tell Blythe."

Dieter shook Reider's hand. "Of course I will stay, and let's dispense with my title. We will soon be brothers-by-marriage."

Ragna liked the sound of that. Pride in her future husband filled her heart.

## CHAPTER TWENTY-TWO

Reider took Ragna's hand. How to explain what must be done before they could be married? "Ragna, if I had my way, you and I would marry today. But Kjartan has discovered that my father was hastily buried in an ordinary grave, like a mere thrall. He will not find peace in the afterlife until he is honoured with the proper burial rites. He will wander as a *draugr*."

Ragna frowned and looked to Dieter who explained, "A revenant."

She shivered and nodded her understanding.

Reider continued. "I cannot be recognised as the rightful heir until my father's spirit is laid to rest. I must drink the *sjaund*."

Ragna again looked to Dieter for help. "The funeral ale."

She squeezed Reider's hands in reassurance. "Of course, I understand. My parents' bodies were never found after they drowned. It was my father's wish to be buried in the crypt at Montbryce Castle in Normandie alongside his father. I have often worried that their souls wander somewhere, searching—"

He embraced her, relieved she understood. "Thank you for understanding."

But he worried about other traditions he must follow that she might not be willing to accept. She had strong opinions concerning thralls, but he owned many, as befitted his rank. He had lain with more than one of the female slaves to alleviate his male needs. It was their purpose, but he had never spilled his seed inside any of them. He did not want to sire bastards who would be born into slavery. He dreaded telling Ragna about his slaves. Better sooner than later.

He looked Dieter in the eyes and gave him an unmistakable signal. The Saxon nodded and took his leave.

~~~

Reider drew Ragna over to a bench in a quiet corner and pulled her onto his lap. "Ragna, you and I are from different places. I have been to your country, but you know little of mine. We have different ways of doing things, different beliefs. I hope those differences will not come between us. You are a woman of strong opinions."

Ragna clutched his hand and gazed at it, brushing her thumb over his knuckles. "I share your fears, Reider. I have never been known for my tolerance of things I disagree with."

Reider moved his legs to change her position. The pressure of her bottom on his *pik* had produced the inevitable result. She must be aware of it. "Your strong-mindedness is one of the things that draws me to you. But there are some things about being a Dane I cannot change."

She turned in his lap and put her hands around his neck. "Such as?"

The ache in his loins intensified each time she moved. "Ragna, in England and Normandie, your great lords have *coloni*. What is their role in life?"

She looked at him curiously. "To serve their master. They are bondservants."

He took a deep breath. "You did not hesitate to answer, yet are they not the same as the thralls who serve us? Your *coloni* are not free to come and go anywhere they please, are they? Neither are our thralls."

He felt her tense. "But a *colonus* is given land to work, protection, and access to justice."

He tightened his grip on her waist. "But whose land, whose justice? He is bound to his lord, is he not? And he must work his lord's land before his own."

She squirmed in his lap, obviously uncomfortable, as was he. "But a bondservant works for all, his master fights for all, and priests pray for all. Each man has his role. A lord cannot sell his bondservants."

Reider glanced around the Hall as the sounds of jovial voices reached his ears. Dieter appeared engrossed in a conversation with Ivar, but his eyes kept drifting in their direction. Reider could not blame the Saxon for his concern for his sister-by-marriage, and he feared this discussion might turn into an argument, but had to persist. "Does Kirkthwaite Hall have bondservants?"

Ragna shook her head vigorously. "No, Aidan is not a great

baron, just a knight. We have tenant farmers who farm our land."

"We too have freedmen who tend farms, but we have thralls who are not free. Some are born into thralldom, others captured—"

"Or rescued," she interrupted angrily.

Reider took a deep breath. "You say bondservants cannot be sold, but if an English lord sells some land, the bondservants must go to a new master, *ja?*"

She got off his lap and sat beside him, tapping her foot. Not a good sign. "If one of your bondservants in England has a child, is the child free?"

She pouted and shook her head.

Dare he go further? "Ragna, if you were a bondservant, would you be free to marry any man of your choosing?"

She looked at her feet. "No."

He held her hand tenderly. "The same is true of our thralls."

Suddenly, she glared up at him. "Do you have thralls?"

This was the moment he had dreaded. "It is my right as the Prince of Strand to own thralls."

Ragna jumped to her feet. He held on to her hand. Dieter had turned to face them, no longer hiding his interest. "Do not judge me, Ragna. You either love me for what I am, or not."

She sat back down, but did not look at him. "What do these thralls of yours do for you?"

Reider touched his fingers to her chin. "Look at me, Ragna. My thralls see to my needs. They feed me, clothe me, bathe me, labour in my fields, my forests. In return I feed them, clothe them, protect them. Most of my thralls were born into slavery, second and third generation descendants of prisoners of war plundered ages ago. They have known no other life. I treat them well. They serve me in whatever way I need them."

Understanding dawned in her eyes and her mouth fell open. "You are trying to tell me you have lain with some of your thralls?"

He clenched his jaw and prayed for her trust. "I am a man, Ragna, with a man's needs. But I have never sired bastards with any of my thralls. I have made sure of it."

A tear trickled down her cheek. "But how can I live with these women you have bedded?"

He took a deep breath. "Ragna, they will be honoured to be your slaves. I am fond of them, but it is you I love. They take great pride in having bedded the son of the king, but they will not think less of you because of it. Did you think I come to our marriage a virgin? Was Aidan a virgin when he wed, or Dieter when he married Blythe? It does not mean I love you less. It means I've learned how to please a woman. Is it not what you want?"

She came to her feet slowly, still not willing to look at him. "I need time to consider what you have told me, Reider."

He stood with her. Dread had settled in the pit of his stomach. Had he lost her? He struggled to keep his voice steady. "We have time. It will take a few days to prepare for my father's funeral."

He hesitated, afraid that what he must tell her next might alienate her forever. "My father will take his favourite thrall with him into the afterlife."

She frowned. "I do not understand."

He cradled her head in his hands, brushing his thumbs along her headband, willing her to look at him. "When my father was murdered, Gorm took his thralls. They resented serving a man who was not their rightful lord. One in particular, my father's favourite, Sigrun, was bereft, and tried to take her life. She loved my father and does not wish to serve another. She wants her life to end. It is a great honour to accompany a chieftain on his death voyage."

Ragna frowned and finally raised her eyes to look at him. The colour drained from her face. "She will be killed?"

"It's what she wants."

Ragna gasped and tore away, a hand clamped over her mouth. "I am going to be sick."

# CHAPTER TWENTY-THREE

Elaborate preparations for the funeral progressed, but Ragna stewed in a fog. She saw little of Reider and Kjartan and spent most of her time wandering along the beach, glad of Thor's company. Often Dieter joined her.

They watched the construction of the stone ship on a headland overlooking the sea. Reider had explained it was his father's favourite place in all his lands. Thralls used shovels to cut the outline of a ship into the earth, then embedded large chunks of rock into the ground. At either end of the ship they erected a stone as tall as a man. It took ten thralls to wrestle each one into place.

In the centre of the ship they built a square wooden shelter. Ragna asked Dieter about it.

"The central structure is the death house, the bier where they will place Reider's father. It will be his funeral pyre."

She shivered. "They will burn his body?"

"*Ja*! The Danes believe the smoke carries the soul to Valhalla. The more smoke, the better the chances Torfinn will reach the end of his journey quickly."

A heavy certainty crept into Ragna's thoughts. "But what of Sigrun?"

Dieter took her hand. "She will lie on the funeral pyre and journey with him."

Bile rose in Ragna's throat again. She dreaded the question she must ask. "Surely they will not burn her alive?"

Dieter's face was solemn, but he kept a firm grip on her hand. "Such used to be the tradition, but it is more likely Reider will make sure she is dead before they light the pyre."

Revulsion shuddered through her and she shook her head. "I cannot live among these people, Dieter. They are barbaric."

Dieter remained silent for a long while as they walked hand in hand. He stooped to pick up a stick and threw it into the water for

Thor to retrieve. They watched the dog plunge into the waves then paddle towards the floating stick.

Dieter turned to look at her, his expression serious. "Ragna, you forget that you are part of this heritage. Vikings have held these beliefs for hundreds of years. Your grandfather four generations ago, the man who carved your beloved dagger, would have accepted these traditions without question.

"He probably took several thralls with him when he was cremated. Because customs are different from the ones you have grown up with does not make them barbaric. Is it not true that William the Conqueror inflicted acts of great barbarity on the Saxon people of England, yet your own grandfather, Ram de Montbryce, fought for him, would have willingly given his life for his Conqueror?"

Ragna nodded mutely. Dieter spoke the truth, but could she live with a man whose customs repelled her?

Thor returned with the stick grasped firmly in his teeth, then dropped it and shook vigorously, showering them with water. She squealed and they both laughed as Dieter picked up the stick to throw it again. "He will probably expect me to do this all day long!"

Ragna took a deep breath. "He will." It felt good to laugh, if only for a moment. She was supposed to be preparing for her wedding. Why did she feel unhappy? Perhaps she was too stubborn and opinionated to change her ideas for a man, even one she loved. Could she have been too hasty in accepting his proposal?

~~~

Torfinn's weapons were gathered, along with his clothing and symbols of kingship. Thralls sewed fine funeral robes for Torfinn and Sigrun. Dry wood was stacked against the sides of the death house.

Reider arranged for Torfinn's grave to be opened, and he returned to the Ringhouse grim-faced after witnessing the task. He said nothing when she took his hand and pressed it to her lips. He strode away quickly, leaving her feeling bereft and useless.

The next day she wandered out to sit on a log on the beach, transfixed by the gaunt sight of the stone ship. She heard footsteps behind her and knew when she turned she would see Reider. His face was grim, his jaw clenched. "All is in readiness. The funeral will be this afternoon, before the sun goes down."

She bit her bottom lip and turned away. Anguish was written in every line of his face and in the stiffness of his body. She wanted to comfort him, but still struggled with what was to happen.

His hoarse voice broke into her thoughts. "You must prepare, Ragna. It is expected for you to attend. You are my betrothed."

She shook her head, tears welling as a lump rose in her throat.

He put his hands on her shoulders. "If this was your father's funeral, I would be there for you."

She gasped, guilt sweeping through her. As usual, she had been too caught up in her own point of view. She came to her feet, but he had already left, striding away. She called his name, but the wind stole her voice. Thor barked, but Reider did not turn around.

She sank back onto the log and sobbed. Thor licked away her tears, and she hugged him. "Thor, I love Reider. I cannot bear the thought of life without him. But somewhere within myself I fear I will have to summon the strength to walk away."

## CHAPTER TWENTY-FOUR

The sea still held Ragna's gaze when she heard footsteps behind her again. Disappointment surged when she heard Kjartan's voice raised in greeting. "Cousin."

Coming to her feet, she sniffled and wiped a sleeve across her eyes, returning his greeting. "Cousin."

"You have been weeping?"

She nodded mutely, still staring out to sea.

He came to stand beside her. "Ragna, the same blood runs in our veins. Our lives have been different. You have your beliefs and Reider and I have ours, but we have many things in common. The manner of your parents' deaths broke your heart. The same is true for Reider. You honour the memory of your parents. Reider seeks to do the same. Can you not understand that?"

She fisted her hands and turned to face him. "Of course I can. But I cannot understand how he can allow a woman to be murdered and tossed onto a funeral pyre."

He put his finger under her chin and tilted her face to look up at him. "Ragna, not only will he allow it, he will be the one to make sure she is dead before the fire is lit. He will make it quick and painless. It is his right."

Ragna gasped and narrowed her eyes, her head pounding. "His right? It's *too much*."

Anger tinged his voice. "Perhaps you have *too much* of the Dane in you. You are too set in your opinions. Why not speak with the woman whose chosen fate you condemn?"

He turned to walk away, but then returned to her side. "If you do not attend the funeral, it will mean the end of your betrothal. Reider could never hold his head high again if he wed you. Will you come with me now to meet Sigrun? I am begging for my friend's sake. If you leave him, you will break his heart."

~~~

Ragna hesitated outside the lodge where Sigrun prepared for the funeral. Kjartan took hold of Thor's collar and pushed the hound to a thrall. "He will take care of your dog." He put his hand on the small of her back and eased her inside.

To her surprise, Sigrun rose to greet her. The slave was dressed in a beautifully embroidered red gown. She was tall and willowy, and looked—serene. She held out both hands to Ragna. "Welcome, thank you for coming. It is a great honour."

Kjartan translated her words. Ragna tried to speak, but the right words would not emerge. She closed her gaping mouth, then rasped, "You are beautiful, Sigrun."

The thrall blushed and bowed. "I want to be beautiful for Torfinn. Kjartan told me you do not understand why I wish to do this?"

Ragna shook her head and averted her gaze from this woman who would die this afternoon, at Reider's hand. She pressed her lips together and wiped her suddenly sweaty palms on her dress.

"Torfinn was my master, but I loved him and he loved me, in his own way. He married two wives, Reider's mother and Gorm's mother. He cared for them both, though he was not Gorm's father. He could never have married a thrall, no matter how much he wanted to, but I held a special place in his heart. Our bodies sang together when we joined."

Kjartan's face reddened as he explained Sigrun's words. Ragna blushed too, understanding perfectly. Her body sang whenever Reider came close, whenever he touched her. "But must you die for him?"

Sigrun smiled. "I would have given my life for him before, why not now? I am not a young woman. I would rather journey with Torfinn. Do not blame Reider."

A chill travelled from the soles of Ragna's feet all the way up her spine. Would she be willing to give her life for Reider? Would she be prepared to die to protect him? Had she not thrown caution for her own safety to the winds in coming to his aid, intent only on his welfare?

As she watched, Sigrun took down her grey hair and another thrall combed it. Kjartan touched Ragna's elbow. "You have probably noticed that female thralls have closely cropped hair. Torfinn thought so highly of Sigrun, he allowed her to keep her hair long. It was a mark of great respect. He gave her the amber beads she wears."

The peace of the small chamber was shattered by the sound of a mournful horn. Ragna jumped, gooseflesh coursing over her skin. A shadow of nervousness passed over Sigrun's face, then left as quickly as it had come. Kjartan's grip on Ragna's elbow tightened. "It is time. The villagers are gathering. You must make a decision, Ragna. All or nothing."

*All or nothing?*

Her lifelong mantra!

She wanted it all! She had always wanted it all!

She smiled at Sigrun, then turned to Kjartan, taking a deep breath to calm her raging heart. "Escort me to my chamber. I must dress for the funeral."

He grinned and whisked her out the door faster than her feet could carry her.

## CHAPTER TWENTY-FIVE

Thralls dressed Ragna in a fine white linen gown, embroidered around the neck and the ends of the sleeves. She pushed away thoughts of Reider lying with any of these women. A blue cloak was fastened around her shoulders and pinned with a *sølje*. Fingering the silver brooch, she suppressed a sigh of disappointment when Kjartan appeared to escort her to the rites.

They climbed the hill to the site of the stone ship. Villagers had assembled, standing to one side of the ship, looking out to sea. Some held unlit torches. They bowed respectfully. Dieter stood among them, his expression solemn. He nodded to her, but did not smile.

Kjartan took her to the entrance of the death house. She dug her nails into his arm, shivering at the sight of Torfinn's body, surrounded by his earthly possessions. A shield lay at his head, his helmet at his feet. His dead hands lay over the hilt of a sword placed on top of his body. Decay lingered in the air.

How difficult it must have been for Reider to complete this ritual that had been accomplished with such obvious love and care.

She appreciated Kjartan's support as they took their places outside in front of the villagers. Shadows lengthened as the afternoon sun made its way to the horizon. The two stone pillars at either end of the ship loomed like giant monoliths. She shuddered and felt Kjartan's hand on her elbow. "Courage, cousin."

~~~

Her heartbeat had slowed, but then the horn sounded again, closer now. She put her hand over her throat, following everyone's gaze down the hill. Sigrun emerged from the lodge, arm in arm with two men. Reider's blonde hair was tightly braided, the bronzed glow of his skin deepened by the white linen of the long tunic he wore. He looked like a golden god. Yearning lit a fire below the pit of her belly and she swayed, but again Kjartan supported her.

As they approached, Reider talked with Sigrun. She smiled. The other man's lips were tightly drawn, his jaw clenched. He was younger than Reider. His fair hair was short, like a thrall's. Ragna did not recall seeing him before.

They climbed the hill slowly and came to stand by the stone ship. Reider did not smile when he caught sight of Ragna, but his brown eyes shone with relief. Sigrun nodded to her, then the three passed through the rocks of the stone ship. Ragna gasped. Reider held a dagger in his right hand, pressed against his leg.

They paused at the entry. The second man embraced Sigrun and walked to one of the monoliths, his head bowed. Reider turned to the thrall. His voice faltered as he declared, "It is a good day for a sail. May fair winds carry you and my father to your journey's end."

They stepped inside the death house, out of sight. Only the sound of the wind broke the utter silence. Ragna held her breath, expecting to hear a scream of pain.

Reider emerged a few moments later, rubbing the back of his neck, the other fist clenched, a trace of blood on his sleeve.

~~~

A thrall handed Reider a horn. He hesitated, took a deep breath, and blew a long note. His weather-tanned fingers turned white around the horn. His face reddened. The mournful sound echoed across the headland.

The villagers formed a processional line and, one by one, families presented gifts to Reider. He handed them to the other man who had escorted Sigrun. Each gift was taken into the death house. They brought cheeses, casks of ale, pitchers of milk, baskets, blankets, chickens, tools. Ragna lost track in her amazement. She could not take her eyes off Reider. His heart must be breaking, yet he stood stoically accepting the gifts, jaw clenched, neck muscles corded, bowing his polite thanks to each donor. Occasionally he rubbed the arm Gorm had slashed.

How hard it must have been for him to help Sigrun on her way, but he had expected no less of himself. The depth of her love for this honourable man shook her to the core. The road ahead would not be easy, but she had never been one to travel an easy road.

When the gift-giving came to an end, Reider sounded another long note on the horn. Thralls brought armloads of cut branches and threw them into the doorway of the death house. Reider came to stand at Ragna's side. His eyes were red, his mouth a stern line. He raised the horn to his lips once more and blew until he had no breath left to blow, an anguished, keening requiem that echoed to the bone. Ragna let the tears flow freely down her cheeks. The villagers wept openly.

The torches had been lit and the men carrying them stepped forward. Reider and the other escort took a torch, thrusting them into the kindling around the edges of the pyre.

"Safe journey, fair winds," Reider shouted, his voice stronger now. He came to stand at Ragna's side again. The flames caught eagerly and the pyre was soon engulfed. Ragna looked out at the waning rays of the sun on the sea below. Soon the red flames glowed on the water and a large pillar of acrid smoke rose skyward. The wind swirled it around the gathering, stinging Ragna's eyes. The heat of the flames scorched her face. She longed to reach out to this grieving man who would be her husband, but was it appropriate? Would he resent her for it? She gasped when he took her hand and squeezed so hard she feared her fingers might break. It would be worth it if it helped ease his pain.

~~~

A thrall bearing a ewer and two goblets approached Reider, who filled the goblets and raised one high above his head. "This is mead, drink of the gods."

Ragna gasped. She knew all about mead! The mead Aidan made at Kirkthwaite rivalled that of Lindisfarne.

Reider was hoarse. "We toast Torfinn Reidersen, a great warrior, father, king and Viking, and Sigrun his beloved thrall. We pray the gods grant fair winds and a safe voyage to this ship. We ask Odin to welcome them into his feast hall."

He poured some of the mead on the ground then drained the goblet. He handed the remaining goblet to the second escort, who cleared his throat then spoke haltingly. "We toast Torfinn Reidersen, a great warrior, king, father and Viking, and Sigrun his thrall, a beloved mother." He too poured mead on the ground before draining his goblet.

What did he mean? Was this man Sigrun's son? Why had he also said *father*?

It was fully dark before the funeral pyre burned itself out and the death house collapsed in a shower of ashes and sparks. Ragna felt a strange sense of peace and completion she had been denied with her parents. Reider still held her hand tightly.

He turned to his people. "We invite you to the feast in honour of my father and Sigrun."

Slowly everyone processed down the hill, led by Kjartan, until only Reider, Ragna and the unknown man remained. Ragna looked inquiringly at Reider. "Ragna, please meet Gregor Sigrunsen."

She knew enough about Danish naming customs to be surprised. "Sigrun was your mother?"

Gregor only nodded, his mouth a tight line.

She looked back at Reider, not daring to ask the question. Her betrothed nodded. "He is my half-brother."

"But—if Sigrun was a thrall—"

Reider inhaled deeply. "You are right in your deduction. Gregor is a thrall, or should I say *was* a thrall. I have freed him, to honour Sigrun—and to please you."

Her mind whirled. She was elated he had freed Gregor, but the man was his half-brother. Why had he not been freed before? Her own father had risked his life on more than one occasion for his half-brothers, Robert and Baudoin de Montbryce.

Gregor stepped forward and held out his hands. His mother's amber beads lay across his palms. "My mother wanted you to have these," he rasped.

She looked in amazement at the amber beads, then quickly at Reider, unsure what to do. His eyes said yes. She inclined her head and Gregor fastened the beads behind her neck. When she raised her head she discerned no malice in his sad eyes. He bowed, shook Reider's hand, then strode away.

She fingered the beads. How could Gregor accept that Reider had taken his mother's life? That he had not been able to bear his father's name? Would she ever understand these Danes?

## CHAPTER TWENTY-SIX

The funeral banquet was bountiful, but the mood subdued. Reider's thoughts went back to the night of his father's murder. His eyes fixed on Ragna, seated at his side. The dread that she would not be at the funeral had torn at his gut. Relief had swept over him at the sight of her standing next to Kjartan on the headland.

Ragna too had experienced heartbreak because of the cruel deaths of her parents. He hoped she would one day find a measure of peace, as he had, knowing his father had been honoured appropriately.

Did she understand why he had helped Sigrun, that it had been his duty as his father's son? He smiled despite his concern. His father must be experiencing great joy with Sigrun at his side as he journeyed to Valhalla.

He prayed his own journey with Ragna would be filled with love and understanding. He had known her only a short time, but could not imagine life without her.

She had been quiet after the rites and looked exhausted. She fingered Sigrun's amber beads at her neck. His home and his traditions must seem strange to her. There would be some lively arguments over the years! He leaned close. "You look tired, Ragna. I'll command a thrall to accompany you to your chamber. Leave Thor here with me. He is too excited."

She squeezed his hand and nodded, her eyes red-rimmed. How strange to see Ragna speechless! He summoned a girl who used to be Margit's thrall. She looked pale and in need of a gentle mistress. She would be a good choice for Ragna.

~~~

Ragna was relieved Reider had sent her to bed, worn out by the conflicting emotions that had warred within her all day. She could barely recall her own name. She smiled at the timid young thrall who had accompanied her to the guest chamber in Reider's ringhouse. He had told her she used to belong to Margit, but now belonged to him. A horrible suspicion had her wondering if Reider had lain with the girl, but she dismissed it. The girl was a child who looked cowed, and unwell. Reider's thralls seemed healthy, happy and willing to serve. She surmised from what she knew of Margit that the girl had probably not been treated well.

"What is your name?" she asked.

The girl flinched. Was she afraid Ragna would strike her? She reached for the girl's hand and pointed to herself. "I am Lady Ragna."

She pointed to the thrall. "What is your name?"

Fear lingered in the girl's tired eyes, but she whispered, "Olve."

"Olve, you need not fear me. I will not hurt you." The girl would not understand her language, but perhaps she would take heart from the kind way Ragna spoke to her.

Olve reached nervously to unpin the brooch holding Ragna's cloak. Ragna relaxed and allowed the servant to disrobe her, then help her don her night attire. She nodded with approval when Olve took the precious dagger and laid it reverently on the sideboard.

The thrall carefully combed out her mistress's hair. Ragna's turmoil gradually left her. "Thank you, Olve. I feel better. Perhaps it is my destiny always to be searching for a way to improve things. Perhaps I am fated never to be completely happy."

Olve tucked her into bed.

Ragna yawned. "You should sleep as well, Olve. You are too pale, and thin."

Olve bowed.

Ragna drifted into sleep.

~~~

Olve curled up on the planking at the foot of her new mistress's bed. She had not understood what Lady Ragna had chattered about, but was grateful she would spend her final days with a gentle mistress.

The pain had been unrelenting since Margit had destroyed her child. Something inside was broken. She was weak, her life draining away. But she would do her best for her new master and mistress. It was an honour to serve them. She cursed Margit as she fell into a doze, trying to identify the night-time noises of a chamber she had never slept in before.

A loud creak sent a cold shiver down her spine. She recognized the footfall and dread filled her heart. How long had she slept? Was she dreaming? How could Margit be here when she was locked away?

She sat up slowly, peering into the darkness. Her mistress snored softly. Olve now had no doubt Margit was also in the chamber. She would know the woman's smell anywhere.

Olve rolled into a crouch, remembering the dagger her new mistress cherished. She cringed when a harsh voice broke the silence. "Wake up, English bitch. I want you to know who it is sends you to *Hel*."

Olve heard the sound of linens rustling and Lady Ragna's indignant voice. "*Godemite!* Who are you?"

"I am Margit Hansdatter and you will not steal Reider from me."

Olve crept silently to where the dagger lay. The penalty for a thrall who murdered a freewoman was death, but she was a dead woman anyway. She would not let Margit kill Lady Ragna.

Her new mistress screeched what sounded like a war cry, raising gooseflesh on the back of Olve's neck. There were sounds of a struggle. A weak shaft of the new moon glinted on the blade of a knife. Olve lunged for her lady's dagger and drew it from its sheath. With strength she did not know she had left, she leapt up onto the bed, plunging the weapon over and over into Margit's back.

Margit grunted and slumped onto the bed. Light filled the chamber as Prince Reider burst in with his torchbearers. A red stain spread on the white linens. Lady Ragna's chemise was spattered with blood. On her knees on the bed, she trembled, staring open-mouthed at the body before her. Olve, panting hard, clutched the dagger in her bloodied hands.

## CHAPTER TWENTY-SEVEN

Kjartan ran into the chamber and quickly disarmed the thrall who looked like she was in a trance. "It's Ragna's dagger," he exclaimed.

Reider stood transfixed, dreading that Ragna had been wounded, perhaps mortally, but Kjartan's voice jolted him out of his daze. He rushed to lift Ragna from the blood-soaked bed, holding her tightly as she keened. "Olve saved me, she saved me. It was Margit. I didn't know her. How did she come to be here?"

He stood her on her feet, running his hands over her. "Are you hurt? Did she wound you?"

She swayed, shaking her head numbly. "Olve saved me."

She collapsed into his arms, sobbing. "Hold me, Reider. I was terrified. I tried to fight her off, but had it not been for Olve—"

Reider smoothed his hand over her hair, whispering words of reassurance, until his gaze fell on the thrall. Two burly guards had forced her to her knees. Dread knotted his gut. This girl had saved Ragna's life, but she would be sentenced to die because she had taken Margit's worthless life in defence of her mistress. Perhaps Ragna was right. Some of his people's traditions needed to change. Ragna would be incensed if the girl were condemned.

"Release her," he commanded.

They obeyed, but the thrall remained on her knees, head bent.

Ragna turned, saw the thrall and rushed to her, drawing her to her feet and embracing her. "Thank you, Olve. You saved me."

She turned to Reider. "Olve must be freed. She saved my life."

*By Thor, if only it were that simple!*

The perceptive Ragna recognised his perplexed expression. Her face reddened and she raked her fingers over her scalp, gripping her hair. "What? Why can she not be freed?"

Olve had sunk to her knees again, seemingly resigned to her fate. The girl looked ill. Who knew what she had suffered at

Margit's hand? The woman had hidden her cruelty well during their brief betrothal.

He put his arm around Ragna's shoulder, but addressed his words to the thrall. "I will return after I have lodged Lady Ragna in another chamber. Remain here until then."

The girl did not look at him, but he knew she would obey.

At the door he turned back. "Thank you, Olve," he rasped.

~~~

Reider wanted to take Ragna to his own bed and hold her tightly until the horror went away. But decorum dictated otherwise.

He took her to another guest chamber. They sat together on the edge of the bed, and he held her trembling hand.

"I don't understand, Reider," she murmured.

"Margit got hold of a weapon and murdered a guard, then escaped from the gaol."

A long breath shuddered through her. "She woke me before she attacked. She wanted me to know my executioner."

"She was mad, Ragna. It became clear a while ago. I wish I had ordered her death before this. I would have given anything to save you this terror."

She leaned into him and he buried his nose in her hair, inhaling the spicy fragrance, once more dreading the explanation he would have to give her about Olve. He noticed the blood spatters on her chemise. "I will send a thrall to help you change your gown."

She pulled away from him. "I want Olve."

He braced his hands on his thighs and looked up at the ceiling, searching for guidance. "I cannot send Olve. I must speak with her."

"What will happen to her?"

He scratched his head. Ragna would not make this easy. "A thrall who raises a hand against a free person must be punished."

She jumped to her feet to stand facing him, hands on her hips. "Punished! She saved my life! The woman she killed was mad. If she had succeeded in killing me who would she have sought out next?"

He looked at his feet. "Me."

She stamped her foot. "Exactly! Olve should be declared Queen of Strand for what she has done!"

He chuckled in an effort to lighten the tension. "That will be your role."

She snorted and turned her back, arms folded across her chest, foot drumming the planking. He could not win this argument. He left while his limbs were still intact.

~~~

Kjartan greeted Reider at the door of the chamber. "Margit's body has been removed."

"Good, thank you. See that her body is returned to Heide as soon as feasible. And send another thrall to assist Ragna."

He strode into the chamber, surprised to see it empty. "Where is the thrall? I instructed her to wait."

"She insisted she must stay here, but when she collapsed, I deemed it prudent to move her to a sick bed. Ragna would not—"

"Collapsed?"

Kjartan nodded grimly. "Some weeks ago Margit kicked her in the belly. She was with child and says something broke inside that has not healed."

Reider's gut roiled. "Whose child was it?" he asked, suspecting he already knew.

"Gorm's."

Shame washed over him. He was reminded again that he had failed to see the depravity under his nose. "I have not been a good prince, Kjartan. I need to be more vigilant in the future."

Kjartan put a hand on his shoulder. "You will be, Reider, with Ragna's help."

~~~

Ragna's eyes blinked open. It was long past dawn. She had not expected to sleep after the events of the night. She stretched languidly, then became aware of Reider sitting in a chair nearby, watching her, his expression guarded.

Would she ever be able to look at him without desire tingling in her breasts and between her legs? She blushed and sat up quickly. "I didn't hear you come back to the chamber."

"You were asleep. I didn't want to wake you."

He had made no move towards her. He still lounged in the chair, his long legs sprawled out in front of him.

A knot of dread wound itself round her heart. "What is wrong?"

He sat up. "Olve is dead."

"Nnnnoooo!" She leapt off the bed and rushed at him, her fists flailing.

He came to his feet, caught her wrists and pulled her to his body, holding her tightly as she beat her fists against his chest. "I hate you all! You're barbaric! I cannot live here. She saved my life and you killed her."

She struggled and protested, but he remained silent and would not let go.

When she could sob no more, she swayed against him. He rested his chin on top of her head, and rocked her. "I did not kill her, Ragna. She was sick. She died because Margit kicked her in the belly when she was with child. She has known for a while that death stalked her."

She took a shuddering breath. "You're lying."

He put his hands on her shoulders and forced her back. "I have many faults, Ragna, but I am not a liar. Do not accuse me of such a thing again."

Again she had opened her mouth without thinking and impugned the honour of the man she loved beyond reason. "I'm sorry, Reider. But she died a slave."

"I freed her before she died."

The enormity of his actions, flying in the face of his people's traditions and beliefs, struck her full force. He had done this out of respect for her, because he loved her.

She fell to her knees at his feet, head bowed, hands resting palms up on her thighs—a supplicant. "I beseech your forgiveness, Reider. I am not worthy to be your wife."

He drew her to her feet. "Ragna, you have the blood of Vikings in your veins, the courage of a warrior and the heart of a lion. It is I who am not worthy of you. I need you by my side if I am to become a better man, a wiser ruler."

He kissed her deeply. She had never felt more loved as he poured his desire into his kiss. She sucked his tongue into her mouth, echoing his growl with a groan of her own.

"Reider—my Viking prince."

## CHAPTER TWENTY-EIGHT

The wedding ceremony lasted three days. Ragna had never seen such a quantity of food and drink in one place, even at the lavish feasts in her Montbryce uncles' castles in England and Normandie. Everyone made merry, and the gathering was boisterous. Reider's people were genuinely fond of him and it gladdened her heart. Their relief at being rid of Gorm's tyrannical rule was palpable.

She and Reider spoke their vows at the end of the feasting. He explained that *Vàr*, the Goddess of Oaths, was a witness to their commitment. To Ragna's relief, a Christian priest was also in attendance to bless their union. These Danes embraced the "White Christ" wholeheartedly, while still holding firm to their pagan gods.

A replica of Thor's Hammer was placed in Ragna's lap and the blessing of the God of Thunder invoked. Thor the hound howled his approval, to everyone's amusement. Then Reider put his hands on Ragna's head and prayed for Freyja's blessings on his wife. "She is the goddess of love and fertility," he whispered.

Ragna felt her face flush and warm wetness pool between her legs. Would the ceremony ever be over? She longed to be abed with this man, experiencing the delights her mother had whispered of. Would she be brave enough to bring Reider pleasure in some of the ways her mother had shared? She shook her head and grinned. What a silly question for a Wild Viking Princess to ask herself!

~~~

Reider sensed something troubled Dieter. His new brother-by-marriage shifted his weight several times, clearing his throat. "Have no fear for Ragna. I will spend my life making her happy."

Dieter smiled nervously. "I see the love you have for her. I am reassured in that regard."

Reider put his hand on Dieter's shoulder. "Then what is it?"

Dieter took another swig of ale and braced his legs. "I am

married to Ragna's sister."

Reider nursed his tankard. "I am aware of this."

"But what you don't know is—the FitzRam women are—unusual."

Reider felt a tingle in his *pik*, but a cold shiver marched up his spine at the same time. He decided to say nothing.

Dieter chuckled. "Let me explain. I want to tell you this for Ragna's sake. You may get the impression on your wedding night that she is an experienced woman, but you know such is not the case. The FitzRam girls had the benefit of a mother who shared everything she knew about pleasing a man."

Reider's *pik* stood to attention. His mouth fell open. Ragna's kisses had already made his knees buckle. He felt his face redden, and feared he might stammer if he spoke.

Dieter slapped him heartily on the back. "I feel better, and I'm sure you do too! We are fortunate men! Enjoy your wedding night, my friend."

Reider caught sight of Kjartan on the other side of the Hall. He strode over to him. "Gather the torch bearers. It's time I took my wife to our bridal couch."

~~~

Ragna fidgeted with the embroidered sleeves of her gown while she waited in the processional line for the torch bearers to assemble, recalling things her mother had instilled. Why had she not paid more heed? Did she have the courage? Would Reider enjoy the same attentions, or did each man differ in his preferences?

Reider took her hand. "They're ready. The torch bearers accompany us to our bridal couch and are thus witnesses to our marriage. This way our joining is a legal marital relationship."

The desire in his brown eyes sent warmth spiralling into her core. Then his words echoed in her head. "But they won't—surely they won't—?"

Reider laughed and trailed his fingers down her throat, adding fuel to the fire. "*Nej*! No one else will be present when we join our bodies, Ragna. That pleasure is for you and me alone."

She licked her lips. "Let's get on with it then."

He smiled and called to Kjartan. "Ready, my friend. Lead on."

## CHAPTER TWENTY-NINE

Kjartan ushered the last of the well-wishers out of the bridal chamber, then turned to his friend. "May I give my good wishes to your bride, my cousin?"

Reider smiled and passed Ragna's hand to Kjartan.

Kjartan took Ragna's hands and kissed her forehead. "May Freyja watch over you, and bless your marriage."

She squeezed his hands. "Thank you, cousin, for everything."

He bowed to his prince, smiled and left.

The silence in the chamber was broken only by the crackle of the hearty fire, casting its glow over Reider and Ragna as they stood face to face in front of the hearth. Though the aroma of roasted food hung in the air even here, Reider caught the scent of female arousal. He inhaled deeply, flaring his nostrils. Before him stood the promise of a night filled with passion. But he must not forget his wife was a virgin. She may know more about marital intimacy than most young women, but had never experienced it. He must do it right and take his time, no matter that his *pik* already ached unbearably.

Ragna swayed, her cheeks red. "I—I know what is to happen this night."

He moved forward to take her hands. "Dieter explained—about your mother."

She seemed relieved and glanced at his arousal, smiling. "I want to touch you, husband."

Reider's heart soared. He pressed her hand to his hard manhood. She kneaded him with her gentle fingers and pressed her palm against him, rubbing her breasts against his chest. He groaned and bent to nuzzle her neck. "Your touch inflames me, wife."

"Am I doing it correctly?" she whispered.

Beneath this woman's veneer of strength beat the heart of an innocent maiden, anxious to please her husband. "There is no wrong way, Ragna."

Her head fell back and he traced kisses down her throat. Hands on his shoulders, she pressed her mons to his arousal. "My breasts long for you to kiss them, Reider."

Whatever he had done to deserve such a wife, he thanked the gods for his reward. He hoped when he replied his voice would sound like his own. "Let me help you take off your gown. I want to see your body," he rasped.

He went down on one knee to remove her shoes. She held on to his shoulders. Taking hold of the hem of her gown and chemise, he slowly peeled them up over her head. She raised her arms, then crossed them over her bared breasts as Reider tossed the garments away.

He put his hands on her waist. "What's this? My brave Ragna—shy? Surely not!"

Her face reddened. She squared her shoulders and let her hands fall to her sides, her fists clenching nervously. His breath caught in his throat as he stepped back to gaze at her nakedness. "You are more beautiful than I remember. I have longed to see you naked again. After the rescue, when I stripped off your clothes and discovered you were not a boy, I thought you were the most beautiful woman I had ever seen."

She wagged an accusing finger at him, a glint in her eyes, and smiled. "I am at a disadvantage, husband. I have never seen you naked. Do you intend to take off your clothes?"

He tore off his tunic, fumbling in his haste to untie the laces of his leggings, and came to stand inches away from her. "Undress me, Ragna. I have something I want you to see."

She tucked her thumbs into the waist of his leggings and pulled them down slowly over his hips. Her eyes widened as his erection sprang free. She knelt to help him step out of his clothing. He rested his hands on her shoulders, then took her hands and pulled her to her feet. She never took her eyes off his shaft. He inhaled deeply, hoping he would not burst into flames when she touched him. "Do you like what you see?"

She grinned, then whispered. "You are even more beautiful than I expected—and bigger."

He wanted to strut like a peacock. "Touch me again, Ragna. Like before."

He braced his legs and she knelt before him, curling her hand around his erection. He showed her how to move her hand on him, and every movement was sweet torture. The silky feel of her beautiful hair brushing against his legs made him weak in the knees. She thrust out her full breasts and he cupped them, brushing his thumbs over the hard pink nipples. She groaned, tossing back her head.

"Use your other hand to lift my sac."

She responded with a touch that sent him reeling. He thanked Freyja for the wise mother-by-marriage he would never meet.

His need threatened to overtake him. He stilled her hand and cradled her body to his chest. "Come to the bed, Ragna. I want to play with you, but if you keep on, I will release too soon."

~~~

For the second time, Ragna knelt at Reider's feet, obeisance she had never offered any man before. Strangely, she liked it. She relished giving her body and her obedience to this man she loved. She had long considered women who allowed men power over them to be weak, but now she felt empowered.

Nothing had prepared her for the sight of Reider's arousal. She had understood he would join their bodies by putting his manhood inside her, but the sheer size of him made her doubt the possibility.

Tears of passion wept between her legs. She arched her back when Reider's finger touched her most secret place. "You are wet for me, my beautiful wife."

She heard a murmuring sound. She had made it! Breathing became more difficult and tingling sensations soared through her body. "Reider...Reider...Reider," she chanted.

He dipped two fingers inside her and suckled her breast, swirling his tongue over the nipple. She crested a wave of intense longing. She dug her heels into the mattress, raking her fingers along his scalp. "I—" she gulped, the words dying in her throat.

Reider kissed her, sucking her tongue into his mouth and the sensations became tantalizingly unbearable. "I want to taste you," he rasped.

A vague memory of something her mother had told her flitted into her recollection, then Reider's head was between her legs, licking her intimate folds. She groaned and put her hands on her breasts, squeezing her nipples. She was drowning in a sea of bliss.

"Come for me, Ragna, that's it. Come for me again."

Her whole body became rigid, yet she felt boneless, as if she floated above the bed. She tried to speak, but strange sounds emerged from her throat. She collapsed into Reider's strong arms, safe from the storm.

His deep voice washed over her. "There will be pain at first, but you're ready now."

She moved her head numbly, in a stupor, then gasped when he slid his manhood inside her. It felt hot and thick. He growled and she cried out, without meaning to. "The pain will pass, Ragna. Hold on to me."

She grasped his hips, digging her nails into his flesh, falling into the deep, hard rhythm of his thrusts. Soon insistent warmth built within her. She clenched her inner muscles on his shaft. It did fit! And felt good—very, very good. She crested another wave of overwhelming pleasure, Reider's guttural cry of completion filling her heart.

~~~

Warm eddies of pleasure whirled slowly up Reider's spine. He had collapsed on top of Ragna, exhausted by the overwhelming euphoria of the deepest connection he had ever felt with a woman.

Making love with his wife had been as completely satisfying as he had expected—and more. She had carried him to a distant shore where love and passion ruled. The tightness of her sheath had both worried and exhilarated him. Somewhere in the recesses of his scattered thoughts, he vaguely hoped he had not hurt her, and was not crushing her now. He was drooling, but did not care.

He was surprised when coherent words emerged. "Sorry. I am too heavy."

Her fingertips traced patterns on his back, but she only hummed a long sigh of contentment in reply. He slid his arms beneath her back and rolled her over on top of him. Her head rested in the crook of his shoulder, her hair a golden curtain falling about them. He gathered it in both hands and twisted it gently behind her nape, enjoying the silky texture of it on his palms. He kissed her cheek and she licked her lips. She was drooling too!

He chuckled and her long blonde eyelashes fluttered open. His *pik* had been softening, but the love he saw in the depths of her blue eyes stirred his interest anew. His heart was so full it made him dizzy.

"Did I hurt you?"

She cradled his face in her hands, causing the full weight of her breasts to press against his chest. "There was pain for a moment, but the pleasure was far greater."

He felt guardedly smug. "I gave you pleasure then?"

She kissed his lips. "And will again! Soon I think? I feel you stirring inside me already."

"By Freyja, Ragna, I could spend my life with my *pik* inside your wet heat."

She laughed. "People might notice when we leave our chamber!"

He hugged her tightly. "Ah, that is the secret. We are never leaving here!"

He could quickly become fully aroused again, but worried she might be sore after losing her maidenhead. Reluctantly he withdrew and lifted her to lie beside him. She curled up against him and reached a tentative finger to touch his *pik*. "I have bloodied you."

He smiled, her knowing innocence filling his heart. He traced his fingers over her thighs. "And I you. We belong to each other now."

She smiled and made a noise that sounded like a kitten purring.

He rose from the bed. He wet a linen cloth with water from the ewer and brought it to her, aware that she watched him. His wife's unabashed interest in his naked body elated him. "This will be cold," he said as he gently wiped the blood from her thighs and her woman's cleft.

"But your touch warms me," she murmured, holding out her hand. "Give me the cloth so I may cleanse you now."

He lay back and gazed at the rafters, clasping his hands behind his head as she washed him. Despite his best efforts to remain unaffected, his *pik* soon stood erect. Through half-lidded eyes he saw a grin on his wife's face. "My mother described how a man's shaft grew, but I never fully understood what she meant, until now. You want me again!" she laughed.

He sat up quickly, overwhelmed with joy at his good fortune in finding this unusual woman. The years ahead held the promise of great love and intimate physical fulfillment. He took her into his embrace. "I have only to look at you to want you," he breathed.

"Me too," she replied.

She leaned away from him and brushed her thumbs over his nipples, sending more blood rushing to his loins. "I remember the first time I saw you. I had never seen such a broad chest!"

He feigned indignation, clamping his hands around her wrists. "And how many men's chests had you seen before?"

Her sky-blue eyes sparkled with mischief. "Many," she lied.

He bent to swirl his tongue over her pouting nipples. "You lie, but I speak truly when I say that I have seen many women's breasts, but nothing prepared me for the sight of your magnificent globes when I first discovered you were not a boy!"

She snorted. "I can well imagine! Hmmm! Many women, you say? You will have to be punished for that."

She quickly came to her knees and tickled him, digging her fingers into his ribs.

He was lost. Soon their cries of fulfillment echoed once more around the chamber.

# EPILOGUE

A brisk wind gusted across the jetty, lifting Ragna's unbound hair. She handed a carefully wrapped bundle to Dieter. She was relieved to honour her mother's wishes, but would miss having the dagger as her talisman. "Tell Blythe I send all my love with this gift."

Reider tightened his grip on her waist. "Not all. Most of it is staying here with me."

Everyone chuckled, easing some of the uncomfortable sadness of the farewell. Dieter was the first to speak. "Blythe will be disappointed not to see you, but will be elated to have the dagger and know you are happily wed. Perhaps someday soon you will both journey to Wolfenberg?"

He tucked the package away safely in a carved sea chest Reider had given him as a token of thanks for Ragna's rescue. He embraced Ragna and shook Reider's hand, then boarded Captain Ivar's vessel for the journey back to Hamburg.

Ivar bellowed orders to his crew, removed his woollen cap and bowed. Reider helped shove the boat off. Ragna's heart pounded loudly at the sight of the bulging muscles of her husband's thighs and broad back. It pulsed in her throat, making it difficult to catch her breath.

This beautiful man was hers. She had already learned a lot about his body, what pleased him, but her mouth watered at the promise of undiscovered delights. There were some things in her mother's arsenal she had not tried yet!

The boat slipped away, the wind readily filling the sails once it cleared the dock. The newly-weds raised their hands in salute until the *knarr* was out of sight, Reider's free arm around her shoulder. He turned her to face him, his hands on her waist. "You are alone now with your wicked Viking."

She pretended to shudder, then smiled. "I'm not afraid, and I have Thor."

He frowned, brushing his lips on hers. "Sometimes you are more afraid than you want anyone to see."

She felt her face redden. "You know me too well. I am a little afraid."

He pulled her into his embrace. "Fear can be a good thing, Ragna. You and I are embarking on a voyage full of unknowns. Life is like the sea, and our love is the boat. It won't always be smooth sailing, but love will keep us afloat in troubled waters. We have witnessed that life can be full of unpleasant surprises, and have much to learn from each other. With Freyja's blessings we'll live an untroubled life here on Strand and sire many healthy children. But we will travel. To England, to Saxony. Vikings love to wander far and wide."

She snuggled into him, relishing the warmth of his big body seeping into her. "I am your lady, Reider, until the rivers all run dry."

He kissed her forehead. "And I am your man until the stars no longer shine."

# HISTORICAL POSTSCRIPT

The Danish island of Strand covered approximately 210 square miles prior to 1634. That fateful year, a disastrous storm tide tore the island apart. 6000 people drowned. Perhaps some of them were descendants of Reider and Ragna Torfinnsen.

One island became three, Nordstrand, Pellworm and Hallegin. Nordstrand today is a peninsula, linked to the mainland by the Beltringerharder, a polder of land reclaimed from the sea. All three islands now belong to Germany.

# GLOSSARY
A complete glossary for Ms. Markland's novels.

CP=*Conquering Passion* (Montbryce Legacy, Book I) © Anna Markland 2011
AMOV=*A Man of Value* (Montbryce Legacy, Book II) © Anna Markland 2011
ILDE=*If Love Dares Enough* (Montbryce Legacy, Book III) © Anna Markland 2012
PIB=*Passion in the Blood* (Montbryce Legacy, Book IV) © Anna Markland 2012
DP=*Defiant Passion* (Sons of Rhodri, Book I) © Anna Markland 2012
DB=*Dark and Bright* (Sons of Rhodri, Book II) © Anna Markland 2012
WTH=The Winds of the Heavens (Sons of Rhodri, Book III) © Anna Markland 2012
CA=*Carried Away* (FitzRam Family, Book I) © Anna Markland 2012
STL=*Sweet Taste of Love* (FitzRam Family, Book II) © Anna Markland 2012
WVP=Wild Viking Princess (FitzRam Family, book III) © Anna Markland 2012
DOL=Dance of Love (Montbryce—The Next Generation I) © Anna Markland 2012

***Abbaye aux Dames***—An abbey for women built in Caen by William the Conqueror ILDE, PIB
***Abbaye aux Hommes***—An abbey for men built in Caen by William the Conqueror ILDE, PIB
***Abbey***—Agneta's mare in AMOV
***Abbot***—Caedmon's roan stallion in AMOV
***Adam de Montbryce***—Son of Antoine and Sybilla PIB
***Adelaide***—Daughter of King Henry I; married Holy Roman Emperor, Henry V CA
***Aediva Melton***—Sister of the Saxon heroine in ILDE
***Aegir***—Norse god of the sea DOL
***Agnes***—Norman scullery maid at Domfort Castle ILDE
***Agneta Kirkthwaite***—English Heroine of Danish and Saxon descent in AMOV
***Aidan Branton FitzRam***—Son of Caedmon and Agneta, twin of Blythe; named for Agneta's brothers who were slain at Bolton. AMOV, CA; hero of STL
***Alexandre de Montbryce***—Eldest son of Robert and Dorianne. Heir to

the title *Comte* de Montbryce. Born in Caen during his father's incarceration PIB

***Alnwick***—Located in Northumbria. Site of a battle in 1093 between Roger de Mowbray, Earl of Northumbria, and Malcolm, King of Scotland. Malcolm and his son were killed. Agneta rescues Caedmon from the battlefield and tends his injuries. AMOV

***Amadour de Vignoles***—Norman comrade of Caedmon during Crusade; hero of Civitote AMOV

***Andras ap Rhys***—Welshman—Friend and comrade of Rhodri ap Owain in CP and DP

***Aneurin ap Norweg***—Welshman—Friend and comrade of Rhodri ap Owain in CP and DP

***Angeline Hugo***—Norman peasant, rape victim of Arnulf de Valtesse CP

***Anjou***—Geographic area of France south of Normandy. Its people are called Angevins. Normans and Angevins were traditional enemies. ILDE

***Anna***—Dieter's housekeeper, CA

***Annalise de Vymont***—Heroine of DB. Niece of the Earl of Chester.

***Antoine de Montbryce***—Norman hero of ILDE; brother of Rambaud and Hugh

***Apollo***—Izzy de Montbryce's horse DOL

***ap Owain***—Welsh patronymic—son of Owain

***Ariel***—Rhodri's Welsh pony DP

***Arnulf de Valtesse***—Norman half brother of Mabelle de Montbryce, heroine of CP. Bastard son of Guillaume de Valtesse. Murdered in CP by Simon Hugo

***Artus Aubin***—Norman steward of Giroux Castle DOL

***Ascha (Bronson) Woolgar***—Saxon mother of Caedmon; in CP and AMOV

***Barat Cormant***—Norman steward brought to England by the Montbryces for Sussex properties; ILDE; son of Michel, brother of Théo.

***Baudoin de Montbryce***—Norman born in England; second son of Ram and Mabelle de Montbryce; becomes 2nd Earl of Ellesmere; marries Carys verch Rhodri; appears in CP, AMOV, DP and PIB.

***Beal***—coastal village in Northumbria close to Holy Island STL

***Bemia Melton***—Saxon sister of heroine of ILDE

***Bernard Chauvelin***—Norman soldier at Montbryce Castle PIB

***Bernard de Montbryce***—Father of Ram, Antoine and Hugh. Dies in 1066 while his sons are fighting in England.

***Bernhardt***—Dieter's valet, CA

***Bileaud***—Norman steward at Domfort Castle ILDE

***Blythe Lacey FitzRam***—Daughter of Caedmon and Agneta, twin of Aidan. Born in AMOV. Heroine of CA
***Boden***—English mastiff in ILDE
***Bolton***—Village in Northumbria; location of Kirkthwaite Hall
***Bonhomme***—Normans; family name of the stewards of Montbryce and Ellesmere.
***Brigantia***—English mastiff in ILDE
***Brindis***—Ram de Montbryce's horse in CP
***Brother Christian***—religious name given to Aidan when he enters the monastery STL
***Brother Tristan***—Cellarer in charge of mead making at Lindisfarne STL
***Caedmon Brice (Woolgar) FitzRam***—Illegitimate son of Ram de Montbryce and Ascha Woolgar. Appears in CP, PIB & CA; hero of AMOV
***Caryl Penarth***—Welsh healer; appears in CP and DP
***Carys verch Rhodri***—Welsh; healer; daughter of Rhodri and wife of Baudoin de Montbryce. Becomes 2nd Countess of Ellesmere. Appears in PIB, DP and DB
***Catherine de Montbryce***—Daughter of Robert and Dorianne PIB
***Civitote***—site of the heroic rescue of thousands of crusaders by Caedmon and Amadour AMOV
***Commote***—A Welsh area of administration, similar to a county.
***Cormant***—Normans; family name of stewards at Alensonne in CP and at East Preston in ILDE
***Coventina Brightmore***—Saxon; friend of hero and heroine in AMOV; marries Leofric Deacon
***Curia regis***—Latin for King's Court ILDE
***Dagfinn Alfredsen***...Dane; ally of Reider in WVP
***Dagfrid***—Dane; cousin of Kjartan in WVP
***Dda***—Welsh surname of Rhonwen and Myfanwy; CP and DP and DB
***de Valtesse***—Maiden surname of heroine of CP
***Denis de Sancerre***—Angevin; son of Sybilla and adopted son of Antoine de Montbryce; dwarf ILDE & PIB
***Devona Melton***—Saxon; heroine of ILDE; marries Hugh de Montbryce
***Dieter Von Wolfenberg***—German hero of CA; marries Blythe FitzRam; appears in WVP
***Dorianne de Giroux***—Norman heroine of PIB; marries Robert de Montbryce
***Earl of Chester***—Hugh d'Avranches. Historical figure. Known by the Welsh as Hugh Vras (the Fat) PIB, DB
***Edgar the Aetheling***—Saxon; historical figure. Claimant to throne of

England taken by William the Conqueror. Aetheling is a Saxon term for "next in line"; appears in CP and AMOV
*Edwin FitzRam*—English; brother of Blythe, Aidan and Ragna; son of Caedmon and Agneta STL
*Elenor de Giroux*—Norman; mother of Dorianne de Giroux; wife of Francois. PIB
*Ellesmere*—Location of castle given to Ram as a reward by William the Conqueror. Ram and Mabelle eventually turn a derelict Anglo-Saxon earthwork into a vibrant, thriving castle.
*Emrys*—Cook at llys Powwydd. DB
*Enid*—Saxon maid of Ascha Woolgar. CP & AMOV
*Espérance*—Cat who brings solace to Robert de Montbryce during his solitary confinement. The word means 'hope'. PIB
*Etienne Robert de Montbryce*—Second son of Baudoin and Carys; DB,STL
*Farah*—Aragonese; heroine DOL
*Fernand Bonhomme*—Norman; second generation of his family to be steward of Montbryce Castle. Father of Mathieu and Honore. Married to Vangeline.
*FitzRam*—Norman patronymic surname bestowed on Caedmon by Ram. AMOV
*Fleurie Mabelle de Montbryce*—Daughter of Baudoin and Carys. Her mother almost dies giving birth to her. DB
*Fortis*—Black stallion; Ram's favourite mount; saves his life at Hastings CP
*François de Giroux*—Norman father of Dorianne and Pierre de Giroux PIB; sworn enemy of the Montbryces ILDE
*Frederika*—Dieter's first wife, CA
*Freyja*—Norse goddess of fertility;WVP
*Gallien Rambaud de Montbryce*—Eldest son of Baudoin and Carys DB, STL
*Gareth Bronson*—Saxon brother of Ascha Woolgar; takes Ascha to Scotland. CP & AMOV
*Gawain Bronson*—Saxon nephew of Ascha Woolgar; CP & AMOV
*Georges de Giroux*—Norman, Crusader. Reappears in DOL
*Gervais*—Norman soldier; Ram's second in command; CP & DP
*Gerwint Isembart de Montbryce (Izzy)*—Second son of Hugh and Devona. Named for his grandfather and great grandfather, and the rat catcher, Joubert. Prefers to be called Izzy.PIB; Hero of DOL
*Gerwint Melton*—ILDE Saxon grandfather of heroine
*Gicotte*—Norman soldier at Montbryce Castle; PIB
*Giroux*—Norman surname of the family sworn to avenge Guillaume de Valtesse's cruelty to their ancestor; CP, ILDE & PIB

***Giselle***—Norman maidservant who accompanies Mabelle to England and becomes chatelaine of Ellesmere; kidnapped with Mabelle; CP
***Glain verch Llewelyn***—Welsh bonesetter in DB
***Gorm***…villain of WVP; step brother of Reider
***Grouchet***—Anglo-Norman baron, villain of STL
***Guillaume de Valtesse***—Norman father of Mabelle; his cruelty begins the feud between the Valtesses and the Giroux family; CP
***Hastings***—Site in Southern England of a historic battle in 1066 that changed the history of England and Normandy CP
***Heinrich***—Historical figure; Holy Roman Emperor; CA
***Hel***—Norse word for Hell WVP
***Hélène de Fleury***—Norman wife of friend of Montbryce brothers killed at Hastings. CP
***Hugh de Montbryce***—Norman-virgin hero of ILDE; brother of Antoine and Ram CP, PIB
***Husembro***—hidden cove on Danish coast WVP
***Hylda***—Christian name of Mabelle's mother, purported to have been strangled by her husband, Mabelle's father.
***Hylda Rhonwen de Montbryce (Rhoni)***—Daughter of Ram and Mabelle born in captivity in Wales; CP, AMOV
***Ingram Maknab***—Scot; son of Neyll. STL
***Isembart Joubert***—Rat catcher from Montbryce; instrumental in saving the lives of Hugh and Devona; ILDE
***Isolda verch Llewelyn***—Welsh healer, heroine of WTH
***Ivar Sigurdsen***—Dane; captain in WVP
***Jennet***—Northumbrian peasant woman STL
***Johann Dieter Marius von Wolfenberg***—Dieter's son by his first marriage, CA
***Joleyne***—Norman mistress of Ram de Montbryce before he meets Mabelle; CP
***King Harald Hardråda of Norway***—Historical figure; pretender to the English throne; killed by King Harold's army at Stamford Bridge; CP
***King Harold II of England***—Historical figure; Saxon brother-in-law of Edward the Confessor. Claimed the throne on Edward's death; slain at Hastings by the Conqueror's army; CP
***King Henry I***—Norman king of England; son of William the Conqueror; known as Henry Beauclerc; succeeded his brother William Rufus on the throne. Historical figure; PIB
***King Malcolm Canmore of Scotland***—Historical figure. CP & AMOV
***King William I of England***—William the Conqueror, Duke of Normandie. CP, ILDE; historical figure
***King William Rufus***—William II of England; son of the Conqueror; AMOV; historical figure

*Kirkthwaite*—Surname of Agneta's family AMOV
*Kirkthwaite Hall*—Ancestral home of Agneta's family, destroyed in a raid by the Scots AMOV
*Kjartan Eldarsen*—Danish; comrade of Reider in WVP
*Kolbrand's Path*—fictitious seat of the MakNab clan on the coast of Scotland STL
*Köln*—German (Saxon) town, known as Cologne in English; CA
*La Blanche Nef*—Infamous White Ship that sank in 1120 taking with it hundreds of sons and daughters of the English nobility, including the Crown Prince, William, son of Henry I STL
*La Cuisinière*—Legendary Norman cook at Montbryce Castle; her name simply means 'The Cook' CP
*Lande Pourri*—A wooded area outside Caen PIB
*Leofric Deacon*—Saxon friend of Caedmon AMOV; badly injured at Alnwick; marries Coventina Brightmore; appears in STL
*Lindisfarne Abbey*—historic Benedictine monastery on Holy Island STL
*Llys* (plural Llysoed)—A building that served as a royal court for a commote in Wales. Stone castles were virtually unknown in England and Wales before the Conquest
*Lothar von Süpplingenburg*—Saxon Duke who became Holy Roman Emperor CA
*Löwe*—Dieter's Rottweiler, CA
*Mabelle de Montbryce*—Norman heroine of CP; wife of Ram de Montbryce; Countess of Ellesmere and Comtesse de Montbryce; AMOV, PIB, DP
*Mabelle de Valtesse*—Maiden name of Mabelle de Montbryce; CP, AMOV, PIB, DP
*Magnus Braunschweig*—Dieter's comrade, CA
*Màni*—Norse god of the Moon
*Margaret, Queen of Scotland* (Saint Margaret)—AMOV, CP; historical figure known for her piety; Saxon; second wife of King Malcolm Canmore; sister of Edgar Aetheling.
*Margit Hansdatter*—Dane; villain of WVP
*Marguerite de Montbryce*—Daughter of Robert and Dorianne
*Martin Bonhomme*—Norman steward at Ellesmere; son of Mathieu
*Mathieu Bonhomme*—Son of Fernand; goes to England to be steward at Ellesmere, father of Martin Bonhomme
*Mathieu de Montbryce*—Son of Antoine and Sybilla. PIB
*Melton Bernard de Montbryce*—Eldest son of Hugh and Devona; named for Devona's family name and Hugh's father. PIB
*Michel Cormant*—Norman steward at Alensonne; father of Barat, Theo and Paul; CP

*Montbryce*—Noble Norman family at the heart of the Legacy
*Mont St. Michel*—Abbey church of Carolingian origin built on an island off the French coast.
*Morwenna verch Morgan*—Welsh; betrothed to Rhodri; villain; mistress of Phillippe de Giroux; CP, DP
*Myfanwy Dda*—Welsh mother of Rhonwen; healer; murdered by Phillippe de Giroux; CP, DP
*Myfanwy Mabelle verch Rhodri*—Eldest child of Rhodri and Rhonwen; becomes a Prioress. DP, DB
*Neuadd*—The communal great hall in Welsh buildings
*Neyll Maknab*— villain of STL: stepfather of Nolana Kyncade
*Nolana Kyncade*—Scot; heroine of STL
*Northumbria*—North east part of England; site of constant conflict between Scots and Normans.
*Oda*—maidservant to Sybilla ILDE
*Olve*—Danish thrall saves Ragna's life WVP
*Paul Cormant*—Norman steward (Alensonne)
*Phillippe de Giroux*—Norman villain; CP, DP, PIB
*Pierre de Fleury*—Norman soldier; friend of the Montbryce brothers; killed at Hastings; CP
*Pierre de Giroux*—Norman villain PIB; brother of heroine, Dorianne
*Ragna FitzRam*—English daughter of Caedmon and Agneta; holy terror; heroine of WVP STL
*Rambaud (Ram) de Montbryce*—Norman nobleman; hero of Hastings; confidant to William the Conqueror. First Earl of Ellesmere; *Comte* de Montbryce; eldest son of Bernard de Montbryce, brother to Antoine and Hugh. Hero of CP. AMOV, PIB & DP
*Regis*—Antoine's stallion ILDE
*Reider Torfinnsen*…Danish hero of Wild Viking Princess WVP
*Renouf de Maubadon*—Norman (Angevin) villain of PIB
*Rhodri ap Owain*—Welsh villain turned hero. CP, AMOV, DP
*Rhonwen Dda*—Welsh/Saxon heroine DP. Healer CP
*Rhun ap Rhodri*—Welsh patriot; son of Rhodri. Twin of Rhydderch. Redhead. DB, hero of WTH
*Rhydderch ap Rhodri*—Welsh patriot; son of Rhodri and Rhonwen. Redhead. Twin of Rhun. DB, hero of WTH
*Rhys ap Rhodri*—Eldest son of Rhodri; hero of DB. Appears in AMOV
*Roar Knutsen*—Dane; henchman of Gorm in WVP
*Robert Curthose*—Son of William the Conqueror; became Duke of Normandie on his father's death; coveted his brother Henry's throne; captured by Henry at Tinchebray and imprisoned for the remainder of his life. PIB

*Robert de Montbryce*—Eldest son of Ram and Mabelle; born in England. Becomes *Comte* de Montbryce. CP, AMOV, DP; hero of PIB
*Ruyton*—Location of Shelfhoc Hall
*Schnell*—Dieter's greyhound, CA
*Shelfhoc Hall*—Ancestral home of the Woolgars in Ruyton, Shropshire, England.
*Sibell*—Mabelle's mare in CP
*Simon Hugo*—Norman serf at Alensonne who murders Arnulf de Valtesse to avenge his daughter. CP
*Stephen Marquand*—ILDE Norman neighbour of Meltons
*Strand*—Danish island principality WVP
*Sybilla de Taloche*—ILDE; heroine; Angevin; widow of Denis de Sancerre, mother of the dwarf, Denis de Sancerre. Marries Antoine de Montbryce
*Théobald Cormant*—Norman steward; brother of Barat
*Thor*...alaunt gentil hound belonging to Ragna FitzRam, named after Norse god of thunder WVP
*Torfinn*...father of Reider in WVP; murdered by Gorm
*Torod*—Norman villain; thug, henchman of Renouf ILDE
*Trésor*—Cook at Ellesmere. The French word means 'treasure'.CP
*Tristan Bonhomme*—Son of Honoré; steward at Montbryce
*Tybaut*—AMOV; steward at Shelfhoc Hall; Norman
*Valhalla*—Norse 'heaven'
*Vangeline Bonhomme*—Wife of Fernand; dies in 1066; CP
*Vàr*—Norse goddess of oaths
*Velox*—Hugh's stallion in ILDE
*Victoire*—Cook at Domfort Castle; ILDE
*Vormund*—Hovawart breed dog; saves Dieter's life
*White Ship*—see *La Blanche Nef*
*Wilona Melton*—Saxon mother of Devona, heroine of ILDE
*Woolgar*—Married name of Ascha Bronson, widow of Sir Caedmon Woolgar, a housecarl of King Harold who died at Hastings; CP, AMOV
*Wyvern*—Caedmon's horse; saves his life at Alnwick. AMOV

# LEXICON

*Fr.*=French
*W.*=Welsh
*G.*=German
*OE.*=Old English
*S.*=Scottish
*L.*=Latin
*D.*=Danish

Abbesse *Fr.* Abbess
Af Odin! D. By Odin!
Alaunt gentil *Fr.* Breed of hound
Ap (or Ab) *W.* Son of
Arrête *Fr.* Stop!
Auf Weidersehen *G.* Goodbye
Au revoir *Fr.* Goodbye
Barm *OE.* Yeast
Bébé *Fr.* Baby
Brychan *W.* Woven blanket
Ceilliau W. Testicles,
Codex *L.* journal
Cog -type of ship
Colonus, pl. Coloni L. Bondservants, later known as serfs
Commote *W.* area of administration in Wales
Comte *Fr.* Count
Comtesse *Fr.* Countess
Cuirass(e) Fr. Breastplate armour
Cymru *W.* Wales
Cymraeg *W.* Welsh language
Derrière *Fr.* Bottom, backside
Dieu *Fr.* God
Ddoe *W.* Yesterday
Draugr D. Revenant, lost soul
Dros Cymru *W.* For Wales
Duw *W.* God
Duwiau *W.* Gods!
Eke *OE.* Extra chamber added to the bottom of a beehive
Enceinte *Fr.* Pregnant
Enfant *Fr.* Child. Mes enfants=my children

Exactement *Fr.* Exactly
Fils *Fr.* Son
Fortæl mig D. Tell me
Fromage cremeux *Fr.* Cream cheese
Fy Nuw *W.* My God
Garderobe *Fr.* Latrines
Godemite *OE.* Saxon expletive, God Almighty
God hund D. Good dog
Godisgood *OE.* Yeast
Gottes segen *G.* Godspeed
Gott sei Dank *G.* Thanks be to God
Gräfin *G.* Countess
Grandmaman *Fr.* Grandma
Gut! *G.* Good!
Hackle *OE.* Conical shaped protection for beehives
Ich bin es *G.* It's me.
Ich liebe dich *G.* I love you
Ja *G.* Yes
Jardin *Fr.* Garden
Je t'aime *Fr.* I love you
Jongleur *Fr.* Minstrel, juggler, medieval entertainer
Kommen *G.* Come!
Knarr D. Merchant ship used by Vikings
Laks D. Smoked salmon
Lamellar Armour made of leather plates
Là *Fr.* There
Léine *S.* Shirt worn by men and women (Gaelic)
Liebling *G.* Sweetheart, darling

Llys *W.* (plural Llysoed) A building that served as a royal court for a commote in Wales.
Ma chère *Fr.* My dear
Majesté *Fr.* Majesty
Maman *Fr.* Mother (affectionate)
Mea culpa *L.* My fault; I take the blame
Méchant *Fr.* Naughty
Meine damen und herren *G.* Ladies and gentlemen
Mein Gott *G.* My God!
Mein Schatz *G.* My darling, my sweetheart
Merci *Fr.* Thank you
Mère *Fr.* Mother
Meth *OE.* ordinary mead
Metheglin *OE.* Spiced mead (for nobility)
Milord *Fr.* My lord
Minnesinger *G.* Minstrel
Misericord *L.* Chamber where monks received their punishment for misdeeds
Mon petit *Fr.* little one
Nein *G.* No
Nej *D.* No
Oes *W.* Yes
Oncle *Fr.* Uncle
Oubliette *Fr.* a small cell where prisoners were forgotten *Fr.* Oublier=to forget
Oui *Fr.* Yes
Pauvre *Fr.* Poor
Pax *L.* Peace
Père *Fr.* Father
Petit baiser *Fr.* a little kiss
Pik *D.* Shaft, manhood
Playd *S.* Woven garment, not tartan (came much later); often brown
Prie-Dieu *Fr.* Kneeler, prayer stool
Regarde *Fr.* Look!
Rundlet *OE.* small barrel or cask
Rute *G.* Shaft, manhood
Rwy'n dy garu di *W.* I love you
Schwarze ritter *G.* Black Knight
Seigneur *Fr.* Lord
Sieg *G.* Victory
Siwrne dda *W.* Good journey
Sjaund *D.* Ritualistic funeral ale in Norse inheritance traditions
Skep *OE.* Man made beehive made of straw
Sølje *D.* Traditional Norse silver brooch
Stridsøkse *D.* battle axe
Sûrement *Fr.* surely.
Tais-toi *Fr.* Be quiet, silence.
Tante *F.* Aunt
Tarse OE. Male genitals
Turaid *S.* Tower (Gaelic)
Ty bach *W.* Latrines
Verch *W.* Daughter of
Vous parlez francais? *Fr.* Do you speak French?
Walhaz- derogatory Saxon term meaning *foreign*; the word *Welsh* derived from it
Willkommen *G.* Welcome
Yr Arglwydd *W.* My lord

## ABOUT THE AUTHOR

Anna Markland is a Canadian author with a keen interest in genealogy. She writes medieval romance about family honour, ancestry and roots. Her novels are intimate love stories full of passion and adventure. Following an enjoyable career in teaching, Anna transformed her love of writing and history into engaging works of fiction. Prior to becoming a fiction author, she published numerous family histories. One of the things she enjoys most about writing historical romance is the in-depth research required to provide the reader with an authentic medieval experience.
*Facebook~Anna Markland Novels*
*Twitter @annamarkland*
*http://annamarkland.com/*
*email:anna@annamarkland.com*

# FAMILY TREE

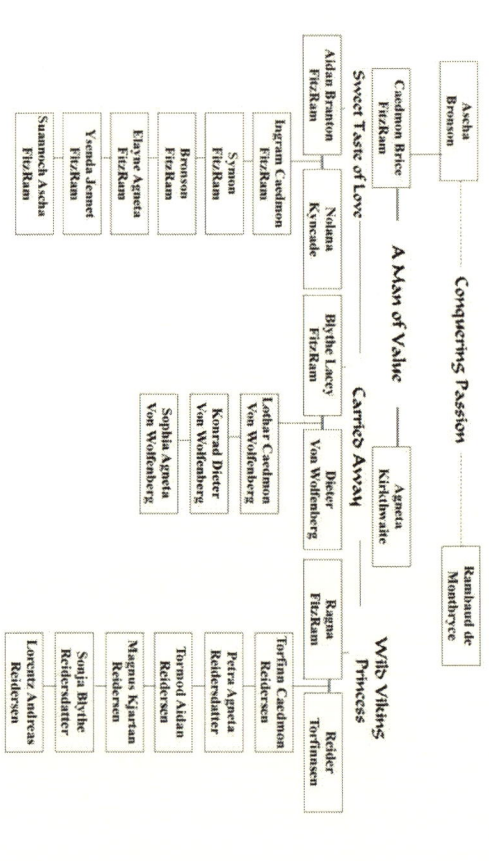

Printed in Great Britain
by Amazon.co.uk, Ltd.,
Marston Gate.